THE STORM

THE STORM

DAN JOLLEY

Copyright © 2017 by Dan Jolley

Cover Design by Melissa McArthur

All rights reserved.

No part of this book may be reproduced in any form or by any electronic or mechanical means, including information storage and retrieval systems, without written permission from the author, except for the use of brief quotations in a book review.

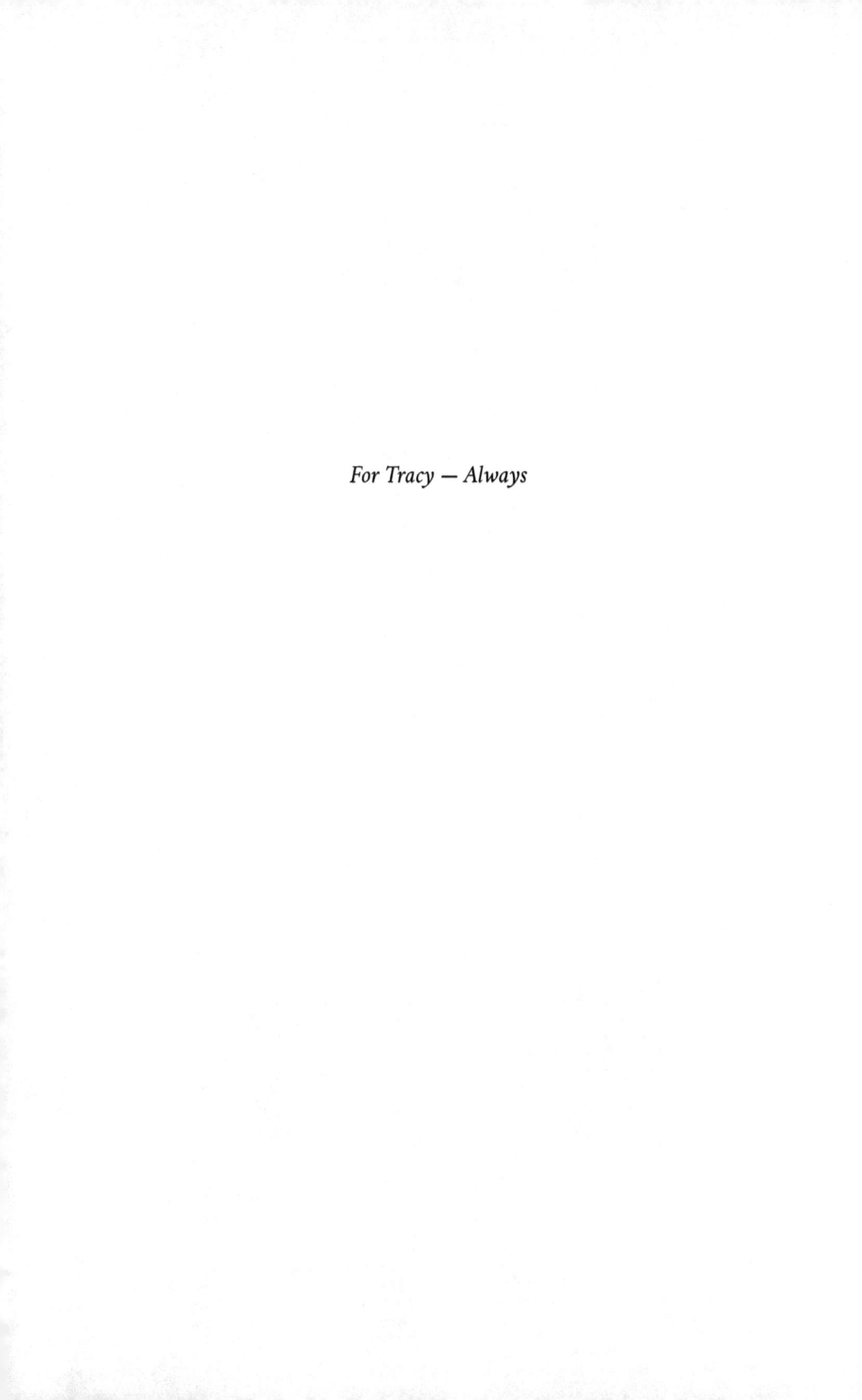

For Tracy — Always

AUTHOR'S NOTE

Once you get into this book, you're going to see a fair amount of characters saying horrible racist and misogynistic things. That's deliberate. Those characters are horrible racists and misogynists.

I grew up in a town that in many ways inspired Red Springs. I left to go to college, and stayed gone for about twenty years, but eleven years ago I came back and have been living here since then. It's sad to say, but I didn't just make up the racism and misogyny in this story. About 95% of it I've heard first-hand, with the other 5% being related to me by the people who did hear it. I was exposed to all of this growing up, and I'm still exposed to it today. It's real. Much of *The Storm* is more journalistic than creative.

That's not to say that everyone in the South is racist or misogynistic. There are plenty of people here who aren't. But there are also plenty who *are*, and it's important to realize that.

You might find the things that some of the characters herein say or do to be upsetting. They might shock you and make you angry.

Good. That's the point.

Dan Jolley
September, 2020

I

CLOUDS GATHER

1

Sunday, August 13, 2017
7:30 a.m.
Nine hours before the storm

A mile and a half down Dahlonega Highway, just west of the town of Red Springs, Georgia, out past the Mega-Star and the Hardee's and the shiny new Zaxby's that hoped to pull traffic from the half-finished community college, sat a rectangular cinder block building. Its parking lot could hold twenty cars if they packed in tight, and its identifying signage was easy to miss: a square white wooden plaque with black letters, set near the front door. It proclaimed the building to be CORKY'S GYM, and in smaller letters below that, stated that it allowed MEMBERS ONLY, and that ADMISSION REQUIRES KEY.

The interior of the building looked at first glance like a place where old gym equipment had crawled off to die. No instructional placards, no shiny yellow or purple or red or gold paint, just worn, cracked leather seats, tarnished steel, and rack after rack of free weights. The gym's one concession to what most of its members considered vanity was that the entire west wall had been covered with mirrors.

Zandra Seagraves glanced toward the mirrors before she lay back down at the Smith machine for her last set of bench presses, but Horace Pounder was in the way, so she couldn't see herself. It didn't matter. It wasn't difficult to use proper form on a Smith machine. Zandra got a good grip on the bar, lifted and rotated its hooks, and gave herself a slow, silent five-count as she lowered the bar to her chest. *Five down... five up. Five down... five up.* She controlled her breathing rigidly, exhaling as the bar slid up, inhaling as it came back down. After the fourth rep, she saw a massive shadow moving toward her and knew Pounder had finished his last set.

She and Pounder were the only two members there. He waited nearby, silent, as she pushed through her last four reps.

Zandra barely got the bar up on the last one. Exactly as she'd intended. She rotated the bar back, hooked it in place, and sat up, reaching for her towel.

Pounder's voice boomed out. "Y'know, you'd get better results if you'd use a regular barbell. And, y'know. Let someone spot you."

Zandra ignored Pounder and took a long swig from her water bottle. When she stood up, he handed her a length of paper towel and a spray bottle, and she spritzed the Smith machine and wiped it down.

Now she had a clear line of sight with the mirrors, and allowed herself a quick glance. An old boyfriend had described her as "a tall glass of Serena Williams." The reflection scowling back at her, clad in a baggy sleeveless t-shirt over a sports bra, bicycle shorts, ratty sneakers, and a ferocious coating of sweat, showed her none of the grace Serena possessed. It did show her power. The morning sun outlined her chiseled biceps and triceps, and when she turned, it highlighted the striations of her thigh muscles. Zandra had long ago decided she preferred power to grace.

She used the hem of her shirt to wipe the sweat from her brow.

Pounder said, "How much you put up? That last go-round?"

Zandra eyed Pounder. She'd never met a larger human being in person. Horace Pounder stood six feet, eight inches tall, had thighs as big around as many men's waists, arms that required specially tailored shirt sleeves to fit into, and a gut of gargantuan proportion. He used another length of paper towels to mop the sweat from his pale, egg-bald scalp. Pounder wore an immense tank-top and huge basketball shorts, and was just as sweat-soaked as Zandra.

"One-eighty," Zandra said, and began taking the plates off the bar. Out of the corner of her eye she saw Pounder's mouth open, and shook her head. "Don't tell me how much you did today, I don't need to know." On more than one occasion, Zandra had seen Pounder walk up to the curl machine—a machine designed for both grips to be used at the same time—put the pin at the very bottom, and curl the entire weight stack with one arm.

"Wasn't goin' to. What I was gonna say was, 'That's a personal best for you, ain't it?'" She turned toward him, and he backed away a couple of steps. "Whoa, you'd best stay upwind, I smell like a durn barnyard."

"And you wonder why I don't want you spotting me."

"Hey, I'm just sayin'. Never usin' a spotter? You're robbin' yourself."

Zandra shrugged and was about to say something else, when the lock clicked and the front door opened. Two men in their thirties, one blond, one with buzzed-off red hair, both of them sporting the kind of physique gained by spending hours in the gym, walked in with gym bags over their shoulders. They caught sight of Zandra and Pounder, and Zandra felt as if the air conditioning had suddenly kicked on.

"Bill. Kenny." Pounder's voice always carried, no matter how softly he tried to pitch it, and it made its way across the gym floor as if he'd spoken through a megaphone. The two men gave Pounder friendly nods as they made their way toward the men's locker room. Their eyes slid over to Zandra. She didn't speak, but she did incline her head a degree or two. The nods she got in return bore no open hostility, but the difference from the greetings they'd given Pounder was unmis-takable.

After Bill and Kenny had disappeared into the locker room, Pounder said, "It might help if you said somethin'. 'Mornin'.' 'Howdy.' Ain't gotta be nothin' big. 'How's your mom an' 'em?'"

"I want some Gatorade," Zandra said, and moved toward the women's locker room. She despised using the showers in there, and usually made do with spreading a towel on the seat of her SUV to keep the sweat off until she got home.

Pounder shook his head, a tiny, rueful grin on his face. "That stuff don't do you no good. Ain't nothin' but colored water."

"I'll see you outside," she called over her shoulder.

The women's locker room was half the size of the men's, infrequently cleaned, and missing half the bulbs in the overhead fixtures. The one working sink poured out rust-colored water. Zandra opened her locker and grabbed her bag out of it.

She had the tarnished metal door half-closed when muffled voices came to her. The lockers took up one wall, and she realized they must share a common wall with the men's, because when she leaned forward and put her head halfway inside her own locker, the voices grew clear.

"...that ass, though. You see it out there?"

"Shit, thing's hard to miss."

"All I'm sayin'. I'd tear that ass all to pieces."

She recognized Bill and Kenny. It wasn't difficult, what with them being the only men in the building besides Pounder.

"Fuck, son, she could crack walnuts with that thing. You'd be walkin' with a limp for two weeks, you get tangled up in that."

Zandra quietly closed the locker door, her face stony, her hands curled into tight fists. Stomach acid threatened to boil up into her throat, but she breathed deeply for a few moments. She'd heard worse. That was the hell of it.

Bill and Kenny hadn't made it out of their locker room yet when Zandra crossed the gym floor and stepped out into the northwest Georgia morning, where Pounder waited for her. It had to be at least eighty degrees already, maybe eighty-five. She gestured with her chin at the Mega-Star up the road. "I was serious about the Gatorade. You want some? I'm buying."

Pounder shrugged. "Got to gas up anyhow. I'll meet you there."

Zandra spread the towel carefully on the front seat of her Chevy

Tahoe and climbed in. It took less than a minute to travel up Dahlonega Highway to the Mega-Star. She parked next to the store, but Pounder pulled his massive Dodge Ram up to one of the pumps. Zandra grabbed her purse, shut and locked the Tahoe, and headed inside. She passed a spinner rack of red "Make America Great Again" hats on her way in, and spent a moment or two considering the benefit of picking one's battles.

Someone hurried toward her, leaving the store, a white man with his head tucked down and his face turned away, but as soon as he said, "'Cuse me," she knew who it was.

All the people in Red Springs knew Augustus Parsons, and they all called him by the same nickname: "Gush." All of them except Zandra. Every small Southern town Zandra had ever been to had someone like Gush Parsons. The loner, usually cognitively challenged in some way, who drifted around the county, wandering, aimless. Sometimes talking to himself. Gush filled that role for Red Springs, but it was a role he'd only occupied for the last eight years—since the day of his motorcycle accident, when he'd slammed face-first into a tree and suffered permanent brain damage. The accident had taken a dozen surgeons many long hours to repair, and they still hadn't gotten it right. The two halves of Gush's pale, waxy face didn't exactly line up anymore, and the few words he could manage came out distorted and strained.

"Augustus?" Zandra called as Gush Parsons hurried across the parking lot. She'd known him since he was a child. She'd spent three summers baby-sitting him, starting when he was nine years old. "You all right?"

Gush straightened up for a second, rising to his full lanky, raw-boned height, and turned his mismatched face toward her. "Gotta go," he called. "Gotta go!"

Zandra watched him scurry past the gas pumps and down the shoulder of the road. Words came to her: *If someone was hassling him, heads will fucking roll.* She was on high alert as she crossed the threshold and looked around.

The usual cashier on Sunday mornings was a college-age white girl named Nicole, who never failed to compliment Zandra on her eyes. Zandra figured it was the only thing Nicole could think of to say to her. That was fine. Zandra had never felt the need to strike up conversations with people she didn't know well, and Nicole always seemed satisfied with getting a quick "Thanks" in return.

Nicole wasn't behind the counter when Zandra pushed through the door, setting off the jangling bell above it. The girl's absence didn't bother her to begin with, since Nicole seemed to spend a lot of time stocking the shelves, or texting, or sneaking off to the back door to have a cigarette. Zandra headed for the glass-fronted case where they kept the cold drinks. She passed the beer and the bottled water, and had opened the case filled with various flavors of Gatorade when she heard a man's voice from back near the restrooms. She couldn't understand the words, but they were followed immediately by Nicole's whimper and the sound of breaking glass, and Zandra moved silently down the aisle and peered around the corner.

A white man stood there holding Nicole. He had Nicole's back pressed against his chest, her throat clamped tight in the crook of one elbow, her fingers clawing at him uselessly. In his other hand he clutched a wine bottle. He'd struck it against the closest wall, leaving the bottle's neck jagged and sharp, and wine sprayed and splattered as he waved the bottle near Nicole's face.

"You're wrong," he said. Maybe to Nicole. Maybe to no one. White showed all the way around his irises. "You're wrong. You're wrong."

Zandra couldn't tell how old the man was. Maybe twenty-five. Maybe forty-five. The lines of his face had dirt ground into them, and his wiry brown hair stood up off his skull as if he'd ridden miles with his head stuck out a car window like a dog. Zandra didn't think he'd changed his clothes for days.

She stood a good fifteen feet from him, but even at that distance she could see easily how dilated his pupils were. Only the narrowest of rings around the black let her know they were normally blue.

"Let me go!" Nicole said through hitching sobs. "Let me go, you're crazy, let me go!"

"*I'm not fucking crazy!*" The man pressed the broken wine bottle against her cheek. Not hard enough to break the skin, but hard enough to dent it. "They can hear me! They can always hear me! They know what I'm going to do, what I'm going to say! They see it all! Through the screens, the mirrors, the TVs, the phones, *they're fucking everywhere* and you don't see it but that doesn't make me crazy!"

"Excuse me," Zandra said, making her voice as smooth as she could. She stepped out around the corner, into the man's sight, her hands raised.

The man jerked Nicole backward, retreating into a corner, and Nicole screamed, and the man said, "Get away! Get away, don't come any closer, are you one of them *are you one of them?*"

"My name is Zandra." She kept her hands up, her bag hanging from her shoulder by her side. "What's your name?"

His eyes got even bigger. "You don't know? How could you not know, you're one of them, they know it all! Everything I've done, everything I'm going to do! They see everything!"

"I'm not one of them," Zandra said, smooth, patient. "But I think I can help you. You've come a long way, haven't you?"

That was hardly a guess. The man's accent held no trace of the northwest Georgia/southeast Tennessee twang. He sounded more like a native Chicagoan. A Chicagoan who had just done a *mountain* of cocaine, if his pupils were any indication. But Zandra's question broke the ice. "Yes! I've been on the road... so long... running from them! Have I gone far enough? Have I?"

It wasn't the first time Zandra had encountered someone from out of state like this, someone who'd just pulled off the I-775 spur, usually heading south to Florida. She said, "It depends. First you've got to tell me your name."

The bell over the door jangled. Zandra cast a glance over her shoulder and saw Pounder staring at her and at the man holding Nicole. She half-turned and put a hand up: *I've got this.* Pounder's face had already begun creasing into a scowl, and it kept getting darker, but he backed off as she directed.

"Why?" The man held Nicole as tightly as ever, but a plaintive note had crept into his words. "Why do you need to know?"

"I need to know because I want to trust you. But I can't trust you unless you tell me your name."

"Are you gonna hurt me? If I tell you? Will you crawl into my brain and lay eggs and turn me into someone else?"

Nicole whimpered again. Zandra swallowed. "No. I promise you. I'm not going to hurt you. I'm not going to do any of those things you just said."

"You swear?"

"I absolutely swear."

"Gordon. My name's Gordon."

"Okay. Okay, Gordon. Good. Now, the next thing I need you to do is tell me who's been watching you."

He jerked Nicole up almost off her feet, and thrust the wine bottle at Zandra in a stabbing motion that sent more wine splashing out onto the floor. "The lizard people! *The lizard people!* At first I thought I was imagining things, I saw them, I saw them when I went to sleep but the doctor said and my mother said they said that was just my imagination, just my imagination, they said, but then on the radio *they said it was true!* They said it was real, it was real, I always knew it was real and *they said it!* And now I'm *fucked*, you hear me, I'm well and truly *fucked*, Zandra, because they can find me now! They can find me no matter how far I go, no matter what I do, I can't get away I can't I can't!"

Nicole's tears had run down her cheeks and streaked across Gordon's arm. Zandra took a slow, careful step forward. "Gordon. Listen to me. I can help you. But first you've got to let Nicole go."

"No! No, I need her! I need her to give to the lizard people! She's younger than me and they'll take her and they'll let me go!"

"No, Gordon. That's not how it works. They don't care about Nicole. But I can talk to them for you. I can explain that they need to leave you alone."

She thought Gordon's eyes might pop out of his skull. *"You do know them!"*

"I just needed to know who you were talking about, Gordon. I figured it was the lizard people, but I needed to know. I can clear all this up. But you need to trust me. And you need to let Nicole go."

A flashing blue glare caught Zandra's eye, reflecting off the metal of a magazine rack, and she realized Pounder had made a call. Her heartbeat sped up. She didn't think Gordon had noticed the blue light.

"How?" Now his own voice had dropped to something like a whimper. "How do you know them? How could you talk to them?"

"I'm going to show you something, Gordon. Okay? It's in my purse. I'm going to get it out real slow, okay, and I'm just going to use two fingers." She reached across her body with her left hand and fished out the black leather wallet.

"What's that? What're you showing me? What's that what's that?"

Zandra let the wallet drop open, displaying the polished gold badge. "My name is Zandra Seagraves, Gordon. I'm the sheriff of Cartauga County."

Emotions chased themselves around Gordon's face. Hope and vindication and disbelief and outrage, in a loop, spinning like a roulette wheel. It finally landed on outrage. "Sheriff? You're trynna tell me you're *sheriff* of this Podunk little shit-stain? They're gonna make a *black woman* sheriff here?"

Zandra kept her eyes on his. The eyes that Nicole never failed to compliment. Eyes so light brown they bordered on yellow and turned a glittering gold in sunlight. "How do you think I got elected, Gordon? I have *connections*. Connections you can use. Now listen. If you'll let Nicole go, I'll take you to them. I'll go there with you. And we'll get this all straightened out. Okay?"

"You'd do that for me?"

"No question. Absolutely."

Gordon's arm relaxed and slid away from Nicole's throat, and Zandra motioned for the girl to get away, but Nicole needed no prompting and bolted out the door like a rabbit fleeing a hawk.

Zandra took a deep breath, and was about to say, "Now you need to put down the bottle, too," when Gordon started trembling. Tears welled up in his eyes.

"I'm not good enough to meet them! I'm not good enough! I'm not I'm not I'm not!"

Gordon stabbed himself in the throat with the broken bottle.

Zandra lunged for him, but in the second and a half it took her to reach him, Gordon jabbed the bottle into his throat again and again, his arm whipping back and forth like a sewing machine needle piercing cloth, and Zandra grabbed the bottle out of his hands and threw it away as Gordon fell.

She caught him, and as she lowered him to the floor, Gordon said, "Praise Jesus, thank you, thank you, thank you Zandra, praise Jesus," and with every word he said, blood sprayed into her face from the holes in his windpipe.

<hr>

Horace Pounder—who held the rank of major in the Cartauga County Sheriff's Department, and functioned as Zandra's second-in-command—stood next to her as the EMTs loaded Gordon into an ambulance. They'd bandaged the man's throat heavily. As the first ambulance pulled away, carrying Gordon off to one of the big hospitals in Chattanooga, Nicole sat in the back of the remaining one, bawling her eyes out.

One of the crew came to talk to Zandra. She had just finished wiping her face clean with the towel from her Tahoe. "So he's going to make it?"

The EMT, a wiry white man in his early fifties, nodded his head and chuckled. "He wouldn't have, if he'd stabbed himself with something meant for stabbing. As it was, that bottle was sharp, but it didn't go in too deep. He'll recover from the punctured trachea."

Not far away, the two men from the gym, Bill and Kenny, stood near a Sheriff's Department cruiser. On the Department's payroll, they were listed as Deputy William Coyle and Deputy Kenneth Roach, both of them part of the Patrol Division. Zandra watched them surreptitiously, and spoke just loud enough for Pounder to hear. "What's their take on this debacle?"

Pounder came out with a hoarse whisper, the only way he could keep his words from echoing around the parking lot. "They wanted to come in guns blazin'. I told 'em you waved me off, and that meant we stayed waved off. Till you said different."

"And they were okay with that?"

Pounder seemed to be choosing his words carefully. "I think they'd have a lot more to say if shit had went sideways."

She nodded, somber. "Thanks for wrangling them."

"You kiddin'? He would'a cut that clerk's face off, hadn'a been for you."

Zandra just shook her head. If she read the deputies' expressions and body language correctly, both of them still disapproved deeply of how she'd handled the situation, whether or not things "had went sideways," as Pounder said. Never mind that a frontal assault would just as likely have hit Nicole as the man threatening her. Zandra figured even if she could've sedated Gordon with a James Bond-style knockout dart, preventing any harm at all from coming to him or Nicole, someone in the department would have accused her of wasting expensive chemicals.

"I'm heading back. Gotta get the report done."

As she walked away from Pounder, past Coyle and Roach, Pounder called after her. "Y'know, you got a secretary for a reason."

She didn't respond.

2

8:45 a.m.

Eight hours before the storm

"It was over 'fore anybody knew what was goin' on good," Belvis Horne said, leaning against his regular booth at the Hardee's. He addressed the three other retirees who gathered every morning to eat biscuits, drink coffee, and fix the problems of the world. The four men had been meeting there for the last seven years, without fail, except when Jerry had his kidney stones out.

Belvis was, to use one of his father's expressions, "of a piece" with his philosophical counterparts. He wore old, battered, intensely comfortable Hush Puppies over black socks, gray chinos secured well above his navel with a cracked leather belt, a plaid shirt stuffed fiercely into his pants since he wasn't a goddamn hippie, a navy blue windbreaker because the mornings were still plenty chilly as far as he was concerned, and a white-and-yellow trucker cap stained brown with multiple oil spots. He hadn't yet turned seventy-five, but could have easily been mistaken for ten years older, so deep were the lines in his tanned, leathery face. Tufts of snow-white hair stuck out from under the cap. His blue eyes had faded, turned rheumy sometime in the last six or seven years, but he still saw perfectly well enough, thank you very much.

Ed and Jerry both wore variations on the same theme—Ed with his salt-and-pepper hair, that wasn't fair, goddamn it, he was older than Belvis—while Thornton wore his favorite pair of overalls and a stained white long-sleeved thermal-underwear shirt. The last of Thornton's hair had finally turned loose right around his seventy-third birthday, so now he was every bit as egg-bald as his giant son Horace.

Thornton had lost a lot of weight since he started his chemo. None of them ever said anything about the chemo.

"How d'you know so much about it?" Ed said as he wiped biscuit crumbs off his stubble-covered chin. "You wasn't even there."

Belvis scoffed. "Don't nothin' happen 'round here without my knowin' it, you know that."

Jerry blew on his coffee. Tommy-June had only given it to him a minute ago, and it was still too hot to drink. "Yeah, well, it ain't right, I'm sayin'. Divide up a man's property like that. He ain't even been dead a month. An' for what? Anybody think we *need* another one o' them subdivisions? All 'at's gonna do's pull in more o' them *tech types* from Chattanooga." Jerry despised the young people who moved to Chattanooga to work, but who picked out more affordable places to live across the state line.

Belvis put on his best condescending face. "Whadda I always say, boys? *All politics is local.* You wantcher voice heard? You getcher ass to the town meetin' an' vote on it."

"I had hay to get up," Jerry said, descending into one of his sulks.

Belvis had drawn breath to say something about Jerry's goddamn hay when Tommy-June called out from behind the counter. "Belvis, honey, your coffee's ready."

Belvis ambled over. Tommy-June Billingsley wasn't a bad-looking woman. Of course, she was too young for him. Not even good into her sixties yet. But she'd kept up her figure for the most part, and he liked the way she piled her silver-gray hair all up on top of her head, and she was always sweet to him, so he put a little swagger in his steps as he crossed the dining room to the counter. Not every man his age could still do that. Sure as hell not Ed, not since they'd put his new hip in, but Belvis could still move. He was still strong. Sometimes he thought maybe he'd take Tommy-June out to a nice dinner, pour on the charm, get her back to his place. Then for dessert he'd *show* her how strong he still was.

Tommy-June slid the brown plastic tray across to him, where a large coffee sat next to a country ham biscuit. "Here y'go, sugar. How's your kids doin'?"

"'Bout like me, I reckon," Belvis said. "Hangin' on like a hair in a biscuit."

Tommy-June laughed and gave him her big sweet smile. "Well, you tell 'em I said hey."

Belvis grinned at her—a lot of confidence rode around in that grin, since he'd had dental implants last fall—and took his tray back to the table. Thornton scooted over enough to let Belvis in.

Ed was saying, "Them tech types you's talkin' about, you know what they bring with 'em, don'tcha?" He rubbed his fingertips together. "Moola. Cold hard cash. An' if they *live* here, they're gonna *spend* it here. We'll get 'em one way or another. Tax revenue alone's worth it."

Belvis thought about a response as he took a bite of his biscuit, but movement from outside caught his eye. He watched as a late-model Ford Mustang, a sharp-looking number with a midnight-blue paint job and broad white racing stripes, pulled up in front of the restaurant. The New York tag jumped out at him. Both doors opened at the same time, and Belvis said, "Well lookee here," as two young black men climbed out.

He figured they might've been college athletes, both of them broad through the shoulders and narrow in the waist. One wore a snug sleeveless t-shirt that showed off the bulging muscles in his upper arms and shoulders. The other one had what Belvis had heard they called "pencil braids," all gathered up at the base of his skull in a big thick ponytail.

The four retirees watched as the two young men came inside. The one with the sleeveless t-shirt headed off to the restroom, while the one with the ponytail walked right up to Tommy-June.

"Mornin'," Tommy-June said brightly, and gave Ponytail the same sweet smile she'd shown to Belvis. "Will this be for here or to go?"

"To go, please, ma'am," Ponytail said. "I'ma wait for my friend to order food, but I know we both want coffee."

Tommy-June obligingly tapped buttons on her monitor. "Two coffees it is. What size, sugar?"

Ponytail gave her a boyish smile. "Big as we can get 'em, ma'am." He glanced around the restaurant and, when he saw Belvis watching him, offered a brief but polite nod. Belvis nodded back slowly, his face carefully expressionless.

Sleeveless came back out of the bathroom, and he and Ponytail ordered a big bag of biscuits and a couple of croissants to go with the coffee. Tommy-June said, "Looks like y'all're on quite the road trip."

Ponytail flashed that grin again. His teeth were white and perfect. "Yes, ma'am. Got to be in Orlando by tonight."

"That's a haul," Tommy-June said, "but you can do it, God willin' an' the creek don't rise. Y'all have yourselves a safe trip, now."

Both of the young men thanked her. Belvis's eyes never left them as they made their way back to the Mustang, climbed inside, and pulled away. Belvis, Ed, Jerry, and Thornton ate their biscuits and sipped their coffee silently for a long moment before Belvis put his coffee down and said, "I tell you what. Shit ain't like it used to be."

Jerry hooked a thumb at the parking space where the Mustang had sat. "I remember back before that damn Martin Luther King showed up, the coloreds knew their *place*. You pass one on the sidewalk, they'd drop their eyes. Show some goddamn *respect*. Now? You get some uppity niggers like those two? Hell, Belvis, that'n with the hair was just lookin' right *at* you."

"World's goin' to hell in a handbasket," Belvis said with a morose head shake. "My daddy always used to say, one o' these days we're gonna have to play cowboys an' niggers."

Thornton stared into space. "Tell you one thing for damn sure. I wouldn't mind puttin' it to that nigger sheriff." When the other three men all sputtered and protested, Thornton raised his hands. "Now, now, you seen her just as clear as I have. That's a woman and a half, right there."

Ed thought about it, and shrugged. "Aw, hell, boys, I ain't never minded niggers. Way I see it, everybody oughta own a couple."

The four of them laughed quietly. Belvis was about to say something else on the subject when the phone in his pocket vibrated. He hauled it out and carefully slid his finger across the screen to unlock it. Ed and Jerry and Thornton had all had a good bit of fun at his expense when he'd first showed up with a brand-new iPhone, called him "Space-Man Belvis" and "Einstein" and such, but once he'd gotten the hang of it—especially after his son, who'd given him the phone for his birthday, showed him how to access Facebook—Belvis had taken to how easy it was to keep up with his family.

He'd never understand why so many people felt the need to tell the world every single little piddle-fart thing they did—nobody's life was that interesting, no matter what they were trying to sell you—but he enjoyed getting messages from his children and his cousins, who he hadn't seen in years, and he'd even hunted up a couple of his old Army buddies.

Belvis tapped at the phone, and squinted at it.

When he was sure of what he was seeing, the blood drained from his face.

"What's wrong, Belvis?" Jerry asked. Ed and Thornton both broke off what they were saying and turned toward him, concerned.

Belvis's granddaughter Savannah, the one everybody called "Savvy," had just "checked in" over at the Civil War memorial park. Savvy had posted a picture, what the kids were calling "selfies," of her and some of her friends, sitting on one of the cannons that dotted the park. Savvy was straddling the barrel, which wasn't ladylike in the first place, but right behind her—with his hands on her waist—was a big goofy-looking black teenager, grinning at the camera with his chin on Savvy's shoulder. She had her head tilted, resting against his, getting his nasty hair-grease all over her face, and Belvis gripped the phone so tight he was surprised the glass didn't crack.

Jerry repeated the question: "What's wrong, Belvis?"

Belvis stood and jammed the phone into his pocket. "I gotta go, boys. I'll see you later." He walked, stiff-legged, out of the restaurant and climbed into his truck, teeth grinding so hard it made his jaw ache, flashes of red splashing across his vision.

3

9:15 a.m.

Seven and a half hours before the storm

The Chickamauga Chattanooga National Military park, or as locals referred to it, simply "the park," lay in Catoosa County, to Cartauga County's immediate west. It was the site of one of the Civil War's bloodier battles. Tour guides gleefully informed tourists—as well as the occasional curious local who'd never gotten around to taking the tour before but had nothing better to do—that some of the fields of battle were so thick with the dead that a person could walk from one corner to the other without touching the ground. The Union soldiers, according to the tour guides, were so much better fed than the Confederate men that when they died, their bodies turned black and bloated. The Southern soldiers, on the other hand, were uniformly malnourished, so much so that their corpses became gray, waxy, shrunken husks.

None of that mattered to Savvy Horne. She'd been coming to the park all her life. Her family and her friends' families had all come here for picnics, and bike rides, and recreational league ball games where Coach Perry would hoot and holler and shout encouragement to all the players. Her father had even taught her to drive, in part, by letting her guide the car for short distances on the narrow, unlined roads that wound through the woods, past the hundreds of scattered monuments to various military companies, and long-decommissioned cannons, and stacks of cannonballs mortared into pyramids. She had poked around the relocated-but-otherwise-authentic one-room cabin along Highway 27, and many times climbed all the stairs of Wilder Tower, the park's biggest monument, which looked like an enormous white rook from a colossal chess board.

No thoughts of hiking trails or historical significance occupied Savvy's thoughts today, though. Today, she and seven of her friends had taken over one of the park's many meadows for a series of four-on-four *Steel Tourney* matches. *Steel Tourney* was an Alternate Reality game that their friend Riley had developed himself, and today was an important part of Riley's beta test. They had all arrived fully hydrated, their phones charged, and now the meadow had transformed into a futuristic battlefield, the AR display on their phone screens planting metallic barriers in a loose, maze-like configuration around the field. It was up to Savvy and her team to find the opposing team's grail—while avoiding exploding traps—and claim it before their own grail fell into enemy hands.

It was also a fantastic opportunity to run around and laugh like a lunatic.

The game had a chat feature. It even had voice chat. But Savvy and her friends simply screamed at each other across the ankle-high grass covering the meadow. They had to get this session done before it got too hot to play, and she'd already broken a decent sweat.

One of her team's traps triggered, and one of the four enemy icons at the edge of her screen turned blood-red and vanished. Savvy peered over the edge of her phone to see her friend Gage standing there, looking legitimately stunned. "Gotta watch your step!" she cried, and Gage shot her an elaborate bird, complete with flourishes.

Cindy shouted, "Guys! I see it! It's over here!"

Immediately Mark, on the now-diminished opposing team, screamed, "Grenade!" and his teammates bolted toward him. Each player got three grenades, which they could lob over the metal barriers with an upward swipe on the phone screen. Savvy was nowhere near Cindy, so she just watched as Staci and Quinton ran in crazy patterns, following the maze. They weren't allowed to run through a barrier or they'd be disqualified.

Savvy's eyes lingered on Mark. She hadn't expected him to climb up behind her on the cannon earlier, when she'd posed for the selfie. The sensation of his hands on her waist stayed with her. She hadn't been close enough to him before today to catch his scent, but now that she had, she wanted more of it. Savvy didn't know if it was after-shave, or cologne, or maybe just something plain like soap or fabric softener, but whatever it was, it combined with his skin into something that made her heart beat faster. Mark had ridden to the park with Gage, but Savvy wanted to offer him a ride home in her car. He'd only been a student at Red Springs High School for about a month. Savvy tried to come up with something plausible. *You can show me where you live,* or maybe *I don't know your neighborhood too well, maybe you can give me a tour.*

She didn't know if she'd be able to work up the nerve.

But then Savvy heard the roar of an approaching engine—one she recognized—and an icy flood washed over her heart. Her guts clenched, and she whispered, "Oh no," just as her grandfather's truck barreled out of the woods on one of the park's narrow roads. She could tell the instant he spotted her. The big red-and-white Chevy skewed to the right, bumped down off the pavement, and to Savvy's utter horror, her grandfather drove out into the meadow, straight toward her.

Everybody else had stopped what they were doing, their phones forgotten in their hands, as Belvis Horne brought the truck to a sliding stop, digging trenches out of the ground. Savvy knew he was violating a ton of laws and codes, and that if a park ranger had seen him do it, he'd be facing hefty fines and maybe some jail time. But none of that mattered as her grandfather threw the door of the truck open and hit the ground practically running. His icy blue eyes raked across her friends, and stabbed holes in Mark before they came to rest on Savvy. Belvis Horne grabbed her upper arm in one vise-like hand and said, "Getcher ass in the truck."

Savvy tried to wrench free, not only because his grip was hurting her, but also because she thought the humiliation might kill her on the spot. She couldn't break his hold, but she did dig in her heels enough to stop him from dragging her any farther. "Grandpa, let me go!"

"Ain't arguin'. Get in the truck."

"Why? What's wrong?"

Savvy knew what was wrong. She wasn't sure how he'd figured out where she was, or who she was spending time with, but she knew it in her heart, had known it as soon as the truck's tires had left the blacktop.

Belvis rounded on her. With his free hand he dug his phone out and shoved the selfie in her face. "Your daddy raised you better'n this," he snarled, and while her friends all stood like statues, staring, Savvy finally pulled her arm free.

"Grandpa, these are my friends!"

Belvis whipped a brick-like hand into Savvy's face. The impact spun her off her feet, blinding pain along her cheek, but he didn't let her hit the ground. His other hand found its grip on her arm again and almost pulled it out of its socket as he yanked her back upright, and this time he put his own face in hers, and though he screamed at Savvy, those icy eyes fixed squarely on Mark. "You listen to me and you listen good, Savannah Michelle Horne! I would rather die! You hear me? I would rather *die* than let you prance around in public with some filthy-ass nigger!"

Savvy whimpered and did her best to choke back sobs, but that was all the resistance she could muster as her grandfather dragged her to the truck and shoved her up into the passenger seat and slammed the door after her. She knew Mark must have been watching her. She couldn't bring herself to look at him as Belvis climbed in, shoved the truck into gear, and sprayed more dirt and grass in the air as he spun around and barreled back out the way he'd come.

4

11:45 a.m.

Five hours before the storm

Service was in full swing at the Red Springs Congregational Gospel Church. Shep Curtis commanded the stage, his piercing voice warmed up now and banging off the rafters, and he stalked back and forth, one end of the platform to the other, waving his arms to accent the words spraying from his mouth.

Not unlike a conductor working an orchestra, in Shep's opinion.

"God said the words, my children! He said the words, just as plain as the words I'm saying to you right this very minute! He spoke, right there in the book of Matthew, the infallible, sacred scripture, He said the words!"

In the second row, a portly middle-aged woman in a pink dress stood up and shouted, "*Yes, Lord!*"

She wasn't alone in her excitation. Shep scanned the crowd, looking not for others who shared in the divine ecstasy, but for any who didn't. The church had twenty pews on each side, and the morning's crowd had filled them about three-quarters full. A little better than half of the flock was already on their feet. Some of them simply held a hand up. Some held up both hands, and swayed a little, back and forth, usually with their eyes closed. Aubrey Griggs had taken his usual seat on the aisle, and any second now he'd leave his spot and start spinning and dancing, up and down the length of the auditorium.

"You all know it's the truth," Shep went on. He took full advantage of the state-of-the-art sound system one of the members had donated, and the microphone clipped to his tie took his voice and channeled it through the massive speakers up in the corners next to the ceiling. "You know the Word of God is the *only* truth! The *only* thing in this wide, wicked world that is *absolute!*"

"*Yes, Lord!*" The woman in the pink dress swayed on her feet.

A man two rows behind her bellowed, "*The Word!*"

"And I'll tell you what God said. I'll tell you right now. It's here, on the page!" Shep hefted the well-worn Bible his father had given him for his twelfth birthday. Its black leather cover bore multiple blemishes and scuffs, and Shep slammed it into the palm of his hand.

"Tell us! Tell us!" That was Aubrey Griggs. Shep knew he was seconds from launching.

"Right here in the Book of Matthew! In the seventh chapter, and the sixteenth verse! *Ye shall know them by their fruits!*"

"*Yes, Lord Jesus!*" Aubrey screamed, and he took off like a top, spinning down toward the big table where the implements of the Lord's Supper lay covered with a white cloth.

"Ye shall know them by their fruits! Jesus's words, y'all, not mine! Not mine! I am but a vessel! A channel, for the divine, incorruptible, undeniable word of the Lord to reach your ears!"

Multiple shouts now, from all around the auditorium. *Yes, Lord! Say it, Lord! Let us hear it, Lord!* And now that Aubrey had left his seat, Shep knew more would follow. He figured Dave Bandy would be next, and maybe Clark Abernathy after that. Clark was a climber. He'd be walking on the backs of the pews once he got started good.

"Ye shall know them by their fruits! And do you know what Jesus of Nazareth meant by that? Do you know the sacred mission He was charging us, his children, with?"

A slim, dark-haired woman in the front row threw back her head and shut her eyes and shouted, *"Sahn didi ai, sahn didi ai, la la la moka ai! Sahn didi ai! Sahn didi ai, la la la moka ai!"*

Shep felt his face turning red as he got more and more worked up. It was hard not to get into it. "Jesus, the son of God, was telling us that it is our mission, our duty, our God-given *right*, to judge our fellow man! *By their fruits ye shall know them!*"

Clark Abernathy clambered up into his seat, got one foot balanced on the back of the pew in front of him, and flung himself forward, the smooth soles of his shiny black shoes guided by the Holy Spirit Itself. He almost fell when Aubrey Griggs bounded back up the aisle and knocked into one of the pews, but not quite, his sixty-year-old banker's body held aloft by God's love.

Shep paced back and forth like the proverbial caged animal. *Slam*, went the Bible into his open palm. *Slam*, with every point he made. "God has put us on the Earth to judge our fellow man, my children! He couldn't have said it any clearer if He showed up right here, this morning, and shouted the words in your ears with His own mouth! We are the ones who are *in* the world, but not *of* the world!"

"Yes, Lord!" the woman in pink screamed. Shep thought she might faint.

"Because I tell you rightly, and I tell you true, straight from God's mouth which is the Word! You know the Word is God, and God is the Word, and He gave us the Word right here!" Shep brandished the Bible like a weapon.

The dark-haired woman in the front row hadn't stopped with her litany—*"Sahn didi ai, sahn didi ai, la la la moka ai!"*—and now two others began speaking in tongues as well. Shep was glad for the sound system, because otherwise they might have drowned him out.

"The Word is the *only* thing you can rely on, my children! The *only* thing you can believe! Some out there will tempt you. Yes they will. Some out there will fill your head with evil. With *lies*. They'll try to tell you wicked things, malicious things, and they'll call it—" Shep summoned up all the bile and hatred he could muster, "—*science!* They'll act like they're the ones who know the truth. They'll spin you lie after lie after lie! They'll tell you the world is millions of years old! Billions, even! They'll tell you it started with a Big Bang! They'll tell you creatures called *Neanderthals* walked the Earth!" He spun his voice up into a scream. "And it's all *lies!* It's the work of Satan himself!"

"Yes, Lord!" "Praise Him!" "Praise Jesus!"

"As if God Almighty doesn't know how the world began! *He began it!*" Shep was about to move on to his next point when he noticed the girl.

She sat about halfway back on the right-hand side. She wasn't standing, wasn't swaying, wasn't speaking in tongues, but her eyes were fixed on him, and they glistened in a way he had come to recognize. In the way that meant she hadn't blinked in a while, because she didn't want to lose sight of him, not even for a second.

Shep didn't let himself falter. "I'll tell you what the Word says!" *Slam.* "Right here! In black and white!"

The girl was slender, with pale skin and thick blond hair that came down just to her jawline, held in place with a couple of pink barrettes. She had blue eyes, the kind of blue that would flash in the summer sun, and a perfect little nose and two of the most luscious lips Shep had ever seen. He couldn't believe he'd never spotted her in church before. She must have been a visitor.

Slam! "The Word says that when you come of age, when you have learned what God wants you to know, you need to *lock your mind!*"

The blond girl wore a simple white dress. She didn't look more than about twelve, maybe thirteen, but that dress couldn't hide what had already blossomed and grown underneath it. A new line of sweat broke out on Shep's upper lip. He could tell the sweet, untouched nipples that crowned those two proud, young, innocent breasts would be the same shade of pink as the barrettes that held her hair. He had a sense for such things.

Slam! "Lock it up tight! Don't let any of the world's wickedness make it through! Lock up your mind and protect it like God's sacred vault, because *that's what it is!*"

"Yes, Lord!" "Speak the truth, Lord!" "Tell us all, Lord!"

Aubrey Griggs made it back to his seat, panting, drenched in sweat, but Clark Abernathy was still going strong, walking the length of the auditorium on the backs of the pews, forward and back, forward and back. Dave Bandy had made it out into the aisle, but the spirit of the Lord had seized him too hard to walk, and he flopped on the green carpet, rolling back and forth, his eyes showing only white.

But Shep didn't care about Dave Bandy. He'd zeroed in on the little blond girl. He finished the rest of the sermon on mental auto-pilot, anxious to make his way to the doors as the congregation filed out, so that he could find out more about her. He'd have to make sure his palms weren't too sweaty.

After church, Shep and his two grown sons, Junior and Zebediah, returned to their house in the Rolling Hills subdivision. It wasn't a bad house, Shep didn't think. Two stories, frame, with a mountain stone front. He parked in front of the closed garage door and, after Junior and Zebediah had laboriously heaved themselves out, he waited for the car to stop rocking back and forth before exiting himself. Privately, Shep wished the boys would lose some weight, but he never brought it up, because that would send Libby on another of her crying jags.

"You want our sons to abandon me," she'd wail, as she had wailed on so many occasions before. "You want to turn them into party-goers, so that wicked girls will swoop in and drag them away from me. Why do you want me to be alone?"

Libby hadn't left the house in the last twelve years. That didn't really bother Shep, since she kept the place spotless and always had some tasty dish ready to eat… though at least part of him admitted that that tendency to feed was part of the problem. Libby's lower half looked as if it belonged to a much, much larger woman. She had what he thought of as "shelf hips." Junior and Zebediah, twenty-two and twenty now, had definitely taken their genes from her, since Shep was tall and thin and couldn't put on weight no matter how hard he tried.

Junior paused before he went inside. "You comin' in, Daddy?"

"Nah, you go on ahead, son. I'm going up to the office. Get some work done."

Zebediah squeezed past his brother. "Hey, maybe we can get in some pickleball practice before lunch," he said, which prompted a wide, gappy grin from Junior, and the boys disappeared into the house.

Shep trudged up the exterior wooden stairs to his office, which perched above the garage. He clicked on the overhead fluorescents—you couldn't have paid him to switch to those ridiculous LED things—and took a seat at his desk. It wasn't much of a desk, really, just a six-foot folding table with a computer on it. But he'd gotten the over-stuffed leather chair at an estate sale where he'd known the lawyer in charge of things, and for a pittance he'd snuck it back and lugged it up the stairs. Shep lounged in the chair for a few moments before booting up the computer. The office smelled like grass clippings and chainsaw grease and dust. It relaxed him.

When the screen popped up ready, Shep tap-tap-tapped with two fingers, sometimes clicking the mouse, until a website loaded. It wasn't the kind of website that showed up on searches with Google or Bing or DuckDuckGo. Shep navigated through a couple of pages until he came to a message board—a stripped-down page of posts not unlike Craigslist.

A list of requests for merchandise.

Shep answered two of the requests, giving dates and times. He left the site and loaded another one, this one highly public. Across the top, in huge gold letters, it proclaimed itself the home of *ADJUNCTIVE BIBLE STUDY*, a series of seminars and prayer meetings organized by Shepherd Shadrach Curtis himself.

Shep scheduled a new seminar in Atlanta, for the date and time he'd mentioned on the merchandise board. The light of the computer's monitor turned his sallow skin yellow and greasy, and reflected off his big teeth.

5

12:15 p.m.
Four and a half hours before the storm

No one knew it, but the town of Red Springs belonged to the Hidden Man.

He moved through the streets unseen. Especially at night, but even in the daytime, the Hidden Man's special powers rendered him invisible to the naked eye.

Sometimes, sometimes a person saw him, just for a second, but then his powers exerted themselves and the gaze slid off of him, past him. No one paid attention to him… unless he *wanted* it paid.

He had that ability.

For better than ten years, Red Springs had been his playground. His game board. His buffet table. Picking and choosing as he saw fit from the blinded citizenry. Sometimes he thought of it as "culling the herd." When a predator culled a herd, it took the weakest. The slowest. The least healthy.

It wasn't a perfect metaphor. The Hidden Man wasn't interested in the unhealthy. He liked his prey young. Vibrant. Trembling with life.

No, what the Hidden Man did was cut away the *lies.*

When he chose a target, the Hidden Man used his powers to spirit the target away, out from under the noses of mothers and fathers, siblings, paramours. So mighty, so cunning, so stealthy was the Hidden Man that, once he had claimed a plaything, no one even realized they were gone.

Now he stood beside the real estate agent's office directly across from the Congregational Gospel Church, watching the beautiful people as they loitered outside it, smiling, talking, laughing. Young and old, big and small, all of them so perfect. He stared at them, raked his eyes over them, drank in the sight of them, but none of them saw *him.* He could walk right up to one of them, and so great was his power that their heads would turn. He could part them like the Bible's Red Sea before Moses's staff.

Oh, yes. He knew their Bible. He knew what it said about the demons. About the monsters. About the *Nephilim.* Those born of human women and fallen angels. The Hidden Man wondered, on occasion, if he had the blood of the Nephilim flowing through his veins. If that was the source of his might. Just as often, though, he rejected that thought.

His strength was his own. His mind. His will. His flesh. He had reached the top of the food chain on his own. The Hidden Man gave credit to no one.

He watched as a pretty young blond girl in a white dress left the church, in the company of two of the elders. He had never seen her before and, as he watched, she turned her head and looked straight at him—

But only for a heartbeat. His power flared, and the girl's eyes darted away, and she quickened her step to walk with the elderly couple. Exactly as if she had never seen him in the first place.

As far as the world was concerned, the Hidden Man didn't exist. He liked it that way.

Casually, he pushed off the brick wall and made his way down the sidewalk. Past the pet groomers. Past the daycare, which during the week was blessed with tiny, pale, shrieking, perfect angels. Some of them were young enough that his power didn't work on them, and so he avoided it during its hours of operation. A meager roadblock in his dominance of the town. Down past the Hyundai dealership, and the furniture store, and the lawyer's office, and on the next corner he paused. Leaned against a telephone pole. Reveled in the sight.

This was his true destination. The pasture in which the healthiest of the cows and bulls grazed and lowed.

Mount Zachariah Baptist Church.

Their blasphemous, imitation services always lasted longer than the real ones, so the Hidden Man sat down on the sidewalk to wait, his back against the telephone pole. He didn't have to wait that long. Soon the cannon-blast of the preacher's voice softened and died away, and amid a rush of organ music, the doors of the church swung wide.

The Hidden Man's guts clenched. Not unpleasantly—more like the butterflies gifted to young lovers. His balls drew up tight against his abdomen, and he felt a stirring, a heat along the length of his shaft. The glorious, gorgeous young men and women emerged into the sunlight, their beautiful skin gleaming like metal, like dark copper and wrought iron, their perfect teeth flashing behind full lips. Their hair dazzling in ringlets and kinks and twists. Their long, graceful, muscular limbs adorned in their Sunday finest. Living, breathing sacrilege. Thunderous profanities, daring to walk and talk and pretend to be real. He couldn't tear his eyes away.

But which one?

Which delicious transgression reached out the most eagerly?

Which one was *perfect?*

He didn't have to make a choice yet. It wasn't quite time. But it never hurt to perform his due diligence. There—a stunning girl of nineteen with enormous gold hoop earrings. There—a lean boy on the high school's track team. Surely one of those. Yes.

Once he'd made up his mind, the Hidden Man knew exactly where and how to move. He knew where both of those youths lived. The Hidden Man knew where *everyone* in Red Springs lived, and tonight, when darkness fell, his essence would take flight and move among them like the sharpest of knives.

He got up and wandered past the crowd, which still grew as church let out.

No one saw him.

He had that ability.

6

2:30 p.m.
Two hours before the storm

Before Zandra could open Mike and Angie Hubble's carport door, Angie opened it herself, and the wave of sounds and smells and the dazzle of Angie's grin washed over her. Angie topped out at five-foot-two, and without fail, left a first impression of wild red curls and pale skin and flashing teeth. She said, "Heeeyyyy!" and flung herself into Zandra's arms.

Zandra returned the hug, but it took no more than a couple of seconds of that for Angie to step back, her eyes narrowing. "Honey. You're shaking. What's wrong?"

Zandra shook her head and tried for a smile, which she could tell Angie found unconvincing. "Nothing, I'm fine." Zandra stepped aside so that her older brother, Perry, could come into the kitchen with her, and Angie gave him a hug too, going all the way up on her tiptoes to do it.

"What has your sister gotten herself into?" Angie demanded.

Perry smiled as he shrugged. "How much time you got?"

Mike Hubble came down the stairs, a suitcase under each arm and two more in his hands, waddling a bit with the weight despite his lean, athletic build. Sweat had plastered his thinning blond hair to his scalp. "We're set to leave in—" He glanced at a wall clock. "Not quite an hour, but these are the last of the bags. Y'all want to hang out in the living room?"

Perry moved forward, his hands outstretched, and said, "Here, let me take one of those."

Mike waddled past him. "Nah, man, I appreciate it, but I got it. No guests in this house're gonna do my work for me." On the heels of his last word, Mike and Angie's two children, seven-year-old Shawn and five-year-old Kristen, came shrieking down the stairs, waved wildly at Zandra and Perry—

"Hi Aunt Zandra hi Uncle Perry!"

—and disappeared into the backyard.

Mike lurched out the carport door to the Hubbles' waiting SUV, which sat with all four doors and the lift gate open. As he went, he said, "Don't mention the D word to them or they'll start climbing the walls."

Mike and Angie had set aside money all year to take their kids on a week-long vacation to DisneyWorld. Angie had told Zandra that they were going all-out: getting FastPasses, staying in a hotel in Animal Kingdom, buying the on-site meal plan, the works. Shawn and Kristen had already begun climbing the walls, as far as Zandra could tell.

Angie said, "Want something to drink?"

Perry's eyes lit up. "You got some sweet tea?"

Angie scoffed. "Like you even have to ask. Zandra?"

"Yes, please."

"Like Mike said, y'all plop down in the living room, I'll be right in."

Zandra and Perry moved from the kitchen to the adjacent living room, each of them taking one of the overstuffed recliners. Zandra let her eyes travel around the room, taking in the framed works of art that covered nearly every square inch of available wall space. Almost all of it consisted of blown-up covers of the children's books that Mike and Angie made their living creating, with Angie writing the stories and Mike supplying the art. The long-running series followed the adventures of a young woodchuck named Chuck Wood, and the title of every book began, *Could Chuck Wood...?*

Could Chuck Wood Win a Spelling Bee? had garnered them several awards, and led to Mike and Angie appearing on *The Today Show*. The two of them even had an honorary plaque engraved with their likenesses, brief bios, and a list of their achievements hanging in the entrance hall at Red Springs High School.

Soon Angie came back in carrying tall glasses filled with deep amber liquid, which Zandra and Perry both graciously accepted. Mike followed Angie after a moment, free of suitcases now, and dropped bonelessly onto the sofa.

Shawn and Kristen's shrieks continued as they chased each other around the backyard, weaving in and out of their swing set's chain-suspended seats. Through a window, Perry watched Shawn with a critical eye. "Y'all think Shawn'll be ready to start playing ball soon?"

Zandra said, "Here we go."

Perry Seagraves had been Cartauga County's head recreational leagues coach for the last twenty-six years. He'd taken the job straight out of college, found it a perfect fit, and gone on to coach the county's children for the last two generations.

Mike dabbed his face with his shirt tail, his blue eyes tracking his kids. "You're barking up the wrong tree with Shawn. You want the athlete of the family, you'll have to wait for Kristen."

Angie took on a far-off expression as she sat down on the sofa next to her husband. "How old is Jamel now? He's about to have his sixth birthday, isn't he?"

Zandra watched as Perry literally swelled with pride. She knew he didn't mean to do it, that he would've been mortified if he realized he *was* doing it, but there it was nonetheless, and kind of hard to miss. At fifty years old, six feet two inches tall, carrying two hundred seventy pounds of mostly-still-solid weight, with a bald head and a goatee that had gone snow-white, any physical action Perry Seagraves took attracted attention. Perry said, "You bet he is. I was fast when I was a kid, but I ain't got *nothin'* on that little roadrunner."

Watching Angie, Zandra said, "Why do you ask?"

Angie ducked her head. "Just thinking about how gorgeous the kids would be if Jamel and Kristen grew up and got married."

Mike chuckled. "Jesus, baby, can't even let them get to puberty before you start matchmaking?"

Angie's pale cheeks went pink, and she drew breath to retort, but instead slapped her forehead with her palm. "Oh shit! I walked through a door and my mind went blank. Zandra, what happened, what's wrong?"

Mike frowned. "Something's wrong?"

Angie twined her fingers through Mike's. "She was shaking when they got here. So? What is it?"

Zandra sighed. Perry said, "Yeah, Zan. Tell 'em what happened."

Zandra set her glass of tea down on a coaster. She leaned forward and rested her elbows on her knees. Her eyes slid closed, and the image of Nicole in Gordon's crazed arms sprang in front of her—but it streaked. Cracked. Wavered and changed, and Zandra saw glimpses of dusty sand lit by moonlight, of a terrified face, felt the heat of blood not her own and heard the screams, the tiny kicking flesh growing still as shrieks of pain and desperation turned to sheerest horror.

Zandra Seagraves hated to cry. She hated it worse than almost anything else she could think of. Hated it worse than vomiting, and she would've rather gritted her teeth and endured the foulest illness than throw up. So when the tears started in her eyes, she clamped down on them with everything she had, shouting silently, rebuking them, until they beat a sheepish retreat.

As soon as her eyes had closed, she felt Perry's hand on her shoulder, and when she opened them again, Angie was right there, kneeling in front of her.

"Zandra, honey, what happened?"

Zandra sat up straight. Breathed deeply. "Sorry. It's just... I didn't..."

It's just been a while since someone's life was in my hands.

Slowly, haltingly at first, Zandra told Mike and Angie about the encounter at the convenience store. When she finished, having taken several long drinks of tea and wishing it could have perhaps been spiked with something stronger, Zandra said, "So of course I've still got a mountain of paperwork to do. Not even halfway through it. But Perry and I wanted to come and see y'all off first. I, uh, I wasn't intending to bring you down before your trip."

Angie said, "Holy jumping Christ, honey. But Nicole wasn't hurt?"

"Not physically. God only knows how much therapy she'll need now."

Zandra glanced outside. The sky to the southwest had darkened, and she pulled out her phone and tapped a weather app. The words TORNADO WATCH flashed over Cartauga County.

Mike said, "And the guy stabbed himself how many times?"

"I wasn't counting. At least ten. Maybe twenty. He was fast. EMT said he punctured his trachea, which is why he was blowing blood every time he said anything, but the wounds were shallow and he didn't cut any major arteries. I've already reached out to a great-aunt who, near as I can tell, is his next of kin, so maybe I can work with her and get him packed off to rehab somewhere. Once he's fit to be released from the hospital."

Angie chewed on her lower lip. "I just—wow. I don't know if I could've done what you did. Face him like that."

Zandra shrugged and tried for a tiny smile, mostly successfully.

Mike said, "Why're *you* reaching out to this guy's family? Don't you have staff for stuff like that?"

Perry snorted. "You forget who you're talking to?"

Zandra shot her brother a dirty look without much malice behind it. "If you want a job done right—"

Perry said the words along with her: "—you've got to do it yourself, I know, I know. You should have t-shirts made. It wouldn't kill you to let someone else help you every once in a while."

Zandra thought about that. She considered saying, "That's why I'm here, instead of home, alone," but decided against it.

Perry grinned at Mike and Angie. "You know she still does her own taxes *and* changes her own oil?"

Zandra's eyebrows shot up in half-feigned indignation. "Forget about those minimum-wage kids at the garage. I'll change my own flat tires, too, thanks very much. And hell, I don't know the people at H&R Block! What if they smoked their breakfast?"

Perry said, "That's why you get an accountant you trust," but he settled back in his chair, clearly letting the argument go.

Angie had gone back to her seat on the couch. Her eyes twinkled. "I remember in high school, everyone always wanted to do group projects with Zandra, because she basically insisted on doing everything herself."

Mike nodded. "That's why you wanted to be a travel writer, right? Just go and do your own thing. Only boss is an editor on the other end of the phone."

Angie gave her a half-sympathetic, half-rueful smile. "Not exactly how things ended up, huh?"

After a careful deep breath—yes, the specter of tears had passed, no chance of her voice shaking—Zandra said, "These days I wouldn't even have to have an editor. Just start a blog. Build a following, God willing, get some advertising revenue going. I mean, it's not like I'd get elected to a second term here, even if I decided to run." She shot a dagger-pointed look at Perry. "Which I won't."

Perry shrugged theatrically.

Zandra gestured toward the window. "Anyway. Y'all better hit the road. You want to get out of the way if a storm does come up."

Mike slapped his knees and stood. "Yeah, we really should get going, baby."

Angie got to her feet as Zandra did, and gave her another long hug. "I'll text you from the road, okay? If you need to talk some more, I'm just a call away."

Zandra nodded. "Thanks."

7

4:30 p.m.

Savvy Horne lay on her bed, belly-down with her head hanging over the edge, her phone on the floor directly below her face. She had Skype open. Cindy looked up at her from the screen, and said, "You know I can't hardly see you."

Savvy's long, straight hair hung down, almost touching the phone, shrouding her face. A heavy chestnut-brown curtain. "It ain't worth seeing anyhow." Her arms lay by her side. She figured she probably looked like some sort of beached fish.

"And you know Mark's heard shit like that all his life."

Savvy groaned. "That don't make it right. And he ain't heard it from me before."

"He didn't hear it from you this time, neither! It was your grand-daddy! We all saw it. We was all there." Cindy chewed her lip. "Wasn't right, how he treated you. How he *treats* you. You thought about callin' DFACS?"

Of course Savvy had thought about it. But bringing the government into personal shit just wasn't something her family did. Ever. The same way they never sued anybody. Savvy's mother had slipped outside the Piggly Wiggly, on that yellow-painted place where the curb turned into a little ramp so you didn't have to bump your buggy down into the parking lot and maybe break some eggs, and when she fell it messed up her back something fierce, but she didn't sue the grocery store. It had never occurred to her or Savvy's father to do something like that. Filing lawsuits was something yankees did. And so was calling the Department of Family and Children Services. It just wasn't *done* when you could handle a problem on your own.

Savvy rolled over on her back and stared at her bedroom's popcorn ceiling. Thinking.

"Okay, now I can't see your face at all."

Savvy spoke with her eyes still fixed on the plastered-on popcorn. "You think we could take care of this ourselves?"

It took Cindy a few seconds to answer. "Take care of what?"

"Of the way Grandpa treats me."

Another pause. "What do you mean, 'Take care of'?"

Now Savvy took her time responding. "Nothing. Never mind." She rolled back over to look Cindy in the eye again, and as she moved, she glanced out the window. It made her sit up quickly.

From the phone, Cindy's voice said, "What is it? What're you lookin' at?"

Savvy's room faced west. Standing at the window, she could see out across the side yard, through the thin little line of trees, all the way to the road. Savvy could always spot the school bus coming, and had it timed so that she could dash downstairs and make it to the end of the driveway just as the bus was pulling up. But now she saw no cars on the road. Instead, her gaze focused on the sky above the trees.

It was black. Black as coal. Black as night.

"Savvy? Hey! Savvy, the fuck you lookin' at?"

From somewhere far off, a thin, weird sound reached her, and grew in volume with each passing second. She'd only heard it a couple of times before, when a class had taken a field trip to the local firehouse.

A tornado siren.

The door to Savvy's room burst open. Her mother stood there, wild-eyed, and shouted, "We've got to get to the basement! Now! Now, Savvy, *move! Now!*"

Savvy lunged for her phone.

* * *

4:30 p.m.

Shep Curtis had finally given in to the low-grade hunger pangs in his belly and headed to the fridge to rummage for a snack. Libby was in the kitchen, working on the early dinner they always had on Sundays before heading back for the evening service. Shep grabbed the cheese ball she'd made for last week's Wednesday night prayer meeting—there was about a third of it left—along with a box of Townhouse crackers and a knife. Libby stood by the stove with her back to him. He watched her as he peeled the plastic wrap off the cheese ball, careful not to let any of the bits of crushed nuts fall to the floor.

Among his group of online acquaintances, Shep had made no secret of the reason he had married Libby. "Well, see," Shep had told them more than once, "being married keeps me from having to masturbate." He carved off a little chunk of the cheese ball, spread it carefully so as not to break the cracker, and popped it in his mouth. As he did, Libby turned from the stove to the sink to wash her hands.

God Almighty, she'd gotten fat. Everything still worked, of course. He still never had to masturbate. But her hips and her ass had just gotten so *huge*. Shep figured he could take that delicious little blond girl from the morning's service, clone her, and fit the pair of them inside Libby's ass cheeks.

Libby shut the water off. "Father?"

That's what she called him. That's what they called each other: "Father" and "Mother." Purely for the boys' benefit, of course.

She said it again. "Father? Could you come and look at this?"

She was staring out the window at something. Probably a raccoon,

Shep thought, as he got up from the table and went to her. Libby was so dumb, she thought every piddly little thing demanded his attention.

"What is it, Mother?"

"Should the sky be that black? It shouldn't, should it?"

A tornado siren went off, and what little color Shep's face had drained down into his neck. He ran to the stairs and screamed at the top of his lungs, "Boys! Get to the basement!"

4:30 p.m.

Zandra Seagraves could've rented one of the nicer apartments in Red Springs. For that matter, she could have easily qualified for a home loan and bought a house, as near-perfect as her credit was. That, plus the sheriff's salary, plus the check she got each month for the twenty years she'd given to the United States Army, would have been more than enough to put her in one of the new homes up on top of Wesley Ridge.

But Zandra had no illusions about the longevity of her position as a public servant of Cartauga County, and had no wish to get herself locked into a mortgage that she might not be able to afford in a few years' time. Consequently, while crashing in Perry's guest room right after she retired from the service, Zandra had launched a search for a decent, secure and, if possible, dirt-cheap place to live.

What she came up with was a 120-year-old house built up on the crest of a ridge on the north side of Dahlonega Highway, accessible via a narrow road that switched back and forth as it climbed up from the valley below. The place had come available after the former occupants, a white couple in their late eighties, had both passed away in a single-car accident on that same road. The couple had had no children, and the lawyer Zandra talked to tried his best to convince her to buy the place and all its furnishings along with it, but instead she'd talked him into renting it to her. She thought he'd ended up auctioning off all of the old couple's belongings.

It wasn't much to look at upon first approach, and she understood why the price had been as low as it was: even though it sat on the ridge crest, dense woods on one side and a massive rock outcropping on the other prevented it from having any kind of view, decent or otherwise. That hadn't bothered Zandra. She figured if she wanted a good view, she'd go up to Rock City on Lookout Mountain.

Now the exterior looked like a 120-year-old house with a fresh coat of paint. The inside, on the other hand, could have passed for the subject of a minimalism photo shoot. Rental or not, Zandra was determined to do the inside her way, and it hadn't hurt anything that the lawyer had agreed to deduct the cost of the improvements from her rent.

It wasn't that she didn't want to have things in her house. It was just that she was very, very, (in Perry's opinion, wholly unreasonably) discerning about what she bought and how she decorated. Plus, once she brought a new thing or set of things into her home, they had to be situated and maintained *just so.*

To say that Zandra liked her house neat was like saying Mike Tyson in his prime punched sort of hard.

Every surface in the kitchen was either brilliant white or blemish-free stainless steel, and after every bit of food consumed, all related dishes were washed and put away immediately. Not so much as a stray fork rested in the sink.

All shoes, Zandra's and visitors' alike, stayed in the corner on a black mat just inside the door. She had a shoe cabinet of polished wood on order from Germany.

New engineered-hardwood black walnut flooring started in the living room and ran through the two bedrooms, but most of the living room floor was covered with a medium-length white shag rug, which matched the white leather recliner and sofa. The coffee table and end tables were also stainless steel, with spotless glass tops, and the TV's remote control stayed in one location on one of the end tables, its edge flush with the table's edge.

The California king bed—made meticulously each day—sported a heavy, quilted black comforter, the edges of which remained precisely seven inches off the floor on both sides of the bed. The single night-stand was also stainless steel and glass, having come from the same store as the living room furniture, and stood near the door to the *en suite*, which consisted of intensely and regularly scrubbed gleaming-white tile and gleaming-white alabaster fixtures.

The house was perfect. Exactly the way Zandra wanted it. She didn't have pets, not even a goldfish, because pets weren't something she could control, and in her own house, by God she *would* have control.

As a girl, at her father's direction, Zandra had taken the first five hours of each Saturday to strip all the wax off the floor of her bedroom and apply a new coating. Only once the job was done could Zandra leave the house. It had become a task she relished.

The only object that seemed out of place was *so* out of place that its incongruous nature instantly came off as deliberate. It was a china cabinet that Zandra had found in an antique store, and which she intended to strip, sand, and stain as soon as she found the exact right color of stain, but it held no china. Instead, the cabinet stood there in her living room, off to one side of the big TV, full of what was commonly known as *murderabilia*.

Clothing. Handwriting samples. A few works of art.

Weapons.

All of them belonged, or had belonged at one time, to murderers.

On Sunday afternoon, hours after the incident in the convenience store, the trip to her office, and the much-needed break at the Hubbles' house, Zandra lounged in her recliner in the living room and stared at the cabinet's contents. She had the chair fully reclined, a glass of white wine on a black ceramic coaster next to the TV remote, and Prince's *Sign o' the Times* playing over discreetly placed speakers.

Her eyes had finally begun to unfocus, relaxing along with the rest of her, when she sat up straight and tapped her phone screen, killing the volume on the stereo. *There.* Not some imagined sound.

A tornado siren.

Zandra bolted to the kitchen door and flung it open, to find herself staring at the blackest sky she'd ever seen. She slid her feet into a pair of boots on the black mat, slammed the kitchen door as she left the house, and sprinted to the angled cellar doors halfway down the house's length.

<hr>

4:30 p.m.

Every tornado siren in the county sang its song. Weather radios spoke urgent words. Sonny Baynes—the meteorologist from Channel 2's Action News, "The One You Can Trust!"— all but shouted at the viewers at home: find shelter.

Perry Seagraves led his wife Sonja and their son Jamel down into the basement woodworking shop he had spent a great deal of money on but hardly ever used.

Tommy-June Billingsley huddled in the walk-in freezer at the Hardee's, deeply regretting having agreed to work a double shift.

Belvis Horne sat in his recliner, staring out the window. His house didn't have a basement, and he didn't trust the place to hold together if it took a direct hit, so it wouldn't have done a damn bit of good to go and crouch in a doorway if the doorway all of a sudden wasn't there anymore. So he sat in his favorite chair and stared down the storm clouds and dared them to come and get him.

<hr>

In seventeen minutes, the town of Red Springs, Georgia, came apart.

The sky southwest of town had already turned black, and at 4:48 the clouds extended a roaring, churning pillar of destruction that slammed into the ground and scraped its way northeast.

The first casualty anyone saw was the Ace Hardware, followed by the Cartauga Citizens' Bank. The winds ripped into the hardware store's metal roof and peeled the sections away like the skin of a banana, leaving them twisted and curled against the brick and shattered-glass storefront. Half the bricks in the front wall tore free and swept up into the funnel cloud, though not high enough that they missed the bank. The tellers and loan officers had taken shelter in the vault. They listened as the rest of the building broke apart around them, engulfed in the tornado's apocalyptic roar.

The pillar continued up Dahlonega Highway. The Krystal had already been evacuated, so no one was harmed when the entire restaurant shuddered and collapsed and blew away, a fate shared by the Sav-a-Ton gas station next to it. The staff at the Ruby Tuesday had unknowingly copied the bank employees, sheltering in the walk-in freezer as the walls split and cracked and tore free around them.

Something in the wind changed when the funnel cloud reached Carter Street. The tornado hitched and pivoted and headed due east, straight up Red Springs' central avenue, destroying hardware stores and furniture stores and law offices, and when it passed over the Mount Zachariah Baptist Church, it paused for thirty seconds, crouched and spun and churned until the building was completely gone, as if the holy place's existence had somehow offended it. Finally satisfied at the church's demolition, the tornado pushed on through the town, ripping through a series of houses and smashing the western wing of the Red Springs Middle School down to its foundations.

Immediately to the east of what could be considered the "downtown" area, as much as a town of three thousand residents could have a downtown, rose Angel Ridge. Red Springs' most affluent residents lived in grand houses atop Angel Ridge, houses with a view that extended over the town and all the way to Lookout Mountain, and it would have made more than one of Red Springs' *less* affluent citizens wickedly happy to see those homes destroyed the way the rest of the town had been. But the tornado spared them. Instead it lifted its pillar, skipped over the top of the ridge entirely, and brought its full force down into the valley on the other side.

Thirty-nine families lived along Fox Valley Road. All but two of their houses had been built by the same contractors, and the plans those contractors followed did not include basements. It was in Fox Valley that the tornado turned cruel.

Moving north now, the massive, coal-black cloud spanned the valley from ridge to ridge, and as it churned along its path, it flattened house after house, crushing them as easily and quickly as a child stomping on a matchbox.

Twenty-seven of the families had heard the emergency weather reports, or received the text messages hooked to the county's emergency services system, and ahead of the tornado they had fled, driving as fast as they could to the north, most of them crossing the nearby line into Tennessee.

But the remaining twelve had had no choice but to, as Sonny Baynes put it, "hunker down" in the middle of their houses, crouching under heavy tables or in bathtubs, trying to get a doorframe over their heads. It made little difference. Twenty-two people died in the raging storm. Some of them crushed by falling timbers. Some of them torn free of their houses and flung away like bits of refuse.

Three of them were infants.

When it ended, the houses along Fox Valley Road had been reduced to little more than driveways leading to bare slabs in the midst of debris fields, the silence that descended in the storm's wake broken only by screams and sobs.

II

THUNDER PEALS

8

Stamford, Connecticut
9:35 p.m.
Five hours after the storm

Colin Massey let the beat of the drums smash into him. The mic waited in the stand. Waited for him. Kylie kept slamming, working both feet, pounding the two bass drums and *there*—Colin didn't look as Brock and Evan came in with the guitar and bass. He reached out as the music filled him up, filled his muscles and his bones, and the mic all but leapt into his hand as he sucked in a great breath, all the way down to the bottom of his lungs—

And Colin *screamed.*

A brittle, grinding, shattering roar, and from the corner of his eye he saw the grin flash across Brock's face.

Because they *had* it. They'd finally come together.

Colin had studied martial arts for a few years when he was younger. He'd never advanced very far, but there was one aspect that always enthralled him. Whenever he'd applied a hold correctly—cranked the joint exactly right, pivoted a limb just as he'd been shown—he'd felt something like a *click.* Not a literal click, but more the

51

sensation of fitting a puzzle piece precisely into place. As if, in that moment, he and his opponent were in perfect synch. Not just with each other, but with the whole universe, both of them in the exact place and time where they were meant to be. A feeling of harmony. It had always delighted him, so much so that even when he was the one being submitted, even when he had to tap out, he'd laughed out loud from the sheer satisfaction of it.

That was how he felt tonight. As soon as he opened his mouth and screamed, he knew the four of them had found the key. Locked into place. A perfectly fitted jigsaw.

Colin knew Brock and Evan and Kylie hadn't invited him to join Rusted Flesh solely because of his vocal talents. At six-foot-two, with his wavy, dark brown hair and perfect white teeth and chiseled abs, Colin looked like a frontman and knew it. One of his sister's girl-friends had once referred to him as a "genetic lottery winner," and he didn't figure he could disagree with her. His mom's blue eyes and cheekbones, coupled with his dad's height and physique, gave him the appearance of a Nordic demi-god and all but guaranteed ticket sales when they went on tour.

Appearance of a demi-god or not, Colin *had* been practicing his vocals. He'd even hired a voice coach. Pleasant, eager butterflies filled his stomach, and he pulled in another breath and launched into the lyrics, belting them out with equal measures of grit and tone.

"Sparrow...

"Smashed against the windows of my mind

"Dying...

"Unfettered, last of your kind

"Canceled...

"The subjugation of your will

"Freedom...

"Never lived a slave and never will—"

The guitar screeched an off-key note and went silent. Colin stopped singing at once, the butterflies in his gut souring, but it took Evan and Kylie a few more seconds to wind down. Once silence had descended, everyone watched as Brock's face, the rapturous grin of a few moments ago gone now, turned a deep shade of red that threatened to go purple. Colin put the mic back in the stand. "What's the problem?"

Brock could barely talk. "What the *fuck* was that shit?"

Evan brushed his hair back behind his ears and said, "Brock, it's—"

Brock went on, speaking to Colin as if Evan hadn't said anything. "Did you just say some shit like '*Never lived a slave and never will*'? Is that what I heard?"

Colin's eyes flicked back and forth between Brock and Evan, and then over to Kylie, who slumped behind her drum kit. Colin said, "Yeah. That's what was on the lyric sheet."

"Oh. No shit? That's what you thought the lyrics were?" Brock shrugged his guitar off and set it on a stand near the keyboard, and turned to face Evan. "Did he think that's what the lyrics were because *you changed them?*"

Evan had shrunk to about two-thirds of his normal size, and Colin got the impression that he wanted to hide behind his bass. Colin had never been in a band with a better bass player than Evan, and at this point—he counted silently—he'd been in eleven different bands.

All of them unsigned, an unwelcome voice in his head muttered.

"I thought it would hit the beat better," Evan said. "With the syllables modified like that, I can really land this new riff I've been working on." He took off the bass and set it aside. "It's just a small change, baby, I—I didn't think you'd mind."

Brock seemed to want to channel early Henry Rollins, at least as far as how he looked. Colin thought he must spend at least as much time lifting weights as he did playing guitar. So he presented an imposing front when he screamed, "You didn't think I'd mind if you changed my fucking lyrics? Why don't I go over to your house and fuck up all your shit? Would you mind that? The line is supposed to be '*Escape the bonds of slavery you will!*' Do you know how long it took me to write that? Do you know how many hours I spent on that shit?"

Evan started crying. Colin edged over to Kylie and spoke quietly. "He's not going to hit him, is he?"

Kylie slithered out from behind the drum kit and motioned with her head: *Let's give them some space.* She might have looked like an escapee from a high school chess club if she hadn't been covered head to foot with expensive tattoos. Colin followed her, stepping away from the lovers' quarrel. She murmured, "Nah. Brock'll yell at him for a bit, and eventually Evan'll get tired of it and start yelling back, and in four or five hours they'll go back to Brock's place and fuck themselves silly."

Brock continued shouting at Evan, obscenities flowing freely.

Colin said, "But tonight's shot, right?"

Kylie stuck her hands in her pockets. "As far as practice goes, I'd say so, yeah."

"And this happens how often?"

Kylie's face scrunched up. "Maybe a third of the time?"

This was Colin's third practice with the band.

Brock had gotten steadily louder while Colin and Kylie talked, and Evan's tears had flowed more and more freely, and Colin was about to step forward and say something when Brock turned and pointed a beefy finger at him. "How do you think our new singer's going to feel, Evan, when he's up in front of some huge audience, spewing shit lyrics that *you* decided you'd *just change a little?*"

"I can answer that," Colin said, conversationally. "Fuck you, and fuck your band. No offense, Kylie, you seem all right."

Brock's mouth fell open. Evan's tears magically dried up. Kylie shrugged, and said, "None taken."

Brock went from a full-throated scream to a mouse-like squeak. "You're quitting? But you only just got here! Colin, you can't quit, you're what's going to get us signed!"

Colin said, "It's sad that you believe that." He walked out of Evan's guest house, into the summer night, and lit a cigarette. He'd never been able to bring himself to use an e-cig.

The guest house stood on Evan's family's estate, about fifty yards from a massive fifteen-bedroom mansion. Colin's Tesla was parked out front, alongside Evan's Escalade. Colin buttoned up his shirt—he'd had it open, displaying his abs and pecs, to get in the right mood for performing—and took a drag off the cigarette as Kylie stepped outside next to him.

"I was expecting Brock. He seems like the kind of guy to run after a singer and beg him to stay."

Kylie gestured toward the cigarette. "Got another one of those?"

Colin shared, and as Kylie lit hers, he glanced back through the glass double doors into what Brock had referred to as their "rehearsal space." The guest house looked to be a good fifteen-hundred square feet. The open-concept design, once all the furniture had been removed, was easily big enough to practice in, but at the end of the day, they were still playing in what was intended to be a living room, and the acoustics sucked.

Kylie said, "Look. Colin. I know Brock's an asshole, but he's a really good guitarist. And I'm not bad. And you heard Evan—he's a fucking beast on the bass."

"True."

"So why don't you give us another shot? With your lungs, man, we've got a real chance."

Colin took another drag and dropped the cigarette onto one of the marble flagstones that made up the guest house's driveway. He ground it out under his heel. "Nah. No hard feelings, I mean, I meant it when I said you seem okay. But I've got one hard and fast rule in my life."

Kylie's face had turned sour, but she kept her voice calm. "And what's that?"

"The second anything I'm doing stops being fun? I stop doing it."

She cocked her head. "Must be nice. Not everybody has that luxury, y'know. Not like you and Evan. Some of us have to work our asses off to get anywhere."

Colin shrugged. "That's got nothing to do with me." He threw one last glance in at Brock and Evan, who appeared to be holding each other, both of them crying now. "I'll see you around, okay?"

Kylie shrugged back.

Fifteen minutes later, the enormous wrought-iron gates at the entrance of Colin's family property sensed the approach of his car and opened silently, closing just as silently behind him after he'd passed through. Colin steered his Model S along the winding, half-mile-long driveway, parked in the ten-car garage behind the main house, and strolled through the kitchen, headed for the downstairs living room. He smiled and bumped fists with the chefs as he passed them. He couldn't tell what they were preparing—something for in the morning, he guessed—but it smelled great, and a smile had found its way to his lips when he walked into the living room where his parents and older sister were all watching TV.

The smile slipped away when he saw their expressions.

"What's up? We in a nuclear war yet?"

His step-father, Diego, silently motioned Colin to join them. Diego sat on the big leather couch next to his mother, Katherine, while Colin's older sister Charity stood behind them. All three pairs of eyes riveted to the TV. Colin walked around the couch and stood next to his sister.

The TV displayed a news report, and at first Colin thought he was looking at the aftermath of a carpet-bombing.

"This is all that's left of many parts of Red Springs, Georgia," a reporter said, and Colin's eyes got bigger the longer he watched. "Meteorologists measured the tornado as an EF-5, the largest, fastest, and most destructive kind. Residents of this tiny town had little to no warning as the storm sprang up this afternoon."

Colin whispered, "Red Springs... I've seen that name before..."

The footage, taken from a helicopter, resembled a cross between a battlefield and a landfill. Colin was pretty sure it showed a residential area, but the field of debris was so thick, he couldn't tell where the wreckage from one house ended and the next began. Trees had been snapped off, leaving only ragged stumps. A truck, flipped upside-down, rested in the branches of one of the trees that had survived. As the camera moved, the remains of a small church came into view, its steeple resting on its side in the middle of the street. The church itself was little more than a crumbled brick foundation.

Downed power lines lay across the streets, a few of them throwing sparks, clustered in deadly black squiggles like a child's scribbling.

Red and blue emergency lights flashed everywhere.

The camera cut to the reporter, a pretty young black woman, standing next to a pale, visibly shaken white man in his seventies, both of them in front of a building that might have at one point been a courthouse. The reporter said, "I'm here with Phil Blackburn, mayor of Red Springs. Mr. Mayor, how bad is the damage? Do you know how many people have been hurt?"

It took the mayor a couple of moments to find his voice. When he spoke, it was with a southern accent so thick that at first Colin thought it was a put-on. "Lindsey, it's too soon to know... to know anything. This just happened. We're tryin' to coordinate emergency services, I know we're gonna be gettin' in help from neighboring counties, but we just... we just don't know yet."

The camera switched to more tornado footage, again from the helicopter. It swept past the rubble field of a destroyed convenience store, and from there to the parking lot of a motel, the entire second floor of which had been torn away.

The TV went silent. Both Diego and Katherine turned to look up at Charity. Diego said, "So you think you can get the whole youth group?"

Charity nodded. "It's perfect timing. I mean, perfect timing for us to help. Of course what happened down there is horrible, that's the whole point. But yeah, the kids don't go back to school till the twenty-eighth, I've got the parents on an email chain, I think I can put it all together."

Colin's forehead wrinkled up. "What're you doing, now?"

Charity made a broad gesture toward the TV. "You know I lead the youth group at church, right?"

Colin nodded. Charity had gone in for the whole religion thing in a big way several years ago, and gotten involved in a mega-church downtown. He thought it had something like five thousand members.

"I'm going to organize a trip with a bunch of the youth, and we're going to charter a bus and go down to that town and help them rebuild." Charity's eyes lit up. "Colin! You should come too! You could be a chaperone!"

Colin circled the couch and flopped down in one of the big leather chairs Diego had had imported from Italy. "Y'know, ordinarily, I totally would, but I'm pretty sure I have plans next week."

Diego turned a bemused gaze on his step-son. "Really? Plans? You?"

"What? I can have plans. For all you know, we got a gig already."

Diego's stare hadn't wavered. "*Do* you have a gig?"

Colin didn't answer. The name *Red Springs* continued tickling something in his memory. He dug out his phone and started googling. While he did that, Charity jabbered away at their parents, talking about helping the whole town, giving out water and sandwiches and whatever, blah blah blah, and really focusing on that church that got hit so hard. Getting them back on their feet.

To Colin, Katherine said, "That does sound like a noble pursuit, son. A few days' hard work for a good cause? It'll enrich your soul."

Without looking up from his phone, Colin said, "How about if I write them a check instead?"

In her Disapproving Voice, Charity said, "How about if you come with us, and you can hand them the check in person, and then help us rebuild the town?"

Colin stood up, stretched, and called one of the chefs on his cell. "Hey, Dario, can you bring something up to my room? ... I don't know, something snacky, but with some protein. I'm kind of hungry. ... Nah, just surprise me. Okay, you're awesome, thanks." He ended the call and saw that Charity had been staring at him the whole time, her hands on her hips. "What?"

Charity said, "You're unbelievable."

Colin gave her a vaguely dismissive wave. "I'm going upstairs. Good luck with your road trip."

Wandering down the hall that led to his wing of the house, Colin grew restless and decided to take the stairs up to his summer suite instead of the elevator. Once he got there, he kicked off his shoes, flopped down onto his bed, and immediately wanted to get up and go out again. His stomach growled, though, so he decided to wait for

Dario to bring his snack up. It was only 10:00. Plenty of time to go out after he ate if he still felt like it.

Colin clicked on the TV that took up most of the far wall, muted it, took out his phone and began scrolling through his Instagram feed. He hadn't gotten very far before he spotted a shot of his friend Bethany. She was in some sort of crowd—she looked angry, and so did all the people around her—some kind of protest somewhere.

A text notification popped down from the top of the screen. Eddie, another friend.

ED-MAN: Colin what up bro

Colin sighed. He didn't really feel like talking to Eddie at the moment. Or anyone, really.

COLIN: U C that shot of Bethany? Fuck she doin?

ED-MAN: She at that protest bro Anti-Trump

The sigh turned into a groan.

COLIN: Fuck's the point of that? Wastin time

ED-MAN: I hear ya bro

Nothing bored Colin more thoroughly or faster than politics. He felt as if he understood more about the current situation than most of his social group did, just from listening to his mom and Diego talk about it, but going to protest the president? At best, all that did was make the protesters look whiny, and at worst it might get them arrested or Tased for no good reason.

Besides, who *cared?* So far, Trump becoming president had affected Colin's life exactly as much as Obama getting elected had. Which was to say, not at all. He and his friends still did whatever they wanted, whenever they wanted. If an orange man had replaced a black man, what difference did it make?

Another text notification popped down, this one from a number he didn't recognize. His thumb hovered for a second before tapping it.

There was no text in the text message, only a photo: a luscious blond girl of about nineteen, wearing not a stitch of clothing, posed in front of her bathroom mirror, phone in hand. Each of her natural breasts was bigger than her head, and she had one lifted up, the hardened nipple suckled into her mouth, her left eye winking lasciviously at the camera.

Colin said, "Oh, for fuck's *sake.*"

Before he could close the message and block the number, words followed the image: *PLEASE DONT BLOCK ME I NEED TO TALK TO YOU COLIN I LOVE YOU PLEASE*

The phone rang, the same number that had sent the text displayed on the screen. Scowling, Colin took the call. "Daphne, you have got to cut this shit out. I mean it." This was the third new number she'd called him from in the last four days.

Daphne McCutcheon never failed to affect a tiny, baby-doll voice, even through tears. Colin had found it mildly entertaining at first, even a little arousing, but now it grated on his last nerve.

"Colin, please, don't shut me out! I love you, and I know you love me, and I just want us to be together! Please, Colin, I'll do anything, I'll let you fuck me in the ass, I'll suck your cock every single day! I saw you looking at my sister, do you want to fuck her too, I can totally make that happen, she thinks you're hot, she'll be into it! We can fuck you together, Colin, please, I love you so much!"

He could *hear* the whites showing all the way around her eyes. "What are you *talking* about? You know I love you? What the *shit?* We only screwed twice!"

"Or, or, or do you want to share me with your friends? You want to watch them fuck me? You want us to put on a show for you, baby? I'll do it! Just say it and I'll do it!"

"Jesus."

"Colin, please, if you could just come out and talk to me face to face, I'll do anything, anything you say!"

He sat up on the bed, the hairs on the back of his neck standing on end. "What do you mean, 'come out'? Where are you?"

"I'm right outside your gate, baby! Do you see me waving? I know it's dark, here, let me turn on the light on my phone! Just come and talk to me, I'll do anything for you, anything, I'll suck your cock right here on the side of the road if you want me to. I *want* people to see! I want them all to know how much I love you! Colin, please!"

Colin muted the phone and walked over to an intercom set into the wall by the door. He pushed a red button. "Frank? You there?"

A deep, gravelly voice responded. "Yes, sir. Is there a problem?"

"You could say that, yeah. A crazy girl is apparently standing out by the gate. Could you and some of your guys escort her back into town, and make sure she leaves me alone?"

"How convincing do you want us to be?"

"Well, don't *hurt* her, fuck. Just make her understand she's not welcome here."

"You got it, sir."

Colin went to his window. He couldn't see the gate very well from this angle, but he thought maybe there was an out-of-place glow that could have come from a phone light. He unmuted the call. "Daphne, this is the last time I'm going to tell you. I don't want to see you. At all. Ever. Go away, and don't bother me anymore. I'll be talking to our lawyer in the morning about a restraining order."

The baby-doll voice elevated to a screech. "I know where you live, Colin! I know all your friends! I know all the places you go! You think you can run from me? I'll find you! I'll make you understand, Colin! I'll make you see that we're meant to be together!" Over the phone, Colin heard the sound of the gate opening, and Daphne said, "Hey, who're you guys? Are you friends of Colin's? What're you doing? Hey! Let me go! Let me g—"

The call cut off. Colin flung the phone so that it landed on his bed. He stuck his hands in his pockets and stared out at the carefully lit, perfectly manicured expanse of lawn. Daphne *did* know all his friends, and probably *could* find him in all the places he liked to frequent. She wasn't as careful with her inheritance as Colin was with his. He wouldn't put it past her to hire a whole private detective firm if the thought occurred to her. Restraining order or not.

Out of nowhere, Colin remembered where he'd seen the name "Red Springs" before.

He went over and grabbed his phone again, and a quick search proved him right. An article came up on the *Huffington Post,* with the headline GEORGIA TOWN GETS FIRST-EVER BLACK FEMALE

SHERIFF. The article described how, in a fluke election, the minuscule northwest Georgia town of Red Springs had elected a recently retired soldier named Zandra Seagraves to the office of sheriff. It wasn't a very long article, and didn't have much in the way of details, but it did feature an excellent photo of the new sheriff. Colin let out a low whistle at the sight of her.

Zandra Seagraves was *stunning*.

Standing there in her sheriff's uniform, straight hair slicked back into a tight bun... flawless mahogany skin... full, luscious lips and —*holy shit*. He blew the photo up larger. Were her eyes *gold?*

In college, he'd dated a girl who'd been into power-lifting. There was never an ounce of fat on her except where it was supposed to be, and she could bend Colin into all sorts of shapes with her bare hands, but though she was in fantastic condition, she'd been too thick-set to fit into the mold of the classic long, leggy model. Zandra Seagraves had that same look about her. A look of strength. Of *power*. She was the polar opposite of Daphne McCutcheon in every possible way— and in a place Daphne would never think of looking.

Plus, as far as he could tell, the ring finger of Zandra Seagraves' left hand was conspicuously bare.

Colin dialed his sister's number, and when she answered, he said, "Y'know what, Char, I've changed my mind. I'm in. I'll go."

He had to hold the phone away from his ear, she squealed so loudly.

9

Cartauga County was the third-smallest in the state of Georgia. A fraction the size of Catoosa County to its immediate west, its sheriff's department staff was proportionately smaller as well. Rather than the larger county's hundred and fifty, Zandra had thirty-five men and women—patrolmen and jailers and investigators and CSIs—on the department's payroll.

In the seven days following the tornado, she got to know all of them a good bit better, since she spent twenty hours out of each day with them. She didn't think the proximity made her any more popular.

The sheriff's department building, constructed only ten years earlier and sharing a campus with the county jail, was commonly referred to as "the Farmhouse." Zandra thought that was because the back edge of the property butted up against a spacious cow pasture. Before the new construction, the sheriff's department and the then-much-smaller jail had occupied the bottom two floors of the Cartauga County courthouse. Now Zandra was plenty glad of the extra room. The tornado had bypassed her house entirely, and right after she called to make sure Perry and Sonja and Jamel were okay, she drove straight to the Farmhouse, barking orders into the radio the whole time. With Pounder's help, she set up a "control center" in the Farmhouse's single large training room. Zandra lined the walls with every whiteboard the department had. The power had only dimmed briefly there during the worst of the storm, so she also set up a bank of landline phones, available cell phones, a couple of satellite phones they'd confiscated from a drug runner they'd busted on the freeway, and an old CB radio.

The sheriff's department swiftly became a crisis hotline. 9-1-1 was overwhelmed—when people could even get through, thanks to the hundreds of downed poles and snapped lines and cell phone towers twisted into mangled metal stumps—and the department's civilian employees, alongside a handful of volunteers, did their best to take every call.

The whiteboards filled up fast.

Call after call came in: property damage. Vehicle damage. Roads blocked by fallen trees. Missing persons. Missing pets. Hundreds and hundreds of families without power, a good chunk of whom had to have it for at-home medical equipment. Even more in desperate need of medication refills and unable to get to a pharmacy. People panicked because they couldn't get to their jobs, many of them only a single paycheck away from financial ruin.

Events began to blur together. By the second day, Zandra felt more like a machine than a human. A decision-making machine, specifically, as she coordinated sheriff's deputies, firefighters, EMT crews, line crews from the North Georgia Electrical Membership Corporation, more line crews from the Red Springs Telephone Company, and a never-ending stream of civilian volunteers.

Order after order she barked out, over the radio and in person, triaging from the life-threatening all the way to the merely inconvenient. She expected resistance. Except for Pounder, the rest of the department regarded her with a cool disdain at best, to poorly veiled hostility at worst. But as the week ground on, Zandra realized why everyone was being as cooperative as they were: first, she actually was handling the county's sprawling and ever-growing list of emergencies. Second, and more important, they knew that if the sheriff's department dropped the ball, the blame would land squarely and forcefully on her shoulders. Zandra accepted that, clenched her jaw, and pressed on.

The civilian volunteers got routed to Horace Pounder. Walker County brought up a mobile command center—a very nice trailer outfitted with a generator, a bathroom, a coffee maker, and interior walls actually made of whiteboard—and set it up in one of the small patches of the Piggly Wiggly parking lot not covered with debris and scattered tree branches and broken glass. As soon as it got there, Zandra installed Pounder in it and made him point man for the deputies in the field. She knew this was no time to play department politics, but facts were facts, and the men liked and respected Pounder. Shifting some of the burden of handing out orders and assignments was just more efficient.

Cable crews from Xfinity had to wait till the roads were clear. Zandra told them all to come back in a week. She let through the technicians from AT&T and Verizon and T-Mobile, because the sooner the cell towers got back up, the sooner people could communicate. That was the worst part. The lack of communication. Not just for people living there in the county, but also for the thousands of relatives from all over the country, trying to get through and find out if their families were okay.

"Sheriff, can you tell me if Trenton Road got hit? My dad lives out there, an' he ain't in good health to start with."

"Sheriff, I can't get through to the nursin' home! My grandma's there—have you heard from 'em? Is everybody all right?"

"Sheriff, I was talkin' to my daughter an' she was sayin' the winds was gettin' real loud, and then the line cut out! Can you send a car out there to check on 'er?"

Decision after decision after decision, what crew went where, which roads to clear first, how to get the ambulance crews where they needed to be. Citizen after citizen, tortured out of their minds with worry, and every time she had to tell them, *We don't know yet. We don't know yet. Please try to stay calm. We're getting information as fast as we can.*

It wasn't until the morning of the next day that she got word about Fox Valley Road. And it wasn't until the fifth day that Zandra could tear herself away from the Farmhouse.

By then the civilian employees, every one of whom had been sleeping there on a long line of emergency cots, finally had the hang of the phones well enough that Zandra felt okay leaving them, if only for a short while. Highway 5 ran right in front of the Farmhouse and into Red Springs proper, where it turned into Lincoln Street, and Zandra drove her Tahoe down Lincoln to the Piggly Wiggly. She found Horace Pounder sitting on the back steps of the command center, sipping coffee from a Thermos and rubbing his bald scalp. He stood up and stretched when he saw her pull into the parking lot.

On the far side of the trailer, someone had set up a couple of six-foot folding tables under the kind of big, open tent typically seen at craft fairs. Both tables were covered with trays of sandwiches and coolers full of bottled water and lemonade, and the line of bedraggled people waiting to get their hands on the food and drink was at least thirty deep. She recognized the beehive-ish hair of Tommy-June Billingsley before she saw the woman's face. That made sense. Tommy-June had been serving food to the people of Red Springs in one capacity or another since Zandra was a toddler. Of course she would have set up a free sandwich station.

Zandra shut the Tahoe's door and went over to stand next to Horace Pounder, and together they looked out at the now-barely-familiar town.

"Your head okay? Saw you were rubbing it."

Pounder took his hand away and revealed a raw, red spot on the crown. "I keep bangin' it against the dang doorframe." He sipped the coffee. "Lots of folks plannin' funerals. Most of 'em goin' to Fort O. Some down to Dalton."

Zandra's lips tightened. The tornado had knocked Red Springs' one funeral home half apart.

Pounder said, "Don't hardly look like the same town, does it?"

Until Sunday afternoon, when you stood in the grocery store parking lot where they were, you could look across the street at the

Walgreens and the fancy automated car wash, but beyond that you just saw trees. The roads and streets of Red Springs made their way through tall, proud pines and oaks and hickories, grown thick enough that only a tiny portion of the town was visible from any given vantage point, unless you drove up to the top of Angel Ridge and looked down.

It wasn't like that anymore. The trees had suffered the brunt of the damage, as far as Zandra could tell, and now she could see past the car wash to the cemetery. Past the cemetery to the old county newspaper building. Past the newspaper to the back of the discount furniture store. The trees lay everywhere, knocked flat and chewed to bits, leaving only ragged stumps.

In the morning light, Zandra thought the stumps looked a little like gravestones. As if the cemetery had crept out in the night, growing and growing, until it claimed the whole town in its greedy grasp.

Pounder handed her the Thermos. "Want some?"

Zandra took it wordlessly. Pounder made good coffee. She took a swig and handed it back. "What's the word on Fox Valley? Fire department out there, getting the road clear?"

Pounder nodded. "Bunch o' ambulances been out that way already, soon as we had a lane open. I reckon they got to ever'body they could by now."

"I think we ought to ride out there."

"Farmhouse can spare you?"

"For a minute or two anyway. You want to go out with me? Take a look?"

Pounder eyed the trailer. "Let me tell 'em I'm goin'. We won't be long, though, right?"

Zandra shook her head. She just needed a few minutes. Half an hour, tops.

It was a ten-minute drive from the command center, around the shoulder of Wesley Ridge, to the intersection where Fox Valley Road dead-ended into Highway 5. Zandra made the left turn, navigated around a fallen tree and topped a small hill—

Her breath left her.

Red Springs had been hit hard. Businesses demolished, houses smashed, and of course the trees. But Fox Valley had been *scraped clean.*

Not literally—not quite. But close. Zandra had read about the Tunguska Event of 1908, when *something,* probably a meteor, had exploded in the sky over a remote part of Russia. The black-and-white photos had shown thousands upon thousands of trees just snapped off at their base, mowed down in endless rows. Fox Valley looked like that now. The north side of Wesley Ridge, all the way across to the south side of Bernard Ridge, had just been flattened.

Zandra drove forward, slowly, toward the sound of chainsaws.

It took her a second to realize they had just passed the Bixley place. Jed Bixley had built the house himself, over seven long, grueling years, but he'd made a thing of beauty, a two-story mountain stone with a shop attached to the back where he could work on his tractors.

The Bixley house was gone. It was just a driveway that led out to a concrete slab, with chewed-up debris all around it.

Pounder said, "Lord have mercy."

Red lights flashed in her rearview mirror, and she pulled over onto the shoulder as a fire truck moved past. Zandra got back onto the road and kept going, slowly. She and Pounder passed firefighters with chainsaws removing fallen trees... a group of three deputies and a man she recognized, Dale Abernathy, as they picked through the shattered remains of his house... a cluster of civilians moving through a field, calling someone's name.

Her voice sounding hollow to her own ears, Zandra said, "We'd better get back."

Pounder nodded, and when she glanced over, she saw that his eyes had turned red and puffy. He sniffled, and wiped his nose on his shirtsleeve. "Yeah. I'll keep sending whatever volunteers I get out here."

Zandra turned around in a wide spot on the shoulder and pointed the Tahoe's nose back toward Red Springs.

She had dropped Pounder back in the Piggly Wiggly parking lot and was headed toward the Farmhouse when a familiar voice crackled over the radio. Since multiple agencies from multiple counties were working in the same area, the Cartauga sheriff's department had set aside the 10-codes they normally used and just spoke in plain language.

"Sheriff? This is Dispatch. We've got a situation at Four Counties. You available?"

"Dispatch, this is Seagraves. Negative on that. I'm on my way back to the Farmhouse."

Her phone rang, and when she answered it, she immediately recognized Bruce Thurley's voice, calling from the Dispatch desk. "What is it?"

"Sheriff, the thing at Four Counties? It's Gush Parsons."

Zandra's brows drew together and formed a tight, pained line. "All right. On my way."

At the northern edge of Cartauga County, where it butted up against the Tennessee line, stood Four Counties General Hospital. The hospital had changed hands several times over the last decade and, if Perry's accounts of it were true, had dipped in quality each time. But it was a good thirty minutes closer than Memorial or Erlanger up in Chattanooga, and the staff still wasn't too picky about who they treated, insurance or not, so it sat there with its outdated equipment and rusty gurneys and kept going.

Zandra pulled up right in front of the main entrance and left the engine running.

She pushed through the big glass doors—they squealed on their hinges—and immediately saw Gush Parsons. He'd folded his long, bony frame into a tight ball and wedged himself into a corner. A couple of scrub-wearing orderlies stood over three young teenage boys, lined up on a bench on the far side of the lobby from Gush, all three of them staring at the floor and looking guilty. Zandra went to the nearest orderly.

"What happened?"

"These three—" he jerked a thumb at the boys, "—found Gush in a bathroom and started teasing him. He didn't take that too well, I don't guess. They said he started crying. Well, that just egged 'em on harder, and by the time we heard Gush screaming, they had him down on the floor, kickin' him."

Zandra caught one of the boys' eyes as he snuck a glance up at her, and she let him have the full force of her glare. He shrank back against one of the other boys as she walked past him, went over and knelt next to Gush.

She couldn't begin to count how many nights she'd babysat him. Gush's father was a traveling salesman back then, and his mother worked swing shifts up at Combustion Engineering, and they both told Zandra time and again what a Godsend she was, keeping little Augustus for them. He'd been a sweet boy, curious and polite and smart, and he'd loved to sing for her.

Years later, once he was grown, he saved up and bought himself a motorcycle, and even though his father cautioned him against riding it after dark, Gus got caught in a rain shower well after the sun went down. His bike left the road and launched Gus into a tree.

Zandra had been in the Army for a while when that happened. She only heard second- and third-hand accounts of the multiple surgeries he'd had to endure. How the doctors did their best to put his skull back together.

The little boy she'd cared for so much had grown up tall, but a broad scar ran down the center of his face, obliterating most of his nose, and Zandra's heart broke a little every time she saw him.

Now, whenever he tried to tell anyone his name, it came out "Gush." That, plus the free-flowing drool that always hung from his lower lip, had ensured that the new name stuck. When Zandra had first come back to Red Springs, she'd run into Gush and his mother in the produce aisle of the grocery store, and he'd recognized her instantly and run to her and thrown his arms around her and hugged her tight.

Gush's face lit up when he saw her now, too, but he stayed in the corner, wrapped up in his tight little knot. He had a black plastic brace on one knee. Zandra figured he'd been hurt in the tornado as well, though it didn't seem to be a very serious injury.

"Andra," Gush said, his uneven mouth splitting into a grin. A couple of strands of spittle dropped from his lower lip onto his shirt.

"It's good to see you, Gus," Zandra said, and realized as she got closer that he stank of urine. He was wearing a pair of black sweatpants with his old, gray sneakers and his tattered blue t-shirt, so it was hard to tell, but she thought he'd recently pissed his pants. No wonder, what with the assault. "I'm sorry those boys were mean to you."

"On't like baffroom," Gush said.

"Bathroom? You don't like what bathroom?"

"On't like Mama's baffroom. Gon' use 'at one." He tilted his head toward a door across the lobby with the word MEN stenciled on it. "But 'ey was in 'ere. Say I can't." He pronounced it *cain't*.

Zandra reached out and touched his arm. Gently. "Gus, honey, I'm going to make sure they don't bother you again. Okay?"

Gush hung his head. "Sorry, Andra. Got my pants wet." He rubbed his nose with the back of his hand and smeared mucus across his knuckles. "Got all upsot. Couldn't hold it no more. Sorry."

"Is there a reason you don't like the bathroom in your mother's room?"

"Small. Real small. On't like it."

"Well, I think it'd be best if you tried to get used to it. And maybe stayed there? In the room with your mom? Do you think you can do that, honey?"

Gush nodded. "Try to."

"Now, can you go with these nice men, and let them help you find your mom's room again? And..." She glanced over her shoulder at the orderlies. "Maybe a pair of pants?"

One of the men nodded silently.

Gush slowly unfolded himself and stood. He towered over Zandra. "Okay."

"Thanks, Gus." Zandra gave him a quick hug. She tried not to make it seem like she was deliberately avoiding touching his pants. "I'll see you later, okay?"

"Miss you, Andra," Gush said softly as he followed the orderlies away.

Zandra watched them go. After half a minute, she turned to the three teenage boys, and this time they *all* flinched. "All right, you little shits," she said, and took a measure of satisfaction as the flinching grew worse the closer she got. "On your feet."

They stood, but one of them had bigger balls than the other two. He stepped forward and sneered at her. "Everybody in this town hates you. You ain't never shoulda been elected."

That emboldened his friends. One of them said, "All your deputies hate you, too. They're gonna get rid o' you. I heard 'em talkin' in the Walmart."

Apparently not wanting to be left out, the third boy chimed in with, "Yeah, all it's gonna take is one shot, Sheriff. An' you ain't never gonna see where it comes from."

As she herded the boys outside, for the millionth time Zandra contemplated how anxious she was to get out of this *fucking* town.

1 0

Six days after the storm left Red Springs in ruins, and twenty miles from the town's city limits, a brand-new charter bus pulled off the freeway and parked at the edge of a strip mall. On the bus, Charity Massey stood up and addressed the three dozen teenagers, seven chaperones, and Colin, who sat in the back row scrolling through his Instagram feed and ignoring the glances and giggles that girls had been throwing his way the entire trip.

"All right, everybody, we're stopping here for lunch. There's—" she twisted and glanced out the windows, "—looks like three or four restaurants to choose from. Take your pick, but be back here at one-thirty. No exceptions. Everybody clear?"

Colin put his phone away amid the chorus of *Yes, Charity*. He stood, stretched, followed the kids off the bus, and walked into a wall of heat and humidity. His clothes instantly stuck to him, but he barely noticed. His eyes kept getting wider as he stared.

Across the street from the strip mall stood a little wood-frame house, small enough that he'd call it a cottage, and in the house's front yard were at least a dozen signs, driven into the red earth, proclaiming the TRUMP/PENCE team. They alternated with more signs that read, "MAKE AMERICA GREAT AGAIN." On the house's front wall hung a wooden pallet that someone had hand-painted to resemble the American flag. They'd gotten the number of stars badly wrong.

Charity walked up to him. His older sister stood four or five inches shorter than Colin. This still left her tall for a woman, but unlike Colin, Charity had always prioritized excellence of food over excellence of fitness. Some would have called her *zaftig.* She said, "You look like somebody just hit you between the eyes with a hammer."

Colin tilted his head to one side and pointed across the street. "That's kind of what it feels like."

Charity followed his line of sight and sighed. "Listen, just because we don't see eye to eye politically with a lot of the people around here, doesn't give you license to act like a jerk. Okay? They need our help, and it's the Christian thing to do to help people who need it."

Colin nodded absently.

"So you're going to be nice?"

"I'm not seven anymore. You're not babysitting me."

"Then don't make me act like it." She softened her words with a grin and took his arm. "Come on, let's sample some of this Southern cuisine I keep hearing about."

Colin and Charity followed a cluster of three of the group's teenagers toward a restaurant at one end of the strip mall. Colin listened absently as the two boys chatted idly about where they'd been that summer. One had spent a month at his family's ski lodge in Vail. The other kept talking about his step-dad's new villa outside Montpellier.

"Aunt Petunia's," Colin read, eyeing the neon sign in the window. He added, "Peddling the finest fried grease since 1978."

"*Be nice,*" Charity said. "These are just hard-working people like you and me. Well, like me, anyway."

Colin let that slide. He hadn't had a job in…well, he'd never *really* had a job. The money their grandparents left them had kicked in on their twenty-first birthdays, and Colin had immediately worked out how much he could pay himself in allowance each week, purely from the interest, while leaving the principal intact. It wasn't as much as a lot of his friends had—a couple of them teased him and called him a cheapskate—but it was more than enough to keep him out of actual employment. He lived in his own wing of his parents' house, he paid his own taxes, and if anybody had anything to say about it, he wasn't interested in hearing it.

Colin studied the three youths walking ahead of them. The two boys were both white, both in private school, both dressed in typical private school attire: boat shoes, khaki shorts, white shirts, and hair that looked like round blobs on their heads, falling down almost to their eyes. They laughed and punched each other and laughed some more.

Walking a couple of steps behind them was a pretty young black girl. Colin thought he'd heard someone call her Mia. He figured Mia came from the same affluence that the two boys did—almost everyone who went to Charity's church had money—but she dressed less conspicuously, just wearing jeans and a nice t-shirt with a pair of Nikes.

All five of them arrived at Aunt Petunia's and pushed through the doors. Inside, two-thirds of the dining area was devoted to tables and booths, while over on the left, a diner-style bar ran the length of the wall. The place was packed and, as Colin swiftly observed, the clientele was one hundred percent white. Young men in work boots and dirty jeans and stained t-shirts sat near older men in fishing vests and trucker caps; young women in flip-flops and tiny cutoff denim shorts and tank tops, their hair shoved up on top of their heads in messy buns, ate next to white-haired women in floral dresses and way too much makeup. Half a dozen tiny children ran around between the tables. One of them wore nothing but a diaper.

Three out of every four of the patrons were, to Colin's eye, *immensely* fat.

A middle-aged waitress in a yellow blouse and skirt came over to them. "All o' y'all together?"

One of the blob-haired boys said, "No, me and Brad're one party."

The waitress's mouth quirked up on one side. "And who's the other 'party'?"

Charity touched Mia's shoulder. "You want to eat with us?" Mia smiled and nodded. To the waitress, Charity said, "We're a party of three, then."

The waitress glanced around. "We've still got the lunch rush goin'. I can seat y'all two—" she indicated the two boys, "—but it'll be a minute till a booth gets cleared. That okay?"

Charity nodded. "That'll be fine, ma'am. Do you have a menu we could look at?"

"Sure do—right there on the end of the bar."

The blob-hairs followed the waitress. Charity and Mia and Colin moved to the end of the bar, where Charity picked up a stained, tri-fold paper menu. Softly she said, "Fried grease might not be too far off."

Mia chuckled, and spoke for the first time. "I bet it'll taste amazing, though."

The door opened, and a big, middle-aged black man came in. He wore a uniform with a name tag that read "KARLOS," and pushed a hand-truck loaded with cases of paper. The yellow-clad waitress came back, and Karlos said, "Where you want these?"

Colin thought he heard the waitress's tone grow cooler. "You can leave 'em right there, that's fine."

Karlos parked the hand-truck and pulled an invoice out of his breast pocket. "Just need a signature."

The waitress started to sign it, but hesitated. "Patti said she wanted to talk to you about next month's order. Can you hang on a minute?"

Karlos grinned and shrugged. "Sure. I'ma step outside and have a smoke, you don't mind."

The waitress nodded and bustled off. Karlos gave a quick look-over to Colin and Charity and Mia, then a polite nod, and stepped outside.

On the edge of the bar, facing the parking lot, sat a small coin-operated vending machine. It was loaded with candy bars—the same selection of Reese's Cups and Snickers and Payday Bars that Colin was accustomed to seeing back home—and Mia drifted toward it.

When she saw Colin watching, she said, "Mom and Dad never let me have candy."

Colin smiled and dug a dollar in quarters out of his pocket. "Why not live a little?"

While Mia examined the machine's contents, deciding which lump of sugar and preservatives to indulge in, Colin studied the patrons seated at the bar. They were all men, all of them older than forty… and as he watched, one by one, they all turned to look at Mia. Colin didn't think she was aware of their attention, since all of hers was focused on the machine, and he decided that was for the best.

Mia dropped in the four quarters and turned the knob.

Nothing happened.

It wasn't that one of the candy bars got hung up on the screw-shaped rack and didn't fall. Simply nothing happened. The knob didn't seem to be attached to anything.

Mia mumbled, "Oh well. Shouldn't have candy anyway."

Colin exchanged a glance with Charity, and stuck a hand out, signaling to the waitress behind the bar. She was younger than the other one, maybe late twenties, white, stamped from the same mold as the young women with the tank tops and sloppy top-knots. Her uniform was a pale mint green. She came over and said, "Yeah?"

Colin gestured at the vending machine. "My friend here just lost a dollar in this thing."

Up until that point, the waitress had been eyeing Colin with an expression he could easily identify: *I'm liking what I'm seeing.* But when her gaze slid past him to the friend he'd mentioned and settled on Mia, that expression changed. Went neutral. Cold.

The waitress again said, "Yeah?"

Colin frowned. "Your machine. It's broken. She turned the knob and nothing happened. It doesn't work."

Without an iota of change in her face or her voice, the waitress said, "Yeah, we know." And she turned and picked up a rag and started wiping the counter.

Colin felt his heartbeat accelerating. He leaned over the counter, wondering if he'd misspoken. "Sorry, excuse me? It took the dollar she put in. Could we get that back, please?"

Now the waitress's face did change. What might have been pretty features turned mocking. "You want a dollar back?"

Colin exchanged another glance with Charity. His sister was staring at the waitress, her brow furrowed, silent. Colin thought, *Okay, so it's not just me,* and said, "Yes, since she lost it in your machine, we would like the money back, please."

He heard a snort. It came from one of the men seated at the bar. The waitress said, "Well, if you wanna make a *big deal* out of it, then hang on," and took her sweet time ambling the length of the bar. She disappeared through a swinging door in the back. Colin stood there, feeling more and more out of place, more and more as if he'd become trapped in some kind of alternate dimension where logic no longer applied. He couldn't make out any of the words, but he realized the men at the bar were all talking, softly, words interspersed with quiet laughter. He saw glance after glance stolen at him and at Mia.

They were laughing at him.

For asking for money back from a broken machine.

Colin Massey had *never* been laughed at before. His mouth went dry, and when he tried to swallow, it didn't work. He could only stand there, trembling, until the waitress came back. She held out a hand and dropped twenty nickels on the bar, which Colin mutely scooped up. He turned to Charity and Mia and said, "Let's find somewhere else to eat."

Charity nodded and slipped an arm around Mia's shoulders, and the three of them walked out of the restaurant.

Karlos stood outside, smoking a cigarette. He raised an eyebrow at Colin.

Colin pointed with a thumb back inside. "Could you hear all that?"

Karlos said, "This glass thin. Heard every word."

Colin tried and failed to say something. He finally blurted out, "What the *hell* was that? What just happened in there?"

"Where y'all from? You don't mind me askin'?"

Charity said, "Connecticut. We're here to help rebuild Mount Zachariah Church, in Red Springs. Because of the tornado."

Karlos shook his head, his lips hinting at a sad smile. "Well, that's mighty kind of you. But shit like this? This every day 'round here. This *life*. What you just seen? Nothin' but one grain o' sand on a big-ass beach."

Inside, a white-haired woman came to the window and tapped on it. Karlos nodded to her. He dropped his cigarette and ground it out with the sole of his shoe. "Y'all have a nice day, now." Karlos went back inside the restaurant, leaving Colin Massey standing there, feeling like a drowning victim.

***

Colin and Charity and Mia trudged across the parking lot in silence, ate lunch at a place Colin had never heard of before —"Bojangles"—still in silence, and got back on the bus. The silence remained.

Colin's head spun. He found himself in a thought loop that started with *These are the people we're trying to help?* and curved around to *It's the Christian thing to do to help people who need it* but then shifted right back to *These are the people we're trying to help?*

He'd never considered himself a Christian. Charity was the convert in the family; their parents had never darkened the door of a church a single day in their lives, and as far as he knew, neither had Diego. But Colin had seen how much joy being involved in the church had brought his sister, and while he never thought it would be for him, he didn't begrudge her her faith.

But surely there were limits.

The bus only drove another fifteen minutes before pulling into the parking lot of a grocery store called—Colin did a double-take —"Piggly Wiggly." The logo was a dancing cartoon pig. He sank down farther in his seat.

At Charity's insistence, he filed off the bus with everyone else, and wandered along after her while she looked for whomever was in charge. There were still piles of debris in the parking lot, but they'd all been pushed over to one side. All but one of the big plate glass windows that made up the grocery store's front had been replaced with big sheets of plywood. In one corner of the lot stood a big windowless trailer. Not like the box on an eighteen-wheeler—more like a utilitarian version of a Winnebago. Outside the trailer, locals were lined up to get to a big open-sided tent, and Colin saw them wandering away with paper plates bearing sandwiches and hot dogs. Most of them juggled bottles of full-strength Mountain Dew.

Like the patrons in Aunt Petunia's, most of them were fat, too.

The person in charge turned out to be an immense individual in a deputy sheriff's uniform who stepped down out of the windowless trailer. An image immediately sprang into Colin's mind: George "the Animal" Steele, the legendary professional wrestler. This guy was cut from the same cloth but, near as Colin could tell, was even bigger. The brass name tag pinned to his shirt pocket labeled him H. POUNDER.

Charity introduced herself to Pounder and told him who they were, where they were from, and what they had come to do. Colin thought he could see the pit stains under Pounder's arms getting bigger the longer he stood there in the afternoon sun. Pounder said, "Okay, let me see if I can get Pastor Jessup on the phone. He'll want to come down here an' meet y'all, I reckon, and I'll let him decide how to put you to work."

Charity and Colin moved away from the trailer while Pounder pulled out a cell phone and dialed. Colin took a closer look at the Piggly Wiggly—at the obvious recent repairs that had been done on the roof—and realized that a huge pile of rubble lying on the far side of the building was the remains of the roof.

Charity said, "I've never seen tornado damage in person before."

He nodded. "Yeah, it tore the shit out of this place."

She nudged him with an elbow. "Being nice means watching your language, too. We're in the buckle of the Bible Belt down here, y'know."

"Oh, like no Southerner ever cursed. I saw *Deliverance.*"

They had been speaking quietly, and Colin almost jumped when a voice from right behind them said, "Y'all must be the ones from that big charter bus, huh?"

They turned to see a middle-aged woman with an abundance of silver-gray hair swept up into something like a beehive on top of her head. She wore a simple blouse and tan shorts, had a sweet, pleasant face with an even sweeter smile, and looked like someone's favorite aunt. She held a hand out, first to Charity, then to Colin. "I'm Tommy-June Billingsley." After they gave her their names, she asked, "Who y'all waitin' on?"

Charity said, "Oh, um, Officer Pounder there is getting in touch with Pastor Jessup. We're here to help however we can, but we really want to get his church back in shape. Mount Zachariah, I mean."

Tommy-June's smile got even broader. "You don't say? Comin' all this way to help out, I swear, the Lord just works miracles, don't He?"

Colin could hear the capital H in "He."

Tommy-June said, "Well, I tell you what, I'm in charge o' the sand-wich stand over here, and it's mighty hot, and we sure could use an extra set o' hands." The hands she had in mind were Colin's, and she took both of his in hers. "Why don't you come on over and help me while you're waitin' on the preacher?"

Colin could think of no response. He saw Charity grinning as Tommy-June led him to the open-sided tent, where a dark-haired woman in her thirties was busy handing out paper plates. "Laura, this here's Colin. That's what you said your name was, right, hon?"

Laura flashed a grin that would have been more appealing if she'd had all her teeth. As it was, she was missing a lateral incisor and a canine on the right side, and the look did her no favors. "Well, ain't he a pretty one? Where'd you find him, Tommy-June?"

"He's come down from up North to lend us a hand. Whole bus-load of 'em."

Laura gathered her hair up into a ponytail and wrapped an elastic band around it. "Well, ain't gonna lie, I could use a break. It's hot as the dickens out here." She picked up a Mountain Dew out of a big barrel full of half-melted ice and wandered off toward a line of parked cars. "Don't worry, Tommy-June, I'll be back in two shakes."

Feeling vaguely kidnapped, and still shaken from the incident at Aunt Petunia's, Colin said, "What do you want me to do?"

"Ain't nothin' to it, honey." Tommy-June pointed at various items. "I hand 'em the plate and the drink, they tell you if they want a sandwich or a hot dog, and you give 'em whatever they ask for."

She was right. It was easy enough. Easy enough that he thought she could have done it by herself, but he knew if he tried to beg off now he'd just look like an asshole, so he put a smile on and handed out the food as people came up to the table. After a few minutes he asked, "What kind of sandwiches are these, anyway?"

Tommy-June glowed with pride. "My specialty. Fried boloney."

Colin repressed a shudder. The salad he'd ordered at the Bojangles had been okay, but he'd had a craving for some good sashimi for several hours now. He doubted he'd find any in Red Springs.

The line of people steadily thinned out, until the only ones left were a black family consisting of a man in his forties, his wife who looked about the same age, and two kids, a girl and a boy somewhere around six and eight. They were the only black people in the whole line. Colin wondered if they brought up the rear just because they arrived later than everyone else, or if it involved some other reason.

The father stepped up, ushering the little boy along in front of him, and Tommy-June flashed her big sweet smile at the family just as readily and easily as she'd shown it to Colin and Charity. "How y'all doin'? Holdin' up okay? Got somewhere to sleep?"

The mother was busy with the little girl, who had stepped out of her shoe and didn't want to put it back on, but the father answered. "Yes, ma'am. We stayin' at my cousin's place. Young'uns 'bout to eat 'im out o' house an' home, though, so we sure do appreciate y'all runnin' the stand like this."

Tommy-June handed out plates and bottled drinks, and Colin obligingly asked the family which they'd prefer, fried bologna sandwiches or hot dogs. Both kids wanted hot dogs, but the adults took the sandwiches. Before they left, the father said, "God bless you, Miss Tommy-June. An' you too, sir. Thanks."

Colin mumbled, "You're welcome."

With no one left to serve, Tommy-June turned and leaned against the table and cooled herself with a fan made out of what looked like a folded sheet of printer paper. Colin considered his words. "I've, um… I have to say, Tommy-June, it was a relief to see you treat that family the way you did."

Still fanning, she turned her head to look at him. "How so, honey?"

Colin hooked his thumbs in his belt. "Well, on the way in, we stopped at this restaurant, this little hole-in-the-wall, mom-and-pop-looking place, and the staff and the customers didn't exactly show us any of your famous Southern hospitality."

Now the fanning stopped. Concern creased Tommy-June's face. "What happened, sugar?"

As concisely as he could, using what he hoped was neutral language, Colin explained the treatment Mia and, by extension, he too had received at Aunt Petunia's. Tommy-June shook her head in an expression of dismay.

"Lord have mercy, there ain't no call for that."

"I didn't think so, either. So it's good to see someone around here just… well, just being nice to African-Americans."

Tommy-June leaned toward him, suddenly conspiratorial. "Well, it don't do no good to alienate 'em! Everybody ought to know that by now. We got to show 'em kindness, bless their hearts. Show 'em how to do right. If they didn't have us white folks as examples, well, they'd just sit around makin' babies and collectin' welfare checks, wouldn't they?"

Colin stared at her. He wondered what kind of emotion showed on his face. Tommy-June didn't recoil from him, so he thought maybe it had stayed neutral. He said, "If you'll excuse me, I need to go talk to my sister."

"Sure thing, honey," Tommy-June said with her big sweet smile.

Colin felt his whole body trembling as he went to find Charity. She was chatting with a knot of the church group teenagers near the bus. He caught her eye and beckoned to her, and when she came over to him, Colin quietly said, "Fuck every single fucking bit of this town. I'm out of here."

11

The Hidden Man watched the news.

His power of invisibility was in full force. No one around him saw him. His influence was so great that it affected their subconscious minds, causing them to veer in their courses on the sidewalk so as not to touch him.

He watched the news on the TV through the plate glass window of the pawn shop and considered what would happen in the wake of the storm. His Workshop was gone now. He'd been there, seen the wreckage, the ruination. It wasn't safe to go back there. And when it was discovered, as it inevitably would be…

Well. That had never been a part of his plan, but wouldn't it be *fun*? Watching everyone scurry around like ants from a kicked anthill.

The Workshop was gone, but he still had his Showroom, unless someone stumbled across that, too. No reason to think they would. Not for a while, anyway.

The Hidden Man strolled down the sidewalk, as was his habit, the waves of power washing off of him, blinding the citizens of Red Springs.

His citizens. They belonged to him. They just didn't realize it.

His steps took him past the parking lot of the local grocery store, the now-devastated monument to consumerism and gluttony. He watched the little lost sheep, driven from their homes by the Biblical funnel cloud, lining up to receive charity from the matronly woman and her snaggle-toothed helper.

Except...

The Hidden Man stopped. He squinted. A girl stood there, accepting food from the matron. Dark skin glistening in the heat, night-black eyes visible even from this distance, wide and deep and beautiful. He recognized her from the church. *Angelique.* That was her name. He hadn't seen her in... it had been a year, at least, and in that time Angelique had grown. Developed. Gone now was the baby fat, the awkwardness. Where had she been? Somewhere that had given her space to grow, for her limbs to become long and slender, for her waist to narrow, for her chest and hips and ass to curve. She wore tight jeans cut off at the knees and a tight white halter top, her hair a bountiful mass of twists, a living embodiment of perfect sin and blasphemy.

Angelique.

Yes.

He knew where Angelique lived.

1 2

Big Harold's Place opened in 1998 in downtown Red Springs, where the old drug store used to be. It occupied half of a long, low, red brick building at the corner of Old Bridge Road and Millis Street, which put it directly across from Norris Brothers Bail Bonds and a stone's throw from the Cartauga County courthouse, and all but guaranteed a steady lunch crowd of county employees. The tornado had missed Big Harold's Place entirely. It hadn't even snarled up the power lines. So Big Harold, who still ran the kitchen as well as all the administrative duties, went ahead and opened back up as soon as the sheriff's department let him know it was safe.

Ordinarily lunch patrons filled the dining room between 11:00 and 2:00. Small business owners and courthouse employees and a *lot* of law enforcement officers made it a habit to eat there every weekday. But the tornado had demolished the courthouse, and of the businesses in downtown Red Springs that were able to open up, only about half of them had yet. Plus, it was a Saturday afternoon, and Big Harold had let it be known to anyone who would listen that it was barely even worth his time to stay open.

Zandra Seagraves sat with her brother Perry at her usual table and surveyed the empty seats around them. She would've felt guilty about coming to sit down and eat a real meal when there was so much left to do back at the Farmhouse, except that the experience so far had been much more like a queen holding court than a noon meal. Citizen after citizen spotted her and, to a person, decided speaking to her directly trumped calling the department's help line.

Big Harold's was one of the few restaurants Zandra would eat in. She had inspected the kitchen herself, knew everyone who worked there, and trusted Big Harold to follow the health code to the letter. She still preferred to cook her own food, but Big Harold's would do in a pinch. She saw Perry watching her, a look of amusement on his broad features, as she ate her Salisbury steak with her usual mashed potatoes and green beans.

Every time Zandra took a bite of food—each item of which was carefully separated from the other items by a small but uniform space —she realigned whatever it was so that everything on her plate was equidistant. It took her a while to eat any meal, and this one was taking longer than usual, thanks to all the people dropping by her table.

"That never gets old," Perry said, as Zandra chewed and swallowed a bite of steak.

"I don't make fun of the way you eat."

"That's because I eat like a normal person. There's nothing to make fun of."

A middle-aged white man stepped up and paused a few feet away. "Uh, Sheriff? My fence got torn plum out the ground, and I don't know where my cows is at now. You think you could maybe get a few o' your men to come help me look?"

Zandra flipped open the notepad beside her plate and jotted down the man's information. "I'll have Major Pounder look into that," she said. It was a response she'd given so many times during this meal that it sounded rote now, but she meant it. She'd have a whole stack of notes to hand off to Pounder when she went back by the crisis trailer after lunch.

The man thanked her and shuffled off, and Zandra shifted the remaining portion of steak on her plate. It was important that she cut off each bite just right, so that what was left was still the proper shape. She and Perry could both see the door clearly from where they sat, each of them taking up an adjoining side of the square table, and she watched as a few teenagers whom she didn't recognize drifted in.

"All these people coming in to help," she said neutrally.

Perry had long since finished his meal. Now he simply sat, keeping his sister company, nursing a glass of sweet tea. "Is that a bad thing? You make it sound like it might be a bad thing."

"I don't know. Maybe. It's just introducing a bunch of random elements into a situation already crammed to the top with more random elements."

Two locals came in. Zandra knew both of them: Jerry Blankenship and Belvis Horne. A couple of good-ol'-boy retirees. They saw her looking at them, but while Blankenship nodded, his eyes had gone frosty. Belvis Horne didn't bother nodding, or disguising the contempt on his face. Zandra didn't react. Instead she scooped up a forkful of mashed potatoes, ate it, and re-sculpted the potatoes still on her plate into a harmonious shape again.

"I couldn't do it," Perry said.

"Couldn't do what?"

"Just not react. I was the sheriff, and I saw a couple of old farts like that giving me the stink-eye? I'd at least have to say something."

"There'd be no point. I know how the town feels about me. The good thing today is, I know Blankenship and Horne don't have anything wrong at their places. If they did, they would've been over here, bitching at me about it." She chewed and swallowed another bite of steak. "I still blame you for all this, you realize."

Perry let a grin spread his lips wide, showing off his flawless teeth. "I don't recall putting a gun to your head and forcing you to run for sheriff."

"Yeah? Well, it damn sure felt like you did. I—"

Zandra faltered. Out of the corner of her eye, she saw Perry pick up on it and immediately swivel his head to see what had caught her attention, and knew in the next second that no matter what happened afterward, Perry was going to give her *endless* shit.

A man and a woman had just stepped into the restaurant. Both white, both young—Zandra placed them around college age—and obviously related. Their eyes, the shapes of their noses, the color of their hair. She was looking at a pair of siblings, unquestionably. The woman projected a librarian vibe. Conservative hairstyle, hardly any makeup, a summer-weight dress so plain that, if it had been longer, would've looked right in place on a Church of Christ member.

The woman's brother, on the other hand…

Zandra knew a term. She'd learned it from one of her little cousins when she and Perry and their mother had gone to visit Aunt Charlaine in Atlanta. The term was *bishōnen*. It was Japanese, and meant "beautiful boy." Zandra's thirteen-year-old cousin Dana had shown her a bunch of manga, and some anime posters, and a video of a Japanese pop group called NEWS. The video had prominently featured a young man named, according to Dana, Tomohisa Yamashita. Though obviously masculine, Yamashita had a fine-boned, clear-skinned, utterly whiskerless face and beyond-perfect hair. Zandra hadn't been able to deny that he was indeed beautiful, to Dana's delight.

The young man standing just inside the door, arguing with his sister, was a brown-haired, blue-eyed version of the same thing. *Bishōnen*. Beautiful. He wore clothes that didn't appear ever to have touched a rack, and he looked as out of place, there in Big Harold's, as a diamond necklace on a hog.

Zandra made this assessment in less than a heartbeat and immediately returned to both her food and the sentence she had broken off—"I never would've agreed to it if you hadn't kept digging at me." But she knew it was already too late. Perry's eyes had gone huge, and he all but squirmed in his seat.

"Something catch your eye, there, Zan?"

"What're you talking about?"

"Oh, no no no, don't even *try* to play it off. I saw you checking out that white boy. I bet the whole restaurant did."

Zandra set her fork down. "Number one, I wasn't *checking out* anyone. I was making note of a couple more people I didn't recognize."

Perry seemed to be holding back laughter, with limited success. "Uh-huh. Go on."

"Number two, there's hardly anybody in here, and the people who *are* in here make a point of ignoring me, so I could jump up on this table and spin a hula hoop and nobody'd notice."

Perry adopted what she instantly knew to be a faux-solemn expression. "Of course. Of course. You're Sheriff Zandra Seagraves. The Zandroid."

"Watch it."

"You can't engage in normal human emotions like the rest of us." Merriment seeped back through. "And you especially can't eye-fuck random white boys."

Zandra said, "*I was not—*" but broke off when she heard someone clear their throat, and looked up to see the *bishōnen* white guy standing there, not five feet away.

He said, "Excuse me, I'm sorry, but are you Sheriff Zandra Seagraves?"

Zandra closed her eyes briefly. She didn't think she could stand to see Perry's face. Under his breath, Perry said, *"White boy's on a first-name basis!"*

As she opened her eyes again, the white guy went on. "I'm sorry to trouble you, but, uh, well, could I talk to you for a minute? If you don't mind?"

Perry quickly stood, grin firmly in place, and held out one beefy hand. The white guy was tall, but massed probably two-thirds of what Perry did, and his own hand got a bit lost in Perry's oversized mitt. "Of course, young man, of course!" Perry said. "This *is* Sheriff Zandra Seagraves, and I'm her brother, Pericles. You can call me Perry. Here, sit down, join us! What's your name, son?"

"Colin. Colin Massey."

He pulled out one of the other chairs and sat down, while Zandra imagined a few creative ways to get her brother back for this. She said, "What can I do for you, Mr. Massey?"

"Please. Call me Colin. I know it's a cliché thing to say, but it's true, Mr. Massey is my dad."

Zandra abandoned hope of finishing her meal in peace. "All right, Colin. What did you want to talk about?"

"Well, Sheriff, I've come down with my sister's church group. We're supposed to be helping to rebuild… I think it's Mount Zachariah Baptist Church? I think that's right."

"Came down from where?" Perry asked. Every word out of his mouth made Zandra want to punch him.

"Oh, sorry. Milford, Connecticut."

Perry seemed eager to take point in this conversation. Zandra let him. Perry said, "Connecticut. Huh. You been to the South before?"

Colin Massey shook his head. "First time. And, well… what I wanted to ask you about—it's just, we only got here about two hours ago, but I've seen a couple of things that're just… well… they're not what I'm accustomed to."

Zandra had been studying Colin Massey, despite her annoyance with Perry, and every single thing about him said *money* to her. She considered saying, "I'll bet you're accustomed to getting whatever you want," but thought better of it. Perry wasn't the only person who'd suggested to her in the past that she could work on her tact. Instead, she said, "All right. What did you see?"

In a sometimes halting manner, the young man described to Zandra and Perry one incident at Aunt Petunia's restaurant involving a coin-operated vending machine, and then another one here in town that centered around a woman with silver-gray hair.

As Colin Massey talked, Perry's grin faded.

When Colin had finished, Zandra said, "Okay. And why did you feel the need to come and tell the sheriff about this?"

Colin made a couple of false starts. "Well, I guess… I guess I just wanted to know if that kind of thing was *normal* around here. And, if it's not normal—I mean, if it's something that doesn't usually happen

—I wanted to tell someone. Let someone know, who's in a position to do something about it."

Zandra let out a long, slow breath. "Since your friend Mia got her dollar back, no crime was committed at Aunt Petunia's. And while I've never heard Tommy-June Billingsley come right out and say what she said to you, her saying it isn't a crime either. Not legally. So I appreciate you wanting to call attention to it, Colin, but believe me, I already know." She cut her eyes toward Perry. "*We* already know."

Colin sat back in his chair and put his hands over his face. Perry said, "Your life's a little different in Connecticut, is it?"

Colin moved his hands, but stared through the tabletop. "Honestly, I think… I never really… I mean, I knew there were people who felt that way." He tapped his temple. "Here? I knew it. The way I know the Earth has a molten core, or that Saturn has all those rings around it. I knew it, but I've never *seen* it. Not till today. Everybody I know, everybody I went to school with—white, black, brown, whatever—we all talk the same. We all act the same. We all *think* the same." His eyes focused, and he lifted them to look at Zandra. "How can you guys *stand* it?"

Zandra considered saying, "That's quite the bubble you've been living in," but once again thought better of it. Instead she said, "Is that what you and your sister were arguing about when you came in? Whether or not you should come and say something?"

"Oh. Uh, no. After the thing with Mrs. Billingsley, I told Charity— that's my sister—that I was going to grab a ride to the airport and fly back to Milford tonight. She was begging me to stay."

Zandra raised one eyebrow a fraction of an inch. "So? Are you going, or staying?"

"I don't… um. I haven't decided yet."

Perry leaned forward. Zandra heard his voice shift into "coach mode."

"Listen, Colin, I can't speak for all white people, any more than I can speak for all black people. I think you know there's as many different kinds of people, different points of view, as there are leaves on a magnolia."

Colin adopted a dry sort of smile. "I don't know what a magnolia looks like, but I get what you're saying."

Perry went on. "What I *can* tell you, though, is the way most of the white people in this particular town think. If you want to know."

"Please. Enlighten me. Because right now it's... it's like I just ran into the boogeyman or something. I can't see how I can believe my own eyes and ears."

Perry folded his arms on the tabletop. "It's like this. There's some white folks in Red Springs every bit as progressive as you are, believe it or not. More the younger ones than the older ones. They don't hold prejudices. They voted for Hillary, for all the good it did 'em. Like pissing in the wind around here."

Zandra said, "Perry—no need for that kind of language around a stranger."

Perry grinned and clapped an enormous hand on Colin's forearm. "Well, he's not a stranger if you get to know him, is he?"

Zandra rolled her eyes.

Perry stowed the grin and took his hand back. "That's one chunk of the population. Then there's another chunk that don't mix with black folks too much, but they don't have strong feelings about us one way or another. Pretty much a live-and-let-live kind of situation."

Colin's eyes had narrowed. "Sounds like there's a third group."

"Yeah. And it's the biggest one. The third group thinks of black folks kind of the way most people think of feral cats."

"I'm sorry—feral *cats?*"

"Yeah. Like, say, every once in a while you'll get a stray cat that shows up, hangs around your house, catches some mice. Does something useful. They're all right, see, the useful ones? You got no problem with those. Now, a lot rarer than that, but even better, you might get one to come inside your house. Turn it all domesticated. Let you keep it as a pet. That's the best-case scenario. You find one of the *good ones.*" Perry drummed his fingertips on the tabletop. "But the rest of the cats out there? They're seen as a nuisance, at best, and a menace at the worst. It'd just be safest for everybody if they were all wiped out."

Zandra watched Colin Massey as Perry spoke. Colin's face had turned a little green.

Perry went on. "They don't say it out loud. Or at least, not when there's any black people around to hear them. But that's how they feel."

Silence descended on the table. Zandra hadn't heard Perry explain the town's mindset in quite that way before. She sat there, trying to poke holes in it, but couldn't. In the middle of the silence, Colin's sister, Charity, walked up.

"Hi, um, I'm sorry to interrupt, but... Colin? Are you, uh, are you going to eat with us? Or—or somewhere else?"

Before Colin could respond, a short, heavyset, ancient black woman in a pale yellow pantsuit came shuffling up to the table. She didn't look at Colin or Charity, or even Perry, but zeroed in on Zandra. "Sheriff! Sheriff, you've got to help me!"

Zandra turned to her. "I know I'll try, Mrs. Daywood. What's wrong?"

"It's a tree, Sheriff. That tornado pulled a tree up out of my yard and laid it down right across my driveway! I can't get my car out! I had to walk all the way down to the road for my daughter to come and pick me up. Can you get somebody out there to get that tree gone?"

Zandra sighed. "We've got tree crews working pretty much around the clock, ma'am. I'm sure you'll be on the list for tomorrow or the next day."

The elderly woman's face sagged. "Two days? It might be two days? Surely you can free up somebody before then? My son left his chainsaw in the garage. I can't lift the dang thing myself, or I would've fixed the problem myself already!"

Colin Massey spoke up. "Ma'am? Mrs. Daywood? Hi, we're with a group of volunteers, and I bet I could grab a couple of the bigger boys and get that tree taken care of."

Zandra saw Charity Massey's eyebrows try to climb up into her hair.

Mrs. Daywood turned to Colin, a grin lighting her face up. "Well, that'd be awful Christian of you, young man! And my oh my, what a fine-looking young man you are! Are the boys you're going to bring along as good-looking as you?"

Colin smiled. "I don't know about that, ma'am, but I bet they'll be thrilled to pick up a chainsaw."

Zandra gave the elderly woman a slip of paper and a pen to write down her address. As Mrs. Daywood was doing that, Perry reached over and fished one of Zandra's cards out of her right breast pocket. Zandra said, "Hey!" and tried to swat his hand away.

Perry slid the card across the table to Colin Massey. Both the grin and the merriment had returned. "Here, Colin, take this. You just give the sheriff a call if you run into any trouble. That has her direct number on it."

Colin took out his wallet and slid the card into it.

Inwardly, Zandra groaned.

Endless shit.

13

harity had almost pitched one of her quiet fits at the mention of the word "chainsaw," but two of the boys in the group, Reg and Andy—a couple of what Colin's biological father, who'd gone back to Dublin, Ireland, after the divorce, would refer to as "big, strapping lads"—assured her they knew how to use one, citing extensive experience at a summer camp in Vermont. With Colin along as chaperone, Charity reluctantly gave them her blessing, and said she'd arrange for one of the local church members to come pick them up when they were done.

They rode out to Mrs. Daywood's place in her daughter's car. Mrs. Daywood's daughter's name was Sharice. She looked about forty, a compact, wiry woman still wearing her Waffle House waitress uniform, and though she didn't smile, Colin thought she sounded sincere when she thanked them for helping her mother. Maybe a little skeptical about their motivations, but sincere nonetheless. Colin reasoned that it wouldn't matter to Mrs. Daywood *why* the tree got moved, just that it did get moved.

Colin wondered if Sharice had the same kind of baked-in antipathy toward white people that, as far as he had seen and

96

according to Perry Seagraves, so many white people had toward the black population. If she did, he didn't figure he could blame her.

Mrs. Daywood's house was in a part of the county commonly referred to as "Treece." It wasn't an official community, he didn't think, and when he asked Sharice and her mother how it got that name, neither of them could tell him. As they drove, he wondered if it was a bastardization of the word "trees," because that's mostly what he saw on either side of the road. Half a mile of trees. Then a house. Then more trees.

The trip was like that until they turned down a long, rutted, gravel driveway, and Colin began to understand why a tree across the drive would have presented such a problem for a woman of Mrs. Daywood's age. The driveway was at least a quarter of a mile long, and snaked back through the woods, so that the Daywood house couldn't be seen from the road at all.

Or at least, that was the way it used to be. The path of the tornado stood out just as clearly as a guardrail-bordered interstate highway. It had come through the woods, smashing and destroying the trees unfortunate enough to stand in its way, cut diagonally across the driveway, and continued through the woods on the other side, headed toward Red Springs proper. Sharice pulled the car up and stopped in front of the gigantic hickory tree that blocked their path. The tornado had ripped it out of the ground, roots and all, and laid it down across the driveway at a near-perfect ninety-degree angle. Hundreds of other trees lay broken and discarded all around them, but by some miracle, this was the only one rendering the driveway impassable.

"You okay for me leavin' you here, Mama?" Sharice asked as Mrs. Daywood opened her door.

Mrs. Daywood came around the car and leaned in her daughter's open window and gave her a hug. "Of course, baby. I know you got to get to work."

Colin and Reg and Andy had ridden in the back seat, crammed in shoulder-to-shoulder, and Colin was grateful to climb out and stretch. He said, "The Waffle House didn't get hit, I take it?"

Sharice *almost* smiled at him. "You know we're part of FEMA, right?"

"I'm sorry?"

"FEMA. The emergency people? They got what they call a 'Waffle House Index.' They can tell how bad a crisis is in the South by whether or not the Waffle House is still open."

Colin had not come even close to learning his way around Red Springs yet, small though it was. "So I guess Red Springs didn't get hit *too* bad, then? If you're going to work?"

Sharice shook her head. "One I work at's in LaFayette." She pronounced it *lah-FAY-et.* "Waffle House in Red Springs ain't there no more. Just a foundation with some rebar stickin' out of it." She shot looks at the two boys. "Y'all take care o' my mama, all right?"

Colin assured her that they would. Sharice backed out to the road and left, and Mrs. Daywood let Colin take her hand and steady her as they picked their way around the enormous root cluster of the tree. Once they were back on the gravel driveway, Mrs. Daywood paused and gazed out at the flattened forest. The tornado's path was almost as wide as a football field. It stretched out in both directions farther than they could see, a broad road paved with broken trunks and littered with splintered stumps.

Colin said, "You okay, ma'am?"

Mrs. Daywood shook her head slowly. Sadly. "I grew up in this house. Ran around in these woods every day as a girl. Ain't never gonna be the same now." She waved a hand and squared her shoulders. "No sense in dwellin' on it. The Lord done looked after me, steerin' that tornado away from my house. There's plenty o' folks need His grace a sight worse'n I do."

Mrs. Daywood guided them the rest of the way up the driveway —they walked at her pace—and she showed them the chainsaw in the garage. "It's ready to go, all full up an' oiled an' such," she said to Reg and Andy. Then, to Colin, "Now you keep an eye on 'em, y'hear? Chainsaw'll get away from you, you don't show it proper respect."

All three of them said, "Yes, ma'am" roughly in unison. She turned to go inside, and as she went, told them, "I'll bring out a pitcher o' iced tea direckly. Reckon y'all'll get plenty hot out here."

Colin eyed Reg and Andy as Reg picked up what looked to Colin like an *enormous* chainsaw. He'd never seen one in real life before. It had the name *STIHL* on the bar. "Were you guys telling the truth about knowing how to use that thing? Or was that bullshit?"

Reg grinned. "Don't worry, Mr. Massey. We spent six straight weeks cutting back trees at Camp Palumbo." He and Andy headed back down the driveway toward the tree.

Colin stood rooted in place. He said, "*Mr. Massey*? How old do you think I am?" But neither boy heard him, or if they did, they elected not to respond, instead pretending to be Leatherface and a victim from *The Texas Chainsaw Massacre.* Colin followed them, grumbling.

The shadows had grown longer, Reg and Andy had both worked up a healthy sweat, and Mrs. Daywood had brought them two pitchers of iced tea when Colin saw the dog.

He was sweating a good bit himself, stacking the cut sections of the tree over by the side of the driveway—Mrs. Daywood had said her son was planning to come down from South Carolina and pick it up—when movement flashed in the corner of his eye. Colin straightened up and found himself looking at the biggest, blackest pit bull he'd ever seen in his life.

The dog barely seemed real. Like a dog-shaped hole in reality, it was so utterly black, broken only by what looked like pale yellow eyes. It stood just inside the tree line, at the edge of the swath of destruction, staring at him from thirty yards away. Colin wiped his face with his shirt sleeve, the rich petroleum stink of the chainsaw filling his nose, and stared at the dog long enough to see it move. Until then he hadn't been convinced it wasn't some kind of cardboard cutout.

When Andy, who had taken over from Reg, throttled down the saw, Colin said, "Hey, guys, take a break for a minute, okay? I'm going to go see if I can catch that dog."

As if it knew he was talking about it, the dog turned and loped along the edge of the tornado's path, away from Mrs. Daywood's house. Reg said, "Dude, are you out of your mind? That's a pit bull!"

Colin raised an eyebrow. "So?"

"So there's, like, dog fighting and shit down here! Right? That dog'll rip your face off!"

One of the charities Colin's mother put a lot of time and effort into was a dog rescue. He'd spent countless days playing with the dogs while she took care of whatever business she had, and his favorites had always been the pitties. He'd never known a breed to be more reliably sweet and good-natured. Colin made a dismissive sound. "Look, when some natural disaster like this happens, it screws the pets. Dogs get disoriented, cats get loose and run off. The point is, it's not their fault. So I'm going to go see if I can figure out who that guy belongs to. See if he's microchipped. Okay? If I can't catch him, I'll come right back. Just—don't cut off any arms or legs or heads while I'm gone. Deal?"

Andy set the saw down and parked himself on the hickory's trunk. They were close to finished, anyway. A couple more good cuts and the driveway would be clear. Reg said, "Don't get killed by hillbillies! If you hear banjo music, run!"

Mirthlessly Colin said, "Ha ha," and took off after the dog, picking his way among the fallen trees and splintered stumps and clumps of twisted undergrowth.

It took him several minutes to reach the spot where the dog had first been standing, and he thought he'd lost the animal. But then it came out from behind a line of bushes not far away, panted at him, and took off again at an easy jog along the tornado's path. Colin had gotten close enough to get a good look at the dog's clear yellow eyes. He was *gorgeous.* His ears had been docked, but he still had his whole tail. Colin also saw, as the dog moved away from him, that he was still very much intact, which made Colin wonder if he'd escaped from a breeder.

The pit bull made his way up a gentle hill and disappeared over the top. It took Colin three, maybe four more minutes to crest the hill, and when he did, he stopped dead, staring. The dog was nowhere to be seen, but his mouth fell open at the sight below him.

Down at the base of the hill, which sloped just as gently on this side as the other one, there had until very recently been a house. Now there was a foundation, situated in the center of the tornado's path, and an enormous field full of debris. Bits of lumber, sections of roof, lengths of random cloth, pieces of demolished furniture, chunks of what might have been drywall… all of it lay spread out, scattered, lifeless amid the felled trees.

Colin could see no sign of the dog. He had vanished as if he'd never been there at all. But—Colin squinted—there was some kind of void in the house's foundation. A basement? He whispered, "Oh shit." What if the dog had fallen down into the basement? He'd be trapped. Colin hurried toward the ruined house.

As he drew close to the edge of the foundation, he passed a tree that, like the one blocking Mrs. Daywood's driveway, had been pulled up by the roots. The violence had left a hollow where the root ball had been, and something familiar and metallic winked at him from the churned-up earth. Colin knelt, reached in between the muddy branches, and his hand touched a smooth, hard object. He pulled it free.

It was exactly what he'd thought it was: a cell phone. Not a great one—Colin recognized the brand, a Chinese endeavor of dubious quality—but aside from a few flecks and specks of mud it seemed to be in good shape, and when he flipped it open, the screen was perfectly intact. *What the hell.* He held the PWR button down, and to his mild surprise, the phone turned on. After a few seconds, the tiny display screen showed him a photo: a man and woman, posed professionally, both of them in late middle-age. She wore a cream-colored pantsuit, but the man was dressed in a sheriff's uniform, the same style that Sheriff Seagraves had worn.

A soft bark made Colin stand up quickly.

The jet-black pit bull stood at the far edge of the foundation, staring at him.

Colin walked over to the edge of what had once been a house, staring right back, and did his best to project warmth and good will and calm at the animal. The dog was bigger than he'd realized, truly a beast, but like almost every pittie Colin had ever encountered, he displayed no menace. He just stared… and then dropped that crystal yellow gaze into the basement below.

Colin followed suit.

It took him a few seconds to process what he was seeing.

When he did, he began hyperventilating. The trees on either side of the tornado's path seemed to draw closer and closer.

The black dog hadn't moved. It stood there, beyond the surreal tableau that had just filled Colin's eyes and brain, and stared at him. From the trees, the drone of cicadas came out of nowhere, like millions of tiny rasping screams.

"This can't be real. *This can't be real.*"

Colin dug in his pocket. He dragged out his own phone, dropped it, picked it back up and almost dropped it again, and forced his trembling fingers to retrieve the business card Perry Seagraves had given him. He had to back up and start over three times to get the number right. "Sheriff? I, this is, this is Colin Massey, I met you today in the restaurant, we talked, you and me and your brother?"

The sheriff's voice came through cool and placid. "What's wrong, Colin?"

"Sheriff, I—I think I need your help."

<hr>

Seven miles away, Shep Curtis's phone pinged at him. He sat in his recliner, in his living room, eating a pimiento cheese sandwich and watching a golf tournament, and he casually reached out and picked up the phone where it lay on the end table. When he saw the words on the screen, the bite of sandwich he'd just taken turned dry and sour in his mouth, and he spit it out into the trash on his way through the kitchen.

Shep left the house and took the steps up to his over-garage office two at a time, and swore at his computer for taking so long to boot up. His mouse clicked frantically, his fingers typed in a password in a blur, and when a map of the county popped up on his screen—a map with a single pulsing red dot on it—Shep sat back in his chair, one hand over his mouth, breathing hard.

"Shit." He ground his teeth. "Shit shit *shit.*"

His left lower eyelid twitching, Shep swiped his phone open and made a call.

14

When Zandra arrived at Mrs. Daywood's place, she found the two teenage boys, Reg and Andy, sitting on a couple of piles of freshly cut wood in the middle of the now-cleared driveway, sipping iced tea amid the remains of a once-great hickory tree. She stopped and rolled down her window.

"You boys doing okay?"

One of them grinned and nodded to her. "Yes, ma'am."

"Looks like you're done here. Why aren't you inside, cooling off?"

The boys exchanged glances. The one who hadn't spoken said, "Colin's pretty freaked out. We just thought it'd be easier to wait out here."

"He's in the house?"

"With Mrs. Daywood, yeah."

"He say what he was freaked out about?"

They both shook their heads.

Zandra thanked them, rolled her window back up, and headed up the driveway to the house. She knocked on the carport door, and Mrs. Daywood stepped outside and closed it behind her. "Sheriff, can you take this nervous white boy off my hands, please?"

Zandra could just make out Colin through the curtain over the window in the door. He sat at the little breakfast table in Mrs. Daywood's kitchen, his elbows on the table top and his face in his hands. "I couldn't make heads or tails out of what he was saying on the phone. What happened here?"

Mrs. Daywood shrugged. "Ain't no tellin'. He won't say a word."

Zandra opened the door. Mrs. Daywood went back inside, past Colin and into the den, where she settled into a well-worn, over-stuffed easy chair. She picked up the remote, and Zandra heard *Judge Judy* start playing on a TV around the corner. Zandra leaned against the doorframe and folded her arms across her chest.

"Mr. Massey? What's going on?"

Colin lifted his face and fixed wide eyes on her. He stood and came over to her, getting closer than Zandra was comfortable with. "I think we need to get out of here. Me, the boys. Shit, the whole group."

Zandra's forehead creased. "Okay. We can probably do that, I guess. Your charter bus is parked over at the Methodist church now. That's where y'all are sleeping, right? But how about you tell me *why* you're in such a hurry to leave?"

He pointed to the northwest. "Just, just go, just have a look out there, you'll understand."

Zandra shook her head. "No, I'm going to need you to show me whatever it is that's got you so shaken up."

He turned even paler. He did seem to have the good sense to pitch his voice low, so his words wouldn't carry over *Judge Judy* to Mrs. Daywood's ears. "I'd really rather not. I mean, whoever did it could be in the woods, right? Watching?"

Zandra took hold of Colin's wrists. That put her even closer, and she tilted her head back to look him in the eyes. "Colin. Calm down. I'm here, and I'm not going to let anything happen to you, but I need you to show me what you're talking about. You said, 'Whoever did it.' Whoever did *what*?"

It took a few more minutes, but Zandra finally persuaded him. When they stepped back outside, Reg and Andy had wandered up the driveway, empty glasses in their hands. Zandra said, "All right, now, who's who here?"

One of the boys pointed at his own chest with a thumb. "Reg." A forefinger jabbed at the other one. "Andy."

Andy said, "Pleasure to meet you, Sheriff."

Zandra pushed the carport door open for them. "Why don't the two of you wait in the kitchen here? We'll just be a minute."

The boys obligingly did as she asked. Zandra nodded in the direction Colin had indicated. "Lead the way."

His eyes drifted down to the gun on her belt before darting out to the woods. "Okay. Okay. But just be alert. Yeah?"

She prodded him between the shoulder blades, and he started walking. Zandra followed him along the fallen-tree-strewn, stump-riddled, churned-up path of the tornado. "How far away is this whatever-it-is?"

He pointed ahead. "It's literally right over that hill."

"Hang on a minute." Zandra stopped and turned in place, getting her bearings. "The old Wilkins place is right over that hill."

"Oh yeah? Did it have a basement? …And were the Wilkinses serial killers?"

Zandra moved past Colin, but as he lagged, she said, "Come on, keep up." He got his feet moving, and they walked side by side up and over the gentle rise, where the massive, depressing debris field that had once been the Wilkins place spread out over what Zandra thought must have been a third of a mile at least. "So what is it you wanted me to see?"

"Down there. The, uh… where the foundation is."

"Show me."

"I'd rather stay here."

"Colin—"

"It's self-explanatory, all right?"

Zandra sighed. "All right, but you don't move, got it? I don't want to have to hunt you down."

"Fine."

She took a step toward the ruins of the house—and froze. Standing on the far side of the rubble, watching her, was an enormous, solid-black pit bull. Zandra didn't take her eyes off the dog, but spoke over her shoulder to Colin. "He belong to you?"

"No. No. He's the reason I found this, though. I saw him. Followed him here."

She frowned. The Wilkins place, as far as she knew, had been abandoned since before she left Red Springs to join the Army. For as long as she could remember, really. She had no clue as to who owned it now. It had just been an old, ramshackle two-story house, sitting in the middle of the woods and getting progressively more grown-over. The kind of place with raccoons in the attic and mold in the walls, not even fit for a homeless person's squat. Definitely not the kind of place that a dog as handsome as the one watching her would call home.

Zandra called out, "Hey. You friendly?"

As soon as the dog understood that she was speaking directly to him, which appeared to be instantaneously, his mouth fell open and a big pink tongue lolled out. He turned and loped around the edge of the foundation, picked up speed, and barreled straight for her. From behind her, Colin called out, "Don't shoot him! Don't shoot him!" But Zandra's hand hadn't gone anywhere near her sidearm. She could spot a big, friendly dog when she saw one, and when the pit bull reached her, he reared back on his hind legs and put his paws on Zandra's shoulders and licked her square in the face.

Quickly Zandra moved the dog's paws, setting him back on all fours, but she crouched down to pet him, scratching his head as she wiped the dog slobber off of her nose and lips and chin with her sleeve. "Hey there. Hey there! Who're you? No tag, huh? So you're a mystery." The dog squirmed with excitement, his entire hind half wiggling back and forth.

Zandra thumped him on the ribs and scratched his sides and petted his head. The dog whimpered and leaned into her.

"Okay. Okay. Now, you be a good boy and go keep that scared boy company while I check this place out. Will you do that? Huh?" She pointed at Colin. "Will you go stay with him for a few minutes?"

The dog whimpered again, but slowly shuffled up the hillside until he reached Colin. Once there, the dog turned and sat and watched her. Colin sat down on the damp earth beside the dog and stroked his back, but while the dog didn't openly object, neither did his attention waver from Zandra. Colin muttered, "Well I guess we know which of us he prefers."

Zandra said, "Stay. That's a good boy."

She got to her feet and walked to the edge of the ruined foundation. When she looked down into it, her breath locked tight in her throat and she forgot about the dog and Colin and everything else.

It was a torture dungeon.

She could think of no other way to describe it.

The top two floors of the house were completely gone, destroyed and spread out across the nearby land. Now the basement lay exposed, punctuated by a row of five broad brick support columns erupting from the floor. Six inches of water stood in the floor, muddy and filthy and littered with bits of debris and pine needles and broken bark, and the north end of the basement had collapsed in something like a mudslide.

But the scene remained clear. The wrought-iron shackles dangling from the red brick walls jumped out at her, as did the X-shaped black metal rack bolted into the bricks between them. As did the table with the clamps: broad bands of metal meant to fit around ankles and wrists and across the forehead. The surface of the table bore long channels that ran down to a hole between the places where the feet were meant to go, and below the hole, a rusty bucket still sat, upright, filled with red-tinged water.

The full strength of the tornado had passed over this place, pummeling it with unimaginable force, drilling into it with punishing rain, but it hadn't been enough to wash away all of the blood. Blood caked on the shackles, streaked down the rack, built up on the restraint table. Blood that had dried. Gone thick and brown. As Zandra took a step closer, a whiff of death reached her nostrils, and the thought of someone standing there in the midst of the savagery, steeped in the decay and putrefaction, *inhabiting* the place, made her gorge rise.

A couple of metal lockers stood against the far wall. They had both come open in the storm, and Zandra caught glimpses of metallic objects in the water in front of one of them. She threw a look over her shoulder to make sure Colin and the pit bull hadn't moved. They hadn't. Colin shouted, "Well?"

Zandra held up a finger. *Wait.* She rolled her pants up to her knees, made her way around to the north side, and carefully maneuvered down the mudslide, lamenting the ruination of her shoes and socks.

The basement floor felt like flagstones under her feet, but she was only guessing. Down at this level, the stench wafted around her, curling everywhere like foul ocean currents, and Zandra did her best to breathe through her mouth. The restraint table and the rack and the shackles didn't get any less authentic or revolting the closer she got to them. She skirted the table, her feet creating nauseating eddies in the standing water, and went to the two lockers.

She tapped the edge of the first one's door with her elbow and it swung wide, revealing shelves and hooks and specialized racks on which rested dozens and dozens of surgical instruments. No—she looked closer. No, not just surgical instruments. Instruments of torture. For every scalpel and box of curved needles, there were hammers and ice picks and pairs of pliers. Many of the shelves and racks were empty, and with her toe she gently nudged one of the metallic objects lying below the surface of the brown water. A scalpel popped up, its deadly-sharp blade winking at her as the foul water ran off of it. She let it sink back out of sight.

Zandra elbowed open the other locker.

Inside were only two shelves, both of them still fairly dry. The top one was empty, but she could see where something rectangular had sat on it for a long time, something now missing. On the bottom one sat a wooden box, roughly eighteen inches wide by six tall and twelve deep. It looked cheap. The kind of thing found in K-Mart's clearance section. By Zandra's rough guess, a similar box was what had caused the discoloration on the top shelf, and she glanced around the basement for it.

She spotted the second box in the far corner, on its side, half-full of filthy water. She'd get to that in a minute.

Zandra shook her sleeve down over her hand, reached into the locker and flipped the lid of the wooden box open.

Staring up at her from inside the box, among other objects, was a teenage girl's driver's license. Zandra leaned in closer, and saw that the license belonged to Shaquana Taylor, eighteen years of age. Piled on and around the license were a number of other small items. A class ring. A pendant. A silver dollar. Zandra let the lid of the box fall back into place, wondering if Shaquana Taylor's blood was on the table, on the rack, smeared on the iron shackles. Wondering how many other victims' blood mingled with hers there.

The taste of dust filled Zandra's mouth. She squeezed her eyes shut, but instantly wished she hadn't, because frenzied screams filled her head. The basement fled, replaced in her mind by dirt-laden wind and screams that turned from pain to horror under moonlight.

Zandra stood there for a minute, maybe two, maybe five, doing her best to control her breathing and her heartbeat. She turned and stared at the table, at the rack. At the scalpel, just visible beneath the water's surface. She waded over and looked at the other wooden box, which she figured the tornado had pulled out of the locker and banged against the wall. It was empty. Careful prodding around it didn't turn up any objects beneath the water, either. Whatever had been inside the box, if anything had, was somewhere else now.

Given the strength of the tornado's winds, "somewhere else" might turn out to be Cleveland, Tennessee.

Her hand went to the radio clipped to her shirt pocket again and again, but each time it dropped back to her side. Finally, slowly, she pulled out her phone and started taking photos. Dozens of them, maybe a hundred, of the whole scene from every angle she could manage. Then she sloshed back out of the basement and walked up the hill to where Colin and the dog waited.

Colin said, "You see why I was freaked out? This is some *Hills Have Eyes* bullshit. Whoever's responsible for that... that..." He swallowed hard. "They could be around here! Watching. Watching us. Watching *me*. Right now! So now that you know, can we all please get the fuck gone already?"

Zandra knelt and petted the dog. He let his floppy pink tongue loll out again, but didn't try to lick her face as she scratched him behind the ears. "No. We're going to wait right here until one of my deputies shows up."

Colin threw his head back, his shoulders slumping. "Oh for *fuck's sake*, Sheriff, are you fucking serious?"

She stood. The dog came around to stand by her side, and sat again. "And after the deputy gets here, I'm going to need you to keep quiet about this. Do not tell anyone what you saw. No one."

"Shit, that's easy. Besides, who in Milford's going to care about what happens down here?"

"You're not going back to Milford. At least, not yet."

Colin's eyes flashed with anger, but he seemed to think better of vocalizing it. "Why not?"

"Because you're a material witness, and I don't want you to leave yet, that's why." She pulled out her phone. Pounder was off-duty, for the first time in a week, so she didn't bother with Dispatch. She tapped his name and listened to the phone ring, and frowned when his deep, slow twang filled her ear.

"This here's Horace Pounder. If it's important, I'll get right back to ya."

Zandra left him a concise message and hung up.

Colin said, "So now what happens?"

"Now we wait."

He blinked at her. "*Here?*"

"You can walk back to Mrs. Daywood's house if you want to."

In the same tone, he said, "*Alone?*"

She shrugged. "Then we wait here until my deputy shows up."

Colin groaned. He went over to a tree stump that wasn't too splintery and half-sat, half-leaned against it, his shoulders hunched. Zandra went back to petting the dog.

Colin said, "So it looks like you have a dog now."

"No. I don't have pets. We'll figure out who he belongs to, or we'll find him a good home. You want to take him back to Connecticut?"

"My sister's severely allergic."

"So? You live with your sister?"

"I do, yeah."

Zandra studied him. "Do you both still live with your parents?"

"Hey, I don't need any judgement, okay? I just—they have the room, and I've got my own wing, and it's really comfortable, so I never—"

"Wait. Back up. Did you say you have your own *wing?*"

He nodded. "My, uh… my grandfather… you know how you can buy water bottles, and some of them are supposed to be sports bottles, and they've got that flippy top on them? Yeah, he invented that. And patented it."

Zandra thought about choosing her next words carefully, and then decided not to bother. "So what's a trust fund baby doing in Red Springs, Georgia?"

Colin folded his arms. It looked like a defensive maneuver. "Trying to leave. Let's talk about something else."

"We don't have to talk at all if you don't want to."

He started to say something, but cut himself off. "Oh shit. *Shit.* I totally forgot I had this!"

"Had what?" Zandra asked, as he shoved a hand into his pocket.

"This." Colin brought out a flip-phone and handed it to her. "I found it over there." He pointed to the hollow beneath a tree's root cluster. "Covered in mud. It still works, though."

Zandra took the phone from him and opened it up—and almost dropped it.

The home screen showed her a photo of former Cartauga County Sheriff Cyrus Bigelow and his wife, Kella.

15

Horace Pounder climbed out of May-Ella Gurnsey's bed and listened to the floor creak under his weight. He kept expecting the whole trailer to tilt with his movement, but it hadn't yet. As he made his way to the bathroom, he corrected himself: this was a *manufactured home*, as May-Ella was quick to point out. He had to take a leak something fierce, but he paused in the doorway of the bathroom and let his eyes drift over May-Ella's body where she lay in the tangle of sheets. Afternoon sun drifted in through the half-closed blinds and slid over her sweat-shined body. She wasn't asleep, he didn't think, but she lay there with her eyes closed, a little satisfied smile on her face, and Horace knew his reputation would stay intact.

May-Ella was forty-one, but looked about thirty-five, and stayed real trim thanks to her floor job up at the Amazon center in Chattanooga. He thought she might be starting to get some varicose veins, but that didn't bother him. He loved her dark blond hair and the little lines on either side of her mouth, like little parentheses, like her lips were about to say something secret, something just for him. Her big tits didn't hurt anything, either, though Pounder considered himself more of an ass man. May-Ella's ass was *tight*. She didn't just give it up for any random good ol' boy with a fancy pickup truck, either.

But then, Horace Pounder wasn't just any random good ol' boy.

He'd bedded half the available women in the county, by his own rough estimate, and always kept his eye out for the next satisfied customer. They kept coming back, too. Once these sweet little things got a taste of Major Pounder—he *loved* being able to call himself that—he got plenty of what he thought of as "repeat business."

Pounder knew he wasn't anything special to look at. His cock wasn't even *that* big. He knew it was plenty big as far as his honeys were concerned, but it was more or less in proportion with the rest of him, which was giant-sized to begin with, so he didn't figure he could brag on it all that much.

The secret lay in a bit of wisdom his daddy had taught him, back when little Horace was about to enter junior high, back when he hadn't gotten quite so fat yet but had a face chock-full of pimples. His daddy had set him down one day and said, "Son, I'm gonna tell you what's the truth. I figured this out for myself, but it took me a long time to do it, an' I aim to save you the pain an' heartache I suffered as a boy if I can. Son, the sexiest thing in the whole wide world is confidence."

Thornton Pounder had gone on to explain that it didn't matter what you looked like, or sounded like, or even smelled like, long as you didn't smell plum awful. If you had confidence, if you knew, down in your heart, that you were rock-solid, it wasn't just that people would like you. People would start to *follow* you.

"But I don't feel confident, Daddy. How do I do it?"

"You fake it, son. You tell yourself how great you are, an' you don't stop, an' you *act* like it. It don't matter if you don't believe it right to begin with. You fake it, and you don't waver with it, an' pretty soon you'll *start* to believe it. After that, you got it made."

It hadn't hurt anything that Horace hadn't stopped growing until he topped out at six-eight—in tenth grade—or that even without lifting weights he could pick the back end of a car up off the ground a couple inches. Then he'd started lifting. Really and truly, his strength was a bit like his capacity for eating shrimp. He hadn't figured out what his honest limit was yet.

So now, even though all his hair had fallen out by the time he was twenty-two, and even though he had a gut the size of a fifty-five gallon drum, that confidence had sunk in, just like his daddy said, sunk in all the way down to the bone. Combine that with being able to carry on a halfway decent conversation, and having developed a genuine fondness for eating pussy, and Horace Pounder hadn't slept alone except by choice in the last ten years.

He turned away from May-Ella and closed the bathroom door behind him. Horace took aim and unleashed half a gallon of urine into the toilet, cleaned up the splatters—that was important, too, women took note of that shit—and washed his hands in the sink.

He was about to dry them on the little pink hand towel May-Ella had hung there when something caught his eye. A single tube of lipstick sat on the counter, uncapped, and it was the deepest ruby-red he'd ever seen. Deeper than May-Ella had ever worn, in fact, at least around him. He picked it up and squinted at the tiny print on the label: it was called *Too Too Red*.

Pounder eased the door open a crack. May-Ella still lay there, exactly where he'd left her, and might have actually gone to sleep now. Pounder closed the door again. He turned to the medicine cabinet mirror above the sink and raised the lipstick...

And drew a symbol with it on his left pectoral muscle. He made the lines thick and wide and bold. First the diamond, just like a diamond on a playing card, but he didn't fill it in, just drew the outline. Then the tilted cross, with the top part poking out of the outline near his left shoulder, and the long center line going all the way through the diamond, pointing at his heart.

Pounder set the lipstick down. He stared at the symbol. A smile danced around his mouth, tugging at the corners. His eyes glistened. He stood up ramrod-straight, all the way to his full height, sucked in his gut as much as he was able and thrust out his chest. His eyes never left the symbol. He loved it. Loved the way the light from the fixture over the sink made it shine and glisten. Loved the way it looked on his skin.

Pounder whispered, "Soon."

"Horace? Baby? You're in the bathroom, right?"

Pounder snapped out of the haze he'd been swimming in. He raked the back of his hand across his eyes, grabbed up a huge wad of toilet paper and a bottle marked "makeup remover," and said, "Yeah, I'm in here. What's up?"

May-Ella's voice got closer to the door. His heartbeat sped up painfully. She said, "Your phone just started makin' a bunch o' buzzin' and rattlin'. Here, you want it?"

The doorknob turned, and Pounder grabbed it and held it tight against the frame. "Whoa, whoa, whoa, now, honey, I'm in here! I mean, I'm *in* here. Let's, uh, let's respect us some boundaries, okay?"

May-Ella giggled. "You want your phone or not? Open the door just a crack an' I'll hand it to you. I promise I won't sneak a peek or nothin'. Kinda cute, you gettin' all modest after what we just done."

Pounder had doused the toilet paper with the makeup remover and was scrubbing his chest as May-Ella spoke. He said, "Uh... well... who is it? On the phone, who's callin'?"

He imagined her squinting at the screen. She was a fine-looking woman, but her eyesight was for shit. "It's your boss, honey. Miss Thang herself."

Pounder had gotten rid of most of the lipstick. He said, "Okay, just a crack," and when the door opened, he took the phone from her and quickly closed it again. Sure enough, there was a little red "1" stuck to the phone icon. Pounder listened to the voicemail Zandra had left while he finished removing the symbol from his chest, and let loose a stream of profanity when the message ended.

From right outside, May-Ella said, "What's wrong, sweetie?"

Pounder made sure no traces remained of the lipstick on his chest, flushed the toilet, and opened the door. "Round two's gonna have to wait, darlin'. It's s'posed to be my day off, but I gotta go to work."

Twenty minutes later, dressed in boots and jeans and a Sheriff's Department polo shirt, Horace Pounder pulled into Mrs. Daywood's driveway. He parked next to the house and, as Zandra had asked him to do, called her. She gave him walking directions. Pounder pulled one of his oversized gym bags out of the back seat of his massive Dodge Ram, along with a couple of big-ass tarps, and set off along the tornado's path.

It didn't take long to find Zandra and a skinny white pretty-boy—Pounder recognized him from the yankee church group that got off the charter bus—sitting next to a beautiful black pit bull, in front of a house that had had the ever-loving shit kicked out of it by the storm. Pounder stopped when he crested the hill, eyeing the wreckage. "God-damn," he said. "That just looks like asshole-bifidus."

The pretty-boy said, "Looks like *what?*"

Zandra made a sort of negative gesture with one hand.

Pounder strode down the hill, approaching the pit bull with respect, but it just wiggled its butt and stayed at Zandra's feet. He said, "I brought all the shit you asked for. Want to tell me what this is all about now?"

"Yeah, Sheriff, fill him in," the pretty-boy said, and Pounder decided he didn't like pretty-boys very much.

"Horace Pounder, this is Colin Massey. You saw him come in with that church group."

Pounder nodded. "Yeah. You and your sister, ain't it?"

"Colin Massey, this is Major Horace Pounder."

Colin Massey sounded sort of bleak when he said, "Pleased to meet you, Major."

"Come with me." Zandra beckoned Pounder toward the wrecked house.

Pounder followed her, and when he got to the ruined foundation's edge and looked down, he had to fight a little harder than he wanted to admit to keep his bowels from turning loose. "This what it looks like?"

Zandra said, "Near as I can tell, yeah."

"Did you—was there—" He stumbled. "So who's doin' it? You find any bodies?"

"No. Not victims, not perpetrators, nothing. Were they here when the tornado hit? Who knows? If they were, they could be in fucking Apison for all we know, wedged in the top of some tree somewhere. In any case, I'm about to put in a call to the GBI."

Pounder let out a long, low whistle. Calling in the Georgia Bureau of Investigation told him how seriously the sheriff was taking this. "I know the storm fucked it all up, but… this looks like it's been goin' on for a good while, don't it?"

She nodded. "Let me have an evidence bag. A big one."

Pounder pulled an evidence bag out of the gym bag and watched as she went and waded into the sludge again. She took a brown wooden box out one of the lockers and bagged it before climbing back up out of the basement. "Okay, let's tarp the whole thing until we get Vocker out here."

Pounder started pulling one of the tarps out of its plastic wrapping. Sergeant David Vocker was the Cartauga County Sheriff's Department's single fully trained crime scene investigator, and Pounder knew he'd shit his pants when he heard about this. "How quiet you wanna keep this, boss?"

Zandra sighed. "If I had any choice about it, the only people who'd know are the ones standing here right now. But I don't see how that's realistic." She looked up at him. "I'm going to get the lieutenants together and bring them up to speed, and we're going to pull the courthouse guys and a couple of the SROs from the middle school to watch this place. I want eyes on it twenty-four hours a day until we know more of what's going on. But this is *not public knowledge*. I'm dead fucking serious about that."

"You got it." Pounder tilted his head toward the pretty-boy. "He gonna keep his yap shut too?"

"I think so. He'd damn well better. Okay, let's get this thing covered."

Working together, they spread the two tarps out over the basement. The truncated brick support columns helped. It wasn't what anyone would have called a careful or all that neat job, but Pounder figured it would keep any further weather from doing any more damage to the scene. Unless another tornado came through, which he couldn't rule out. Surveying the job they'd done, Zandra said, "God, I'm going to have to burn these shoes."

Pounder thought about that. "Aren't they sort of evidence now, too, though? Since you were down there walking around?"

She flashed him a grin. "I'll burn them once the case is closed."

Pounder lived for those grins.

He walked with Zandra and Pretty-Boy Colin and the big black pittie back toward Mrs. Daywood's house. About halfway there, he said, "What're you going to do with the dog?"

Zandra answered distractedly. "I don't know. Maybe Perry'll take him. I sure as hell won't have a dog."

Colin had barely said a word since Pounder had arrived, but now he spoke up. "Won't? Or can't?"

She speared him with a look. "I have chosen not to have pets. It's a decision I'm going to stand by."

Colin lifted defensive palms. "Okay, okay, just curious."

"Horace, once Mrs. Daywood's gone, use that winch on your truck and drag a couple of big trees across the driveway, down by the road. I don't want anybody just showing up here."

"You got it."

When they arrived at the house, Mrs. Daywood and Reg and Andy had come out onto the carport. Mrs. Daywood said, "Sheriff, what in tarnation is going on out there?"

Zandra threw pointed glances at Colin and Pounder before she spoke. "Turns out, the tornado picked up a chemical tank from God knows where and dumped it on the old Wilkins place. So we've got ourselves a dandy chemical spill on our hands."

Andy had knelt down to pet the pit bull, who'd obligingly walked over and let him, but now he stood back up. "What kind of chemical?"

"The dangerous kind," Zandra said without missing a beat. "So if you don't want cancer, and you don't want your hair to fall out, and you don't want your balls to shrivel up and drop off, I wouldn't go out there."

The two boys went pale. Mrs. Daywood said, "Land o' Goshen! Am I safe here? Should I go someplace else till you get it cleaned up?"

Zandra said, "Do you have somewhere you can go?"

The old lady nodded. "My cousin lives up in Knoxville. I reckon I could stay with her, till you tell me it's okay to come back. It will be okay to come back, won't it? Is it safe for Sharice? Does the whole town need to leave?"

"It's not going to spread, I don't think," Zandra said. "Especially as long as nobody goes out to the site. We'll let you know as soon as it's all clear."

Mrs. Daywood went inside to pack. Neither she nor the boys questioned what was in the gym bag Pounder had brought back from the "chemical spill," or why he no longer had the tarps.

16

Zandra left Pounder at the dungeon—a word she never thought she'd use in real life—and took Colin, Reg, Andy, and the pit bull back to the Methodist church where the volunteers would be sleeping. The congregation had set up the fellowship hall like a makeshift barracks, with three rows of cots, and a clipboard on the wall displaying a schedule for use of the shower across the parking lot in the pastorium.

Reg and Andy had been petting the dog, all three of them in the back seat, but when they got out, the dog showed no sign of wanting to follow them. Zandra watched as the boys made a beeline to their friends, several of whom were hanging out near the church's back entrance, but Colin hesitated, perched there in the shotgun seat. Zandra said, "Something else I can help you with?"

He turned to face her, and the waning afternoon sunlight caught the blue of his eyes and turned them a shade of violet Zandra had never seen before.

She chastised herself for noticing something so pointless.

"I can't say anything to anybody else, right? And you won't let me leave town."

The pit bull crowded forward and put his big muzzle on Colin's shoulder. Colin scratched the dog's chin absently.

"That's the long and short of it, yeah."

He gazed out at the parking lot. Now even the charter bus was gone. "I've got to have transportation. I've got to know I can at least move around. Does anybody rent cars here?"

"Sure. The Enterprise here got shut down from storm damage, but you can take your pick of some local dealerships that do it, or you can go up to the airport in Chattanooga, they've got three or four rental agencies there."

"Could I prevail upon you to give me a lift to the airport, then?"

"You can prevail upon Lyft. I've got shit to do."

Colin's head tilted just slightly to one side. "You're serious? Lyft operates in Red Springs?"

"We're not fucking savages, Mr. Massey. Now if you'll please get out of my truck." He did, and she leveled a finger at him. "I'm serious. No scampering back to Milbanks or wherever it is you come from."

He said, "Milford," sounding miserable, and closed the door. As soon as he did, the dog scrambled up into the shotgun seat and panted at Zandra. He seemed to be smiling.

Zandra drove slowly around Red Springs for twenty minutes, not really paying attention to her surroundings, just giving herself time to think. Eventually she made her way back to the Farmhouse. She logged the wooden box and its contents into evidence, as well as the cell phone Colin Massey had found. Wearing a pair of latex gloves, trying to disturb the contents as little as possible, she took dozens of detailed photos of the items inside the box. Then she called a meeting of the department's three lieutenants.

One of them, a tall gray-haired man named Williams, was already on-site, and just had to walk over from the jail. The other two, Dunn and Belcher, were out in the field, doing the same thing they'd been doing all week: helping put the county back together. They both grumbled and bitched, but they agreed to come in, and twenty minutes later all three men stood there in her office.

She'd also called in David Vocker, her CSI.

Vocker had turned forty less than a month ago. He stood almost as tall as Pounder, but weighed about a third as much, and his uniform hung on him the way it would on a clothes hanger. He had the garden-variety brown hair and brown eyes of most white folks in the area, and from what she understood, loved to fish above all else in the world, which explained the tan and the premature wrinkles on his face.

Vocker's face lit up when he walked in and saw the big pit bull. "Whoa, you got a dog?" His accent was just as thick as Pounder's. The word came out *dawg*. Vocker dropped to one knee, and the pit bull got up and padded affably over to him, and Vocker stroked his back and scratched his head above his ears. The dog appeared to know a sucker when he saw one, and quickly turned around, offering the spot just above his tail and looking over his shoulder as if to say, *There, there's the spot, now scratch it.*

Vocker did. The dog closed his eyes and whined a little.

Williams, Dunn, and Belcher all watched Vocker pet the dog with varying degrees of apathy and disdain.

Zandra cleared her throat. Vocker jumped up to his feet and said, "Sorry, ma'am," and the dog wandered back over and stretched out on the carpet again.

Belcher cleared his throat. "What'd you wanna talk to us about, Sheriff?"

The word "sheriff" coming out of Belcher's mouth sounded sour. Zandra ignored that. Using short, clipped words, she described what Colin Massey had found, and what she and Pounder had done about it so far. When she'd finished, Dunn folded his arms and pursed his lips. "So you're sayin' there's some kind o' crazed torture-murderer out there?"

Zandra drummed her fingers on her desktop. "I don't know. Maybe. I know what it *looks* like. It looks like we found some kind of..." She wanted to use the word *lair*, but she also wanted these men to take her seriously, which none of them did on her best day. If she started throwing around the kind of language found in comic books, she could kiss any chance of their cooperation goodbye. "...some kind of place used by a serial killer. But we have no suspect, and more important than that, we have no bodies."

"Yeah, speakin' o' that," Belcher said, "we ain't got enough bodies of our own. Sheriff, the town's still torn to shit. We're startin' to get the power back on now, an' they got all the cell towers back up, but there's still lootin' goin' on, an' people missin' shit, an' all kinds o' property damage. We ain't got enough people to do the jobs there already are. Now you want us to put deputies t'investigatin' somethin' that *might* be somethin'?"

"I want Lumpkin and Bills from the courthouse. And until school starts back up, I want the SROs. They're going to work shifts out there, keep an eye on the site."

Williams said, "You think if there *is* a killer, he's gonna come back to that spot?"

Zandra shook her head. "Maybe. I don't know. But that's not the point. It's more about keeping this from the public. Last thing I want right now is to start a panic, when we're already in the middle of another panic."

That rang true to the lieutenants. She could see it in their faces. But doubt cropped back up with Dunn. He said, "All right, but say this place is the real deal. You don't want the public to know if there's somebody dangerous runnin' around?"

She'd seen that coming. Damned if she did, damned if she didn't. "We can't have it both ways. Either we keep it quiet or we don't, and for now, we keep it quiet. Until we figure out what we're really looking at."

Belcher shrugged. "Okay. But who's gonna be doin' the figurin' out? You pullin' the detectives off their cases for this one?"

"No. You've all got your hands more than full, putting the county back together. I'm going to look into this myself."

The three lieutenants exchanged glances. Belcher said, "No offense, ma'am, but you sure you wanna take that on? On your own, I mean?"

"Why, Lieutenant? Do you not think I'm qualified? Or capable?"

Belcher's eyes narrowed a fraction of an inch. He took a moment before he spoke. "Not what I meant at all, ma'am. It's just a touch unusual, the sheriff handling a case like this directly."

Zandra stood. "We've never had a case like this. But look at it this way: if I screw it up, I'm likely out of a job." A silent moment turned into several more silent moments. None of the lieutenants said anything. She had no doubt that each of them had plenty he'd *like* to say, but no one stepped up. "Thank you, gentlemen, that'll be all. Sergeant Vocker, if you'd stay behind, please."

Vocker had stood apart from the lieutenants, almost over in a corner, nervously quiet the whole time. After the three other men left, Zandra gestured to a chair. "Have a seat." He did, still silent, and Zandra indicated the box and the phone. "I want to know everything there is to know about all of this. I want to know everything about the entire scene, but these items especially. And, Sergeant, concerning this cell phone—I want whatever you find out to stay between us."

Without hesitation: "Yes, ma'am."

Zandra stood and leaned forward, hands on the desktop. "*Just between us.* You are to mention your findings to no one else. No one. Show the report to no one. Talk about it to no one. It stays here. Do you understand?"

Vocker blinked. "Uh… yeah, I get it, but why—"

Zandra opened the phone and showed him the home screen. Much like Pounder, Vocker wasn't stupid, and she watched all the possibilities dawn on him as he stared at the photo of the former sheriff. "This was at the crime scene? At the, uh, the torture dungeon?"

"It's password-protected. I need you to get around that password. Once you've done that, nobody needs to know what you take off this phone but me, Sergeant. Nobody even needs to know you *have* it. Work off the clock if you have to." She paused. "Keep this between you and me, and I'll see about getting you an extra week's vacation. Say, beginning of June?"

Vocker swallowed hard. It seemed to take an effort for him to drag his eyes from the phone up to hers. "There's a fishing tournament the first week of June. Down at Weiss Lake."

She kept her voice neutral. "Is there? How about that."

"Sheriff… ma'am… I appreciate it. But, uh… you don't gotta bribe me. I'll do it. An' I'll be discreet."

Zandra sat back down, wondering if she'd underestimated him. "I appreciate that. How soon can you get me some results?"

He shrugged. "Most o' the cases the boys're bringin' in, they don't require all that much in the way o' CSI business. You catch a looter with a van full o' TVs, it's kind of open-and-shut."

"Which means?"

"Which means, far as the stuff in the box goes, I'll likely have somethin' for you in a day or two. For the phone—are you lookin' for prints, stuff like that, too? Or you just wanna know what's in it?"

"Prints. Trace evidence. Contents. Everything. How long do you think it'll take?"

"Well, far as external stuff, 'bout the same as the rest of it. I ain't got the right equipment to crack a password, though. Reckon I'll have to send the SIM card down to Rome."

Zandra sighed. The limitations of a small county's small operating budget. "Do you know the technician in Rome who'll work on it?"

Vocker nodded. "I can make sure my buddy Wes gets it. We go fishin' together 'bout twice a year."

"And you trust him to be as discreet as you are?"

"I can get him that way." Vocker grinned. It made him look about ten years younger. "*Him* I can bribe."

She didn't like that, but didn't figure there was much to be done about it. Vocker gathered up the items and put them in the gym bag, per Zandra's instructions. He waved goodbye to the dog before he left. Zandra stood and said, "All right, you, come on," and the dog jumped up, tongue lolling out. He followed her out to the parking lot, and when she opened the Tahoe's passenger door, he leapt up into it as nimbly as a giant black cat.

Ten minutes later she pulled into Perry and Sonja's driveway. Jamel rushed outside to greet her—he always did, whenever he spotted her truck turning in—but when he saw the dog, his eyes threatened to bug out of his head.

"Aunt Zandra! You got a dog! He's awesome!"

The dog appeared to be just as excited as Jamel. He scrambled over Zandra's lap and down to the ground as soon as she opened the door, and before she could even say anything, the pit bull had covered Jamel's face with licks as the boy all but screamed with laughter. The two of them immediately began running around the yard, playing a ragged sort of tag.

Perry came out of the garage, watching his son with the dog, a bemused expression on his face. "Since when do you want a pet?"

"I don't. He's for you." Watching her nephew, she went on, "Well, I guess he's for Jamel. In any case, I can't keep him."

Perry put his hands on his hips and did his best to look exasperated, but Zandra watched him watching his son with the pittie, and knew the battle had already been won. "What am I supposed to do with a dog that size? I'll have to get him his own couch!"

Sonja stepped out of the kitchen into the garage, and her jaw dropped when she saw the enormous black canine streaking across her yard, her seven-year-old barreling after him. "Zandra. You didn't."

Zandra tried and failed to repress a grin. "I sort of have to. Y'all, I'm in the middle of something right now, and I don't have time to deal with this animal. If you don't want to keep him, I'll find somewhere to put him, but just for a night or two, can he stay here?"

Perry exchanged glances with his wife. "Just for a night or two, she says." To Zandra: "You want to break your nephew's heart?"

Sonja's forehead creased sort of haplessly. "I guess we could train him? Turn him into a guard dog. Maybe. Where'd you get him? Doesn't he belong to somebody?"

Zandra had been watching Jamel frolic around the yard with the pittie, but the thought of where she'd found the animal brought the horror of the situation firmly back into her mind. She repressed a shudder. "He was a stray. Or at least he seemed to be. If y'all want to take him over to the vet, see if he's chipped, I'll pay for it."

Perry looked at Sonja again. "Probably ought to do that sooner than later. Before someone gets any more attached than he already is."

Zandra touched Perry's arm. "Thanks. I owe you for this."

"Damn straight you do," Perry said, grinning.

Zandra waited until Jamel and the dog were at the other end of the front yard before she climbed back into the Tahoe and took off.

When she glanced in her rearview mirror, she saw that the dog had stopped dead still in the driveway, and was standing there, staring after her.

Back at her office, Zandra pulled the file on the death of former sheriff Cyrus Bigelow. A cell phone registered to Bigelow had been recovered at the scene—an iPhone. Which meant the sheriff had had two cell phones. Considering who was riding with him at the time of his death—which had led to the biggest local scandal in anyone's memory—the second phone had almost certainly been used to arrange illicit activities. Zandra put in a call to the sheriff's widow, Kella, but the call went to voice mail. She left a brief message asking the widow to call her back.

Next, Zandra combed through tax records until she found the Wilkins place. That was how she'd always known it: simply "the Wilkins place," no more information than that. As it turned out, the house had been built in 1934, and in 1972 was sold to Abraham Wilkins, who then left it to his son, Jeffrey, in his will. Jeffrey and his wife Gwen were also dead, but ownership of the place had transferred to Jeffrey Wilkins's only child, Finn.

Finn Wilkins still lived in Cartauga County, but nowhere near the dungeon house. According to the information on Zandra's laptop screen, he had a small farm down at the southern end of the county, right next to the Whitfield County line. She grabbed up her keys and headed back out to the Tahoe. It was 4:45 in the afternoon, but the day had plenty of light left in it.

On her way through town, the stark difference in Red Springs before and after the tornado jumped out at her again. Zandra had always navigated by landmarks. She had never thought of houses or buildings as standing on the corner of such-and-such street, or west of such-and-such intersection. She had always pictured them in her mind as being at the bottom of that one curvy hill, or just past the bridge, or right before that bend with the cornfield on the right.

Now her cognitive map had been severely damaged. The curves

and hills were still the same, which was the only reason she didn't get hopelessly lost. Everything else about the town was almost unrecognizable—mainly because of the trees, and the lack thereof. On a basic, gut level she didn't really feel as if she knew Red Springs anymore.

Thinking about the dungeon underneath the ruined house, she wondered if she ever had.

Zandra took Dahlonega Highway two miles south and east before turning left onto Verity Road. That led her out into one of the parts of the county that was more cow pastures and hay fields than anything else. The tornado hadn't touched down out here, but the area had suffered some high winds, and a few trees had blown over. Zandra turned down a narrow, unlined road with a big yellow DEAD END sign at the entrance. A driveway more dirt than gravel led off of the dead-end road through a tangled thicket of wild blackberries, pokeweed, and overgrown Bermuda grass, and deposited her at Finn Wilkins's house.

"House" was being generous. The place had started its life as a single-wide trailer, and with the addition of a rickety porch, some steps, and what appeared to be a couple of decades' worth of neglect, had become a single-wide trailer in grave need of maintenance. The trees grew tall and thick right up to the back of it. A GMC pickup with no wheels rested on concrete blocks outside the front door, next to a metal barrel blackened from repeated trash burning, alongside a mildewed couch and a wooden deer-shaped target with a couple of arrows sticking out of it.

Zandra shut off the Tahoe's engine and opened the door. Immediately loud rap music washed over her from inside the trailer. Somewhere behind the house, the location distorted by the blaring music, a dog barked. Then another. She climbed the unsteady steps, crossed the porch—wincing as the boards creaked and sagged under her weight—and banged on the door.

The music shut off. She heard a couple of muffled voices through the door, male and female. The female voice approached. "Who's there?"

"Cartauga County Sheriff's Department, ma'am. Could you please open the door?"

The lock clicked, and when the door swung open, Zandra realized it was just a piece of spray-painted plywood hung in the frame. No wonder she could hear the occupants talking through it. A young, wretchedly skinny, bleach-blond white girl with wide, watery blue eyes and a Porky Pig tattoo on her left shoulder peered at her from inside. When she spoke, Zandra noticed the girl was missing about half of her teeth. She had *meth-head* written all over her, but that was an issue for another visit.

"Whatchu want?"

"I'm looking for Finn Wilkins. Is he here?"

The words had barely left Zandra's mouth when she heard a loud bang from the back side of the trailer, and the watery-eyed girl turned and looked over her shoulder, which allowed the plywood door to swing just wide enough for Zandra to see a tall, lean, shirtless white man in jeans and work boots hauling ass away from the trailer's back entrance. Zandra shoved the girl out of the way, crossed the width of the trailer in three sprinting strides, and hurled herself after the man.

The woods did crowd up to the back of the trailer, but a trail had been cleared from the back door straight out through the trees, and it was down this trail that the man—Zandra assumed it was Finn Wilkins—was doing his best impression of Usain Bolt. Zandra pounded after him. Her legs weren't as long as his, but she doubted he got up and ran ten miles every morning, either, not if he was living with Jenny Meth Whore back in the trailer. Steadily, Zandra gained on him, but as they ran, the barking of the dogs got louder, and she almost lost both her concentration and her footing when they burst out into a clearing and the barking launched into a frenzy.

The clearing was round, maybe twenty yards across, and rusty, badly kept, chain-link kennels took up about a third of that space, one cluster at the east edge and another at the west. That left the center open, and Zandra recognized it as a dog-fighting pit as soon as she laid eyes on it. Her teeth ground, her eyes flashed, and with a guttural roar in her throat she shot forward and tackled the lean man around the knees. He face-planted and skidded to a stop in the dirt, but before Zandra could clamber up and jam a knee in his back, he twisted around and thrust a booted foot into her face.

Or he tried to, anyway. Zandra saw the kick coming and torqued to the side, catching a glancing blow on her shoulder that was still painful enough to make her grunt. The man drew back his foot for another try, and Zandra surged up and punched him square in the balls as hard as she could. His face turned a sickly shade of green, and he tried really hard to curl up into a fetal position, but Zandra shoved him back over onto his face—she noticed then that his nose was bleeding freely, she guessed from the face-plant—and now she did lodge one knee in his back. He didn't put up much resistance as she cranked his arms around and handcuffed him.

Zandra stood, breathing hard, and took a second to absorb her surroundings. Only the cages on the east side of the clearing had dogs in them. The other kennels, while anchored to the ground admirably well, had put up no resistance when a tall, slender pine tree had fallen and smashed the back half of them, leaving them open to the elements and utterly devoid of dogs.

Without looking at him, Zandra said, "Finn Wilkins, I'm guessing?"

Finn Wilkins vomited onto the dirt. "Fuck you."

The dogs in the intact kennels all appeared to be pit bulls, though none of them were as big or healthy-looking as the one she'd dropped off at Perry's house. Zandra walked over to them, and saw that the kennels were home-made, little more than chain-link stretched between whatever kind of posts Wilkins had had at hand. A half-assed canine cell block. The dogs were going crazy, jumping up and down and howling in their cramped little cells.

Zandra heard the thump of booted feet on the ground and turned in time to see Finn Wilkins, his hands still cuffed behind his back, charging at her with his head lowered like a bull. She thought, *He's a determined one* as she pivoted in place, grabbed Wilkins's belt as he passed her, added her considerable strength to his speed, and flung him full-force into the nearest post of the kennel.

It didn't have the effect she'd expected. Not on the kennel, anyway.

It looked as if it hurt Wilkins a great deal, but the impact of his shoulder knocked the post askew—unlike some of the others there, it was *not* anchored to the ground very well at all—and before she could react, the chain link sagged and bowed…

And left a foot-high opening at the bottom of the kennels.

Zandra couldn't get any kind of accurate count of the number of dogs that wrestled free of their confines and dashed off into the woods. She thought maybe a dozen, maybe fourteen or fifteen. For a moment or two she feared they might attack her, but the dogs were interested in one thing and one thing only: escape. They vanished into the trees, barking and howling, gone in seconds.

Movement caught Zandra's eye. She turned to see Jenny Meth Whore standing on the far side of the clearing, recording video with her phone. Zandra called out, "Hey. Hey!"

The girl sneered at her. "What? You want me to quit videoin' you? No fuckin' way, bitch! This shit's goin' on Instagram!"

"I just want you to go back to the trailer and shut the door. Unless you're a hundred percent certain none of those dogs are going to come after you."

The girl appeared to think about that. It didn't take her long to turn and hurry back along the trail. Zandra went over to Finn Wilkins, who had gotten up to his knees. He turned and sank down against one of the still-upright kennel posts and grimaced at her. She squatted on her haunches in front of him.

"Okay. Now. Are you Finn Wilkins?"

"Just name it, okay?"

Zandra's eyes narrowed a fraction of an inch. "Name what?"

"Name your fuckin' price! How much? How much to forget about all this?"

"Forget about what, exactly?"

"Are you fuckin' dense or somethin'? The dogs! And the, and, I guess, what, resistin' arrest?" He spat a wad of vomit- and blood-streaked spittle off to one side. "Bigelow always had the good sense not to look a gift horse in the mouth."

"And you think I'm like Bigelow?"

"You wearin' his badge, ain'tcha?"

"Mr. Wilkins, I came out here to ask you about your house. The one out in Treece. The one your parents left you."

The gears in Finn Wilkins's head took a while to turn. Zandra watched them clicking over, tooth by tooth. He seemed genuinely puzzled. "Whatchu wannna know about that place for?"

"When was the last time you were there?"

He squirmed against the post. A huge, ugly bruise had already begun to form on his shoulder, and he had flecks of vomit on his chin. "Fuck, I don't know. Ten years? Fifteen? I never even went inside. Place was a fuckin' dump."

She got a tiny bit closer. "Come on, now, Mr. Wilkins. When was the last time you were down in the basement?"

Wilkins's brow beetled. Either he was genuine, or his theatrical talents were being sorely wasted, living in a shitty trailer and running dog fights. "What fuckin' basement? You sure you got the right house? Listen, I never lived there. My daddy thought it was just as big a fuckin' dump as I did." He paused. "Never even knew it *had* a fuckin' basement."

Forty-five minutes later, once Finn Wilkins had been charged in relation to the dog-fighting and deposited in a holding cell, Zandra sat at her desk, fingers steepled, staring at nothing.

She believed Wilkins when he said he'd never known anything about the basement. The question had cropped up in her mind as to why the Wilkins family had never sold the property, but it didn't bother her that much. Nobody in the South who *had* land was quick to give it up. Not if they didn't have to. And a house cut off from the grid and left to rot… well, that was just what some people *did*. It fell in line with the abundance of ancient, rotting barns that dotted the countryside, abandoned and slowly caving in on themselves. If the unwanted house just sat there, troubling no one, until it disintegrated, what was the harm?

Of course she'd run down Finn Wilkins's associates—the ones she could establish, anyway, since he was already proving tight-lipped about who'd helped him run the dog-fighting ring—but Wilkins already smelled like a dead end.

A soft knock at her door almost made her jump. A college-age black girl named Doreen stood there, and someone Zandra couldn't quite see around the corner of the doorway stood right behind her. "Sheriff? Ma'am? You've got a visitor."

Doreen was her secretary, technically. She came in each day and sat at the desk right outside, but Zandra had never asked her to do anything—not make any coffee, not schedule any appointments, nothing. When Doreen had protested that she was essentially getting paid to do nothing, Zandra had said, "You're in college, right? You need money, and you need to study. So sit there and study. I'll call you if I need anything."

Zandra didn't want to fire Doreen, not only because she knew Doreen needed the job, but also because, if she eliminated the position, the allocation for it would disappear from the department's annual budget, most likely permanently. Zandra didn't think she'd ever *need* a secretary, but as her father had often said, "Better to have something and not need it than need something and not have it."

Zandra straightened up in her chair. "That's fine, thank you," she said, and when a middle-aged black woman moved around Doreen and stepped into the office, Zandra got to her feet. "Come in. How can I help you?"

"I'm Maxine," the woman said, in a tentative, just-barely-not-quavering voice, and Zandra took note of how red and puffy her eyes were. "Maxine Currant. It's about my daughter. Angelique."

Zandra waved toward one of the chairs in front of her desk. "Have a seat. Please. What about Angelique?"

Maxine Currant pulled out a cheap Walmart smartphone and showed Zandra a photo. It looked like an official class portrait, and showed a beautiful young black woman with the lean features and long limbs of an athlete. "She ain't come home. Left day before yesterday, and I ain't heard from her since. Sheriff, somethin's happened to her. Somethin' terrible. I feel it in my heart, Sheriff."

Gazing at the image on the phone screen, Zandra felt her guts tighten and cool. Angelique Currant bore a superficial resemblance to Shaquana Taylor. "Can you email me that photo?" She handed Maxine one of her cards and waited until the email showed up on her laptop.

"She a good girl, Sheriff," Maxine said, and the tears that had ravaged her eyes returned. Zandra fished a couple of Kleenexes from a desk drawer and handed them to her. "She been livin' with her father in Augusta. I just got her back this summer. She gonna live here now, do her senior year at Red Springs. Help out at the house. I got my mama with us now, and it's hard takin' care o' her with just one pair o' hands, but Angelique a *good girl*, Sheriff, she ain't mind helpin' out none. She glad to do it. She said, 'Mama, it ain't fair, you bein' here by yourself.' She just got a job at the Piggly Wiggly, right before the storm hit. Sheriff, why she get a job and then run away? It don't make sense. It don't make sense."

As carefully and compassionately as she could, Zandra asked Maxine Currant the questions she needed to. Had she contacted Angelique's father? Who were Angelique's friends? Did she have a boyfriend? After she'd finished, Zandra said, "All right, Mrs. Currant, we'll get a BOLO out with Angelique's photo and information. We'll do everything we can to find her."

Maxine Currant sniffled. "You promise?"

"I promise we'll do everything in our power."

"All right." She stood. "Angelique a *good girl*, Sheriff. Whatever she goin' through... she don't deserve it."

Zandra hugged her, and asked Doreen to walk her out.

17

Colin Massey squirmed in the driver's seat of the Hyundai Elantra he'd rented at the Lovell Field airport in Chattanooga. The rental agent had suggested something nice, something like an Escalade, and Colin had readily agreed, but then thought better of it. He already felt as if he stuck out like the proverbial sore thumb in Red Springs, and didn't want to draw any more attention to himself than he had to. So he rented a much smaller, cheaper vehicle than he was accustomed to, and followed the Waze navigation on his phone, taking 153 to I-75, down to the 775 spur, and back over to Red Springs. Before he got to the spur, he decided to fill the tank, since they'd given it to him about a third full, and pulled off the interstate. The closest gas station was a RaceTrac.

As the tank filled, Colin casually gave the other customers a look-over. They reminded him of the patrons at Aunt Petunia's restaurant, for the most part. All white. Many of them grossly overweight. He counted the Trump/Pence stickers—out of thirteen cars filling up, nine had them on either their back bumpers or, in the case of the many pickups, the back windows. Two of the trucks had truck nuts dangling from their trailer hitches: big, veiny, rubber scrotums housing oversized rubber testicles. Both sets were colored to mimic

Caucasian skin tones. Colin had never seen truck nuts in real life before. His own balls tucked themselves tighter up against his abdomen.

Partly because he was thirsty, partly because a morbid fascination drove him to explore the local fauna in further detail, Colin paid for his gas at the pump and pulled the Hyundai up into one of the station's parking spaces. He went inside, found the cold drinks cooler, and pulled out a big bottle of water. A line had formed at the register, six or seven people deep. It extended back past the case of hot dogs turning placidly on their heated rollers, and continued between the aisles offering candy on one side and magazines on the other. *Men's Health* and *Guns & Ammo* took the most prominent spots. Two registers sat behind the counter, but there was only one clerk, an overweight white boy who looked about fifteen.

Colin got in line right behind a lithe young woman in flip-flops, cutoff denim shorts, and a snug tank top that bore a large Confederate flag on the front. She turned, her dark blond hair piled up in one of the messy, top-of-the-head buns he'd seen on many other women in the area, and gave him a bold head-to-foot once-over.

"You must be passin' through," she said, in a voice he would have liked if it hadn't been soaked in north Georgia twang.

"What gave me away?"

Her eyebrows rose. "Just a feelin'. 'Course, you done proved me right when you opened your mouth. I said to myself when I saw you, I said, *He looks like a yankee.* An' I was right."

Colin wasn't sure how to respond. "You get a lot of us? Yankees?"

"Yeah. Y'all stop off here comin' an' goin' from Florida, mostly. Don't worry, hon. We don't bite too hard."

A second cashier, a wrinkled white woman who seemed to have gone out of her way to make her dyed-black hair look as jarring as possible, appeared behind the counter and fired up the second register. "Y'all can form another line here," she called, and the people who'd gotten in line behind Colin—he hadn't even noticed anyone come in —obligingly split off and went to the second register.

There were three people in the second line: an overweight white man with an enormous beard and a pair of camouflage-patterned overalls, a black man in his mid-twenties, and a young white girl with close-cropped red hair and, near as Colin could tell, seventeen facial piercings. The redhead had a "Don't Tread On Me" back tattoo partially obscured by her halter top.

"Hey there, Deshawn," the blond woman in front of Colin called out, and the black man in the other line glanced over.

He said, "Yolanda," and gave her a small, polite nod.

Yolanda gave Colin a brief, playful wink, and called out to Deshawn again. "Hey—Deshawn—you gonna take the Mexicans with you?"

Deshawn had faced forward again, since the big man in the camo overalls was stuffing his change in his wallet, but he looked back at Yolanda with a puzzled frown. "Say what now?"

"I said, you gonna take the Mexicans with you?"

"How you mean?"

"You know! Take 'em back to Africa! When Trump sends you back to your own country!"

Colin felt bile rise in his throat. He didn't think Deshawn knew how to react any more than he himself did, and Colin could only watch as Deshawn faced forward again and silently made his way up to the cashier. Yolanda gave Colin another playful wink and a smirk over her shoulder.

Colin set the bottle of water on the nearest shelf and left the store. He almost ran back to the rental car, and got out of the parking lot and back on the freeway as fast as he could without running down any pedestrians.

In the same way that a certain kind of car seems to appear everywhere once you've taken an interest in it, now Colin noticed Trump signage at what felt like every turn. More Trump lawn signs. Every car seemed to sport a Trump sticker now. Just before the 775 split—and he had to stare at this to make sure he wasn't hallucinating—a massive black billboard reared up beside the freeway that proclaimed in huge white letters, "TRUMP. GOD BLESS OUR COUNTRY. MAKE AMERICA GREAT AGAIN." It shared advertising space with another billboard directly below it, clearly placed by the same company, that read, "JESUS IS LORD. AND YOU KNOW IT."

By the time he pulled into the parking lot of the Methodist church, the sun had almost set. He saw Charity standing just inside the door to the place he'd heard someone refer to as the "fellowship hall," talking with an early-middle-aged white couple. Colin parked and intended to saunter over to them, but the after-effects of the most blatant display of racism he'd ever seen in person must have been lingering on his face. Charity looked alarmed when she saw him, and the middle-aged man came out to meet him, one arm extended as if to keep him from falling down.

Charity said, "Colin, what's wrong?" at the same time the man said, "Son, you look like you've seen a ghost."

Colin politely waved away the proffered support arm. "Where's all the kids?"

The unfamiliar woman spoke. "They're over at Mount Zachariah. The preacher's showing them what'll need to be done first thing Monday morning."

Colin started to say, "Monday? But it's Saturday night," but realized church-going folks wouldn't want to engage in heavy labor on Sunday. Then he tried to say, "So what're we all going to do tomorrow?" but the words got jumbled up in his mouth and he had to take a second to collect himself.

Charity said, "Colin—uh, this is my brother, he's helping us chaperone—Colin, this is Brother Paul and his wife Ruth. Brother Paul is the minister here."

Colin made some noises that he hoped sounded like a polite greeting. Brother Paul said, "Why don't we get into some air conditioning? You look like you're about to get heat stroke, you don't mind me saying."

Colin nodded and let himself be led inside. Charity said, "Seriously. Dude. Are you okay?"

Colin despised feeling out of control. *Despised* it. That was one reason he'd never bothered trying to find a job. His life, the way he'd set it up, was one hundred percent on his own terms. No boss. No deadlines. Nothing that he didn't set up and follow through as he saw fit. But since he'd arrived in Red Springs, he'd felt more like an alien from outer space than a human. At the moment, he was sure he'd have more in common with some extraterrestrial species than he did with Yolanda, or with the waitress at Aunt Petunia's. And because of that, he wanted—desperately wanted—to get the hell out of there. Take the rental car back to the airport, buy a plane ticket, and get his ass back to Milford where it belonged.

But he couldn't.

And he couldn't tell anyone *why* he couldn't.

That thought opened up a can of worms in his brain as well. There was a killer in Red Springs. A *torturer*. Why didn't he have police protection? Why weren't the police all over everything? How could he know he and Charity and the teenagers, and for that matter Brother Paul and Ruth, would be *safe?*

"Just stay in groups," Sheriff Seagraves had told him. "Stay in public. That's the kind of advice you'd give to a bunch of out-of-town teenagers anyway, isn't it? Besides, for all we know, whoever's responsible for this got carried off and chewed to bits by the tornado."

Brother Paul led Colin through a couple of doors to a small sitting area outside what Colin guessed was his office. Green-tinted shades filtered the evening sunlight, and the small couch he sank down onto was *super*-comfortable, and Colin suddenly very much wanted a nap. Charity and Brother Paul and Ruth took seats as well, and Brother Paul said, "Want to tell us what's troubling you?"

Haltingly, Colin described what Yolanda had said to Deshawn at the RaceTrac. "I guess I was still hoping what I'd seen so far were isolated incidents. But I'm realizing that's not the case."

Ruth sighed, her expression troubled. "There's a wave of ugliness moving through the country. And I fear our president isn't helping it any."

Colin let his hands flop into his lap. "I don't know. I don't know, maybe I've been—" He looked at Charity. "Have we... have I been *that* sheltered?"

Brother Paul said, "Colin, if this exposure to racism is the first you've ever seen up close and personal, I'd say you've been brought up properly. In a good environment. The Lord loves all of us. Every last human. We are all His children, and a lot more of us would do well to remember that."

Colin let his head fall back against the top of the couch and stared at the ceiling. "I just don't understand. I mean, obviously that orange moron is there in the White House, so lots of people must like him."

"Three million fewer than liked his opponent," Charity said softly.

Colin went on. "But how? *Why?* What do people in, in, in Red Springs, Georgia, think they have in common with a billionaire from New York?"

"He speaks their language," Ruth said without hesitation. "Yes, he's a billionaire, but he talks the way they do. Or, more accurately, the way they'd *like* to. The way they wish they could. He seems fearless to them. And that goes a long way for someone raised in poverty."

Colin shook his head. "I can't believe I'm having this conversation. I can't believe I *want* to have this conversation. Until I got here, the news—current events—I kept them at a distance. They were something I clicked away from. I mean, yeah, I talked about stuff with my online friends, college buddies, sh—" He started to say *shit like that,* but caught himself. "People I know. And we'd laugh at all these miserable rednecks, soaking in their own squalor, actively swatting away the hand that was trying to help them up. No, no. No government assistance for us. Can't accept something that might actually do us some good." Colin sat up straight and traded eye contact back and forth between Brother Paul, Ruth, and Charity. "But now I'm face to face with it, and I—" He rubbed the bridge of his nose. "I feel like someone just proved leprechauns were real."

"I'll give you an example," Brother Paul said, leaning forward. "Shed some light on the subject. You know how popular camping is. Among some demographic segments, anyway. It gives people a sense of independence. Self-reliance. It says, *I can go out into nature with nothing more than what I can carry on my back, and bend nature to my will. I don't need electricity or running water or indoor plumbing. I don't need beds and chairs and air conditioning. I'm too tough to need any of those things.* Does that make sense?"

Colin nodded. "Yeah. I mean, I've never been camping, but I get what you're saying."

"So then, have you heard of 'glamping'?"

Charity said, "Oh, yeah—glamorous camping. Big fancy insulated tents with electricity and indoor plumbing and all that. Right?"

Brother Paul bobbed his head. "Exactly. It's like taking a hotel room and plunking it down in the middle of the woods. And do you know what the traditional kind of campers say when they see people who prefer glamping?"

Colin let out a long exhale. "I can't imagine it'd be anything good."

Brother Paul said, "Exactly. They say, wow. What a bunch of losers. All those men and women and boys and girls humping a four-person tent and some charcoal and a hatchet out into the wilderness? They're thinking, *This is all we need. Because we're strong. We don't need fancy electrified tents. And anybody who does is pathetic. Worse than pathetic.*"

Colin groaned. "So… you're saying… people don't want govern-ment assistance because it hurts their sense of independence to take it?"

"In part. Yeah. It also connects to a sense of inferiority that I'm afraid has plagued the South since the Civil War. We didn't have as much money or power or education as the yankees did, and for the most part we still don't. We got the stuffing beaten out of us in the war itself. And, often—very often—people from up north come down here and take every chance they can to criticize and condescend to Southerners."

Ruth offered Colin a sad smile. "My father always used to tell me that yankees thought every Southerner spent their days barefoot, lounging on the riverbank with a piece of straw between their teeth."

Brother Paul said, "I've seen people online commenting on the deep-seated streak of anti-intellectualism in this country, and at least some of it goes back to that sense of inferiority, coupled with pride. You get some kid born in a mobile home, with no chance of being able to pay for college, and he's not a bad student but he's not good enough to get scholarships. And the best he's ever able to do employment-wise, thanks to where he lives and what education he could get, is drive a truck. But he works himself half to death driving that truck, because he's got a family and by God he's going to provide for them. And he *does*. He provides. He puts food on the table and keeps the power on and puts presents under the tree at Christmas. Maybe once a year they take a trip to the beach. It's a good life."

Colin let his eyelids slide shut. "And that truck driver sees someone like Bernie Sanders or Hillary Clinton, and they seem like aliens to him. But the foul-mouthed bully is someone he can maybe relate to a little bit."

Ruth said, "Exactly. To that truck driver, Trump is what happens when a regular guy makes good. Self-made billionaire. To that truck driver, Trump is what they would love to be. To a *lot* of people that's what he is."

Colin made a sort of vague strangling motion in the air with both hands. "But Trump isn't self-made! He got all his money from his father! His old man bailed him out over and over again! He lost money running a *casino!*"

Now it was Brother Paul's turn to sport a sad smile. He waved a dismissive hand. "Fake news. Trump is self-made. Because he said so."

Colin sighed. "Well, I'll say this much. It's… really refreshing. Meeting you guys. Knowing someone down here who knew better than to vote for him."

Frowns flitted across Brother Paul's and Ruth's faces as they exchanged glances. Brother Paul said, "But we *did* vote for him. We had to."

Ruth nodded. "Much as we didn't like Trump, Hillary was pro-abortion. We couldn't support that."

Silence descended.

Colin avoided looking at Charity. He knew where she stood on abortion, and it was a lot more in line with Brother Paul and Ruth than it was with his own values. He felt himself crumpling. Physically and mentally and emotionally. Still not looking at her, he said to

Charity, "I'm suddenly exhausted. Are there cots made up yet? Do I have a cot?"

Charity stood and beckoned to him. "C'mon, I'll show you."

Brother Paul and Ruth stood, too, and Colin hoisted himself up off the couch. Mechanically he shook Brother Paul's hand, and then Ruth's. "Thank you. This was an enlightening conversation."

"That's at least partly why we're here," Brother Paul said with a warm smile.

Ruth grinned too. "It was a welcome change of pace."

Colin followed Charity out of the sitting area, feeling as if he were plummeting into a bottomless pit.

18

Bright and early Monday morning, Zandra called Kella Bigelow's number again, and this time the woman picked up. Zandra kept it short, just asking if she could pay her a visit. Minutes later she was behind the Tahoe's wheel.

Approaching the former sheriff's house emphasized the primary reason why so many of Red Spring's citizens had had a problem with him. The home Mrs. Bigelow had shared with her husband was well beyond the means of most of Cartauga County's residents, and compared with Zandra's modest rental, it looked like Buckingham Palace. It sat out at the end of Ware Valley Road—already one of the few truly affluent parts of the county, one touched not in the slightest by the tornado—and put every other house along the way to shame. Zandra knew she was almost there when a low, decorative brick wall sprang up by the side of the road. The wall, which looked expensive but wouldn't have kept out a determined Basset hound, led to a pair of mighty granite pillars topped by roaring stone lions. An enormous black metal gate stood behind the lions, and Zandra watched a security camera follow her as she pulled up. The gates opened for her. She didn't even have to use the touchpad mounted on a steel pole next to the driveway to announce her identity.

Past the wall and the lions and the gate, every bit of which Zandra found unbearably ostentatious and tacky, the wide, freshly paved blacktop driveway led through a vast, perfectly manicured lawn up to the three-story beige brick house with the slate roof. That was the only part of the Bigelow place that Zandra envied. Her father had often spoken, in her childhood, about how amazing slate roofs were. "If you can keep them from breaking—keep limbs and such from falling on them—they'll last you a lifetime." A slate roof symbolized wealth to Zandra. The kind of wealth that people in her family, in her life, didn't have and never would have. It was something unattainable, ephemeral. Something that would turn to fog if she tried to take it for herself.

She pushed the button next to the Bigelows' twelve-foot-tall front door and heard a deep, resonant chiming from somewhere inside the house. It surprised her when Kella Bigelow herself answered the door. Zandra had never been to this house before, but expected Kella to have at least one servant.

"Sheriff Seagraves," Kella said, with a small, perfunctory smile. "Please come in."

"Thanks." Zandra walked past her into a foyer that looked like someone's ill-informed idea of an Italian villa. Her shoes squeaked on marble floors, fluted columns supported white marble statues and huge, carefully maintained potted plants, and an actual honest-to-God fountain sat in the middle of it all, a statue of a little girl in the center, surrounded by fish spewing water from their mouths.

That's not how fish work, Zandra thought absently.

Kella Bigelow was sixty-five, according to the department's files, but appeared to have had some quality work done on her face, so that, while she couldn't seem to move her forehead, she looked roughly Zandra's age. She either had good genes or a competent personal trainer, too, as the yellow silk sundress she wore showed off arms with the kind of long, well-defined muscles a lot of women get from Pilates classes. Her hair was silver. Not white, not gray, actual silver. It shimmered and flashed in the sunbeam coming down through one of the foyer's skylights.

"Can I get you anything, Sheriff?" Kella asked. "Coffee? Have you had breakfast?"

Zandra followed Kella into the biggest kitchen she'd ever seen in a private home. She counted four ovens, two massive sinks against the wall, and two marble-topped islands that had smaller sinks built into them. Zandra realized this was what people meant when they said "professional kitchen." The kind of place where caterers could come and set up shop while Kella hosted an event. Kella motioned to a round table—also marble-topped—off in one corner with four expensive-looking leather-and-mahogany chairs set around it.

"I wouldn't turn down a cup of coffee," Zandra said, settling into one of the pricey chairs. She watched as Kella went to an espresso machine.

Normally Zandra drank instant coffee. She'd never paid much attention to how espresso machines worked, so she couldn't really follow all of the steps Kella Bigelow went through, but a couple of minutes later Kella came back with two steaming cups. She set one down in front of Zandra, but instead of taking another chair right away, Kella stood over her for a solid ten seconds, sipping her own coffee. Looming. Asserting dominance. *You are in my house.*

"So what brings you here this morning?" Kella asked, finally settling into the chair opposite Zandra's. "Surely anything you might have to tell me could have been said over the phone."

"It could have, but it's a potentially delicate matter, and… I never properly paid my respects, either. So this is a two birds, one stone deal."

Zandra watched the tiny tremors of motion in the muscles of Kella's face. The immobilized forehead made her hard to read, but her eyes tightened. "I understand why you ran against my husband, Sheriff. Those who opposed him made no secret of why they wanted him gone."

Kella had barely any trace of Red Springs twang in her voice. That came from money, too, Zandra supposed, though wealth clearly hadn't bought her any taste.

"Well, your husband's death is why I'm here. My office recently came into possession of a cell phone that belonged to him."

Kella Bigelow's fingers whitened, just for a second or two, around the handle of her coffee cup. Zandra got the impression that her breathing, which stayed even and measured, took an effort of will to remain so. Kella seemed to choose her words with care. "And… why are you telling me this?"

"Well, I'm sure you're aware, the sheriff's iPhone was found at the scene of the accident. So the phone in question appears to be a second one."

Kella took a sip of her coffee. "Yes? And?"

If Kella Bigelow knew how bad it looked to be discovered with a second, probably secret cell phone, she gave no indication of it.

"So we're not sure how it ended up where it was found. It could be evidence. Which means the investigation into your husband's death may need to be reopened. I wanted you to hear that from me, and not in the news."

Kella looked away. "You mean you wanted to tell me in person that all of the pain and suffering and humiliation might get dredged back up and paraded around out in public again."

"It won't come to that if I can help it. Mrs. Bigelow, I had issues with your husband, but I never had and do not have any animosity toward you. I only want—"

"Only want *what?*" Kella said, still looking away, abrupt bitterness flooding through her words. Her forehead never moved, but her lips thinned. "Only want to gloat? Only want to drag Cyrus's name through the mud some more? Get it so filthy nobody'll ever remember anything positive about him?" As she spoke, her Red Springs accent quickly seeped back in. "He was a damn good husband. He loved me, he doted on me, anything I wanted, he did his level best to get for me. No, he wasn't perfect." *Wasn't* came out *wuddent.* "But Jesus Christ, can you not show the dead some respect?"

"Mrs. Bigelow, I only want the truth. If anything on that phone makes us see the circumstances in a different way… well, wouldn't you want to know that?"

Kella Bigelow pushed her coffee cup away, sliding it slowly across the table with both hands, until her arms were straight. She took a few long, deep breaths, and just as slowly pulled the cup back. Took another sip.

"Call me Kella," she said, the accent gone again.

"All right. Kella."

The sheriff's widow sipped her coffee, still not looking at Zandra. "You don't know what's on the phone?"

"Not yet. Do you know what your husband's password was? Or did he maybe keep his passwords written down somewhere?"

Kella set her cup down on the table and looked Zandra in the eye. "You know what I didn't know until just now? I didn't know he *had* another cell phone. As you said, the one he usually carried was at the scene when he and that little... that little boy died."

Zandra would have bet money that Kella had almost just said *that little nigger boy,* but had caught herself.

"So no. I don't know what the password was. Good luck figuring it out." She stood. "If there's nothing else, Sheriff, I've got a pretty full schedule ahead of me today, so I'll walk you to the door."

When they stepped out onto the broad flagstone front porch, Zandra was about to say goodbye, but broke off at the sound of a decidedly un-muffled engine approaching out on the road. She figured it was still a good quarter of a mile away, and considered going after the driver for noise pollution, but couldn't bring herself to care all that much.

As the engine grew closer and louder, she said, "What my mama always used to say when she heard foolishness like that—*I hope I can be as cool as he is when I grow up.*"

Kella laughed politely.

Zandra went on, "Wonder if that's somebody headed to the Rod Run over in Chickamauga? I heard they were having one to raise money for the tornado victims."

Kella had turned to go back inside, and over her shoulder, another bit of twang slipping through, she said, "Nah, that's no classic. I'll see you later, Sheriff."

The big front door closed, and Zandra watched as a battered but definitely later-model Camaro finally came into sight and zoomed past the ridiculous stone lions.

She went to the Tahoe and climbed in, thinking about the last words Kella had said.

***

Zandra never saw the tall, lean, angular man watching her from one of the Bigelow house's upstairs windows. He ran a finger through his graying blond hair, his narrowed eyes tracking her every move, until the Tahoe drove away. At the last second, the sheriff cast a glance back at the house, and the tall man moved away from the window, letting the gauzy curtains drop back into place. Keeping him hidden.

19

Back at the Farmhouse, Zandra had just set her coffee down on her desk when David Vocker rapped lightly on her office door, a big evidence bag under one arm. She sat and waved him in.

"Close the door."

Vocker did, and took a seat. She said, "What do you have for me?"

He pulled the wooden box from the dungeon out of the bag. "You can look at this now. Just return it to lockup when you're done. Our guy? Whoever's responsible? *Super* careful. Must've been wearing gloves the whole time. I got two sets o' prints, other'n that Massey guy. One's on the driver's license, and surprise surprise, it belongs to the girl the license was issued to. The other one's on the cell phone. Again, obvious."

"Sheriff Bigelow?"

Vocker nodded. "Man's prints're on his own phone. Don't help us none."

"No prints on any of the other..." She stopped short of calling them *souvenirs*. "...items in the box?"

"Nope. He must've wiped 'em all off. I swear, Sheriff, I think he bathed 'em in alcohol, too. Only one he didn't bother with was the license. Guess he figured what's the point, since her name's on it?"

"I'll take a look. Now, what about the cell phone?"

"My buddy in Rome's got it. Said he'd get it done quick as he could."

Zandra drummed her fingers on the desktop. They were itching to open the wooden box and dig into its contents. "I appreciate your discretion on this."

Vocker sat a little taller. "Absolutely, ma'am." He stood and turned to go, but paused with his hand on the doorknob. "It, uh, it may not be my place to say, ma'am, but… it ain't all of us in the department that don't like you. It's just, y'know, you want all the other boys to have your back. And that's easier if everybody acts like we're all on the same page."

Zandra let that percolate for a few seconds. "Well. Just so you know. I've got *your* back, Vocker."

He grinned. It turned his face boyish. "Thank you, ma'am."

Once Vocker was gone, Zandra locked the office door, closed the blinds on the window that looked out into the parking lot, and opened the wooden box. It held—she counted, moving each one from the left side of the box to the right—fourteen items. The driver's license, a big class ring, what looked like a navel piercing, a silver dollar. A gold chain. Two different earrings. A belt buckle. Zandra sifted through them. For the most part innocuous—a cheap plastic fountain pen. What looked at first glance like a gold wedding band, but which revealed its base-metal nature where the electroplating had worn off. A charm off a charm bracelet, in the shape of a running shoe. A purple hair pick, a copper-colored metal bottle cap, and a Pez dispenser in the shape of the character Gollum from *The Lord of the Rings.*

Zandra picked up the driver's license and murmured, "Low-hanging fruit."

Shaquana LaToya Taylor stared sullenly at her from the tiny, low-quality photograph, all full lips and brown skin and attitude. Zandra figured the license had most likely been produced at the nearest

Department of Driver Services office, a tiny little affair down in Rock Spring. Idly she thought of how often people called the place "Rock Springs," with the unnecessary "s" on the end, and how that had irritated her father every time he heard someone say it. Shaquana Taylor, according to the license, was seventeen years old, a pretty girl who might have been even prettier if she hadn't looked ready for a fight all the time.

Zandra turned to her laptop and tapped the keys. Shaquana Taylor's last known employer was CVS Pharmacy, and her last known address was out in Treece, not two miles from Mrs. Daywood's house.

Zandra sat back in her chair. She had no bodies. This looked for all the world like the souvenirs kept by a serial killer, but with no bodies, how certain could she be?

She sat back up and fished out the class ring. It was big, masculine, stainless steel with a solid black stone, and featured the name of one of Chattanooga's better private schools emblazoned below the stone. Engraved on the inside were three initials—JGB—and a serial number. That plus the school, plus the ring's manufacturer, and two phone calls later she had a name: James Gregorius Biddles. The school's administrative office gave Zandra an address. They also let her know that James Biddles had dropped out last year.

On the off-chance that identifying the other items' owners would be as easy, Zandra examined each one under a magnifying glass, but had no further luck. Everything else seemed to be what it looked like at first glance: a random piece of junk. Zandra put the items back in the box, put the box back in the evidence bag, and as Vocker had requested, returned it to the evidence locker.

On the way to the Taylor residence, she called Clive Lumpkin. The old man answered on the first ring. "Morning, Sheriff."

"Clive. What's the word? Any movement out there?"

"No, ma'am. I've got myself tucked up in a deer blind that Davey Crocket himself couldn't spot, and I ain't seen a goddamn thing. Pardon my language."

Zandra felt some small measure of relief. "That's impressive. Good thinking. I appreciate you taking initiative like that."

Lumpkin chuckled. "Ma'am, I sat in that goddamn courthouse for three decades without shit happenin', pardon my language. I hate what brought me here—the storm, I mean, and whatever the hell this is we're keepin' an eye on for you—but it's a welcome change, t'be honest."

"Just keep your eyes peeled."

"Yes, ma'am."

It didn't feel right to Zandra for someone as old as Clive Lumpkin to call her "ma'am." But she *was* the sheriff, and her grip on the office was tenuous enough already. She said, "How much longer do you have on this shift?"

"I'm here till five, ma'am."

Zandra drove out past a public works truck, where men in bright yellow vests loaded segments of fallen trees into the bed. She didn't know where all the wood was meant to end up. As long as it got off the roadways, she didn't much care at that point, but it was easier to think about that than to consider how she'd feel if one or more of the men she'd assigned to watch the dungeon got hurt.

The Taylor house sat on a small parcel of land that took up a corner of an intersection, where one seldom-used road crossed another seldom-used road. Zandra thought the place qualified as a cottage. Small, quaint, and gray, covered with a worn shingle roof and asbestos siding. The house she'd grown up in had had asbestos siding, and she remembered coming home from school one day, full of alarm. "Mama! Mama, asbestos is poison! We got to get rid of all this siding, it's bad!"

Her mother, standing at the kitchen sink, peeling a potato, hadn't looked away from her task. "For one thing, it's 'we've.' 'We've got to get rid of all this siding.' And for another thing, no we don't. It's bound up in about ten layers of latex paint, and it's not hurting anything, so relax."

"We've," Zandra whispered as she parked in front of the Taylor house.

She knocked on the front door. Or rather, she knocked on the screen door mounted in front of the solid-wood front door. A few seconds later, a black woman in her fifties cracked the wooden door and eyed Zandra through the screen, her brow furrowing. "Sheriff Seagraves?"

"Are you Shaquana Taylor's mother?"

The woman threw the front door open and unlatched the screen. "Yeah. Name's Jillene. Why? Somethin' wrong? Is Shaquana okay?"

Zandra let that process for a second. *Is Shaquana okay?*

"Would you mind if I come inside?"

Jillene Taylor held the door open for Zandra, but concern made her voice increase in pitch. "Sheriff, if somethin's happened to Shaquana, you gotta tell me. Okay? You gotta tell me!"

Zandra walked into Jillene's living room. The place was spotless, but the furniture looked like something out of the Sears catalog circa 1974, with as many worn and threadbare spots as one would expect. Zandra said, "Please, have a seat. I'd like to talk about Shaquana."

Jillene perched on the edge of a wing-back chair. "What about her? Sheriff, you scarin' me!"

Zandra wasn't sure how best to proceed. She said, "When's the last time you heard from her?"

Immediately, Jillene said, "Last night."

Zandra blinked. "I'm sorry—what?"

"Last night. She sends me messages on Facebook. Sheriff, what's happened to my daughter?"

Zandra's mind whirled. She took a while to respond, and chose her words carefully. "Maybe... nothing. Her name has come up in an investigation. Do you... could you call her? Or give me her number? I would love to speak with her."

Jillene seemed to have calmed down a bit. Enough for concern to slide into bitterness. "I'd love to call her myself, Sheriff, but she ain't give me her number. Facebook's the only way we communicate now."

"Only way you communicate *now*? What do you mean? What happened?"

Jillene Taylor rolled her eyes. "Little Miss Hot Pants ran away from home six months ago. Walked out of school and hitched a damn ride to Fort Lauderdale. Now she's down there workin' at some resort, says she needs her *space*, can't have me callin' her all the time. She just checks in with me on Facebook to let me know she's still in one piece. Sends me pictures." She pronounced it *pitchers*.

Zandra heard a sort of roaring in her ears. Her head spun. She sat down on a couch with springs visible through the seat cushion. "Could you show me some of Shaquana's messages?"

"Sure thing." Jillene picked an iPhone off an end table and started swiping the screen. "How her name come up in an investigation? Somebody sayin' somethin' about her? Here." She held the phone out to Zandra, who took it gingerly.

"I'm afraid I'm not at liberty to discuss details," Zandra said quietly, staring at Shaquana Taylor. Or at least, a grainy image of her, the kind of low-resolution photo taken by cheap, off-brand phones. The girl had on too much makeup, which made her look a lot older than seventeen, but it was her, no question about it. She stood on a dock, with the ocean behind her, the setting sun over one shoulder. Shaquana was leaned forward, in the midst of blowing a mischievous kiss, her eyes closed. Below the image was her message:

DOIN GR8 MAMA HUG DADDYS NECK 4 ME

Zandra scrolled through Shaquana's other messages. They had come roughly once a week, never more than a line or two, always reassuring. Every third one had another grainy photo. Shaquana on a balcony overlooking a city. Shaquana with a starry night sky behind her. Always happy.

"So this is the only way you have of getting in touch with her?"

Jillene nodded. "Mostly it's her gettin' in touch with me. She don't always answer when I write to her. Off playin' grown-up." She sighed. "I won't lie, sometimes I'm jealous. I never had the heart to just take off like that. Much as I wanted to now an' then. But she doin' okay, far as any of us can tell."

Zandra stood and handed the phone back to Jillene. "All right, well, thank you for your time."

Jillene stood with her. "So she's not in trouble?"

"No, no, not at all. I just wanted to talk to her. Which resort does she work at?"

"She wouldn't say. Same as with the phone—didn't want me smotherin' her. Like knowin' where she at's such a big deal."

"Okay. Well, I'll reach out to my colleagues in Fort Lauderdale, then. And maybe I'll send her a friend request myself. Thank you for your time, Jillene."

Shaquana's mother walked Zandra to the door. "If you do get in touch with her, tell her we'd love to see her for Christmas, at least, okay?"

"I'll do that."

Zandra drove away from Jillene Taylor's house with the roaring still in her ears. It struck her as off, as *wrong*, the whole thing, and yet there was Shaquana Taylor, very much alive, very much sending her mother photos and messages employing the kind of clipped, online shorthand that made Zandra's teeth grind. She pulled into the parking lot of a Gas-N-Go and looked up James Gregorius Biddles on the Tahoe's department-issued tablet.

Zandra had to go beyond Cartauga County to find the Biddles family. They lived over in Fort Oglethorpe, a decent-sized town a few miles west of I-75, but she didn't hesitate to cross the county line. Sheriffs had jurisdiction everywhere in the state of Georgia, and she knew she wasn't going to step on anyone's toes. Especially if all she was doing was asking questions.

The Biddles house sat in a subdivision off Dietz Road, a new development nestled between a horse farm and some property that belonged to one of the local Baptist churches. Zandra thought of places like these as "house orchards." The houses were undeniably big and nice, but they'd all been built to roughly the same plan, and had no more than eight or ten feet between them. Zandra parked the Tahoe on the street and walked up the steep driveway, taking in the surroundings as she went.

The laughs and shrieks of playing children reached her from farther into the subdivision. A single-head sprinkler came on two houses away, watering the postage-stamp lawn. Bikes and scooters and Big Wheels lay here and there, cast into stasis by their young owners, dormant but ready to roll again at a moment's notice. It all looked so *normal*. Zandra felt the pores of her skin contract. That something like the torture dungeon had crouched there, hidden, breathing and bleeding, while life carried on around it…

How many more horrors dwelled just beneath the surface?

How much more horrific death and destruction would Zandra simply never know about?

She tried to shake off the icy net that seemed to have settled over her and rang the doorbell. Almost immediately, the door swung open, revealing a small black boy of seven or eight, dressed in what looked like either a dragon or a Godzilla costume. Someone had shaved the boy's hair into an impressive Mohawk. Before Zandra could even take a breath to speak, the boy screamed, "*Dad! The po-po's here!*"

The boy stayed rooted in place, staring up at Zandra with enormous deep-brown eyes, the doorknob in his hand, as a black man in his forties came up the hall. He stood a couple of inches taller than Zandra, had a bald head and a thick chin beard, and wore dress shoes, perfectly pressed slacks, and a white button shirt with the sleeves rolled up and a loosened tie around his neck. He didn't look alarmed, just a bit cautious. "Is there something we can help you with, offi—" She saw the recognition spark in his face. "Sheriff?"

Zandra said, "Is this the home of James Gregorius Biddles?"

The man shrugged. "It used to be. I'm his father. Clifford Biddles." He stuck out his hand, and Zandra shook it. "This is Jimmy's little brother, De'von. Say hello to the sheriff, De'von."

The boy gave Zandra one of the best gap-toothed grins she'd ever seen, and said, "Hello to the sheriff, De'von!"

Clifford pulled De'von gently away from the door. "Smart-ass. Go play some video games." De'von needed no further persuasion. He turned and bolted down the hall, growling fiercely, his arms up above his head and his fingers hooked into claws. Clifford sighed. "You know the truest thing my mother ever said to me? 'Boys are weird.'"

Zandra smiled politely. "May I come in, sir?"

Clifford Biddles made a sweeping *welcome* gesture and held the door for her. "Just in there to the left."

The living room she entered looked like what would have

happened to Jillene Taylor's place if she'd updated her furniture and coated everything with toys. Clifford said, "Just shove whatever's in the way out of the way and have a seat." Zandra did, sitting straight-backed in a very plush recliner, while Clifford dropped onto a sofa. "So what's this about? Is Jimmy in trouble?"

"His name came up in an investigation. I have no reason to believe he's done anything wrong," Zandra said, hating herself a little for omitting so much. "But I would like to talk to him. Do you know where I can find him?"

Clifford Biddles seemed utterly untroubled. "San Diego. His ungrateful, scrawny, ambitious little ass up and hauled out of here last fall. Now he's tending bar at one of those fancy hotels, right on the water."

The skin pucker Zandra had felt out in the driveway skittered across her neck and shoulders. "Are you still in touch with him?"

"He sends me updates. On Facebook."

Zandra kept watching Clifford's face. "Isn't Facebook a little outdated for young folks now? Aren't they all on Instagram or Snapchat or whatever?"

"Jimmy said that's why he's using Facebook. 'Cause he knows it's the only social media platform his mother and I are comfortable with."

"Is his mother around?"

"She's at work. De'von goes back to school next week, and I'm in sales—the kind that has me running up and down the road. I'm working half-days this week. Shaunda's coming back at lunch."

"Do you have Jimmy's phone number?"

Clifford frowned. "No. He wants to keep us at arm's length. Remember when I mentioned the ungrateful part? Wouldn't kill him to let his mother hear his voice now and then."

The skin pucker got slightly worse. "When's the last time you heard from Jimmy?"

Clifford reached over and picked up a laptop, which had been leaning against the couch. "Hang on and I'll tell you." He clicked and typed, clicked and scrolled, and turned the laptop around so Zandra could see it. "Wednesday of last week. He likes to rub our noses in his 'glamorous life.'"

On the screen was a grainy image: a handsome, rail-thin young black man stood alone on a gorgeous beach, a huge smile on his face and a pair of stylish sunglasses over his eyes as he sipped a Corona out of the bottle. The message below the photo read:

BET U WISH U WAS HERE

"May I?" When Zandra beckoned, Clifford handed her the laptop. Much like Shaquana's page, it had photo after photo of Jimmy Biddles and his thousand-watt smile, living it up on the beach, never without his shades. All the images were relatively low-quality, but Zandra didn't think their graininess looked quite the same as Shaquana's photos. Maybe taken with a different kind of cheap, off-brand phone?

"Thinks he's such a big-shot. He's not even nineteen yet. Drinking in public. Still, he seems happy and safe enough. And he's a legal adult, even if he's not old enough to drink."

Zandra nodded. "Not too much you can do about it, huh?"

"He's paying all his own bills, too, which is a damn sight more than I could say about myself when I was his age. So we worry about it, but we decided not to throw stones."

Zandra thanked Clifford Biddles for his time, and waved goodbye to De'von as he peeked around a doorframe at her, and walked back down the driveway to her SUV. She drove to the end of the road and parked in a wide cul-de-sac and stared into space.

What kind of scenario would explain this? Yes, it was weird as shit, but as Jimmy's father had pointed out, these kids seemed safe enough. At least Shaquana and Jimmy did. Was she going to find the same kind of story with all the other items?

But how would that make any kind of sense? Speaking to no one, she said, "Hi, I'm going to hang out with you in your dungeon for a while, and you can strap me to your rack and your table and I guess I'll bleed a lot while I'm at it, and you can take this thing that means a lot to me, yeah, just pop it in that box over there. But now I'll be on my way! Thanks for everything, goodbye!"

Was the dungeon's owner some kind of... facilitator? Helping kids get out of situations they didn't like? She whispered, "Sure, I'll help you. I just need to get my rocks off first... you don't mind a little sado-masochism among friends, do you..."

Zandra pulled up Facebook on her tablet and found both Shaquana Taylor's and Jimmy Biddles's pages. She saved four or five good profile photos—good enough for other sheriff's departments to recognize, maybe good enough for facial recognition software to register—and looked up phone numbers in both Fort Lauderdale and San Diego.

A stream ran by Perry and Sonja's house, about thirty yards from their back door, and when Zandra and Perry settled down into the wicker chairs on Perry's screened-in back porch, the night air sang with the crickets and katydids and frogs. Perry had put a cold Dos Equis in Zandra's hand as soon as she'd stepped into the kitchen. Zandra took a long swig and slid down in the chair, the bun gathered at the back of her head providing a compact, not terribly comfortable cushion as she tried to relax. Her eyes slid closed.

When she opened them, she saw Perry staring out into the darkness of his backyard. He said, "Am I wrong for wanting to pack Sonja and Jamel into the car and run off after the Hubbles?"

Sonja and Jamel were at the grocery store, but Zandra had laid out the whole situation for Perry, the two of them standing there in the kitchen. He'd listened, wide-eyed but never interrupting, and had only asked intelligent questions so far.

"No, you're not wrong. Part of me wants to evacuate the whole town. But if I do that, this fucking... *dungeon freak* knows I'm onto him, and I'll probably start a panic, and more people get hurt than if I'd kept my mouth shut. At the same time, if I *don't* let anyone know about it, and I can't catch this son of a bitch, then God only knows who he'll hurt until I do catch him."

"*If* you catch him."

"Thanks for that vote of confidence."

Perry grinned. The oil he used on his beard made it sparkle in the light pouring through from the kitchen window. "Not what I'm saying. You ever see that movie—what was it. Starred Jack Nicholson, and, uh… Princess Buttercup. Claire Underwood."

"Robin Wright?"

"Yes! Thank you! Yeah, Robin Wright, and damn if she didn't look rougher than I'd ever seen her. *The Pledge!* That was it. Shit. I swear, way my mind's going, Sonja's going to have to get me tested."

Zandra scoffed. Perry's mind was as sharp as it had ever been. "What about this movie?"

"Okay, so Nicholson plays a cop. And he makes a pledge to this family that he's going to catch the guy who killed their kid—I think it was their kid. Yeah, a little girl, I'm pretty sure. Anyway, in the course of shit, he meets Robin Wright, and she's a single mother, and she's got this little girl who's *just* the killer's type. And Robin Wright and Jack Nicholson, they start up with each other, like it's going to be a real thing, but he's still hung up on this pledge he made. And he ends up using Robin Wright's little girl as fucking *bait*. Trying to lure this killer out into the open. And, of course, Robin Wright finds out and kicks his worthless ass to the curb."

"Do people say 'kick to the curb' anymore?"

Perry shrugged. "I do. Not the point. The point is, Jack Nicholson's plan *worked*. The killer was on his way to try to take Robin Wright's little girl—but he died in a fucking car wreck before he could get there! And Jack Nicholson never knew that. Never found out the killer was dead. And it drove him sort of batshit. Like, crazy old man talking to himself all alone batshit."

"I appreciate the spoiler warning."

"Movie came out when Dubya was in the White House."

Zandra sat up. "So what you're saying is that whoever's responsible for that mess in the Wilkins's basement might've gotten swept up in the tornado along with the rest of the house. And we might find him spread out over the northern half of the county."

"Maybe some in Tennessee, yeah."

"I've thought about that. And if that's what happened, then great, Hallelujah. But as long as I don't know for sure, I've got to keep looking. And I've got to keep it as quiet as possible."

Perry drained half his beer in two long gulps. Zandra waited for what she knew was coming, and after he let out a thunderous belch, he said, "Yeah, I get it. But two of those doodads in the box belong to kids who're still taking breaths, right?"

Zandra frowned. The whole Facebook-only thing bothered the shit out of her, but she couldn't deny the kids in question were alive and well. "I'll feel better once I've talked to them. Got deputies in both cities looking for them."

"So what you're looking at is a place where people—you don't know for sure how many—bled all over some props that look like they're used for torture."

"The blood's real enough. I'll know more once the GBI crew gets in."

"And when's that supposed to be?"

Zandra grumbled. "They said it'd be a week. At least."

"So for now, what you know is there was some bleeding going on, and some stuff that looks like it wasn't used for any kind of wholesome purpose, and some things that seem like the sort of shit a serial killer would take off his victims. But you got no dead bodies, and two supposed victims alive and well."

Zandra's mouth wrinkled in distaste.

Perry went on. "So maybe it's not what it looks like at all. Maybe you're gonna find out somebody was shooting some kind of low-budget horror movie there. I've heard of those. 'Micro-budget.' Kind of thing you can film all in one room. Stick it in a RedBox, make your budget back in no time. Or, hey, maybe it's not about killing anybody. Maybe it's a sex thing."

Zandra tapped her fingertips against the beer bottle. Her nails were natural, and she didn't keep any real length on them, but they stayed healthy enough. *Tink-tink-tink-tink*, rapid, like drops of rain on a metal roof. *Tink-tink-tink-tink.* "I was on leave in Rammstein one time, and a bunch of us, I don't even remember how, but we wound up at this hotel where there was this BDSM convention going."

Perry's eyes got huge. "You never told me about that!"

"I never had *reason* to tell you about that. We were all drunk, it seemed like a good idea at the time, so we paid the admission fees and in we went. Let me tell you, I saw some things that night that I had never seen before, and have no burning desire to see again."

"My little sister!" Perry cackled with laughter. "Dommin' it up! Tell me more!"

"Well… there was this little old man, covered head to toe in metallic gold paint, wearing nothing but this sort of wire-filigree penis sheath." Perry's laughter got louder. "And somehow we got on an elevator, this thing was packed, we were jammed in there tight. It went up to the third floor—I think we were heading for the fifth—but it stopped at the third, and the doors opened, and there was this stocky white guy standing there in fur boots and a fur loincloth, and sticking out from the loincloth was this two-foot-long polished wooden dick. I mean, it looked like a table leg or something. But, like I said, there was no room on the elevator, so we all just stood there and stared at him, and he stood there and stared at us, until *ding*, the doors closed."

Perry howled with laughter. Zandra wasn't sure he was going to stay on his chair.

"Then, up on the fifth floor, there were these girls serving drinks, but the way you got a shot was one of *them* took the shot, held it in her mouth, and then kissed you and let the liquor fall into your mouth."

Perry slapped his knees a couple of times, but the laughing spasm had passed, and he straightened back up. "Well, that's just unsanitary."

"And some college-age girl wearing a cloak, an honest-to-God cloak, lifts the cloak up and she's topless underneath, and she says— my German was pretty terrible, but I think this is right—she says, 'Would anyone like to suck my nipples?'"

Perry snorted. "Did she get any takers?"

"Guys were on her like flies on roadkill."

"Why are you telling me this?"

"Because, eventually, we made our way down to this grand ball-room place. And they had these… I guess you'd call them *stations* set up. Like a trade show, except instead of booths, there'd be a table with a naked girl getting shocked with a cattle prod, and then a table where a girl dressed as a cheerleader sat on a naked guy's back and whipped him, and there was this big X-shaped rack. A guy had this nude, morbidly obese girl shackled to the rack, and… I don't know what he was doing to her. I think it was supposed to be about humiliation. Anyway, that X-shaped rack? The one in the Wilkins basement looks a lot like it."

"That's a long way to go to draw a comparison."

"I wanted to give you context."

Perry shook his head. "With those two kids not just alive, but doing well? I don't think this thing is what you're afraid it is."

Zandra took another swig of her beer. "I hope you're right."

Lights raked across the backyard, and Zandra heard the sound of the garage door opening. "They're all back," Perry said.

"All two of them?"

An expression Zandra couldn't quite read passed across Perry's face, but before she could ask him about it, the kitchen door flew open and she heard the frantic clicking of claws on the tile floor. Jamel and the huge black pit bull both came charging out onto the porch neck-and-neck and flung themselves on Zandra, and amid the giggling and the panting and the sudden wetness all over her hands and lap, Zandra could scarcely breathe.

It took her a second to realize that some of what she thought was slobber was more than likely the product of Jamel's extremely runny nose. Zandra put her hands on Jamel's shoulders and gently but firmly pushed him back to arm's length, then pointed at the dog and said, "Sit, you."

The dog sat. And put his head on Zandra's knee. And looked up at her with the biggest, clearest, saddest yellow eyes she'd ever seen. She fished a Kleenex out of a pocket and wiped her nephew's nose, taking into account how puffy his eyes looked. From the doorway to the porch, Sonja said, "Well?"

The unreadable look on Perry's face grew more intense. Zandra said, "Well, what?"

Sonja sat down in an empty wicker chair, eyeing her husband. "You didn't even ask her, did you?"

Perry averted his gaze. "It didn't come up."

Jamel, who hadn't stopped grinning the whole time, said, "I'm allergical!" He scratched the dog's head behind the ears. "Mom and Dad say I can only come and visit him at your house!"

The dog, who hadn't stopped staring at Zandra, whined softly. His tail thumped on the painted plank floor. Zandra sat back, and the dog took the opportunity to put one paw on her thigh, next to his face. She held her hands up. "No. No, no, no. No way."

The dog whined marginally louder.

Perry said, "Zan, Jamel can't take the dog being here. He loves him. He named him. But he can't keep him."

"And you expect *me* to? I'm not set up for a pet! I don't even know anything about how to take care of a dog! Is there a good vet around here? Who knows? I don't! Forget it!"

Sonja leaned forward and put her elbows on her knees. "Zandra, I hate to surprise you with this. But after you left him here, you know what that animal did? He went out to the driveway where your truck was parked, and he just laid down there and waited for you. For hours. It took everything we had to convince him to come inside."

Zandra shook her head. "I don't need a dog, y'all."

Perry said, "I don't guess you do, no. But it's looking like the dog needs *you*."

"We'll help!" Jamel piped up. "We went to the pet store, and got him a bowl and a leash and some dog toys, and a big floppy dog bed, and a great big bag of dog food! It was so big I almost couldn't carry it! It's all out in the trunk. And Mom and Dad said they'd help with the vet if he needed it." As he talked, a rivulet of snot ran down out of Jamel's nose, and he thoughtlessly wiped it away with the back of one hand. "His name is Jordan. That's a great name! Isn't it? Isn't it? He already answers to it!"

To no one in particular, Zandra said, "No one knows who *Jordan* belongs to. As healthy as he is, he's probably someone's pet. Do we know if he's microchipped?"

Sonja shook her head. "There's a Banfield attached to the PetSmart. They checked. No chip. Though they did *very* strongly suggest we get him neutered."

Zandra had avoided looking at the dog. Slowly, reluctantly, she lowered her head until she met his eyes. Hundreds of pets went homeless after every natural disaster. She knew that. And without a microchip, the odds of getting the dog back to his rightful owner, if he had one, were slim at best. She reached out a hand, and the dog lifted his head and put his chin in her palm, panting not-entirely-objectionable dog breath up into her face. "I'm putting up 'Lost Dog' fliers," she said. "They're going to say, 'Anybody missing a big black smelly dog? Call the Sheriff's Department.'"

Jamel's mouth had fallen open. "He's not smelly!"

"You'd be doing us a serious favor," Sonja said. "Jamel's right, we've got a whole pit bull starter kit ready for you."

Zandra groaned. "All my furniture is white. Even my rugs are white." She pointed in the dog's face. "You sleep on *your* bed. Not mine. Got it? And you stay on the floor. No getting on the couch." The dog sat up straight and panted. The enormous pink tongue she'd seen before flopped out the side of his mouth, the size and shape of an Odor Eater shoe insert. Zandra narrowed her eyes at him. "Jordan, huh? Is that for Michael? Or Michael B.?"

Jamel grinned. "It's for Jordan Peele!"

Perry softly cleared his throat. "That might have been my suggestion."

Zandra scratched Jordan's neck. He whined again, and his tail thumped against the floor faster. "Not bad," she said.

Across town, at the Congregational Gospel Church, Shep Curtis stood in the fellowship hall, watching. Like every other church across Cartauga County, they'd had their doors open to the public since the tornado, giving out food and drink to citizens who were still without power or water or both. A decent number of homes outside the Red Springs city limits ran off wells, almost all of which used electric pumps, and when the electricity went out, those homes had no water either.

Shep checked the time. The "kitchen" was set to be open for supper from 6:00 p.m. to 9:00 p.m. It was only 5:30. He groaned inwardly. *Three and a half more hours.*

The lunch crowd had dwindled away, and it was still early for supper, but a few stragglers still hung out, clumped together like clotting blood cells as they crammed food in their mouths. Shep had no patience for them. He knew he had to let them come, had to feed them, but more and more, the older he got, the less he found he could tolerate in the way of public association.

Two kinds of people made it onto Shep Curtis's "acceptable" list. The first were the ones initiated into his private endeavor.

The second were the children. The beautiful, blameless children, placed on Earth by God for Shep to show them the way. The proper way. The respectful way. Like that splendid little blond girl he'd seen last Sunday morning.

Idly he considered the ones who'd resisted. They'd had to be disciplined, hadn't they? Disciplined thoroughly. But he and his associates had special ways of doing that. And until recently, a special place to do it in.

He eyed one of the human clumps.

There was Mary Teems, every bit as fat as Libby and only half as appealing. And Mary's two little half-breed young'uns, both boys, neither capable of communicating at any level other than the tops of their lungs. Shep hid the sneer he wanted to throw Mary's way. No surprise she'd plop out a couple of nappy-headed carpet lizards. No white man would touch her, he knew that much. And where were the fathers now? Did she even know? For that matter, did she even know who they were?

Still, Mary was better off than Gush Parsons, who sat by himself a couple of seats down from the Teems family, slobbering into his plate. Shep didn't know what had happened to Gush's mother, but Gush had shown up an hour or two ago, and had behaved himself so far. Shep could barely look at him. The uneven nature of the young man's face brought the bile up into Shep's throat.

On the other side of the table, down a few more seats from Gush, sat a rail-thin young blond woman with bad skin, missing teeth, and a Porky Pig tattoo on one shoulder. She had clustered together with a couple of young men—birds of a feather, all of them, with *meth-head* practically stamped across their faces—and was busily showing them something on her phone, her empty paper plate and Styrofoam cup shoved off to one side.

Shep's attention snapped away from the human detritus when Will Bigelow walked into the fellowship hall. Tall, lean, with an angular face and graying blond hair, Will embodied what Shep secretly wished he could be. If a genie showed up and granted Shep three wishes, one of those wishes would be, "Make me look like Will Bigelow."

Will made his way through the tables. When he got close enough, he said, "Shep. Ready to talk?"

Shep shook Will's hand. "Come on upstairs."

The two men took the stairs to the church's second floor, and had turned on the landing to climb up to the third, when Shep said, "Oh, hey, before I forget." He opened the stairwell door to the second-floor hallway and beckoned Will to follow him.

Shep led Will into the church office, where a FedEx envelope sat on the corner of one of the desks. Shep pulled a flier out of the envelope and handed it to Will. The flier featured a photo of Shep, doing his best to look solemn and authoritative, along with the slogan, *CURTIS FOR SHERIFF.*

"What do you think?"

Will Bigelow's eyes ticked from the flier to Shep's face and back. "Not a bad likeness. You didn't want any kind of campaign slogan?"

Lightly miffed that that was Will's whole reaction, Shep took the flier and slid it back into the envelope. "It's just a proof." He cleared his throat. "Personally, I'm not convinced it's the way to go. I think I could do more good for us on the county commission."

Will shook his head. "County commission isn't hands-on like the sheriff is. We need somebody in that spot. Not that goddamn nigger bitch. Besides, you saw what my brother accomplished."

Words came to Shep's mind—*What your brother accomplished till he got careless and started sampling the product*—but he bit them off. He said, "Yeah. I s'pose. It's just gonna be really fucking embarrassing if I run and don't win."

Will clapped him on the shoulder. "You just show up. We'll take care of the rest. Now come on."

Shep and Will left the office and went up to the third floor, strode down the hall to the old choir robe room, and stepped inside. Shep closed the door. He didn't lock it, but then, he didn't need to, as they could hear anyone coming thanks to the hallway's shriekingly loud floor joists. The old nails in the joists sang like an alarm whenever the slightest pressure bore down on them.

Will said, "So. *Real* business. Saturday?"

Shep nodded. "Fifteen-passenger van. Already got the venue secured. *Adjunctive Bible Study Seminar. Registered and paid attendees only.*" Shep didn't think anyone in his right mind would wander into such a function off the street, but just in case, once they were all there, he'd lock the doors. "You got the merchandise coming?"

"A dozen of the sweetest young things you've ever seen. All taken care of—except, of course, for my cut."

"Nope, got that taken care of too. Hang on a sec."

The old choir robe room was a long, rectangular affair that had at one time been part of the building's attic. It held six long racks of choir robes, many of them more than a bit moldy, and at the back of the room stood a deep, wide, cedar wardrobe. Shep went to the wardrobe, opened the stout padlock that kept it shut, and threw the doors wide.

A different kind of robe hung there. Not moldy in the slightest, and in comparison with the ones for the choir, practically sparkling. All of them snow-white, with their accompanying peaked white hoods draped carefully over each hanger's cross-bar.

All of them bearing a unique symbol in the upper left quadrant of the chest: a hollow diamond with a tilted cross lying over it, the cross's long central bar pointed straight at the wearer's heart.

Shep reached past the robes of the Holy Brotherhood of Red Springs and opened a drawer, from which he took a fat envelope of cash. He was always glad to pay Will his fair share, considering the good work he did.

2 1

The police thought they were so smart.

Hiding, up in the trees, watching with their binoculars and their radios, ready to spring whatever puny trap they had tried to set. But the Hidden Man knew about traps. He knew *all* about them. He'd spotted the old cop first, crouched up in his deer blind like some little boy playing cowboys and Indians. Then the other ones. The second old man from the courthouse. The three that usually spent their time at the schools. There was always someone there now, always someone watching his Workshop.

Fine. That was fine.

Irritating, but fine.

Especially since none of them had discovered the one secret it still held.

The Hidden Man walked into his Showcase. The Workshop was gone, everything about that location compromised, but as long as he had his Showcase, it didn't matter all that much. He didn't like the thought of making his Showcase into a dual-purpose location. It was supposed to be pure. Clean. He didn't want the smell of brain oil anywhere near it... but he didn't think that could be helped now.

He waved cheerily to Angelique as he walked past her. She didn't say the words, but he could tell she was grateful for the courtesy. No reason not to be polite, yes? No reason to make her feel unwanted or unwelcome.

The Hidden Man crossed the floor, moving past his Showpieces, to a curtained-off section at the back of the room. He slipped through the curtain and sat down at the desk, the bright glow of the computer monitors reflected in his eyes, and he worked the magic that let his vision expand. The Hidden Man's sight reached out, and out, along the cables and through the airwaves, until it arrived at Sheriff Seagraves's computer.

He wasn't sloppy. He had never been sloppy. About anything.

He didn't make the kind of amateurish mistakes that could get him caught. The sheriff's webcam light didn't come on, even though he peered out of it. There was no slow-down on her end, no irregularities of function, no traces of code that would arouse suspicion. No, his private telescope into Zandra Seagraves's life returned crystal-clear, full-color video, and the monitor to his right mirrored the sheriff's desktop, right down to the movements of her mouse.

The Hidden Man stood. He left the computer, walked out through his collection of Showpieces, and entered the Tunnel.

He was proud of the Tunnel. Almost as proud as he was of the other things he'd accomplished. It had taken him the better part of two years, working alone, and was a formidable feat of engineering, if he did say so himself. The Hidden Man strolled down its length to the door at the far end. His hand hovered above the latch.

No.

No good could come of seeing whether that door would open now.

If there was one thing the Hidden Man understood about the human race, though, it was that humans *excelled* at forgetting. Lessons faded... wisdom failed to catch hold... knowledge slipped away like morning mist.

Perhaps in a few years, he could reclaim some measure of what had pleased him most about his Workshop. Once everyone had forgotten.

An alert sounded out on the Hidden Man's phone. He pulled it from his pocket, sat down with his back to the tunnel door, and tapped the screen with both thumbs for a few moments. The signal was weak, thanks to the earth overhead, but he was able to do what he needed to.

When he got back to the Showcase, a different sound came to him from out on the floor. A thumping. He stretched and cracked his knuckles, and went to find the source of the noise.

To his complete lack of surprise, it came from Angelique. She was trying to move, trying to inch the heavy wooden chair to which she was shackled closer to the door. The Hidden Man put his face next to hers, and watched as the tears welled up in her eyes. "Are you bored?" he asked. "Is that it? Am I not providing you enough stimulation?" She couldn't answer him, of course. He had become far too proficient at the crafting and placement of gags to allow for that. "Here. I know just the thing." The Hidden Man tilted the chair backward onto the heavy casters he had installed for this specific purpose, and Angelique looked up at him and saw his face upside-down, and the tears spilled out of her eyes. The Hidden Man rolled her into the far corner, where he'd cobbled together a makeshift work table, the blood channels routed out that very morning.

When he set her back upright, Angelique grunted, shook her head, her big dark eyes pleading and crying, and something about her struck the Hidden Man as so unbearably pitiful that he surprised himself. Before he realized what his hands were doing, they had unbuckled the gag.

But he held one hand over her mouth. Kept the ball in place. He said, "I want to hear no screams from you. Do not even raise your voice. If you cooperate, I will let you speak. That's what you want, is it not? You want to communicate?"

Angelique nodded. Carefully. Respectfully. The Hidden Man removed the ball from her mouth. Let her work her jaw, move her tongue. He even offered her a sip of water, which she graciously accepted.

"Please, mister," she said when she was able to. "Please. I can't be here. My folks—they need me. They need my help. That's the whole reason I came back to Red Springs. My granny, she's sick, and it's too much for my mama. She can't, they, there's not enough money for a nurse or anything, it's all on my mama, and I came back to help. If you take me away from them... it's..." She swallowed, and coughed. "It'll be like you're killin' me and my granny both."

A second surprise: Angelique believed he was going to kill her. He could tell she had accepted it. The level of maturity required to face one's own mortality with that degree of calm was a rare thing to see, especially among those he chose. "You misunderstand, Miss Currant," the Hidden Man said. The black ski mask he wore only muffled his words a tiny bit. "I do not consider what I do here to be *killing*. On the contrary. I am *improving*." He spun the chair around so that she could see the rack of tools he was about to use on her, and put his mouth right next to her ear, speaking just above a whisper. "After all, one cannot kill that which never truly lived, yes?"

The Hidden Man slipped the ball gag back into Angelique's mouth just before her screams began in earnest.

22

By the time the sun had slid far enough overhead to begin thinking about dipping toward the horizon, Colin Massey would have given his left pinkie toe for a long, hot shower and a massage, followed by another long hot shower. He'd applied sunscreen twice, but he felt pretty sure that at the very least his nose and ears and shoulders had burned to a boiled-lobster red. His muscles ached. He had more than one blister on each hand. Colin dumped what seemed like the thousandth armful of trash and broken bricks into the huge metal bin on the edge of the church's lot as Charity came over to him.

He thought she might have had the right idea after all, with her broad-brimmed straw hat and long-sleeved white shirt and old jeans. She looked ridiculous, yes, but he knew she wasn't even a little bit sunburned, and the sopping-wet shirt probably kept her a lot cooler than the snug black tank top he'd chosen to wear. Charity had a paper cup full of water in each hand. Colin accepted one graciously.

"Tell me again why I'm still here?" he said, after chugging most of the cold water. He poured what was left onto his head.

"You're the one with the rental car. I can only guess you're here

177

because you want to be." She drank from her cup. "I'm grateful, though. And so is the church."

He cocked an eyebrow at her. "The church as a whole?"

"No. This church. Mount Zachariah. I was just talking to Reverend Jessup—his congregation have been giving what they can, of course, but they also put together a GoFundMe, and they're about to have enough money to hire a contractor. Pretty sure the church'll be better than before the tornado hit, once they're done with it."

As if speaking his name made the man appear, Reverend JaPatrick Jessup pulled up and parked behind the waste bin in his ancient land-barge Cadillac. For a man of (according to Charity) seventy-one years, the reverend seemed to be *made* of energy. He bounded out of the huge car as nimbly as a twenty-year-old and headed straight for Charity and Colin, an ear-to-ear grin splitting his face and his right hand extended.

"I don't believe I've had the pleasure, young man," he said, and Colin shook his hand, wincing as the reverend's grip squeezed his blisters. "'Course I've met young Miss Charity, here, and don't the Lord in Heaven know, don't nobody deserve that name more than she does! She's been a right boon to us, organizing y'all's group like she did!" Jessup held on to Colin's hand, studying Colin's face, the whites of his eyes exactly matching the puff of white hair on his head. "You have *got* to be Miss Charity's brother. Colin, isn't it? That's what you told me, correct, Miss Charity?"

Charity gave him her sweet smile, and Colin couldn't help but mirror it. Reverend Jessup's energy was infectious. "Guilty as charged," Colin said.

"Look like you done worked up quite the sweat." Jessup wore a pair of work boots, tan jeans, and a white button shirt that wouldn't have looked out of place with a three-piece suit. Nonetheless, he rolled up his sleeves and took a pair of work gloves out of his back pocket. "I been out tendin' to the flock all day, so to speak. Lots of folks have trouble leavin' their houses, and it's up to us to make sure they got what they need." He cast an eye toward the afternoon sun. "Hot as blazes. I reckon it'll get up past a hundred, most days this summer. Old folks, we got to make sure their AC's workin'. Don't want 'em fallin' out from the heat. Colin, you been carryin' off trash all day?"

"That I have, sir."

"And why ain't you wearin' gloves? A man carry broken brick an' pieces o' glass without gloves, he ain't got the sense God gave a gnat."

Under other circumstances, Colin would have been offended. But Reverend Jessup said the words with an easy grin and a twinkle in his eye, and all Colin could do was chuckle. "If I'm being honest, Reverend, this might qualify as the first day of honest work I've ever done in my life."

"Hard to believe that," Jessup said, and squeezed Colin's right upper arm with a hand that felt like an industrial vise. "Got these big shiny muscles. Best believe you got the attention of plenty o' the young ladies around here." While Colin tried to think of a good response to that, Reverend Jessup handed him his own gloves. "Here. Take these. I got another pair in my trunk. Let's see how much o' this here *detritus* we can clear off before Shep Curtis's bunch shows up with their soup-and-sandwich fixin's."

While Reverend Jessup went back to his car, Colin turned to Charity. "Is that what we're doing for dinner? Soup and sandwiches?"

She shrugged. "I guess. I heard another church was going to come by and set up a food station. I think it's supposed to be for us and whoever else needs it. Open to the public-type thing."

Colin grunted and, when Reverend Jessup came back, returned to the cleanup effort. He wasn't entirely sure why they couldn't have just gotten a bulldozer in to scrape all the trash and wreckage off the concrete slab the church was built on, but he wasn't here to question anyone's methodology. Maybe it was a cost-saving thing? Why spend hundreds of dollars renting a bulldozer when people would do the work for free?

He would've paid thousands of dollars to get out of the heat and not thought twice about it. Colin paused, looking around for another cup of water—

And saw Reverend Jessup working, alongside the teenagers Colin and Charity had brought down here. At first Colin thought the man might have been on drugs, but he was too steady, his movements too quick and self-assured. Colin watched as Reverend Jessup, all seventy-plus years of him, scooped up armload after armload of trash and carried them to the dumpster. In the heat. *With a smile on his face.* And he did it as if it were nothing. No complaining. No pauses for rest. Just sheer, smooth energy.

Colin watched the reverend work out of the corner of his eye for the next hour. The man was a dynamo. He put Colin to shame, and the shame made Colin work faster.

As he worked, Colin thought about why exactly he was there.

Because he couldn't leave. That was why. According to Sheriff Zandra Seagraves, he needed to stay put for now. Simple as that.

But Reverend Jessup kept working, never lost the smile, and had a kind word or gesture for every single person he encountered.

Colin's thoughts ran in a loop of confusion and resentment, mixed with some righteous indignation that slid into awed admiration, until people started showing up for the free food. No one from the neighboring church was there yet, but word had clearly gotten out, and a few dozen citizens of Red Springs arrived, many in cars but a lot of them on foot as well.

A skinny white woman with oily blond hair, bad skin, missing teeth, and a Porky Pig shoulder tat sat down on the grassy strip between the sidewalk and the parking lot, and Colin overheard her talking to a knot of local white teenagers. He couldn't make out every word she said, but it seemed to revolve around pit bulls, so after he dumped his latest load of debris in the bin, he strolled over and pulled his gloves off.

"Excuse me," he said, and every eye turned to fix on him. "What were you guys saying about dogs?"

"We-e-ellll, ain't you a *GQ*-lookin' white boy?" said the skinny blonde, which confused Colin, since she was every bit as white as he was.

One of the other teenagers, a hulking boy with bad acne and

stringy brown hair that hung down in his eyes, said, "What're you, some kinda yankee?" He turned to his friends. "Y'all hear him talk?"

The boy's friends laughed.

That put Colin right back in Aunt Petunia's, and he realized he'd made a mistake by interacting. "Sorry," he said, for some reason, "I'll just get back to work."

"Nah, here," the skinny blonde said, and patted the grass next to her. "Set a spell. Everybody needs to hear this anyhow."

Colin hesitated. "Hear what?"

"'Bout the dogs. You was askin' about the dogs, wasn't you?"

Colin lowered himself to the grass. The blonde looked over her shoulder, saw that Reverend Jessup was too far away to hear her, and said, "That damn bitch nigger sheriff. She come bustin' in at my boyfriend's place, damn near beat 'im to death, and set loose all o' his pit bulls while she was at it. They's all up on the ridge behind his trailer now."

The boy with the acne shook his head. "My daddy brought home a pit bull couple o' years ago. Wanted it to be a guard dog. All it done was chase our chickens an' tear shit up."

Colin got the sudden feeling of having been dropped into the ocean with weights around his ankles. The blonde's casual use of the word "nigger" put a sort of cold pit into his stomach, but the boy's mention of his family's pit bull gave Colin something familiar to latch onto. Struggling to keep his voice calm, he said, "Well, y'know, they're smart dogs. All you have to do is spend a little time training them. Maybe you could put yours in an obedience class. Most of the big pet stores offer those. There's a PetSmart or something around here, isn't there?"

The boy's friends laughed, as if Colin had suggested something ludicrous, like maybe dressing the dog in a deep-sea diver's suit and sending it to hunt for buried treasure. The acne-faced boy said, "Nah, the dog wasn't no good. My daddy just took him out back and shot him."

The blonde nodded sagely as the boy's friends made noises of assent. One of them said, "That's what you gotta do."

Scalding tears started in Colin's eyes, to his surprise and dismay. He stood up abruptly and turned to get back to work, but the boy called after him. "Hey. You cryin'? What the fuck, man? It was just a damn dog."

Colin wanted to scream. He wanted to scream at the acne-faced boy. Call him a savage, call his father a savage, call everyone in the entire goddamn town a bunch of fucking brain-dead backwoods inbred dumb-as-shit worthless barbarians, but the words crunched together into a logjam in the back of his throat. All he could do was wave incoherently as he walked away, hating them, hating this place, and hating himself for saying nothing.

T he free food showed up thirty minutes later and, at Reverend Jessup's suggestion, Colin got in line with the rest of the volunteer group. He didn't have much of an appetite at the moment, but as hard as he'd been working all day, he knew he needed to eat, hungry or not.

Standing in front of him was a slim, pretty white girl of about seventeen, and in front of her—Colin tried to size him up without being too obvious—was a living, breathing embodiment of the stereotypical Grumpy Old Man, all the way down to the worn Hush Puppy shoes and the faded trucker cap. The GOM turned and spoke to the girl.

"Get three sandwiches. We'll take 'em back to your mom an' dad."

The girl wore what seemed to be the official Red Springs warm-weather uniform: flip-flops, cutoff denim shorts, and a tight t-shirt. Unlike most of the rest of the teen female population Colin had seen, however, she had spent a bit of time on her straight, dark brown hair, and she pushed part of it back behind one ear. "Grandpa, I don't think we're supposed to take extras." She pitched her voice low for the next words, but Colin's hearing was excellent, despite all the time he'd spent in garages and storage units with sub-standard indie rock bands. "Besides, we've had power for three days now. We don't need this stuff to begin with."

The old man turned cold, steely blue eyes on the girl. "You gon' argue with me, Savvy? Again? You tryin'a test me?"

Savvy's face fell. "No, Grandpa."

The old man went on. "We're gon' need all our strength anyway. Them pit bulls loose in the hills? Shit." He dragged the word out. *Shiii-iit.* "Bunch of us're headed up there. Gonna meet at the old fire-watch tower. Hunt those animals down, 'fore they come out o' the woods and maul some helpless child."

A lump rose in Colin's throat. It got worse when Savvy said, "Grandpa? You really goin' huntin'? …Can I come, too?"

"Huh?" Sarcasm saturated his words. "What're you gonna shoot with? Your phone?"

"No, I, I can borrow Daddy's rifle."

The grandfather raked his eyes up and down Savvy's body. Devoid of emotion. Like a buyer at a cattle auction sizing up a calf. "Well…" He hesitated long enough for them to advance a couple of places in line. "Yeah, I reckon you can come along."

His appetite obliterated, Colin left the line and scrolled through his call history until he arrived at Sheriff Seagraves's number. It didn't take long.

* * *

Zandra slouched in her office, staring at the oversized sketchbook on her desk, while Jordan snored softly in the corner.

She felt grateful for every single man and woman on the payroll. Almost everyone had their power back on now, but the complaints still rolled in, and Zandra still had her deputies scattered all over the county addressing them.

The computer on her desk displayed a site advertising deals on travel packages. One had caught her eye earlier, offering a week's stay in the Shetland Islands for what looked to her like a reasonable price.

Zandra reached out and closed the browser window. Not the time nor the place, she told herself, no matter how tempting.

The big sketchbook on the desk in front of her displayed the flowchart that she'd spent the last two hours working on. She hated it. It was sloppy, and incomplete, and told her nothing. In the center was a box with the word DUNGEON in it. Radiating off the top edge, lines connected the DUNGEON box to two other, smaller boxes that held the words TORTURE and SURGICAL INSTRUMENTS. Two arrows sprang from the TORTURE box's bottom two corners, one leading to a circle with JIMMY BIDDLES in it, the other to one labeled SHAQUANA TAYLOR. Two more arrows led from Jimmy and Shaquana's circles to a diamond shape with the word ALIVE scrawled over it.

Zandra traced and retraced that word. ALIVE.

It didn't make sense.

Maybe it was like Perry had suggested, and the dungeon was some sort of violent but consensual sex thing. Except, from what she'd been able to determine, neither kid had shown any signs of being interested in that kind of thing. For that matter, neither of them had shown signs of wanting to run away from home, either.

Could she call it "running away from home," if they were eighteen? Legal? Wouldn't it then just be called "leaving?"

The style of the messages bothered her, too. Shaquana and Jimmy, who didn't know each other as far as she could tell, both sending updates on Facebook at roughly the same intervals, accompanied by all-caps messages written in styles that might be too similar to be a coincidence. If she didn't know they were both alive and well, she would've thought the same person had been writing on behalf of both of them.

But she kept coming back to the photos. Photos where the boy and the girl were posing on the beach, sipping drinks, enjoying the sunset. There was no question that it was Shaquana and Jimmy, either, despite the images' low resolutions. Jimmy had a distinctive spray of vitiligo spots on his right biceps, and Zandra had seen it peeking out from his shirt sleeve in a number of the photos.

"Maybe this is all nothing," she said quietly. Jordan raised his head and thumped his tail on the floor. "Maybe whoever's responsible is just playing some kind of elaborate joke."

Her cell phone rang. She didn't recognize the number, but answered on the third ring. "Seagraves."

Zandra instantly recognized Maxine Currant's voice. The worry that had eaten it up when they'd first spoken had been replaced with pure jubilation. "Sheriff! Sheriff, my Angelique okay! You can call off whatever kind o' investigatin' you was doin', she just fine!"

Zandra sat back in her chair. "That's fantastic news, Mrs. Currant!" Maybe something could go right for a change. "Where was she?"

The jubilation faltered, but not by much. "Well, she done acted plain stupid, you ask me—takin' off like she did—but she okay, so now I'm not so worried my heart give out."

Zandra swallowed before she spoke. "Mrs. Currant, if you don't mind me asking, what's she done to make you say she's acting stupid?"

"Sheriff, call me Maxine, please! She done took off with some o' her friends from Augusta. They headin' out to Las Vegas, can you believe that shit? Oh, I'm sorry, pardon my language."

Zandra sat up straight. The hairs on the back of her neck had come to attention. "Angelique left town without telling you?"

"Ain't that just like a young girl? Get a fool notion in her head, you can't tell her nothing."

"And... how do you know she's all right? Did she call you?"

"No, ma'am, Sheriff, she sent me a message on Facebook. Said not to worry, she'd only be gone for just a little while. 'Less she found some sweet job out there, she said, and if that happens, she'll send money home so I can hire a nurse to help me take care of her granny."

"And did you try to call her?"

"I did, but it just went to the recording. That's okay, Sheriff, I'm just so awful glad she okay, the Good Lord done answered my prayers! Praise His name!"

Zandra's throat felt tight. "Maxine, I'd love to send Angelique a message myself. How does she show up on Facebook?"

"Her name on there *Angelique Aphrodite.* Aphrodite her real middle name, she just left off the Currant part. You talk to her, you tell her you be checking up on her, would you mind? I bet she listen to you a lot better'n she listen to me."

"Thanks, Maxine."

Zandra ended the call, pulled up her own personal Facebook page, and typed in *Angelique Aphrodite.* Immediately a profile popped up featuring Maxine's daughter. Zandra sent her a friend request, stared at the screen for a few moments, and sat back in her chair again.

Was Maxine Currant about to start receiving status updates from her daughter? Featuring Angelique on some balcony, sipping a hurricane, living it up? Accompanied by one or two lines in all caps?

Zandra buried her face in her hands and whispered, *"What is going on?"*

When her cell rang again, she almost jumped. The name *Colin Massey* appeared on the screen. She answered after a couple seconds' hesitation. "Sheriff Seagraves."

For the next several minutes, Zandra listened to Colin Massey vent. She heard a lot about the racism in Red Springs, and how it just kept getting worse the longer he was here, and about the general insensitivity and cloddishness of the natives, and how he wished he'd never heard of the place. When he'd finished unspooling all of that, he finally said something that made her pay attention.

"And now a bunch of these gun-toting congenital idiots are going to go and *hunt the escaped pit bulls.* Like they're all man-eating tigers or some ridiculous bullshit. They're just dogs!"

Zandra glanced over at Jordan. He was watching her, his yellow eyes clear and full of understanding. "Did you hear these 'congenital idiots' mention where and when this hunt was going to take place?"

"I don't know about the when, but they said something about a fire-watch tower. Does that mean anything to you?"

"Thank you, Colin, I'll take it from here." She ended the call and punched a button on her desk phone. "Doreen, can you come in here, please?"

Minutes later, with Doreen looking after Jordan, Zandra sped down Highway 5, heading back toward Finn Wilkins's trailer. The only fire-watch tower in the county was on the ridge immediately west of his place, and while Zandra wasn't *that* worried about the escaped dogs, she had less than zero interest in some kill-happy good-ol'-boy mistaking his neighbor for a pit bull and blowing someone's head off.

Her fingers tight around the steering wheel, she had to suppress a smile. It felt good to be *doing* something. Anything.

In his Showroom, the Hidden Man stood up from his computer, which displayed Zandra Seagraves's now-empty office chair. He went to a closet, pulled out a long gun, and hurried for the door. He passed Angelique along the way, but now she didn't protest, or try to escape her bonds, or make any sound at all. He winked at her as he left.

2 3

Having waited until the line died down to just kids from his sister's church, Colin took a paper plate with a couple of hot dogs and a Styrofoam cup filled with purple Gatorade and sat down on an as-yet untouched pile of rubble at the corner of the church lot. He had gnawed his way through the first dog, trying to think of it as fuel and not as cheap animal by-products, when he noticed a big white truck approaching the church. The truck slowed down when it pulled abreast of him. Colin's skin prickled. His breathing grew shallow.

But then the window rolled down, and he found himself looking at the broad, grinning face of Perry Seagraves. "Young Mr. Massey!" Perry called out. "How goes the work?"

Colin glanced around as he stood. The teenagers were all grouped off, giggling and flirting, some of them groaning with tired muscles, and Charity and Reverend Jessup stood by the reverend's car, chatting and smiling. As Perry eased the big truck into the partially-cleaned-off parking lot, Colin took a bite of his second hot dog. He chewed it and swallowed as he walked over to the truck, trying to decide how much to say.

"Has, uh, has your sister said anything to you about what I found?"

Perry's grin dwindled. "She's filled me in, yeah."

Colin shook his head. "I've been trying not to think about it. That's what she said to do. Just go on as usual—except at the same time, she won't let me leave town, and I can't say anything to anybody about it." He took a gulp of Gatorade. "Tell you the truth, when you pulled up just now, I didn't recognize the truck, and I was thinking, *Oh shit oh shit he's found me I'm about to die.*"

Perry silently took in the ruined church. After a moment, he said, "Zandra likes to use me as a sounding board sometimes. Never about anything as serious as this before. I understand why she doesn't want the public knowing about it, but..." He eyed Colin speculatively. "I'm thinking maybe putting a couple of extra brains together couldn't hurt. You wanna go grab a beer? See if we can hash this out?"

"If I can get some good Mexican food to go along with it, you've just made my night."

"Oh, we've got some authentic Mexican cuisine around here, don't you worry. Once our friends south of the border got wind of the jobs to be had in the carpet mills, the whole area got browner in a hurry. Well, not Red Springs so much, but definitely a little south of here."

Colin's forehead had creased up. "Carpet mills?"

"Dalton. Twenty, twenty-five miles south of here. Carpet capital of the world."

"I'll take your word for it. Listen, let me go tell my sister what I'm doing and I'll be right with you."

"And I'll be right here. Tell her I said 'howdy.'"

<hr>

Zandra tore past the driveway to Finn Wilkins's trailer. Less than a minute later the road took a sharp turn to the right and began to climb, making its way up Grey Ridge, and a few minutes after that Zandra found the rutted dirt road that led up to the fire-watch tower. The Tahoe slid and bumped its way up to the worn gravel patch—it could hardly be called a parking lot—around the tower, and she felt her stomach sink when she saw close to a dozen pickups and Jeeps parked there, deserted.

The hunt had already begun.

Zandra got out of the Tahoe, but kept the microphone connected to the loudspeaker in her hand, and her words echoed off the hillside. *"Everyone! This is Sheriff Seagraves! You all need to return to your vehicles! This is an illegal hunt! Return to your vehicles right now, and there won't be any trouble!"*

At first she thought she must have been alone on the ridge, but after a few moments she heard distant shouts, followed by a couple of even more distant rifle shots. Zandra recognized the flat crack of a 30-06. If the dog-hunters had heard her, they'd paid her no mind. Zandra cursed as she pulled on a hunter-orange vest and took the narrow, overgrown, winding trail from the tower up the side of the ridge.

She'd only been climbing for ten minutes when clouds scudded across the lowering sun. That, along with the shade provided by the trees themselves, dropped the temperature by several welcome degrees, but it also brought out the mosquitoes in greater force. Zandra had her sidearm, three extra clips, a Taser, and a flashlight, but no bug spray. She slapped at the back of her neck as one of the cursed little creatures punctured her skin. Her hand came away bloody.

Grey Ridge ran north-to-south, and Zandra steadily climbed its western face, the sun—when its rays could get to her—shining down on her back and shoulders. It wasn't a terribly tall ridge, probably no more than two hundred feet from the base of the tower to the ridge's crest, but the trail she'd been following had quickly petered out, leaving Zandra to navigate her way upward through thick trees, thorny underbrush, and a sharply tilted forest floor rendered treacherous by the thick layer of pine needles and decomposing fallen leaves.

"My ankles're gonna be covered in chiggers, I just know it," she grumbled. Zandra had always preferred the straightforward blood-thirsty predation of mosquitoes to the prolonged torture inflicted by chiggers, the near-microscopic red insects that drilled into the skin and made her want to claw her flesh off to escape the itching.

Overhead, the clouds grew thicker, and in the distance Zandra heard more shouts. Male and female voices echoed through the trees. She cursed and scrambled upward faster, wishing she'd brought a battery-powered megaphone with her, and wondered how quickly her own voice would get lost if she tried to call out to the hunters. Were they staying together as a group? With her luck, no. Would they even be wearing orange? Again, she figured, probably not. Of course, that was the larger part of the point—to try to keep gun-toting drunks from shooting each other.

Abruptly Zandra broke through a line of trees and found herself at the crest. The land fell away more sharply on the eastern side than the way she'd come up, and—there! Maybe an eighth of a mile to her right and halfway down the ridge, she spotted movement. Zandra cupped her hands around her mouth, drew as deep a breath as possible, and bellowed, *"Everyone! This is Sheriff Seagraves! Stop what you're doing immediately! This hunting trip is over!"*

To her ears, that sounded like a pronouncement booming down from the Heavenly Host itself. Her words rolled down the slope, echoing, growing. Surely everyone had heard her. They couldn't have *not* heard her.

She got no response. Zandra waited a full minute, and the sound of faint, distant laughter wafted up to her, followed by a couple more 30-06 shots.

Snarling, Zandra said, "I'm going to break my damn neck up here," and started down the slope toward the last place she'd seen movement. As she traversed the loose, uneven soil, dislodging pebbles and bits of pine cone—most of which lodged inside her shoes, from the feel of it—the clouds grew even darker, and a drop of rain touched her cheek. Zandra had taken breath to say, "Shit," when the ground beneath her right foot gave way completely, and in less than a second she was sliding, rolling and slipping down toward a wall of trees, and she threw her arms up in front of her face just as her torso slammed into the trunk of a tall, slender pine.

She didn't black out as she hit the ground.

Or at least, she didn't *think* she blacked out.

Wincing from the pain, Zandra sat up and gingerly did a body check, finishing up with a few exploratory deep breaths. No ribs cracked, she was pretty sure, which made her sigh in relief—which, in turn, made her wince in pain. She couldn't turn her head very far to the right without sending stabbing pulses down into her arm. Something had gone wrong with her neck during the fall.

Not as wrong as what had happened to her radio. The microphone, caught between her chest and the tree, wasn't much more than scrap now, and she could already feel the bruise forming where it had smashed itself apart against her skin.

The rain came in earnest as she mourned the radio's loss.

Zandra shakily rose to her feet and made her way into the woods. The footing wasn't much better here than farther up the slope where she'd fallen, but she could catch herself on tree trunks if she lost her balance. She clicked on her flashlight, did her best to figure out where she'd last seen any of the hunters, and headed in that direction.

The clouds overhead had gone black. The rain fell in frigid little slaps, each drop a shock to her skin, and every so often the wind burst through the trees in a mad rush that whipped the rain straight into her face. Clouds, rain, canopy of trees overhead—all of it, combined with the sun setting on the far side of the ridge, plunged the woods into a murky sea of shadows. Zandra's flashlight barely penetrated the darkness. The trees around her became a sharply tilted labyrinth, and for the first time she began to consider the possibility that she had made a terrible, terrible mistake.

A series of mistakes, if she were being honest with herself. She counted them off in a bitter litany.

I shouldn't have come here without proper gear.

I shouldn't have come here without backup.

I should have let someone know where I was going.

It was supposed to have been a simple matter. Show up before everyone left their vehicles, tell them their ridiculous endeavor was getting shut down, watch them all drive away, go back to the Farmhouse.

The rain soaked through her shirt and undershirt. A painful, unwelcome word bobbed to the surface of her mind: *hypothermia*. Unlikely in August, but still. What if she got caught out here overnight, in a storm? An intelligent woman would stop dead in her tracks, turn around, make her way back up and over the ridge, and return to her truck. If the fear-filled, pack-motivated, beer-soaked citizenry ended up shooting a few dogs, or themselves, well, she'd done all she could, hadn't she? Zandra couldn't help it if some trigger-happy townsfolk wanted to see natural selection in action.

She sneered at herself. What kind of cowardly sack of shit would she be if she gave up? If she was feeling this much distress, how must the dog-hunters feel? How many of them had any kind of survival training at all? If she turned around now, and one or more of them died, how could Zandra ever look herself in the mirror again?

She wiped rainwater out of her eyes, clenched her jaw, and heaved forward—

—just as a chunk of the tree she'd been leaning against exploded.

Zandra whipped around as the sound of the gunshot rolled across the ridgeside. "Hey!" she screamed, "it's me, you dipshits! Sheriff Seagraves! Watch where you're *fucking* shooting!" She scanned back and forth through the woods, trying to pinpoint the son of a bitch who'd just almost blown her head off, when her brain fully processed the sound of the gunshot. Zandra's guts turned to ice.

That wasn't a 30-06.

That was a .308. The rifle used by the Cartauga County Sheriff's Department.

Zandra ducked behind another tree. Had the racism and anger and resentment in the department finally come to a head? Had one of the deputized good ol' boys she'd been legally compelled to retain finally decided to get rid of her? It was a terrible plan if the shooter actually was using a department rifle, because ballistics would nail his ass to the wall...

Unless forensics was in on it, and falsified the report.

Or, even more likely, if whoever had shot at her was too dim to think through the consequences.

Zandra stared up the face of the ridge, through the trees, trying to spot the shooter. Because of that, she didn't pay sufficient attention to where her feet were planted, and when she shifted her weight, both of them slipped out from under her.

Zandra's grunt of pain coincided perfectly with the second explosion of bark and splintered wood, and as the report of the rifle sounded out, any doubt she might have felt evaporated.

Someone was hunting her.

Zandra scrambled farther down the slope, zigging in and out of tree trunks, staying as low as she could while still keeping her balance, and a third shot sounded out, slamming into the forest floor ahead. She spotted a rocky outcropping and threw herself behind it. It wasn't great cover, but it was between her and the shooter, so it would do for a few seconds at least.

She risked a look around the rocky edge. The darkness was growing thicker by the second, but adrenaline had slowed time down for her, sharpened her senses, and—

There. Someone. Barely a glimpse. Just a flash of the distinctive shape of a head and shoulders, outlined against the dimming sky. Zandra flinched as another bullet cracked against the rock above her head and sprayed her with jagged stone shrapnel.

She had no advantage here. The shooter was on higher ground, bearing a weapon with far greater range and damage than her department-issue Glock. She had no body armor, but for all she knew, the shooter was decked out head to foot in Kevlar. She only had one option here.

Run.

Run, and call for help.

Zandra flung herself down the slope, half-sprinting, half-sliding, her lungs hot, her breathing ragged. A rifle shot rang out. Then another—

She stumbled, white-hot pain searing across her thigh, slammed into a tree and bounced off, and came to a teeth-rattling halt against a boulder half-covered with moss and decayed leaves. Zandra shoved herself up and continued her mad plummet down the slope. She had no time to look down at her thigh, to try to gauge how badly hurt she was, how much she was bleeding. Ahead of her, a gigantic hickory tree had toppled, ripping its enormous ball of roots up out of the hillside's rocky soil, and she slid behind it, digging her heels in. She hadn't heard a gunshot in the last thirty seconds. Maybe the shooter had lost sight of her?

Zandra dug her phone out of her pocket with shaking fingers. Somehow dirt had packed into her pocket, and she had to claw through it to get a grip on her phone, but when she slid the screen open it still worked, and she stabbed Pounder's name with her thumb. She couldn't think of anyone else to call. Pounder was the only one in the department she truly trusted.

The phone rang.

And rang.

Zandra regulated her breathing through sheer will. *Come on. Come on. Answer the damn phone.*

"You have reached Horace Pounder. Leave a message."

Zandra whispered, *"Fuck,"* and tried again. More ringing. Still more ringing.

As Pounder's voice mail message began to play again, light flared through the trees ahead of her, splashing off a familiar sight, and Zandra's breathing stopped entirely as she realized where she was. The illumination came from a car's headlights cutting through the dusk, and it flared off a huge Chick-Fil-A billboard. Zandra had made it all the way down the ridge. She was crouched not even ninety feet from the edge of Apison Highway.

That helped. And it didn't. She knew exactly what stretch of road she'd fetched up against, and there were no businesses out here, no houses, nothing but woods and long-unused cow pastures. The rain had let up at some point during her break-neck descent, and she strained her ears, listening for footsteps. A rustle of clothing. The sound of breathing.

She heard nothing but the patter of water droplets falling on leaves.

Overhead, the clouds parted, and the world entered the black-and-gray gloom just before true night fell. Zandra wriggled farther up under the fallen tree. There was only one person she could think of who could help her now. She dimmed her phone's screen as low as she could get it and tapped out a text to her brother.

Somewhere above her on the ridge, she heard a voice. Then another. Just as they had been earlier, faint, distant—but not agitated. Just conversation, called out over a short distance. Even a burst of laughter.

Zandra tried to imagine the logistics of the situation. Block out the scene. She was crouched, hidden, or at least she hoped she was hidden, at the bottom of the ridge. Somewhere nearby, the shooter lurked—or did he? Had he given up? Had she lost him? Had the approach of the dog hunters scared him off?

Should she call out to the hunters? There was no way to tell how near or far they were from her position. If she stood up and shouted, the killer could shoot her and be done with it before any of the hunters had a clue what was going on.

Zandra remembered what the shitty little teenagers had said to her at the hospital. *All your deputies hate you.* And *They're gonna get rid of you.* And *All it's gonna take is one shot.*

Minutes dragged by. Ten. Fifteen. She risked another look at her phone. The oppressive gray gloom deepened. More voices reached her. The hunters had made it down to the base of the ridge and gotten close enough for her to make out a few individual words. Someone said, "Goddamn dogs." Someone else said, "Soaked through."

Zandra heard a vehicle approaching. It sounded big. Like Perry's truck. She crept out of her hiding place, but stayed low, her head beneath the top of the underbrush as she moved closer to the edge of the road. She'd told Perry to come to the billboard. *Don't stop,* her text had read. *Just slow down, I'll run out and jump in.*

The voices behind her drew closer still.

Perry's big white pickup came around a corner, slowing as it approached the billboard, and Zandra was up, running, sprinting full-out toward the truck, and there was Perry behind the wheel and—someone in the back seat? Who? She didn't have time to worry about it as Perry leaned way over and opened the door, and Zandra swung it wide, her foot finding purchase on the running board.

Perry said, "Zan, what the f—"

Then her world exploded into streaks of pain and broken glass and blood.

2 4

While Zandra was on her way to the fire-watch tower, Colin Massey sat with Perry Seagraves in a Mexican restaurant called *Los Magueys*. They had driven over to Highway 41 and taken it a few miles south to another tiny town called Tunnel Hill. Colin had laughed when he saw the town's name.

"Is there actually a tunnel in a hill in Tunnel Hill?"

"There is," Perry had said. "It's an old railroad tunnel. But I've never gone to see it."

"Why not?"

"No good reason. Kind of like people who grow up in New York but live their whole lives without ever going out to the Statue of Liberty. I think when things like that are local, they just sort of enter your mental landscape. Get taken for granted. Not that special."

"But we're going to Tunnel Hill for margaritas?"

"And burritos. You won't regret it."

Colin didn't. He sat in a booth across from Perry, a big margarita glass half-empty beside his plate, and a beyond-generous portion of chicken burrito, yellow rice, and refried beans mostly gone. Perry was making his way through a dish that involved chicken, strips of steak, and chunks of chorizo, all drowned in a white cheese sauce. Colin eyed Perry's plate. "Next time, I'm ordering that."

Perry belched, and took a swig from his own margarita. "I just figured, if we're going to try to make any sense of this dungeon business, we'd need full bellies. Can't think on an empty stomach."

Colin chewed a bite and swallowed. "Unless I pass out after this. I don't know when I've worked hard all day under the sun. Maybe never. Probably never." He took a sip of his drink. "Okay, definitely never."

Perry smiled around a bite of chicken and chorizo. "So what do you *do* up in Connecticut? You still in school?"

Colin thought about his answer. He took a look around the restaurant, taking in the intensely blue-collar clientele, and thought about the parking lot full of battered old Chevys and Fords, the mud-spattered Jeep Wranglers, the work trucks with the corrugated steel toolboxes bolted into the beds. "I don't really... do... anything," he finally said. "Not anything worthwhile, anyway. I'm afraid I... well, there might not be any better word for it. I think I'm a dilettante."

"Trust-fund baby?"

Colin rubbed the back of his neck. "Kind of?"

"No shit. You mean I'm sitting across from one of those mythical 'idle rich' types I've read about?"

"Please don't hold it against me."

Perry took another bite. Chewed and swallowed. "You sound like you regret it."

"More like I'm starting to get embarrassed by it. When I first got here, I could barely see the locals. I mean, I was just looking *all* the way down my nose at them, y'know?"

"Did something change that?"

"I don't know. Maybe. Hard to say. But I will say this: I've never met anybody like Reverend Jessup before."

"No black preachers in—Milford, right?"

Colin shrugged. "There might be. I'm not a church-goer. But it's not religion I'm talking about. Here's a man whose whole livelihood is taken up by that church, and it just got torn to *shit*, I mean, it was fucking leveled, and this little old man came rolling in like a ball of sunshine. It never even seemed to *touch* him. He just came in and pushed up his sleeves and worked circles around the rest of us, easy and grinning."

Perry nodded. "One thing I try to instill in all the kids I coach is the belief that hard work is its own reward. That hard work can be *fun*. That the sense of accomplishment you get will give you a rush just as good or better than beating some boss in a video game. Or getting high." He waggled his fork at Colin. "Reverend Jessup shares that. And you can damn sure believe he appreciates all the hard work you and your sister and her youth group are putting into the clean-up."

Colin gazed at the tabletop between his plate and Perry's. "This is not to say that I haven't been absolutely fucking horrified at some of the things I've seen and heard since I got here. Like that incident I told you and the sheriff about, at Aunt Petunia's."

"I remember."

"Do you know what Mrs. Billingsley said? When I was helping her hand out food? She said, and I'm only paraphrasing a little, 'We've got to show these black folks how to be. If not for us setting an example, well, they'd just stay home and have babies and collect welfare checks.'"

"Yeah, you told us at Big Harold's." Perry's eyes hardened around the edges. He set his fork down and drank from his margarita. "That right there, Colin. That right there is the biggest thing working against us, you want my opinion." He put his elbows on the table. "We ain't dealing with skinheads or fucking tiki-torch Nazis in Red Springs. It's this Old Guard mentality. *I think this way 'cause my daddy thinks this way, and his daddy before him, it's just the way the world works.* People who believe, all the way down to the marrow of their bones, all the way into their DNA, in their *souls*, that black people are less than white people. That we're—and I know this is gonna sound dramatic, but I mean it—they think we're not really *human*."

Colin winced.

Perry went on. "They believe it the same way they believe the sky is blue and water's wet and you need air to breathe. It's a given for them. A fact of nature. Of *course* black people are inferior. Of *course* they are." He leaned forward. "But they also think, if they're *nice to black folks anyway*, that means they ain't racist. They think they're being all magnanimous and shit, speaking to us politely, working alongside us. When they wouldn't no more have their son or daughter marry one of us than they'd shoot their own foot off."

Silence fell. Colin took a long pull from his drink.

Perry slowly unclenched. "Too soapboxy for you?"

"No. No, I believe every word you're saying. I just... fuck me if I know what to do about it."

"Most of the time I get drunk."

Colin grinned. "We're not making much headway about the dungeon, are we?"

"Shit. I keep trying to convince myself it's all just a hoax. If it's real... what do you do about something like *that*? Especially when Zandra wants to try to keep it away from the public?"

Colin opened his mouth to answer, but before he could, Perry's phone buzzed. He'd set it on the table next to the little square tub that held all the artificial sweetener packets, and when he picked it up and looked at the screen, his jaw dropped open. Wordlessly he turned it around so Colin could see it. A text from Zandra read *I'M IN TROU-BLE. COME TO THE CHICK-FIL-A BILLBOARD ON APISON HIGH-WAY. HURRY.*

Colin and Perry both pulled bills out of their wallets, threw them on the table, and all but sprinted out of the restaurant. Perry said, "You comin' with me?"

Colin had no real time to consider whether he should, but he didn't want to get left behind, so he just grunted assent and clambered into the back seat. Perry threw him a quizzical glance as he buckled his seatbelt, but Colin just said, "The sheriff'll want to sit up front with you, won't she?"

Perry gave him the briefest of shrugs as he cranked the engine. The tires squealed as he tore out of the parking lot and barreled north on

41. Colin heard a tremor in the older man's voice. "Zandra don't *ever* ask for help. Not ever. This's got to be bad."

Perry had clicked his phone into a holder attached to the dash, and as they sped up the road, another text popped up on the screen: *Don't stop. Just slow down, I'll run out and jump in.*

"What the hell're you into," Perry said softly.

Colin didn't know what to say, so he kept quiet, but he leaned forward and rested his arms and chin on the back of the front bench seat, peering out through the windshield. Perry crossed the line into Cartauga County and almost tipped the truck over as he made a hard left at an intersection with a flashing yellow light. Colin said, "Is this— what was it? Addison Highway?"

"Apison," Perry grunted, speeding up.

It looked more like a regular road than a highway to Colin, just two lanes running north through trees and open fields. The day had almost ended, and Perry's headlights came on, illuminating the road ahead and occasional deer crossing signs. They'd been on Apison Highway for right at four minutes, making their way around some serious winding curves, when the trees on the left fell away to reveal a huge, rolling pasture, and a ridge sprang up on the right. Toward the end of the pasture, someone had erected a billboard, currently occu-pied by a Chick-Fil-A advertisement with two three-dimensional cows standing on the catwalk, exhorting people to eat more chicken.

"That's the one she was talking about?"

"It's the only billboard like that between here and Apison, so yeah." The truck's nose dipped slightly as Perry applied the brakes, his head swiveling back and forth. "Come on, Zan, where are you?"

Colin caught movement off to the right and shouted and pointed. "There! I see her, she's right there, right there!"

Perry slowed the truck to barely fifteen miles an hour, and out of the darkness the sheriff sprinted across the shoulder and threw the door open.

Perry said, "Zan, what the f—" and the sheriff's body torqued forward, her face twisted in pain, and something sprayed into Colin's face and eyes and from somewhere he heard a high, sharp *crack*, and before he could get whatever it was out of his eyes, the truck lurched off the road into a ditch and slammed to a stop and Colin's head banged off the driver's-side door handle.

Someone started screaming.

Colin didn't think it was him, his head hurt, but it didn't hurt *that* bad, and he finally got his eyes clear and pulled himself up so that he could see into the front seat. At first nothing made sense. The light from outside, weak and gray and diminishing, barely made it into the cabin, and random, disjointed images came to him that didn't seem to have any connection to anything.

The sheriff had a gouge dug out of her shoulder, and that was bleeding. And her leg was bleeding. Colin didn't see any spurts, like when an artery got cut, but her whole right side was soaked with blood.

Everything sparkled. It took a few seconds to realize the passenger side window had shattered, and tiny crumbs of glass covered the sheriff and the seat and Perry—

Perry lay slumped against the door, and his head wasn't the right shape. The back of it ended right behind his ears. And the window it lay against had turned a red so dark that in the dim light it looked black. And one of his eyes was gone.

The sheriff called out Perry's name, over and over and over. Tears carved channels in the blood that had sprayed across her face, and the pain that scraped and carved its way out of her throat made Colin want to scream himself. Colin heard *Perry* and *No* and *Please* amid the agony, and as she tried to move Perry's body, tried to cradle him, the bleeding from her shoulder got worse and worse.

The rear driver's-side door was wedged against the side of the ditch they'd crunched into, so Colin climbed up and opened the passenger door, and had to stand on the edge of the seat to crawl out of the truck. His feet hit the ground as the door slammed shut, and he jumped up onto the running board and pulled open the passenger door. He had to let it rest against his back as he reached in and took hold of Sheriff Seagraves, his fingers hooked into her belt, and as he pulled her toward him she twisted around and fought him, drove fists at his face and clawed at his hands, but there was no strength to it. He pulled her to him, and put his face to hers, and said, "Sheriff, we've got to get you an ambulance."

She went silent. Colin thought she might have been going into shock, and as carefully as he could, he slid her down and over so that she sat with her back against the front tire. He heard someone say something behind him, and whirled around, and yelped when he saw a bunch of locals standing there holding rifles, all of them planted like statues, all of them staring open-mouthed and wide-eyed at the grisly sight.

There was the Porky Pig tattoo girl, and the vile old man from the hot dog line, and Tommy-June Billingsley, and a bunch of other people Colin had never seen before. All of them standing and staring, their hands gripping their rifles with white knuckles.

"Get away!" Colin bellowed. "Get away from us!" He grabbed his phone and called 9-1-1, and hit *Speaker*. Then he dropped the phone on the ground and wrapped his hands around the wound in the sheriff's shoulder, squeezing tight, horrified at the blood that seeped through his fingers.

The sheriff didn't move. Her head tilted back, and her eyes slid closed.

One of the locals said, "We can help—"

"*Fuck you!*" Colin screamed. He unleashed the full jet-engine fury of his voice, so loud and powerful that it slammed into them and drove them backward. "Fuck you, you fucking *shits!* You hate her this much? You hate her so fucking much you've got to fucking shoot her? *Her brother's dead!*"

Another local, a woman, said, "Ain't none of us shot her—"

"You fucking *animals*." He dialed it up further. "You fucking shit-sucking inbred fucking *parasites!* Get away! Get the *fuck* away!"

The small crowd took another few steps back. Colin heard a siren in the distance, and a minute later an ambulance screeched to a stop next to the truck. A couple of EMTs jumped out—a pair of young white men—and one of them said, "Holy shit, that's the sheriff." For a second Colin thought he was going to have to scream at them, too, to get them to do their fucking jobs, but they both rushed to the sheriff's aid, and seconds later had lifted her and put her on a gurney. As they slid her into the back of the ambulance, two Sheriff's Department cruisers approached at high speed, sirens and blue lights splitting the night air, but Colin never left the sheriff's side.

One of the EMTs said, "You'll probably need to stay and talk to the cops."

Colin snarled at him. "Fuck that. I'm going with her."

The EMT shrugged, and the ambulance door slammed shut as the first of the deputies left their vehicles. Colin sat next to the sheriff. Some part of him that he didn't fully understand insisted that he stay with her, to make sure no one else hurt her, and he kept a hawk's eye on everything the EMTs did as they cut the cloth away from the wounds on her shoulder and thigh and applied pressure bandages.

The sheriff opened her eyes. She turned her head, and saw Colin, and he flinched when she took his hand and squeezed it. Fresh tears spilled down her cheeks. "Perry," she said in a tortured whisper. "Is that... did that... happen? Is he... gone?"

Colin wrapped his other hand around hers. Lost, flailing, drowning, he reached for any words he could find. "I'm so sorry, Sheriff."

The sheriff sobbed. Once. Hard. Her eyes closed again, and she fell silent, but the tears didn't stop, and she didn't let go of Colin's hand until they got to the hospital.

III

LIGHTNING STRIKES

25

In Zandra's dream, Shaquana Taylor and Jimmy Biddles and Angelique Currant posed together on a beach at sunset. The flash of an unseen photographer lit them like bolts of lightning, and Shaquana's hair waved and played about her face, lifted by the winds as the sky beyond grew darker and darker. Jimmy had his shades on. Brilliant smile shining. Angelique had an armful of leis. Jimmy and Shaquana twined their arms together and sipped each other's cocktails, playful, intimate, while Angelique slipped leis over their heads.

Shaquana never opened her eyes. She turned her head, and Zandra knew the girl was looking at her, but the eyelids stayed shut, and when Shaquana spoke, it was Sonja's voice, cracking like thunder as the teenagers kept smiling.

"Why? Why, Zandra? You're the goddamn sheriff! Why did you call your brother?"

Zandra tried to explain, but she couldn't speak. Couldn't move. Couldn't close her ears and block out the voice of her brother's widow.

"You were getting shot at, and instead of calling the cops, you called Perry? What the fuck were you thinking?"

Zandra wanted to answer her. Wanted to say, *I couldn't reach Pounder, and I couldn't trust anybody else.* But the words locked up in her throat.

Jimmy and Shaquana slid their arms around each other, and sipped their drinks, and kept their grins, and blood began to seep out from between Shaquana's eyelids. Down from behind Jimmy's shades. Angelique's face shriveled and shrank and became a skull, and all three of them said, *"It's your fault Perry's dead. You killed your brother. You killed him. You should burn in hell for that."*

Zandra woke to the simultaneous sounds of Jordan softly whining and someone rapping on her door. She shifted her weight in the recliner, wincing at the pain in her thigh and her shoulder, and folded the footrest back up into the chair's body.

After the funeral, it had taken four days of near-nonstop ringing for her finally to answer the phone and talk to Angie Hubble. Four days of Angie, and then Mike, and then Angie again, trying to get through to her. When she'd finally answered, Angie had said a lot of things along the lines of *This isn't healthy, Zandra,* and *Please let us come and see you,* and *We want to help you,* and *You can't keep hiding from the world.*

Yeah, Perry's funeral had been all she could stomach of the world, thanks very much.

That last one-sided conversation with Angie was two days ago. Zandra hadn't spoken to anyone in those two days, and didn't think she'd eaten anything, either. She couldn't remember. In any case, she had run completely dry on willpower, and whoever kept knocking showed no signs of stopping, and Jordan padded along beside her as she finally shuffled to the door.

Zandra peered through the mullioned window and said, "Ah, shit." She glanced down at herself, took in the 3X t-shirt and the stained sweatpants, remembered that her hair was down and that she didn't have even the tiniest fleck of makeup on, and decided she couldn't care less.

The *bishōnen* kid stood there. Colin Massey. With a double-handful of grocery bags in his hands, half-silhouetted against the late-after-noon sun. Zandra opened the door, but didn't move aside.

"What do you want, Mr. Massey?"

Colin shifted his weight from one foot to the other. "You haven't answered any of my calls."

Zandra eyed him evenly. "That's correct."

"For a week."

She said nothing.

"So I thought I'd come by."

"How did you know where I live?"

"You're the sheriff. You're not hard to find." He peered over her shoulder into the house. "Damn, the inside of this place does not match the outside. You're going for, what, minimalism? Stark mini-malism? Is that a thing?"

Her eyes dropped to the plastic Piggly Wiggly bags. "Mr. Massey, what on earth possessed you to go out and buy groceries for a woman you barely know?"

A vertical line appeared between his eyebrows. "That's, uh... it's what you're supposed to do. Right? When there's been a, um, a death. They said you were on leave. I mean, I know how bad your shoulder is. I didn't figure you'd feel like doing much in the way of food preparation."

Zandra sighed. Her stomach might have growled. "No point in just standing here letting the bugs in and the cool out." She pushed the door wider. "Come on."

She led Colin through the living room and into the kitchen, and as he followed her, he let out a low whistle. "What's beyond minimalist? 'Spartan'? 'Antiseptic'?"

"You can set those bags there on the counter. Anything perishable in them?"

"Um. Yeah—some frozen stuff. To be honest, I didn't really know what I was buying, I just grabbed a bunch of stuff that looked like it might go together."

As he set the bags down, Zandra said, "Don't do much cooking?"

He shook his head. "Dario and Lupita take care of that."

"Who're they?"

"Our chefs. Well, a couple of them." Colin began un-bagging the groceries, but must have felt Zandra's eyes on him, because he turned and saw her and his face went pink. "Yes. We have chefs. Like I was telling…" His voice faltered. "…telling Perry, I've never had much in the way of… responsibilities, look, Sheriff, I'm so sorry. I'm *so* sorry. I didn't get a chance to know Perry as well as I would've liked, but every second I spent with him—he was an *excellent* person. It was obvious. In every way."

Zandra leaned against a counter. She stared at the floor. Her left hand absently traced the line of stitches under the bandage on her right shoulder.

Colin went on. "Anyway, y'know, since it's been a week, I figured I'd come and check on you."

She dragged her gaze up to look him in the face. "Mr. Massey, you may or may not have prevented me from bleeding to death. And I heard about your valiant efforts to defend me. For that I'm grateful. But what's going on in Red Springs is none of your concern, and you really don't have to waste any more of your t—" A thought occurred to her. "Your group. The church group. Y'all were only supposed to be here for seven days. You should've been back on the bus to Connecticut already. Why're you still here?"

Colin didn't look at her. He just kept unbagging groceries. "I, uh, I might've… rented a townhouse, up on Angel Ridge. Just. Y'know. Month to month."

Zandra ignored the pain in her thigh as she crossed the kitchen and spun him around to face her. "Why the *fuck* would you do that?"

She expected him to back away. She had on her angry face, and used her angry voice, and people backed away from her when she did that. But Colin Massey didn't. Zandra couldn't decide if it came from a lifetime of the most egregious kind of entitlement, or if the boy actually had stones. He just stood there, his nose inches from hers, and looked her dead in the eyes. "Sheriff, I think you can call me Colin. I'd prefer it if you did."

Zandra took in a breath to speak, and some kind of rich, dark scent flowed off of Colin Massey and into her nostrils, and she became abruptly and acutely aware that she looked an utter mess and wasn't wearing a bra and didn't smell all that fresh. She scowled and moved away from him—to the side, she did *not* back away—and used her left hand to begin sorting through the items he'd brought. The doctor had said the muscle in her right shoulder would heal up just fine, but at the moment it hurt to raise her arm enough that she didn't if she didn't have to. "You haven't answered my question."

"I'm staying for Perry."

She paused. "Excuse me?"

"When we went and had Mexican food. The reason I was with him —the whole point of that—was we were trying to help you figure out this dungeon thing."

Zandra's sorting slowed. "Did you? Figure it out?"

"No. No, we didn't, but he said... he said you were, uh, very independent, and often choose not to let other people help you—"

She faced him. "Oh, bullshit. Perry said I was pig-headed. Right?"

The corner of Colin's mouth twitched. Zandra thought it looked as if he were trying to decide whether any display of humor would be in good taste. Or even permitted. "He might have used that term, yeah. But what I'm getting at is that he said he was your sounding board. Like, your *only* sounding board."

"Mr. Massey. *Please* do not tell me you think you can step into my brother's shoes."

This time he did backpedal, his hands up. "No! No, of course not! But I do want to help you figure out what's going on. As poor a substitute as I'd be. I'd like to try."

Zandra separated the perishable from the non-perishable items, and further divided the frozen from the refrigerated. Mildly she said, "Hungry Man microwave dinners? You trying to say something?"

Now he did smile. A little. "I plead ignorance."

"Frozen meals, a bunch of random vegetables, and orange juice. I believe you when you say you've never cooked before. How are you supposed to eat, up there in your fancy townhouse?" Zandra actually knew exactly which place Colin must have rented. There were only a handful of townhouses on Angel Ridge, and only one empty one that she'd seen. "Don't tell me you're going to live off KFC and Hardee's."

"I've subscribed to a meal service. Food shows up in insulated boxes. I just have to heat them up." He cleared his throat. "And Merry Maids comes twice a week."

Zandra put the frozen and refrigerated items where they needed to go. "Look, there's no point spending any more time on this dungeon nonsense. Pounder's doing just fine running the department while I'm gone, and they've called in the GBI on everything else. It's out of my hands."

"The hell is the GBI?"

"Georgia Bureau of Investigation."

"Are you serious? That's a thing?"

Zandra glared at him. "Yes, Colin, we have a state investigative agency. Not all of us spend our days picking cotton and fucking our cousins, despite popular opinion."

He lost his smile. "I meant no disrespect. I apologize. Please forgive me."

"Look, I… thanks for the food. But, truly, there's no point in you trying to help me do anything. I'm done. Even after I heal, the town's lost what little scrap of faith they had in me to start with. I'll be stepping down as sheriff."

Colin surprised the shit out of her by moving close and putting his hand on hers, where it rested on the countertop. Surprised her to such an extent that she didn't think to pull hers away. "Sheriff. I don't know what's really out there. But whoever it is, the dungeon asshole, that's *got* to be who shot your brother. Right? And Major Pounder, and the GBI, they haven't caught anybody, have they? You'd know about it. Right? So let's try. Let's at least try our damnedest to put an end to this."

Jordan padded over and sat down next to Colin. He looked up at Zandra with his clear yellow eyes, and *whoofed* at her, and panted with his tongue flopped out. Colin knelt down. "See? This guy agrees with me. You know what's up, partner." He held his hand out. "Put 'er there."

Jordan raised his paw and plopped it into Colin's.

Zandra groaned. "Pour yourself a glass of wine if you want. I'm going to go see if I remember how to dress myself. And then I'll show you how pointless this all is." When she walked out of the kitchen, Colin had sat down on the floor, and Jordan had stretched out on his back to let Colin scratch his belly. Under her breath, Zandra muttered, "Traitor."

Twenty minutes later, after Zandra had pulled her hair back into a sleek ponytail, put on a bra and a pair of jeans and a halfway decent t-shirt, and applied about ninety seconds' worth of makeup, she and Colin sat at her dining room table and stared at her laptop. Jordan lay under the table with his head and front paws on Colin's feet. Every so often Colin reached down and scratched him behind the ears.

Zandra watched him do that, and said, "You know, you can take that animal with you if you want."

One of Colin's eyebrows twitched. "Really?"

She rolled her eyes. "Ugh. No. He stays here, the ungrateful mutt." Jordan whined and thumped his tail against one of the legs of Colin's chair, and Zandra said, "Yeah, you know when I'm talking about you, don't you?"

Smiling, Colin cleared his throat. "Okay. So, basically, you've got the dungeon, which appears to have been used to torture people. And you've got the souvenirs. Two of which you traced to their owners, who are alive and well. Has anybody in forensics come back with anything else on the others? The earrings and such?"

Zandra shook her head. "No. Not even the GBI's lab turned up anything, according to the last call I got from Vocker, which was yesterday."

Colin put his elbows on the table and rested his chin in his hands. "Can you show me those Facebook walls again? Shaquana's and Jimmy's and Angelique's?"

Zandra obligingly pulled up Shaquana's. She opened another window and put Jimmy's side-by-side with it. "Still no luck from any law enforcement where these kids are supposed to have gone, but see, they've all sent updates in the last couple of days."

"What happens when you try to reach out to them on Facebook?"

"No response. Every now and then they'll respond to their families, but they're just ignoring me."

Colin leaned forward, staring at the latest photos. There was Jimmy Biddle, still with his grin, still with his cool shades, tipping back a forty-ounce malt liquor on the beach. Beside him, in the other window, Shaquana Taylor appeared to be in the midst of a dance move in someone's living room, her eyes closed, her brow creased with concentration. There weren't any recent photos of Angelique Currant.

Colin stood up, carefully extricating himself from Jordan, and stretched. Zandra said, "Going somewhere?"

"Just moving around. If I sit in one spot for too long, I tend to get sleepy, and that doesn't do us any good." He wandered from the kitchen into the living room, and Zandra heard his footsteps come to a stop, and realized after it was too late to do anything about it that he must be standing in front of her display cabinet.

"Um… Sheriff?"

Groaning inwardly, Zandra stood and moved to the broad doorway between the kitchen and the living room. She leaned against the frame. Colin was indeed standing in front of the case, staring at it, probably wondering if maybe *she* was the dungeon freak. "It's called 'murderabilia'."

Colin turned toward her, his face pale. "What—what's—why do *you* have it?"

She came over and stood beside him, staring at the case's contents. "It started six… no, eight years back. My best friend from high school, Sharmelle Buckley, was murdered."

"Holy shit. I'm sorry to hear that."

"I found her. I was home on leave, and I found her, right in the middle of Red Springs, dumped out in a field behind the Walgreen's. She'd been raped and stabbed to death."

"Jesus. Did they—uh, was the killer, did they catch who did it...?"

"No. I found a section of his shirt. There at the scene. Sharmelle fought back, and must've cut him and ripped his shirt, because I know that material wasn't part of anything she owned. But the police... and by 'the police,' I mean Sheriff Cyrus Bigelow... he refused to believe it wasn't hers. Just dismissed it, said it wasn't evidence. Enough of us raised enough stink to get him to test it for DNA, but he just said the blood was all Sharmelle's. And then the bastard *gave* it to me. And I kept it."

Zandra tapped one nail on the glass, in front of the case's centerpiece: a roughly rectangular, ragged white piece of cloth with ancient brown bloodstains on it.

"I took it back with me. Don't ask me why. Maybe I didn't want it to get destroyed. Then, I don't remember who I told about it, but some of the guys started bringing me things. Items from murders. 'Here, here's a sandal that an Afghan guy wore when he cut his best friend's throat.' 'Here, have a scarf that an Iraqi woman wore before she blew up a checkpoint.' Shit like that." She paused. "It's fucked up, I know, but at this point it seems disrespectful to get rid of it."

Colin's forehead had become a mass of wrinkles. "Is it even legal to have this stuff?"

Zandra shrugged her left shoulder. "It is as long as no one reports it."

"Did you ever have the blood tested?"

"That was one of the first things I did when I got elected. Sharmelle's case is still officially open, but it's gone cold. The blood didn't match anybody in any database. Might as well belong to a ghost." She cleared her throat. "Come on, enough of one morbid thing. Let's get back to the other morbid thing."

Colin nodded. "Happy to."

When they'd settled at the kitchen table again, Colin said, "Something's bothering you about these photos. Isn't it?"

"Why? Something jump out at you?"

"I don't know. Coming back to them with fresh eyes, there's… shit, I don't know." He sat back in his chair, staring.

Zandra said, "Eyes *are* a part of it."

"What do you mean?"

She scrolled through, and pointed. "Shaquana's got her eyes closed in every single photo. And Jimmy never takes off those sunglasses."

Colin nodded slowly. "Huh. Yeah. What do you think that means?"

"Shit if I know. There's that, and… like you said, something else. Something's not right."

Colin squinted. "Wait. Go back to that last one." When Zandra clicked back to the previous photo, a shot of Jimmy Biddle on the beach, this time in the afternoon, Colin said, "Look at that shadow." He pointed at the shadow cast by a beach umbrella, stretching across the sand.

"Okay. What about it?"

"Now look at Jimmy's shadow."

Zandra's eyes widened. *"It's too short."*

"Either that, or the umbrella's shadow is too long."

Her heart began pounding. "Holy shit. Holy *shit*. The photo's been altered."

"Can you put some of Jimmy's photos side by side? With each other, I mean, not with Shaquana's."

Zandra clicked on several. Seconds later she had half a dozen lined up, and Colin snapped his fingers rapid-fire and tapped the screen. "Do you see that? Do you fucking *see* that?"

It finally fell into place. It was subtle, because the intensity of the light varied from photo to photo. But the source of the light in every single photo on Jimmy Biddles's wall came from the exact same direction. Zandra said, "Hang on, let me do this with Shaquana's." More clicks followed, and when she lined Shaquana Taylor's photos up in the same way, the similarity stared them in the face. "Holy fucking shit. If you know what you're looking for, it's right there."

Colin said, "These photos were all staged. Those backgrounds are fucking Photoshopped! But what does *that* mean? These kids are *posing* for the guy?"

Zandra turned in her seat and rested her elbow on the table, looking at him. "Maybe they are. Maybe they're doing it against their will. We might be looking at a kidnapping case instead of murder. Maybe they're being held somewhere." She took a deep breath through her nose and exhaled slowly, remembering all the souvenirs she'd found in the wooden box. "Maybe a lot more kids than just Shaquana and Jimmy and Angelique." Zandra turned back to the computer and accessed the department's database.

"What're you doing?"

"Looking for missing persons reports on kids Shaquana's and Jimmy's age in Cartauga County in the last year." The results appeared on the screen, and Zandra frowned.

"How many?"

"Two. And one of them was white."

Colin tilted his head to one side. "Okay. You don't think any of the, uh, the souvenirs could've come from a white kid?"

Zandra drummed her fingernails on the table. "It feels like he's targeting black kids. Can't say exactly why. From my gut." She went back to the database and expanded the search to Catoosa and Whitfield Counties. It still only brought up seven names. "That's not enough."

Colin watched her. "What're you thinking?"

"I'm thinking, if this guy went to all the trouble to kidnap these kids and made them pose for photos and rigged up the backgrounds, he's smart. He's really *fucking* smart. No wonder he didn't leave any traces on the souvenirs. And if the other missing kids are doing the same thing, sending messages home? Telling their families they're fine, that nothing's wrong? There wouldn't *be* any missing persons reports."

"So how do we find who the other souvenirs belong to, if nobody thinks anything bad's happened to them?"

Zandra folded her arms across her chest, grimacing at the twinge in her shoulder. "I've got an idea. You free tomorrow morning?"

Colin grinned. "As if I have anything else to do." Growing more sober, he said, "You going to share your insights with Pounder? Or whoever's there from the GBI?"

She nodded. "I'll write it up. You head back to your townhouse and get some sleep. Does it have an alarm system?"

"It does, yeah. Does this place?"

"Like you said. I'm the sheriff. Of *course* it does. So make sure yours is on. We haven't heard a peep out of this guy, but that doesn't mean he's not still out there." Colin stood and headed for the door, but Zandra caught up with him. "Listen. Colin."

He stopped, and turned, and looked down at her, and that scent found its way to her again. "Yeah?"

"Perry was right. You were right. I am pig-headed. But… thanks. This helped."

"Any time."

"You were… you were there. With Perry, when he—at the end. And you helped me. You *are* helping me. So I guess you can call me Zandra."

Colin's blue eyes sparkled. "Zandra. It's a beautiful name."

Her heart beat faster. She hoped it didn't show in her face.

He said, "See you in the morning, Zandra," and walked out. She locked the door behind him.

Zandra watched through the window as he started his car and pulled out of the driveway. When she turned around, Jordan was standing in the middle of the living room floor, watching her, his tail wagging and his tongue flopped out the side of his mouth. Zandra said, "Oh, shut up, you," and activated her own alarm system.

26

Zandra had barely knocked on the townhouse's front door when Colin opened it. He wore a loose, off-white linen shirt French-tucked into a pair of faded jeans, and what appeared to be a brand-new pair of Nike sneakers. Zandra, dressed in a UGA t-shirt and an old but very comfortable pair of khaki pants over work boots, pondered how unjust it was that Colin was the prettier of the two of them.

"New outfit?"

He shrugged lightly. "I have a delivery service."

Zandra paused, her mouth open, but closed it again and made her way back to the Tahoe, where Jordan waited on her. As Colin locked the front door, he said, "You know I can *hear* your eyes rolling."

Once they were in the truck, cruising down another of the battered two-lane roads that seemed to crisscross Cartauga County, Colin said, "Hey, so, can I ask you something?"

"I guess."

"How did someone like you wind up in a gritty reboot of *Blazing Saddles?*"

Zandra couldn't help it. The laughter escaped from her, and

though it felt wrong so close to Perry's death, at the same time it felt so *good*. "I love *Blazing Saddles*."

"Everybody loves *Blazing Saddles*. It's Mel Brooks and Richard Pryor at their finest. But seriously, how did the people of Cartauga County elect a black woman sheriff?" He paused, and spoke more quickly than necessary. "Or do you prefer African-American?"

"'Black' is fine. And the details of my election are public record. You could google them."

"Nothing like hearing it from the horse's mouth. That's horse in the most complimentary sense. Well, at least the least negative."

"Are you a nervous talker? Or is this what you're like when you finally relax?"

He shrugged with his eyebrows and looked at his feet. "I don't know that I'm ever going to relax again."

"That's fair."

"So? How?"

Zandra let out a long, slow breath. "I just retired from the Army a little more than a year ago. Did my twenty and came home."

Colin's eyes got big. "You *retired?* When did you join, when you were ten?"

"I'm thirty-nine, Mr. Moneybags. Do you want to hear this story or not?"

"Yes, yes, by all means, please continue. It's just that I thought you were in your late twenties. Thirty, tops."

Zandra had Colin pegged for twenty-two, *maybe* twenty-three. She wondered if he would have come and spoken to her so boldly in the restaurant if he'd known how much older than himself she was. "So, yeah, I came home, and I hadn't decided what I was going to do yet. But there was a sheriff's election coming up, and… well, you already know how I felt about the old sheriff. Turns out I wasn't alone in that."

"What did the people not like? Aside from the way he didn't handle your friend's case?"

"All the corruption, basically. Sheriff Bigelow was for sale. And if you were one of his poker buddies, or had connections to one of his poker buddies, well, you could do whatever you wanted. Permanent get-out-of-jail-free cards. He'd just hand them out, so to speak. Some people in the county wanted to get rid of him, but the man had run unopposed for the last thirty years. Then Perry got the bright idea that *I* should run."

Colin thought about that. "Protest candidate?"

"No one in their right minds thought I had a chance of winning. You've seen the lay of the land around here. But a black-owned printing business down in Dalton got wind of my campaign and donated a shit-ton of signage, and word of mouth started to spread, and all of a sudden I was running for sheriff."

"Wait… you were in the Army, I get that, but don't you have to have at least a little bit of background in law enforcement?"

"My twenty years? I was an MP for every damn one of them."

"Wow…"

"All we were trying to do was show the people that someone *could* oppose the man. That it wasn't just a given that Cyrus Bigelow would be the sheriff of Cartauga County forever."

"So what happened?"

"Four days before the election, Bigelow died in a single-car accident on Highway 5. And when the EMTs showed up, they found him in the wreck next to a thirteen-year-old black boy. And they both had their pants down."

She watched as that sank in. Colin's mouth quirked upward a few times. "So… you're saying… you beat a dead pedophile?"

Zandra snorted. *"Barely."*

Colin laughed. She almost joined him. She said, "Four days was just enough time for word of Bigelow's death, and the circumstances of it, to circulate around the county, but not enough time for how much everyone hated me to overcome their disgust. Most of the voters just stayed home. But we got everybody who wanted Bigelow gone to show up, and I got 50.2% of the vote."

"I don't know whether that's sad or impressive."

Zandra shrugged.

Colin said, "So where are we going, anyway? What's this idea you had?" He reached back and scratched Jordan between the ears. The big black dog sat in the center of the back seat, and when Colin touched him, he leaned forward and rested his chin on Colin's shoulder.

Zandra slid her shades on and adjusted the sun visor. Once they'd come down off of what she'd begun to think of as "her ridge," they'd turned east, and the sun flooded straight in through the windshield. Colin tilted his head and held one hand up to keep the glare out of his eyes. Zandra said, "We may or may not have a bunch of missing kids. What we know for sure is that Shaquana's and Jimmy's and Angelique's families all said they weren't expecting the kids to run off like they did. But since they're alive, as far as we can tell, and since we don't know who the other souvenirs belonged to, there aren't any missing-persons reports."

"Right, I got that."

"And you know you're in the buckle of the Bible Belt, too, yes?"

"I know most of the people around here attend church, yes."

"Well, that's where we're going."

"To church?"

"To a bunch of churches. Talk to a bunch of pastors."

Colin nodded slowly. "Reverend Jessup said he'd spent the whole day attending to his congregation. Visiting people who couldn't get out. Making sure they had what they needed."

"Yeah, that's a pastor thing. It's part of what they do. Or if they don't do it themselves, they have people that *do* do it." In a lighter tone, she said, "For God so loved the world, that He did not send a committee."

"I'm sorry—what?"

"Nothing. Baptist humor." She pointed ahead of them. "There's the closest one."

Coming up on the right was a small red-brick church with a black shingle roof and an incongruously large white wooden steeple. Zandra guided the Tahoe into the small gravel parking lot. Colin said, "It's a weekday morning. How do you know all these church people will even be there?"

"I made some calls."

"Yeah? How many churches are there around here?"

"In this county? Twenty-seven." She thought that, if Colin had been drinking something, he would have spit it out.

"*Twenty-seven?* Are you serious?"

"Cartauga's a small county."

"How many're in a big county?"

"Well, none of Georgia's counties are what you'd call *big*. Not compared with, say, South Carolina. Because we've got so many of them." She parked beside the church, and looked past Colin at a trailer set up behind the building. "Come on, follow me. But *let me do the talking*. Got it?" Colin nodded. Zandra rolled the windows down and spoke to Jordan. "Okay, you stay here, and don't let anybody take the truck. Got it?"

Jordan gave her his best floppy-tongue-panting grin and curled up in the backseat.

As they walked past the church, toward the trailer, Colin said, "Okay, I'll bite. How many counties does Georgia have?"

"A hundred and sixty."

"Jesus. How do you keep track of them all?"

"You look at a map. And to answer your question, Catoosa County's over to the west. It's a smaller one—bigger than we are, but smallish—and it's got sixty-five churches last time I checked. Don't worry, we're only talking to the black churches. That cuts the number *way* down."

"How far down?"

"Try seven. That's not so daunting, is it?"

Colin ran his hands over his face. "I guess this is what culture shock feels like."

"At least everyone here speaks English."

"I've heard people around here talk. It's debatable."

Zandra climbed the three wooden steps to the door of the trailer, and took in the vast difference between this one and the one where she'd found Finn Wilkins. The Wilkins trailer was dirty, the metal parts were rusted, and the sheet metal skirt around the bottom had fallen half apart. This trailer, on the other hand, basically looked like a neat, conscientiously maintained little cottage that just happened to be long and rectangular. Zandra pushed a button beside the door, and from inside came a cheery three-note bell. Pastor Klark McNabb answered the door seconds later.

"Sheriff. Good to see you. I sure am awfully sorry to hear about what happened to your brother."

Zandra inclined her head. "Thanks. I appreciate that."

"Who's your friend?"

"This is Colin Massey. He's consulting on the case."

Klark McNabb was forty years old but looked about twenty-eight, with close-cropped black hair, hazel eyes, skin a couple of shades lighter than Zandra's, and the trim, hard, quick physique she could spot as ex-military from a mile away. He wore a white undershirt, charcoal gray slacks, and house slippers, and he held the door open wide for them. Colin came up the steps behind Zandra and shook McNabb's hand.

"Colin. You can call me Brother Klark, or just Klark, if you'd prefer. Pleased to meet you."

Colin just said, "Likewise," apparently taking Zandra's instructions to heart.

The inside of the trailer gave no indication that it was anything other than a small middle-class home. McNabb's taste in furniture seemed to run to muted, earth-tone plaids, and he gestured for Zandra and Colin to take seats on an overstuffed plaid sofa. "Can I get either of you anything? Cup of coffee? I've got some doughnuts."

"I'd love a cup of coffee," Colin said, and McNabb veered into the kitchen.

"Doughnut to go with it?" he called out.

"No thanks."

"You sure? They're Krispy Kreme. Top o' the heap."

Colin smiled. "No, thanks, just the coffee'll be fine."

McNabb peered around the kitchen doorframe. "Sheriff? Anything?"

"I'm good, thanks."

McNabb came back, handed Colin a coffee mug with "WWJD"

emblazoned on it in huge letters, and sat in a big plaid-and-leather recliner across from them. "All right, then, what is it you wanted to talk to me about, Sheriff?"

"Your church takes prayer requests, I assume."

McNabb half-laughed. "Yes, ma'am, we certainly do." He lost the tiny grin that had curved his lips. "Do you want us to pray for someone?" He scooted forward in the chair. "Do *you* need our prayers, Sheriff? I know bereavement is a terrible thing, but I can assure you, the good Lord has a plan for all of us."

Zandra saw Colin's knuckles whiten around the handle of the coffee mug, but he didn't say anything.

"That's very gracious of you, Brother Klark, but we're not the ones I'm concerned about. What I'm looking for is families who've come to you because a son or a daughter has run away from home. Somebody maybe seventeen or eighteen years old. And it wouldn't be that they went missing. More like they moved to a different city, probably far away from here, and got a job of some kind."

McNabb didn't hesitate. "That'd be the Florians you're talking about."

Zandra felt an icy rush in her chest. She pulled out a small, spiral-bound notebook, clicked open a ball-point pen, and began making notes. "Tell me about the Florians."

"Tommy and Dana. Their daughter Freeja left home last year… early spring, maybe late winter. Just up and left one day, went to Chicago, got a job as a hostess at some high-class steakhouse."

Zandra successfully kept the excitement out of her voice. "Does she still contact her parents?"

"They say she does. Sends them messages on the computer. Facebook, I think."

Zandra felt Colin looking at her, and when she cast a glance his way, his expression conveyed what she was feeling: *bingo*. She said, "This is helpful. Do you remember any other instances like this? Other members asking for similar prayers?"

McNabb shook his head. "Not here, no. But I know I've heard Reverend Jessup comment on—" He broke off.

Zandra said, "What? Brother Klark, have you thought of something?"

McNabb's eyes narrowed. He stared into nothing. "I was going to say, Reverend Jessup described a similar situation to me at his church, four, maybe five years ago. But there was another one."

Colin had leaned forward, his elbows on his knees. "When?"

McNabb said, "Day before yesterday. Girl named Angelique Currant. Her mama told Reverend Jessup she'd gone all the way out to Las Vegas. Just hopped a bus, out of nowhere. She let them know she was all right, though. Sent them a photo."

Five minutes later, as Zandra and Colin climbed back into the Tahoe, Colin said, "Shouldn't you have gotten the Florians' address?"

Zandra cranked the engine. "The department's got it." She pulled out of the gravel lot and back onto the road. Jordan sat up and put his chin on Colin's shoulder again.

"Well… shouldn't you be calling this in? Getting, I don't know, getting a deputy or something to go talk to them? The girl's family, I mean?"

Zandra shot him a quick look, and realized in that half-second that Colin was smarter than she'd given him credit for. He said, "Oh, fuck me. This isn't an official police thing we're doing, is it?"

"I have reason not to trust the department." She paused. "Not the whole department, anyway. So no, this isn't official. I'll turn over what we find to the GBI, once we're done finding it. Agent Hirsch. I only know the man a little bit, but from what I've been able to tell, he's got a good head on his shoulders. Still—I'm supposed to be on medical leave, and everyone's aware of what happened to Perry." She took a moment to steady her voice. "We need to be able to convince Hirsch. We need to *overwhelm* him."

Colin settled back in his seat and folded his arms across his chest. He stayed silent for a solid minute. Then he said, "Okay. Then let's overwhelm the bastard."

By four o'clock that afternoon, Zandra and Colin had visited all seven black churches in Cartauga County. After the second one, Colin had begun to have a hard time sitting still. By the fourth, Zandra felt like joining him in his fidgeting. The picture emerging was horrific, to be sure, but it was also *coherent*. They had found the pattern. In church after church, one or two or even three teens had gone missing over the past seven or eight years, and in one case the church secretary remembered an instance from a full decade ago. Every one of them had assured their families that they were just fine, and proved it with regular photos and updates on Facebook.

Zandra had guided the Tahoe out of Cartauga, over into Catoosa, heading for another church, when Colin's stomach audibly growled. He said, "Sorry. Been a while since breakfast."

"You want to stop and get something to eat?"

"I can function on an empty stomach if you can."

Zandra surprised herself by flexing her left biceps. "You think I keep these guns loaded by fasting?"

Colin's mouth dropped open in cartoonish astonishment. "Sheriff Seagraves—was that *humor*? I didn't think you were allowed to make jokes!"

"Then you haven't hung out with enough cops." She pointed at something ahead of them and to the right. "See that place?"

"Oh God. You're taking me to a Waffle House."

"Have you been to one?"

"I have not. Closest I've come was Mrs. Daywood's daughter Sharice talking about them. And listening to Conan O'Brien make jokes about their waitresses."

"Then don't pass judgment. At least not yet." She pulled into the Waffle House's lot and parked. "What're you doing watching Conan, anyway? I thought all the young folks looked at was shit on YouTube. Dolan Twins or some other nonsense."

Colin flashed a dazzling grin at her as he opened the door. "Damn you kids! Get off my lawn!"

She rolled the windows down. "Jordan, you want some bacon?

Yeah? Then don't go anywhere." The dog flopped down on the back seat and rolled over, and Zandra reached in and scratched his belly for a few seconds.

Colin came around the Tahoe, following her as she approached the restaurant, but Zandra stopped when a familiar figure pushed the door open and walked out. Every bit as tall, gaunt, and oily as when she'd last seen him. Shep Curtis didn't have dentures, Zandra didn't think, but his smile still looked like a badly fitted set, the teeth coffee-stained and too big for his mouth.

"Sheriff Seagraves! It's so good to see you out and about! Please allow me to pass on condolences, not only from myself, but also from my sons, and Libby, and the rest of our congregation. If there is anything we can do to help you in this time of need, you only have to ask."

Zandra said, "Shep Curtis, Colin Massey. Colin, this is Shep Curtis. He's a preacher in Red Springs."

Shep shook Colin's hand. Zandra noticed as Colin tried surreptitiously to wipe it on his jeans afterward. "Lay preacher only, I'm afraid," Shep said. "I was called to lead our church when the pastor took ill. When God calls, well… one cannot resist such a desire, can one?" He gestured at the Waffle House. "Blessing in disguise, I'd say, that the sister location in our beloved hometown bowed to the might of the tornado. The bacon here is *par excellence*, wouldn't you say, Sheriff? And the pecan waffles are beyond compare. Doesn't it just have that, that…" He made an elaborate grasping gesture in the air. "*Je ne sais quoi?*"

"Oh," Colin said. "*Parlez vous français? J'ai étudié pendant quelques années. Est-ce que vous avez été en France?*"

The greasy smile on Shep's face fled as if blown away by a stiff wind. "Yes, yes, great. Sheriff, it's been a pleasure." Zandra watched him scurry across the parking lot to a fifteen-year-old Buick and disappear inside.

Colin stepped ahead of her and held the door open. "After you."

As she passed him, she said, "What the hell did you say?"

"I said, 'Wow, you're a pretentious asshole. Why don't you get lost?'"

Zandra let her lips curl upward. "Convincing."

At 5:30, after Zandra had dropped Colin off at his rented townhouse, she and Jordan went back to the Farmhouse. She sat in the parking lot and typed up a report on her department tablet, the windows down, a few precocious katydids chattering from the tall grass in the field across the road. A rare cool breeze blew through the Tahoe. Zandra hated that it made her fear another tornado.

When she was done, she took the tablet and the dog and walked through the side entrance right outside her office. She knew GBI Agent Wayne Hirsch would most likely be sitting at Zandra's desk. She would've preferred it if Horace Pounder could've taken the office while she was out, but as much as the rest of the department looked up to him, Pounder didn't seem to have a whole lot in the way of ambition, and stayed at his own desk where he was comfortable.

Zandra rounded the corner and headed for her office, Jordan at her heel, but slowed when she saw Pounder standing outside it. He heard her coming and shifted, and when he did, he revealed Wayne Hirsch leaning against the office doorframe. Both Hirsch and Pounder might as well have had voice balloons hanging in the air next to their heads reading, "Oh shit." Pounder started toward her, but Hirsch—a tall, blocky white man in his early fifties with an iron-gray horseshoe of hair—put his hand on Pounder's arm and stepped past him, stopping Zandra in the middle of the hallway.

"Agent Hirsch," Zandra said. Jordan sat down, watching Hirsch with his clear yellow eyes, but all the man did was size the dog up for a second before returning his full attention to her.

"Sheriff. There's been a development. Why don't we go into your office?"

Zandra followed Hirsch, past Pounder, Jordan at her heel again, and when she turned left into her office, she didn't try to stop the scowl from clouding her face. A woman she didn't recognize sat at her desk. Small, Asian, with a short, masculine haircut and a severe navy pantsuit. The woman stood and came around the desk, but didn't bother extending a hand. "Sheriff Seagraves. I'm Special Agent Danette Yu. Federal Bureau of Investigation. Is that dog safe around strangers?"

Zandra looked over her shoulder at Pounder, who lingered in the doorway. "Can you keep Jordan for a few minutes?"

Pounder nodded. "Sure thing. We'll be at my desk." He bent and held a hand out. "C'mon, boy. Let's see if I've got some dog treats."

Jordan cast an uncertain look up at Zandra, but followed Pounder. Agent Hirsch left along with him, and closed the door behind him. Agent Yu went back and sat down in Zandra's chair again, gesturing at one of the straight-backed wooden visitor's chairs. "Why don't you take a seat, Sheriff?"

"I'll stand, thanks. What the fuck is going on? Why is the FBI here?"

Agent Yu put her hands on the desktop. "The better question would be, 'Why wasn't the FBI called immediately?'"

"Because it wasn't a federal case."

"Evidence of a sado-masochistic serial killer didn't trip any alarms for you? Didn't make you think maybe our resources or expertise could be of use?"

"There's no indication that the person responsible for that—" she hesitated to use the word *dungeon* "—for the objects found in that basement crossed any state lines." She held up her tablet. "In fact, as I've detailed in a report that I was just about to give to Agent Hirsch, there's no indication that anyone even died. Kidnapped, maybe, yes. But we've got no bodies, and we *do* have evidence that at least two of the people involved are alive and well."

Agent Yu stared at Zandra for a few long moments. She reached into a jacket pocket and brought out a business card, which she slid across the desk. "Email me that report. Do it now, please."

Feeling more and more like a little kid called to the principal's office, Zandra tapped in Agent Yu's address and sent the file. Yu made no move to verify that she'd received it.

"Now, Sheriff, I do understand that condolences are in order. To say you've undergone trauma in the last week would be an understatement, and I'm not unsympathetic. So here is what I would very much like you to do: go home. Take another week. Take a month if you'd like, fully paid, of course. But this investigation is out of your hands now, and I would ask that you not interfere with it."

Zandra took a deep breath and relaxed her jaw, which she hadn't realized she'd clenched. "It's *my* investigation."

"Not anymore. We're exerting federal jurisdiction."

Zandra put her hands on the back of the nearest wooden chair. It trembled under her touch. "I'm the sheriff of this goddamn county, like it or not. Don't expect me to act like some obedient dog."

"All we're asking is that you stay out of our way. If you interfere…"

"What? What if I 'interfere'?"

"Then you can be charged with obstruction. I don't want that. I'm pretty sure you don't want that. But I won't hesitate if I think you're deliberately damaging this case any further."

Zandra stood there for… she wasn't sure how long, glaring at Agent Yu, but if Yu found that intimidating, she gave no outward sign of it. Finally Zandra said, "Fine. No interference. I'm assuming I can still do the rest of my job?"

"If you want to. I still think taking a leave of absence to recuperate is the best course of action, but if you want to work, by all means, go ahead."

"And you're going to read my report?"

"I'll get right on it."

Zandra just barely managed to keep from slamming the office door on her way out. She leaned against the wall in the hallway to steady her hands on the tablet, and sent a slightly modified version of the report to both Horace Pounder and Wayne Hirsch. She found both of them standing at Pounder's desk, while Jordan sat in Pounder's chair, panting and grinning as Pounder spun him in slow circles.

"Hey, boss," Pounder said carefully. "How, uh… how you holdin' up?"

"I just sent both of you a report. Please read it." She threw a stabbing glance back toward her office, then stepped closer to Hirsch. "I'm serious about the warrant."

Hirsch said, "Uh…what?"

"It's in the report. In the version I gave you two, anyway. Read it. I'll be in touch. C'mon, Jordan." At the sound of his name, the dog jumped out of Pounder's chair and came over to her. He licked her hand when she reached down to pet him.

Hirsch said, "Where're you going to be?"

As she left, Zandra said, "Out of the goddamn way."

27

Several hours later

Zandra recognized the pattern of Colin's knock. She heaved herself up off the couch and, as Jordan whined nearby, made her way to the door on unsteady legs. When she opened the door, staring up at him with eyes that didn't want to focus, Colin said, "Whoa. Sheriff. I didn't think you were supposed to bathe in whiskey."

Zandra had decided to go for comfort when she got home. She wore an old, ratty pair of gym shorts and a threadbare pink t-shirt, her hair was down around her shoulders again, and to absolute fucking hell with a bra. She was dimly aware that Colin noticed her bralessness. "What do you want, Colin?" Zandra felt a burst of pride that the words emerging from her mouth actually matched up with the words that had formed in her head. She'd given that about a fifty-fifty chance.

"I wanted to find out what was going on, but once again, you're not answering your phone. And if you're going to drink yourself into a stupor, why isn't your alarm system turned on? Was this door even locked?"

She shoved the door wide and shambled back to the sofa. Colin came in and shut and locked the door. He went over and sat down on the floor next to Jordan, who immediately flipped onto his back and asked for belly scratches. Colin obliged.

Zandra didn't think she could call the activity in her head "thoughts." That would have been too generous. It was more like a huge swirl of room-temperature soup. She picked up the bottle of Evan Williams from the coffee table and splashed more of it into her glass. "You want some? There's glasses…" She gestured vaguely toward the kitchen. "Somewhere over there."

"I think I'll pass, thanks. Look, Sheriff, you're out here in the middle of nowhere. And I'm guessing from your current state that you're not working on the case anymore, or at least not anymore tonight. So why don't you and Jordan come back to my townhouse? It's in a brightly lit area, lots of people around, much less likely that some deranged killer's going to stalk you. And I'll actually engage the security system."

She looked at him over the rim of her glass. "I said you could call me Zandra."

"Okay. Zandra."

"I'm not going anywhere." She nodded at the dog. "Neither is he."

"Then at least tell me what happened after you dropped me off this afternoon."

Zandra took a long sip of bourbon. She nestled back into the corner of the sofa where the back met the arm, and with the flat of her bare foot patted one of the sofa cushions. "Come sit on the furniture. Like a grown-up."

It took Colin a moment to unfold his long, lanky body and move to the sofa, and when he did, he sat down on the edge. Zandra said, "God Almighty, Colin, I ain't about to bite you. Try and relax."

"Zandra…"

She took the same foot she'd used to pat the cushion and pressed it against his midsection, pushing him back, and after a second or two he gave in and settled back into the sofa. She stretched her legs out so that her calves rested on his thighs. "You sure you don't want a drink?"

The only light came from the kitchen. She hadn't bothered to turn on any lamps in the living room, and the TV was off, but she saw the sparkle of his blue eyes clearly enough, and felt it when his breathing quickened.

"Zandra… Sheriff… this isn't why I came here."

Zandra twisted over and set the glass down on the coffee table. She scooted farther down on the couch, so that her knees were over his thighs now, and she watched him from under her lashes. "Just mind that bandage, all right? Leg's still a little sore."

Colin's hand touched her knee. Light, tentative. As if she might fly apart if he exerted too much pressure.

The voice in Zandra's head spoke much more loudly now, and spread south through her body. It said, *Fuck it. I need a win.* She pivoted on her ass, swinging her legs down to the floor, slid over and wrapped her arms around Colin, and before the poor white boy knew what was going on, she was kissing him. The pain from the wounds in her shoulder and thigh seemed distant, negligible, not a part of her world anymore—no more than Perry's death was—and as soon as she felt Colin's tongue in her mouth, she pivoted again and straddled him and felt him grow instantly hard against her grinding crotch.

"You been wantin' this," she said between kisses. "I seen you lookin' at my tits. You want 'em? You want 'em now?" Zandra pulled up her t-shirt, exposing her breasts. She cupped one in each hand and lifted them to his face. "You got 'em. They're yours. Take 'em."

Colin surged up off the couch, his hands under her ass, and Zandra's head swam as he supported her weight, carried her *easily*, and she knew in the next minute he'd be inside her, fucking her hard and fast, and she could finally, finally get something she wanted.

Instead Colin turned and set her down on the couch and backed away a step. Zandra blinked up at him, reorienting herself, and when the room stopped spinning, she said, "Oh, you want some o' that first? Fine, bring it here." She licked her lips as her fingers found the buttons of his jeans.

Colin took another step away from her. Out of reach. He said, "Zandra, this isn't right."

Zandra's t-shirt was still up around her neck, and she arched her back, and with a deep satisfaction, she heard him groan, the bulge in his jeans growing larger. She went to stand, so that she could stalk across the floor like a majestic leopardess, but she misjudged where the edge of the sofa was and instead of standing, she put her hand in the wrong place and pitched over sideways.

Colin was there in an instant. As he helped her upright, he tugged the edge of her t-shirt down again.

Before she even realized they were building, the tears spilled over. "You don't want me?"

Colin was still breathing hard. But she saw his jaw set. "Zandra, I've wanted you in my bed from the first second I saw your photo. You're half the reason I came down here. But I want *you*. The real you. Not the… the you that's going to regret something."

The room was spinning again. Slowly she reached over to the far end of the sofa, grabbed a quilt her grandmother had made, and pulled it around herself. Tucked her legs up underneath her and wrapped the quilt around her whole body so that only her head stuck out. She wanted to cover her head, too, but a tiny scrap of dignity still hovering around somewhere prevented her. She said, "I think I might already have some regrets."

Colin knelt in front of her. "Zandra. Let's get you dressed, and let's go over to the townhouse. Do it for me? So I'll feel better about both of us?"

She sniffed. "Where're you thinkin' I'm gonna sleep?"

"The place has four bedrooms. And it's furnished. You'll have your choice."

Colin's image swam in front of her. "Four bedr— Jesus God, boy, how much is rent on that place?"

He said, "Come on," and helped her get up. "What do you want to wear? I'll help you."

Jordan followed them as Colin took Zandra's arm and guided her into her bedroom. Under her breath, she muttered, "No win tonight," but when Colin asked her what she'd said, Zandra replied, "Nothing. Never mind."

Forty-five minutes later, dressed in a sweatsuit (with underwear and a bra underneath it), Zandra sat on Colin's rented couch in his rented townhouse, drinking a cup of rented coffee. Her buzz had left her, but the bourbon had begun seeping out of her pores. The living room had a big gas fireplace in it, which Colin had turned on once he'd gotten her settled, and now Jordan lay on the hearth in front of the flames, stretched out. Every ten minutes or so he rotated to expose a new side to the warmth.

"Well, he may never leave," Zandra said, watching the dog. "Silly to have a fire going in August, though."

"Yeah, but look how much he likes it." Colin sat down in a big chair on the other side of the fireplace. "So. You feel up to talking?"

"Depends. Are you going to bust my balls over that mortifying display back at my place?"

He gave her an easy grin, and Zandra wondered what it must be like to have that kind of confidence. It just poured off of him in waves, as easy as sweating. He said, "I was thinking more about the status of the whole investigation thing."

Zandra closed her eyes and made a soft snorting sound. "I'll tell you what the status is. I've been shitcanned."

"They *fired* you?"

"No, no. Sheriff's an elected position. Lots of red tape to go through if anybody wants to get me out of office sooner than the next election. No, they called in the FBI. It's a federal case now. Hotshot young agent, sitting in my own goddamn chair, telling me I bungled shit up so bad they don't want me anywhere near it."

"Damn. Okay. Huh." He pulled an ottoman closer and propped his feet up. "So what're you going to do now? Just let them handle it?"

"That's what they want me to do. Step away completely. Take a long leave of absence. Recuperate."

Colin hesitated before he responded. "You think maybe they're right? Have you, uh… have you talked to anyone? Gotten any counseling?"

Zandra didn't answer. She stared into the fire. Only the crackle of flames and the occasional tiny whimper of contentment from Jordan broke the sudden silence. She was safe. She knew she was safe.

So why did the room rip and tear in her mind? Why did it shred, letting her see the moonlit sand beyond it, letting her hear the screams?

Zandra had no idea what horror must have passed across her face, but Colin was there beside her in a heartbeat, his arms around her, and he took her coffee cup and set it down and said, "Zandra, what's wrong? What is it?"

She wanted to cry. She *hated* to cry, but she'd already done it in front of him. Why couldn't she cry now? Why had the tears locked themselves in tiny vaults filled with pain, denying her even that much release?

"I joined up right out of high school. Did twenty solid years, like I said. But you know what a black female MP gets to do? Or, well, I can't speak for all of us. You know what *I* did an awful lot of?" Colin shook his head. "I stood at doors and checked IDs. One base to the next, I'd get transferred and *bang*, right back on door duty. Did you know a lot of soldiers fucking *hate* MPs? Yeah. Think we exist to make their lives harder. Hassle them for no reason. So after the sixth or seventh year, I started angling to get patrol duty instead of door duty."

She couldn't stop the words now. She hadn't spoken of it in so long, and now the words marched forward, inexorable, undeniable.

"Patrol what?"

"MPs're in charge of base security. So part of what we do is patrol the perimeter. Except I guess that was too big a leap, so they put me and a guy named Schiller out at one of the base's gates. Instead of stopping soldiers on foot and asking for IDs, I got to stop whatever vehicle traffic came through. See if they were on the list or not."

"Where was this?"

"Afghanistan. And there we were one night, Schiller and me, making sure everything was kosher. And here came this car, this beat-to-hell piece of shit old Peugeot. We could tell something wasn't right, 'cause it was weaving a little, and then maybe twenty yards from the gate it just veers off the road and dies in the sand. And the driver's door opens, and I can tell somebody gets out, but it's two-thirty in the morning and really fucking dark, and all I hear are these *screams*. Worst sound I ever heard in my life."

"Jesus."

"So it turns out the only one in the car was this Afghan woman, and she's fucking *giving birth*. She went into labor and tried to make it out to the base, 'cause she thought we could help her. And I go out there and I'm screaming at Schiller to call somebody, get some help, I get out there to her and she's lying there in the dirt with her dress hiked up around her hips and there's this little tiny pair of *feet* coming out of her."

Colin's face got paler. "Breach birth."

"Okay, you know what that is. And you know it's bad." He nodded. "Well, not only is she giving birth the wrong way, but she's *bleeding*. There's blood coming out from around those little feet, and the mother's awake and she's looking at me and she's screaming, and she starts gesturing at her crotch, she's fucking frantic, and she's screaming like it's killing her. And Schiller, I don't know what the fuck Schiller's doing, I don't hear anybody coming, it's just me and this Afghan woman and her breach baby, but she's bleeding something fierce, and I figure if I don't do anything she's going to bleed to death right there and it'll be her dead and the baby dead too."

Colin swallowed hard. "What'd you do?"

"I pulled. I got a good a grip on those tiny little legs, and I pulled, trying to be as gentle as I could and still get the job done. And I look up at her and she's nodding, she's like, *Yes, help me*, she's nodding and I'm pulling and the baby slides out a little bit, I got it up to the waist, and I can see it's a little girl, I'm gonna help this woman give birth to a little girl out there in the fucking desert, and God there was so much blood. And she's nodding, and moving her hands like *Keep going, keep going…* but the baby wouldn't come out any farther. I didn't want to hurt it, y'know, I didn't want to mash anything that shouldn't be mashed, but I knew I had to get it out, and I pulled harder, and pulled harder, and I heard this *sound*, and the baby slid the rest of the way out."

The night sky lived there in Zandra's mind. The living room and the fire and the dog and the boy finished shredding themselves and fell away, and the smell of dust and blood filled her nose and the screams of the mother drilled into her ears, and something that felt like a steel claw reached into her chest and squeezed and squeezed until it cut her heart into ragged strips.

"Except… except… I didn't know anything about breach births, I didn't know anything about what the umbilical cord could do. I just knew I had to try to help that woman. I had to get that baby out of her. So they could both live."

Colin's breathing had grown shallow. "But you did. Didn't you? You got the baby out?"

"I held the baby up, and right then I saw these flashlight beams come bobbing across the ground at us, it was Schiller, he'd called the medics, and they were all coming out to help, and I held that baby up for them to see." Zandra's throat tightened, and all the blood and pain of her shredded heart finally forced its way out of her eyes. "And it *didn't have a head.*"

"Oh God. Oh, God, Zandra—"

"That was the sound I heard. Like… like a *ripping*. I pulled too hard. And I tore that baby's head loose and left it inside the mother."

Colin held her, and gently rocked her back and forth, and she let him, but it didn't lessen the pain. "And I called Perry, I called my brother, I put him in harm's way and he's dead because of me. Just like that baby. *Just like that baby.*"

Colin held her and stroked her hair. Zandra soaked his shirt with her tears and pressed her cheek against his chest and felt his heartbeat in her bones. She waited for him to say something. To tell her that it wasn't her fault, to tell her that she was only trying to help, that she was only trying to survive. To tell her something that she knew she wouldn't believe. But he didn't say anything, just held her and stroked her hair, and Zandra cried herself to sleep in his arms.

Zandra woke before Colin the next morning. He'd put her in the guest bedroom nearest the living room, and when she'd gone upstairs to his room and made sure he was still asleep—he didn't snore, but his door was cracked, and she heard his deep, even breathing—she crept back down, got her shoes, and made for the door. Except the number pad for the alarm system was right there, with a little red light staring at her and the words, "SYSTEM ARMED" scrolling across a green LCD display.

Zandra searched the place, quickly and methodically, and in a drawer in the kitchen she found the owner's manual for the system with the PIN written inside the front cover. Zandra called a Lyft, deactivated the system, and slipped outside with Jordan. While she waited for the car, she let Jordan do his business past the edge of the parking lot where the trees started.

Standing there, she turned in a slow circle, taking in the townhouses and the ridge rising beyond them. She and Perry had spent long summer hours around there when they were kids, hiking along Angel Ridge's trails. Zandra wondered how many of the trails were left, and how many had been bulldozed.

It had rained at some point during the night. Water glistened on the cars and shallow puddles dotted the lot. Zandra savored the feel of the air—the sun hadn't risen high enough yet to turn all that moisture to steam. From somewhere higher up the ridge, the scent of honeysuckle caught a ride on a breeze and made its way down to her, and she turned her face up toward the morning sun. For a minute or two, she pretended her town hadn't been torn to shit, and that there wasn't some kind of depraved maniac out there doing God only knew what to innocent kids.

She sat down on the sidewalk outside Colin's townhouse. No one else was up and moving, or they were already gone to work. Either way, Zandra was alone and grateful for it. Jordan came over and pushed his muzzle up under her hand until she petted him.

When the Lyft showed up, the driver—a white woman in her mid-thirties who might as well have had a sign on her forehead reading *BORED HOUSEWIFE*—took a look at Zandra and Jordan and said, "No, uh-uh. Sorry. I can't have an animal in the car."

Zandra realized the woman had no idea who she was, and after thinking about it for a second, decided that was just fine. She didn't have her badge with her anyway. It was a miracle she'd remembered to bring her phone. "Look, I don't have that far to go, and he's very well-behaved. What if I threw in a big tip?"

The driver looked skeptical. "How big we talkin'?"

"How big would do the trick?"

Ten minutes later, the most expensive Lyft ride Zandra had ever taken ended as the driver dropped her off in front of her house. She hadn't brought her keys with her, either, but she punched in the code on the pad next to the garage door and listened to it clunk and rattle its way up. With the alarm set, she rarely bothered to lock the door from the garage into the kitchen, and she walked past the parked Tahoe and into the house.

Zandra stopped in the middle of the kitchen floor.

Something seemed... off.

She couldn't put a finger on it, but she turned, scanning the kitchen, Jordan panting beside her, searching for something out of place. Anything. Anything to justify the hairs standing up on the back of her neck.

Nothing.

Jordan trotted over to his bed in the living room and flopped on his side and stretched, but as soon as she started pouring dog food he sprang back up and charged into the kitchen, his whole face disappearing into the bowl as he ate. Zandra frowned. "If you're not agitated, then I'm probably over-reacting."

She searched the rest of the house, room by room, and still found nothing. Finally, twenty minutes later, with all the doors and windows locked and her alarm system activated, Zandra relaxed enough to get undressed and take a shower. She felt better after that, though thoughts of her humiliating escapades with Colin the night before kept swatting her, slapping at her, making her cringe. She got dressed in work boots, khaki slacks, and a Sheriff's Department polo shirt, and ate a couple of microwave sausage-biscuit sandwiches while Jordan sat and stared at her. Zandra sipped the instant coffee she'd made to go with the food and gave the dog side-eye. "You're not getting any biscuits," she said, "so don't even bother asking."

Jordan whined and pawed at her thigh, but not with much enthusiasm.

Zandra finished her breakfast, slipped her Glock into a concealed holster tucked inside her waistband, and headed for the garage with Jordan at her heels. She opened the Tahoe's front passenger door for him and let him jump inside, went around and got behind the wheel, and cranked the engine. The feeling that something wasn't right still nagged at her, buzzing around her head like the tiniest of gnats, but she could find exactly nothing to back it up, so she raised the garage door and headed out.

Her phone rang: VOCKER. "Seagraves here."

"Uh, Sheriff, I guess you know about the Feds? Showing up? Right? And, uh, taking over?"

"I'm aware."

"And you know my buddy Wes, down in Rome, was working on that cell phone."

"Yes...?"

"Yeah, well, his results came back, and that li'l Oriental lady grabbed 'em up first thing. Except I, uh... well... I sort of made a copy."

Zandra wanted to say, "Bless your rule-breaking heart, Vocker," but instead she just said, "And?"

"And I've got some info for you. There wasn't much on the phone in the way of photos or files or such, but I got quite a few text messages. I can send 'em your way."

"Were you doing this work on a department computer?"

"No, ma'am. My personal machine."

"Well then let's keep it personal. Send it to my Gmail address. You've got that, right?"

"I do, ma'am. Sending now."

"Thanks, Vocker. I owe you one." She ended the call, and her phone immediately dinged with the sound of incoming mail.

Zandra parked in a little pull-off at the top of the ridge, about an eighth of a mile from her house, from which she got a pretty decent view of the town.

Vocker had copied all the text messages into a Word doc. She turned her phone sideways and blew the screen up to get a better look.

Most of what she saw made very little sense at first glance. Vocker had highlighted the number belonging to the phone Colin had found, and Zandra saw exchange after exchange with a bunch of other phone numbers. At the top of the list Vocker had left her a message: *All the numbers with Atlanta area codes are burners.*

She scrolled through the messages. They looked like gibberish for the most part. She could pick out dates here and there, and a few sequences of numbers that she figured were probably times, and a mass of what appeared to be random words. Zandra muttered, "What kind of code were you using, Sheriff Bigelow?"

She got into the second page of the transcript and stopped short. Vocker had highlighted a group of messages that had all come from a number with a Red Springs exchange. Seven messages, a few minutes apart, dated...

"Wait. What?"

Zandra switched over to her phone's web browser and did a quick search, and when the results came up, she said, "Holy shit on a saltine." Jordan stretched out and put his chin on her thigh and looked up at her with his yellow eyes, and as she scratched his head, she said, "At least part of this is starting to make some sense, boy."

The Red Springs number had sent the former sheriff seven messages, two days before he died in a car wreck, and each message read either, *YOU BASTARD* or *WHERE ARE YOU?*

Scrolling further, she saw that Vocker had looked up the number, confirming the search she'd just done. It belonged to Kella Bigelow. The dead sheriff's wife.

Zandra spent a few more minutes poring over the gibberish texts, which she knew good and well were anything but gibberish, and for a moment she thought she'd seen something noteworthy. But the screen was too small and the letters too cramped and her eyes still too gritty to give it the attention it deserved, so she resolved to look at it on her home computer as soon as she could. As soon as she went and had a talk with Sheriff Bigelow's widow.

Zandra put her phone to sleep, shifted the Tahoe into Drive, and nosed out onto the road. It was steep, the way up to her house, with several sheer drop-offs that she'd lobbied the county commission to reinforce with some guardrails. Each time she'd been told the matter had been "taken under advisement." Zandra entered the first curve, tapped the brakes—

—and the pedal sank all the way to the floor.

Zandra said, "Oh *shit.*"

She stomped on the emergency brake pedal, felt the ratcheting as it tried to engage, but it didn't work. The Tahoe picked up speed.

On her right, the ground dropped away, a nearly sheer slope dotted with old trees and boulders. On her left, a series of driveways flashed by, each of them steeply slanted as they climbed up the side of the ridge to houses above the road. Another curve came up, this one bearing sharply to the right, and Zandra skidded around it, feeling the Tahoe shift hard onto the left-hand tires.

Beside her, Jordan sat up straight in his seat and whined and barked.

"This is about to get bad, boy," Zandra said, and swung into the next driveway on her right at forty miles an hour. The two-story house at the bottom of the driveway loomed in front of her like a mountain.

The Tahoe mowed down the mailbox, side-swiped a tree next to the driveway, and skidded off the pavement and across the front yard, digging enormous trenches in the grass. Zandra tried to steer the big vehicle around the house, and mostly succeeded, but glanced off the corner, scraping the shit out of the whole passenger side and leaving the side mirror embedded in the house's mountain stone foundation. The Tahoe shuddered as she plowed down a concrete bird bath, and Zandra gritted her teeth and gripped the wheel as tightly as she could as the vehicle's path took it straight into the side of an above-ground pool in the house's backyard, triggering the steering-wheel airbag.

Seventeen thousand gallons of water erupted around the Tahoe, shoving it farther back up into the yard, but since the house was built on the side of the ridge, the miniature flood ran down and away from her, smashing small trees flat and scraping the hillside clean of grass and flowers. Zandra watched, breathless, as the pool's walls collapsed, pulled free of their moorings, and slid away down the hillside, following the path of the water.

Jordan whimpered. One of the impacts had knocked him into the backseat. "Jordan!" Zandra fought aside the now-deflated airbag, stepped out onto the rutted, muddy earth, and yanked open the back door. "Jordan! Are you hurt? Are you okay, boy?"

The massive pit bull whimpered again, but she couldn't see any cuts, there was no blood anywhere, and after a few seconds he came forward and licked her face, his hindquarters wiggling. Zandra hugged him and stroked his back—and a scent reached her.

She bent over. Peered under the SUV and took a deep breath.

That was what had bothered her so much when she'd come back home this morning. She just hadn't put it together. Standing there inside her house, vanishingly faint though the scent had been, Zandra had smelled brake fluid.

She pulled out her phone and called Horace Pounder, just as a bewildered middle-aged man emerged onto the house's back deck.

"Uh… Sheriff Seagraves?"

She waved at him. "Don't worry, sir. The department has excellent insurance."

29

Zandra was sitting quietly at Pounder's desk, in one of his visitor's chairs, typing up the incident report about the crash, when Special Agent Danette Yu found her. Jordan lay at Zandra's feet, and looked up at Agent Yu for a second, but then laid his chin back down and closed his eyes. Zandra said nothing as Agent Yu turned the other visitor's chair to face her and delicately perched on it, ignoring the huge dog.

"Sheriff Seagraves, this is not what I meant when I said you should rest and stay out of trouble."

Zandra set the tablet she'd been typing on to one side. "Believe it or not, I didn't wake up this morning and say to myself, *Hey, I think I'll cut my brake line and almost get me and my dog killed.*"

Agent Yu sighed. "I don't suppose you did. I would like to know, though, if this has anything to do with the—" she said the words with clear distaste, "—torture dungeon."

Zandra folded her arms across her chest. "You tell me. You've had a Bureau forensics team crawling all over it, right?" Yu's brows drew together. Zandra said, "Yes, yes, I'm off the case, I know, you're not telling me shit. But I guess it'll make you happy to hear that I don't think this brake line business has anything to do with it."

Yu cocked her head to one side. "What does it have to do with, then?"

"I'll let you know after Vocker has a look at exactly what was done to my Tahoe. And after I have a conversation with someone."

Zandra stood, and Yu popped up beside her, and for the first time Zandra realized that Special Agent Danette Yu only came up to her shoulder. The difference in height seemed to irritate the smaller woman. Yu said, "So you're just going to blow off the whole 'take a leave of absence' thing."

"Agent Yu, I have already stepped back from one case. You go ahead with it. I won't interfere. But I'm going to keep working."

"That's fine. Work. But you're behaving as if you're a detective. You've *got* detectives. Assign whatever case you have, whatever lead you want to pursue, to one of them. I may not know all the ins and outs of how a sheriff's department is run, but I do know that every sheriff I've ever talked to has been a lot more preoccupied with budget concerns than with clearing cases. They have to be. That's the job."

Zandra didn't get any closer to Agent Yu, but she straightened up to her full height, looming over her, and spoke in the same low, dangerous tone she'd used when convincing drunken soldiers that she meant business. "This is *my* department. The job is what I say it is."

Jordan followed her as she walked away from Agent Yu, who watched her go in silence.

One of the patrol officers, a skinny white boy in his mid-twenties named Holcomb, took Zandra and Jordan to a storage unit out in the western part of the county. Holcomb spoke only when spoken to.

That silence was more than fine with Zandra. Just being around one of the department's deputies—she couldn't bring herself to think of them as *her* deputies now—brought back the whole experience of being hunted. Of Perry dying right in front of her. It was broad daylight, a few minutes past noon, and she did her best not to let any tension show, but Zandra's hand never strayed far from her sidearm.

Halfway to the storage unit, the cruiser passed Gush Parsons, shuffling along on the shoulder of the road, staring at the ground. Zandra turned to look at him as they rolled by—he had on a different pair of stained sweatpants, with a long, shiny strand of drool hanging off his bottom lip—and considered asking Holcomb to stop so they could offer Gush a ride. Instead, after a few seconds, she settled back into her seat without saying anything. The teenagers who'd picked on Gush at the hospital were the exception rather than the rule; most of the county's populace was happy enough to let him shuffle along his way unperturbed. With a brief, perverse pang of envy, she wondered what that would feel like. No one caring enough about you to bother you.

Zandra thanked Holcomb perfunctorily and sent him on his way, found the unit she'd rented right after coming home from the Army, and was about to turn the key in the lock when her phone buzzed. Colin Massey's name flashed across the screen, and Zandra stared at it long enough to let it go to voice mail. A few seconds later, a text from Colin popped up: *Whered u go? U ok?*

Zandra grumbled, "Millennials," and quickly responded using complete words and sentences, the way she thought anybody with an IQ higher than their shoe size ought to do. *Don't worry, I'm fine.* She hit SEND and, on what she acknowledged to herself as an ill-advised impulse, followed that with, *I'll call you later. Z.*

That last single letter stared back up at her from the phone screen. She was, what, fifteen years older than Colin? At least? On top of that, he had more money than her entire family combined had ever seen. He was a yankee. And he was the liliest of lily-white.

Z.

What business did she have, not only being on a first-name basis with someone like him, but using a stupid flirty initial like that?

Still…

She'd behaved abominably last night. She remembered every second of it—Zandra had never gotten black-out drunk in her life—

and part of her cringed when she thought of how she'd thrown herself at him, grinding on him, rubbing her tits in his face like some ten-dollar crack whore.

Still...

She remembered his words, too. *"I've wanted you in my bed from the first second I saw your photo."* And, *"You're half the reason I came down here."* A thrill coursed through her at the memory, settling in her stomach, and she all but ripped the lock off the storage unit's roll-up door, muttering, "Stupid, stupid, stupid," under her breath.

She remembered how he smelled, and did her level best to ignore it.

Inside the storage unit, covered with a tarp, sat the car that Zandra had saved money for throughout her high school years, bagging groceries for long hours at the Piggly Wiggly: a 1992 Camaro Z-28. She pulled the tarp off, revealing the paint job that was supposed to be a solid, perfect matte black, but was instead a misbegotten combination of matte black, red, gold, primer, and rust. Regardless of how it looked, Perry had kept it maintained for her, and when she turned the key in the ignition, the engine roared to life.

Jordan eagerly jumped into the passenger seat. Zandra rolled down the windows. "Sorry, boy, the air conditioner never has worked in this thing. Just don't jump out when we're tooling down the road, okay?"

Jordan *whoofed* at her. Zandra pulled out of the storage facility's parking lot and headed for Ware Valley Road, and Jordan stuck his head out the window, tongue flapping.

When she got to Kella Bigelow's place, pulling up between the stone lions, she half-expected the big black gate to open up with no prodding. But this time it just stood there, looking imposing, as it was designed to do, and Zandra hit the CALL button on the security keypad. After half a minute, the widow's voice crackled out at her. "Sheriff Seagraves? What can I do for you?"

"You can let me in, Mrs. Bigelow. We need to talk."

Fifteen seconds passed before the gates opened. Zandra wondered what kind of thoughts must have been going through Kella Bigelow's head. She'd been prepared to nudge the gates open with her car if she'd needed to, since any scratches or scrapes would hardly make the paint job look any worse.

Zandra parked in front of the massive house and told Jordan to stay put. He jumped over into the driver's seat and put his paws on the wheel, but made no further move to follow her. As she walked up to the front door, Zandra muttered, "Look at me, I'm a human, I can drive. Honk honk." She rang the doorbell, and Kella Bigelow opened the door before the chimes had finished sounding out.

"Come in, Sheriff. What did you want to talk to me about?"

Zandra spotted a couple of suitcases in the foyer that looked as if they'd cost as much as her Tahoe. "I'm sorry, did I interrupt vacation plans?"

Kella blinked at her. "What?"

Zandra pointed. "The suitcases. Are you going somewhere?"

"No, I'm not going anywhere. Here, come and have a seat." She led the way into a sitting room, and the gears turning in Zandra's head threatened to come off their shafts and crash into each other. For a woman who'd done what Zandra suspected her of doing, she was playing it *intensely* cool. Kella gestured toward a couch, and took a seat in a wing-back chair. "So what's this about?"

Zandra took a deep breath. Might as well dive in. "The last time I was here, you and I heard a car approaching as I was leaving. Neither of us could see it, but it was loud. Extremely loud. Do you remember that?"

Kella looked more and more confused. "Vaguely. So?"

"So I thought it was on its way to the classic car show in Chicka-mauga, but you said, and I quote, 'That's no classic.' You said that without even seeing it."

"Uh. Okay. Again—so?"

"So it made me curious. And I did some digging. Your father was what people call a 'shade-tree mechanic,' wasn't he? Had a shop out behind his house? Worked on cars, nights and weekends? Extra income?"

Kella sat back in the chair. "Yes, that's right. It was more of a hobby than a second job, though."

"Okay. But my point is this: you knew that car was no classic *just by hearing it.* That takes some knowledge. You know a *lot* about cars, don't you, Kella? More than the typical *nouveau-riche* PTA mom. More than your sisters down at the Daughters of the American Revolution."

One side of Kella Bigelow's face wrinkled up, and the Red Springs accent emerged. "I'm startin' to feel like a broken record here, Sheriff, but *so what?* I grew up with a mechanic. You can't do that without pickin' up a thing or two. What's that got to do with the price of fuckin' tea in China?"

"Well, the thing is, I went back and took a look at the file on your husband's death."

Some of the color drained out of Kella's face, but otherwise she didn't budge. "Still bound an' determined to drag that all out into the spotlight again, huh? What is this, a plank in your campaign platform? You gonna solve all the county's cold cases?"

"No. Just this one. Because *you* cut your husband's brake line, didn't you? You knew how to make it look like normal wear and tear. Like it tore loose in the wreck. Right? I saw the texts you sent to him. *You bastard. You bastard.* Over and over. And I'm betting that's because of what you saw on his phone, isn't it? All the code? The times and dates?"

The rest of the color had dropped out of Kella's skin as Zandra talked. "I didn't see shit on his phone. I only overheard that miserable sumbitch *talkin'* on it. Heard 'im all romantic-like, talkin' sweet, that's when I knew he was cheatin' on me. So I waited till he was out of the house, and I rooted around in his shit till I found where he had the number hid. Secret fuckin' phone, an' he was so addle-brained he had to write shit down for it. So yeah, I sent those texts, and I shouldn't've, but I was fuckin' *blind* I was so mad, you hear me?" She folded forward, hugging herself, her head between her knees. "And what'd he do? Fuckin' *denied* it. Denied all of it. But I knew. I knew how to make 'im pay for it."

Kella sat back up, consumed with fury. "How was I s'posed to know he'd have some goddamn little nigger boy in the car with him? How was I s'posed to know they was suckin' each other's cocks? He was just supposed to run off the road and *die*. 'Single car accident claims the life of local sheriff, film at eleven.' I didn't ask for that whole fuckin' three-ring circus, them throwin' around words like *pervert* and *pedophile* and *nigger-lover*. I never asked for none o' that shit."

Zandra had to fight to keep her mouth from falling open. It felt a bit like watching a gruesome train wreck.

"Well, now, hold on, Mrs. Bigelow—"

"Oh, for fuck's sake, Sheriff. Call me Kella. You're makin' me feel fuckin' ancient."

"Fair enough. Kella. If you didn't see any of the things on your husband's phone… then why did you pull the same stunt with me?"

Kella frowned. "Huh?"

"The brake line. On my Tahoe."

"What the *hell* are you talkin' about?"

If the widow was acting, it was the best performance Zandra had ever seen.

"Last night. Someone cut the brake line on my Tahoe. Almost killed me."

Kella Bigelow burst out laughing. "And that's why you came out here, all determined an' shit? Sheriff, last night I was at the casino in Cherokee with the Red Hat Club. We just got back this morning. I hadn't even been home half an hour when you got here. That's why the luggage's still sittin' there."

It was Zandra's turn to frown. "And I suppose all of the other Red Hat ladies will swear you were with them?"

"Shit fire, Sheriff, I won seven thousand dollars at the blackjack table. They got it on video. You want receipts? I got 'em. I ain't done *shit* to your Tahoe."

Zandra heaved a long, drawn-out sigh and stood up. "All right, Kella. On your feet. You're under arrest for the murder of Cyrus Bigelow."

Kella stood and held out her hands. "That bastard made my life miserable for twenty-seven years. Bring him back from the dead and I'll do it again."

Zandra clicked the handcuffs around her wrists. "I'm sure the jury will appreciate that."

Zandra had just gotten Kella Bigelow situated in the Camaro's passenger seat—Jordan had obligingly settled himself in the backseat, and seemed to be actively ignoring the widow—when Zandra's phone made a noise she'd never heard before. She pulled it out of her pocket and saw an alert from Facebook Messenger.

"Hang tight a minute," she said to Kella, and moved a few paces back toward the house, just enough to step into the shadow. Now that she could see the screen clearly, she opened the Messenger app, and almost dropped the phone.

At the top of the screen was the name *Angelique Aphrodite*, and the tiny portrait next to the white message bubble showed her Maxine Currant's daughter. The message was in all caps.

Y U LOOKIN 4 ME

Zandra hit the phone-handset-shaped icon at the top of the screen. It didn't work. There was no phone number associated with Angelique's account. Slowly, she typed in a response.

Are you all right, Angelique?

The answer came back swiftly.

LIVIN MY BEST LIFE

Then,

Y U TRYNA TALK

LEAVE ME B

Zandra typed as fast as her thumbs would allow. She kept having to backspace and correct errors.

I need to talk to you. It's part of an investigation. Can I call you? Or FaceTime?

IM FINE LIKE I AM

LEAVE ME B

QUIT COMIN AT ME

Zandra sighed.

It would make me feel a lot better if I could talk to you. Hear your voice. I know you told your mother you want space. I just need to know you're really all right.

BITCH U BLIND I SAID IM FINE LEAVE ME ALONE

Despite the summer sun, and the humidity, and the sweat already soaking through her shirt, Zandra felt a chill play across the back of her neck and down her spine. She tapped in a response even more slowly and deliberately than before.

Is this really Angelique?

No response. She stood there, waiting, for a full minute, the chill growing worse. When Angelique still said nothing, Zandra went to her page on Facebook—

And couldn't. She whispered, "Little bitch blocked me."

When she got back in the car, Kella packed all the sarcasm she could into her words. "You done checking your tweets?"

Zandra drove away from the Bigelow house, wondering exactly who she'd just been talking to.

That night, Shep Curtis stood at the entrance of the loading dock at the back of a Ramada Inn on the southern edge of Marietta. All the arrangements had been made; the latest Adjunctive Bible Study Seminar was set to kick off in forty-five minutes, the whole "ballroom" had been rented out for the event, and Shep had just finished setting up better than fifty folding metal chairs. The seminar attendees, all of whom had paid in advance, were starting to filter in. Shep could hear their quiet voices floating in from the ballroom proper. All that was left was the arrival of the merchandise.

That was Will Bigelow's job. He had taken over from his brother after the accident, and Shep thought Will might actually be better at it than Cyrus. Shep checked his watch, but saw that he didn't need to, as headlights splashed across him. The van pulled right up to the loading dock. Will got out and came around to the back, and Shep walked down the four concrete steps to join him.

"Any trouble?" Shep asked.

"Nope. I slipped 'em all a little something in their Cokes. Nice and cooperative."

Will opened the van's rear doors, revealing the latest batch of merchandise, orders for which Shep had taken on his website. They all looked to be between eleven and thirteen—Shep thought of that age range as "the sweet spot"—and represented a healthy mix of blondes and brunettes, redheads and Asians, even some Mexicans. One little girl looked like she might have been of Middle Eastern extraction. Maybe he'd save her for the auction portion of the evening.

Shep clapped Will on the shoulder, thinking of the fat envelope of cash they'd exchanged. "Money well spent, my friend. Let's get them inside."

30

Zandra sat at Colin's breakfast bar and stared at her laptop. Colin sat on the floor, his back to the couch, with Jordan stretched most of the way across his lap, belly up, his tongue hanging so far out of his upside-down mouth that it touched the carpet.

"So, does this put you back to square one, or what?"

Zandra didn't turn away from the computer. "I don't know. Maybe. I'm not even supposed to be on a square. But I thought for sure Kella Bigelow was the one who cut my brake line. I mean, I found it kind of hard to believe that she would've been out there on the ridge... shooting..." Mention of the incident put Perry's face front and center in her mind. She took a few deep breaths. "But then, we never ruled out that the dungeon could've been used by more than one individual."

"And the Messenger stuff..."

"Not enough there to do anything with... other than give me the creeps. Maybe it was Angelique Currant. Maybe it wasn't."

She knew Colin could see the screen of her laptop from where he sat. He said, "And what you're looking at now—that's a thing you're not supposed to have. Right?"

"It's the text messages Vocker got off Cyrus Bigelow's phone. There's the ones from his wife, and then all this… I'm assuming it's code." She scrolled down through the list. "A lot of code. Sometimes there are little random phrases here and there. This is the first time I've had a chance to take a good look on a screen bigger than my phone." She looked over her shoulder at him. "You're aware this is embarrassing as shit, right? That I'm reduced to using your place as a, a clubhouse?"

Colin shook his head. "Think nothing of it. Yours is all taped off, right? I mean, whoever did the job on your truck was *there*. In your house."

Zandra turned back to the screen. What Colin said was true enough. Special Agent Danette Yu's forensics team was in the process of climbing all over the place. Zandra would never admit it out loud—she barely even admitted it to herself—but even when the place was declared no longer a crime scene, she didn't know when, or *if*, she'd be comfortable going back to it. Once she realized what had happened, the feeling of violation and betrayal that came with the house ran deep. "Don't worry about it. It's only a rental."

She scanned the codes and the random terms and phrases. They made no sense to her. Amid the numbers, suddenly there'd be the words—random shit, like "mountain high," or "spring-loaded," or "glib jack." On one line she saw, "the meek shall inherit." On another, "catnip to the masses."

Zandra sighed and, with her elbows propped on the bar, rested her face in her hands. Colin said, "You okay?"

"I'd be better if I knew what I was doing. I've been grasping at straws this whole time, at best, and now that Agent Yu's taken over, I feel like I'm sitting in the middle of the ocean on a tiny little iceberg, just watching it melt."

Colin gently slid Jordan off his lap and got to his feet. The dog rolled over, moved the eight or so feet to the hearth in front of the fire, and turned his belly to the flames. Zandra looked up as Colin sat down on the stool next to hers. "I'm glad you're here. Even if you don't know what you're doing."

She narrowed her eyes at him. "Hey, *I* can point out that I'm floundering. I don't know that *you* can."

He smiled. Sitting this close, his scent reached her, and to her horror, the fluttering stirred again in her stomach. She stared rigidly at the computer and made sure no part of her body was close to touching any part of his. She said, "I don't know. Maybe Yu's right. Maybe I should just take a big fat leave of absence. They all hate my guts down there anyway. Well, almost all of them."

"But you won't, because…"

Zandra frowned and cracked her knuckles, slowly, first her left hand, then her right. "Because this shithead has been squatting here, in *my town*, for God only knows how long, and I've got no real faith in that tiny little Asian woman. Forgive me if that sounds racist."

Colin traced patterns on the bar with one index finger. "May I make an observation?"

"Depending on what it is. And how fast you can run once you've made it."

He flashed that smile of his again. Zandra wondered how much it cost to get teeth that perfect. "I think you don't have much in the way of faith in *anyone*. Anyone who isn't Zandra Seagraves, anyway."

Zandra turned and looked him square in the eye. She maintained that eye contact, her brows slowly drawing closer together, as she leaned an elbow on the counter and propped her head up on the heel of her hand. "You're not completely wrong."

"So… any interest in changing that? Maybe expanding your, ah, *personal circle?*"

Zandra shrugged with her eyebrows. "I'm sitting here, ain't I? Instead of some hotel room somewhere?" She leveled a finger at him. "Don't make me regret it."

Colin checked his watch. "I'd like to make you dinner, actually. If you're up for it. I have a couple of gourmet meals set to arrive in about half an hour."

Zandra sat up very straight. "You already ordered two meals?"

Colin put up easy hands. "Number one, you know I can't cook, so any meals I get are ordered several days in advance. Number two, if you say no, then I'll have one of them for dinner and the other one for lunch tomorrow."

Zandra turned back to the laptop. Thoughts bumped and scraped against each other in her head. Was he asking her to *dinner*, dinner? Or just offering her food? If he was asking her to *dinner* dinner, was it supposed to be a date? Was he the kind of boy who thought providing a woman with food entitled him to sex? If so, she had a Taser in her purse with his name on it. No, screw that: she had *knuckles* with his name on them.

But then... after she'd thrown herself at him in that drunken display that still made her cringe, he'd said he *did* want her. Just not drunk her. He wanted the Zandra that wouldn't regret anything.

Just being blunt with herself—she hadn't gotten laid in *so* long.

And he smelled *so damn good.*

She realized she'd let her eyes relax, staring through the laptop, and when she brought them back into focus, the words sat there, on the screen. Laughing at her. Mocking her. *"Cannot resist such a desire."*

Zandra said, "Holy shit."

Colin leaned closer, squinting at the computer. "What? What? What'd you see?"

She tapped the screen with one fingernail hard enough to distort the resolution. "This. These words. I've heard them before. I heard someone say them. Fuck. *Fuck.* Who was it?" She slid off the stool and paced the length of the kitchen, her hands waving and grasping. "Come on, come on, *fuck.* You found this phone outside the dungeon, right? And it belonged to Sheriff Bigelow, who died in a car wreck with a teenage black boy. And we know two, at least two, black teenagers are connected with the dungeon. Shaquana and Jimmy. Maybe Angelique Currant. And if anybody ever bothers to match the other souvenirs in that box with that list of names we got from the preachers, I bet they all belong to black teenagers, too."

Colin watched her. "So you think the last sheriff was involved in the dungeon?"

Zandra gestured wildly. "Who knows? Maybe? Why was the phone there? I mean, okay, it could've been dropped there, the tornado could've picked it up from anywhere, but what if it just picked it up from inside the house? If the sheriff had that boy in the car with him… where was he taking the kid? Is that what all those dates and times in the text messages are about?"

Now Colin said, "Holy shit. So Sheriff Bigelow might've been involved in… what, you think, like, child trafficking?"

Zandra kept pacing. "In other trafficking rings, they use code when they communicate with each other. The ones doing the selling, not the girls. They'll refer to the girls like 'Mulan,' or 'Ariel,' or 'Sleeping Beauty.' Asian, redhead, blonde."

"Are you fucking serious? That's…" Colin's pale skin took on a mild green tinge.

Zandra came back over and tapped the screen again. "So, what if all these bullshit jumble words are a different kind of code? What if we're looking at the sheriff helping someone set up times and places to trade black teenagers?"

Colin stared at the list of messages. He said, "Oh my God."

Zandra stopped and whirled to look at him. "What?"

"'Cannot resist such a desire.' I know who said it. I was *there* when he said it, we both were!"

"Who?" She fought back the urge to grab him by his collar and shake him. "Who?"

"That oily guy. Outside the Waffle House." He snapped his fingers rapidly. "What was it, you introduced me, the fuck was his name?"

Zandra's world narrowed down to a single point. "It was Shep Curtis."

S eriously. We could've taken my car."

Zandra glanced over at Colin. Under other circumstances she might have laughed at the sight of Jordan more or less sitting in Colin's lap, again with his head jutting out the window. She said, "You shouldn't be coming with me at all."

"And if we'd taken my car, you could've been giving me that admonishment in the *air conditioning*."

Colin had insisted on coming with her to talk to Shep Curtis, but she'd made him agree to stay in the car this time. Zandra figured as long as Jordan was with him—in broad daylight, out in the open—he'd probably be fine. She said, "I should've brought Pounder."

Colin shook his head. "You said it yourself. Not official police business. What's it, 'fruit of the poisoned tree'?"

Zandra didn't respond. The legal term didn't exactly apply, but Colin wasn't wrong. She wasn't supposed to have had that cell phone information. She wasn't supposed to be working on anything to do with the dungeon. Going to talk to Shep Curtis was a hundred percent off the books.

But she'd *tried*. She'd called the Farmhouse and asked to speak to Agent Yu. Instead she'd wound up with some functionary taking appointments, who'd told her that Agent Yu was very busy, and that if she had something to report, he'd be glad to make a note of it, and that Agent Yu would get to it in due time. At which point Zandra had hung up on him.

It came down now to a question of carefully following up an unofficial lead, or putting her job in jeopardy and risking jail time.

Well, no. The third option was to turn over what she knew, claim she stumbled across it somehow, and wash her hands of it.

Zandra and Colin had already dropped by Shep Curtis's house, where his timid, subservient, morbidly obese wife had told them in her little mouse voice that Shep was at the church. Zandra didn't have time to think about unpacking all of the pathology that Libby Curtis represented, at least not right now. It didn't take long to get from the Curtis house to the Congregational Gospel Church, where Zandra spotted Shep's car parked near one of the side doors.

She parked the Camaro under a metal awning. "Here, at least you and the Ferocious Guard Dog'll be in the shade."

Jordan seemed to know that he was the Ferocious Guard Dog. He squirmed around in Colin's lap until his belly was exposed, and Zandra obligingly gave it a few scratches before she got out of the car.

When she opened the door, Colin said, "Hey—why don't you call me, and leave your phone on, and just stick it in a pocket or something, and that way if you get in trouble I'll hear you, and I can come and help?"

Zandra took a breath to rebuke the boy. She was a twenty-year Army veteran, better trained in both armed and unarmed combat than Colin could ever dream of being, she had her sidearm in the concealed holster tucked into her khakis, and she was the *goddamn sheriff.* But after a second's consideration, she didn't figure it could hurt anything, either, so she nodded, called Colin's number, and tucked her phone into a breast pocket, screen facing inward. "All I'm going to do is feel him out. I don't want him to think he's in trouble, and risk him going and getting rid of evidence."

"Fine. I'll be here. Mr. Ferocious and I will come running if we need to."

Jordan whined and thumped his tail against the driver's seat as Colin took over the belly scratches.

Zandra peered through the glass side door near Shep Curtis's car. She saw no one. The lights were all off, typical of a church in mid-day during the week, but when she pulled the curved aluminum handle, the door opened readily enough. Zandra slipped inside and made her way down the hall. She wasn't exactly moving stealthily, but neither did she want to announce her presence.

The ground-floor hallway proved as empty as it had looked from outside. Classrooms, the fellowship hall, the kitchen, the choir room —all dark and unoccupied. She glanced out into the auditorium and saw nothing but empty pews.

From somewhere over her head, she heard a floor joist squeal.

The church had three levels. Zandra climbed the stairs to the second floor, slowly pushed the stairwell door open, and peered up and down the hallway. She figured this would be mostly classrooms, used for Sunday School, and wasn't surprised to find most of them dark. But light shined from one at the end of the hall, and she padded down toward it, her shoes noiseless on the tile floor.

The small office she found was deserted. Just like the first floor.

She was about to leave and head back to the stairs when a FedEx envelope on the corner of the desk caught her eye. The corner of something bright and colorful stuck out of it, something printed on heavy paper stock, and when she took a step closer to get a better look, she saw the letters *RIFF* printed on it.

A frown crept onto Zandra's face. She picked up the envelope, slid the brightly printed paper out of it, and the frown deepened into a scowl.

"Curtis for Sheriff." The words tasted foul on her tongue, even as the knowledge and ramifications slid down her throat like the bitterest of pills. "Shit. *Shit.*" Zandra slid the flier back into the envelope. "Shit fucking *dammit.*"

From directly overhead, another floor joist squealed.

Zandra took the stairs up to the third floor as quickly as she could while staying more or less quiet. As she opened the door from the stairwell, another, louder squeal—unmistakably the sound of a footstep on an old wooden floor—came from down the hall. The first step Zandra took produced a similar shrill sound as a nail moved in the joist beneath her foot, and she heard a voice from a room four doors down.

It was Shep Curtis. He said, "That's probably Will."

Zandra moved quickly down the hallway. Another voice, muffled but familiar, said something that sounded like, "...he supposed to be here for this?"

Shep Curtis, close now, from right behind a thin wooden door, said, "No, but it doesn't surprise me." Then, louder: "C'mon in, Will. Get a good look at our newest brother. I think Libby got the fit just right."

Zandra pushed open the door, saw the two men standing there in the long, rectangular room, and almost screamed.

Closest to her was Shep Curtis, in his normal, too-boring-for-words dark slacks and white short-sleeved button shirt, his brown shoes polished to a gleam. As Curtis looked at her, realizing who she was and that she was not "Will," as he'd expected, a vile sort of understanding swept across his face. His beige, too-big teeth bared in a nasty smile, and he turned to the room's other occupant. "Well, would you look who it is!"

Standing at the back of the room was Horace Pounder. Wearing a white Ku Klux Klan robe. Holding a peaked white hood in his massive hands. Pounder gaped at her, his face turning a horrible purple-red, and he said, "Boss—Boss, wait—"

But Zandra had already turned, stomach twisting, acid in her throat, and she bolted down the hallway, each footstep marked by a shrill metal-on-wood scream.

31

Zandra drove aimlessly.

She'd dropped Colin off back at his townhouse. She felt bad for him, in that he kept asking her what the hell had happened in the church, and she couldn't tell him. Couldn't get the words to come out. Hell, couldn't get the words to line up properly in her head. Zandra had only muttered something about being okay, and that she had to think about things, and that she'd call him later. "Thanks for going with me," she was pretty sure she'd said. At her last sight of him before she'd driven away, he'd thrown his arms up in frustration and stomped up the steps to his front door.

Jordan lay with his chin on Zandra's thigh, ignoring the wind rushing past the open windows. He seemed to want to maintain physical contact with her at any cost.

Horace Pounder. In KKK robes.

"C'mon in, Will. Get a look at our newest brother."

Horace Pounder, the boy Zandra had known all her life. The boy Perry had spent hundreds of hours coaching. The boy who'd become the only member of the Sheriff's Department Zandra had truly, fully trusted.

She felt as if she had just walked off a cliff.

All her life, Zandra Seagraves had wanted one thing: to know where she stood. Other kids thought her parents were ridiculously strict, but what they hadn't realized was that Mr. and Mrs. Seagraves were meticulously, relentlessly *consistent*. Yes, the rules they'd established were harsh. Sometimes even draconian. But Zandra had never minded that, because she knew *exactly* what was expected of her, *exactly* where the boundaries lay, and *exactly* how she'd be punished if she broke any of her parents' rules.

It was why she had gravitated to the Army. The structure. The rules. That was what had let her survive for two decades, despite the soul-numbing dissatisfaction of spending almost every day standing beside a door and checking IDs.

Zandra had never had more than three genuine friends at a time, outside of her family. Never in her whole life. She knew there were people who had "dozens of close friends," people who threw parties for their vast social circles, people who never met a stranger. She'd never understood those people. Because in Zandra's experience, most humans were unreliable and would lie at the drop of a hat. She had made a point of identifying people like that and forcibly stripping them out of her life, which led to one, *maybe* two solid, dependable, honest friends. Until today, she considered those friends to be Mike and Angie Hubble, and Horace Pounder.

Zandra would have died for those friends.

She would've died for Horace Pounder.

Perry, the best judge of character Zandra had ever seen, had decided that Horace Pounder was good people, worthy of a shit-ton of attention and care and respect.

She wanted to talk to Perry about the horrible thing she'd just seen. Wanted to talk to him *so bad*.

The ground beneath her tires yawned away from her. Zandra felt her mind falling. Plummeting, tumbling heels over head, and if Jordan hadn't been there in the car with her, she would have screamed and pounded her fists against the steering wheel and screamed some more. She drove, aimlessly, prowling up and down the streets and roads of Cartauga County as the sun crept closer and closer to the western horizon.

And as if Horace Pounder joining the *fucking* Klan wasn't bad enough, Shep Curtis was about to run for sheriff.

She felt herself falling, yes. And the thought of Shep Curtis sitting in her office at the Farmhouse clamped shackles around her ankles and fixed a giant weight to them.

After a couple of hours of summer heat and no air conditioning, Zandra caught a whiff of something unpleasant, and realized she'd become a tad ripe. That led her to the realization that she had only grabbed a few items of clothing when she'd decided to stay at Colin's place. She pulled over to the side of the road—a cell conversation would be impossible over the sound of air rushing past the open windows—and called Agent Yu's number.

Hirsch answered. "Danette Yu's desk."

"Holy fuck, Hirsch, you're taking calls for her now?"

Agent Hirsch chuckled. "Not officially. Yu's in the shitter. What's up?"

"Well, I've got a practical question for you, but first—how's the case? Turn up anything?"

The good humor left Hirsch's voice. "We've turned up jack and shit."

"Were you able to get that warrant…? The one I suggested?"

He sighed. "Yeah. I'm sorry, Sheriff, it was a dead end. Though the guy I talked to at Facebook was more willing to cooperate than I was expecting. I sort of got the impression he thought I was calling about something else."

Zandra had closed her eyes and leaned her head back against the headrest. "Dead end how? What'd the guy say?"

"All twenty-eight accounts, the last known activity for them was the old Wilkins house. The one that got demolished."

"The fuck're you talking about, dead end? That fucking proves my point!"

"Hang on. You didn't let me finish. The most recent one? Two days ago."

Jordan whimpered. Zandra scratched his head without looking at him. She said, "That doesn't make any sense. That's—that's not possible."

"He swore up and down he had it right."

"So somebody was posting status updates from a shithole water-logged basement?"

"A shithole waterlogged basement that we've had under constant surveillance. I don't know what to tell you, Sheriff. Obviously there was some kind of glitch in the system. Hang on a second." She heard him lean away from the phone and blow his nose. "Sorry. Pollen. What was the practical question you said you had?"

Zandra once again felt like screaming and pounding the steering wheel, but instead, in a level voice, she said, "I need some clothes. Is it going to ruffle any federal feathers if I drop by my house and grab some?"

Hirsch thought about it for a moment. "Nah, go ahead. Yu's forensics people are done with it. Just touch as little as possible while you're there."

"Thanks." Zandra ended the call, got the Camaro back on the road, and pointed its nose toward her house. Well… toward the place she still had a lease on. She'd already decided to find a new place to live, decorations and improvements be damned.

Night had fully fallen by the time she crested the hill—having driven past the house where she'd crashed into the pool, the wreckage of which she couldn't see because of the blessed darkness. Zandra turned in to the gravel drive and crunched her way to the house, stopping short thanks to the yellow-and-black crime scene tape that still circled the place. To Jordan, she said, "You know the drill, pal. Stay here. Don't let anybody steal my car."

Jordan didn't whine this time. His tail didn't thump. He just sat in the passenger seat and stared at the house. Zandra couldn't help wondering if he felt as creeped out by the place as she did. She ducked under the tape and let herself in through the front door, avoiding the garage.

As she walked into the living room, a chill made its way up her arms and down her spine. Softly she said, "Fuck, I should've just bought some new shit at TJ Maxx." She flipped on lights as she made her way down the short hall to her bedroom.

It didn't take long to pack as much as she thought she'd need. An old duffel bag shoved onto the narrow little shelf high up in her closet provided more than enough space for the lightweight summer clothes she grabbed off hangers and out of drawers. She dumped most of the contents of her underwear drawer into the bag, and to her mild surprise it only bothered her a little that the delicate, silken items landed in messy little heaps. The house felt alien to her now. She had zero desire to stay and fold everything properly.

Bag in hand, Zandra walked back out into the living room, and paused in front of her murderabilia display cabinet. She pondered taking a couple of the items with her. Set them up in the spare room at Colin's place, maybe. They'd make her feel more at home. And freak him out. The thought made her smile.

Zandra had reached out to open the cabinet when she saw the moving reflection in the glass, and she threw herself to one side as something flashed past her head and smashed apart the glass doors of the case. She hit the floor hard on her wounded shoulder, and the pain struck her so fiercely she thought she might vomit, but she didn't stop, knew if she stopped she was dead, and she rolled and came up to her feet with her Glock in her hand.

The thing that had smashed the display case crashed into her gun hand. Her fingers blazed in agony as the Glock flew away from her, and she staggered backward until she came up hard against the break-fast table and finally got a look at what had attacked her. A sound escaped from her throat involuntarily. A hitch, a sobbing noise, filled with shock and pain.

A tall, lean man dressed in black from head to foot rushed toward her. He had a black ski mask over his face, and underneath the ski mask he wore a pair of mirrored sunglasses. In his hands he held an aluminum baseball bat with flecks of Zandra's blood on it from where he'd pulverized her fingers. The mirrored lenses beneath the black mask took away his humanity, turned him into a demon, a thing dredged up from nightmare, and Zandra saw her own wide-eyed, shrieking face reflected in them as he drew back the bat.

Zandra lunged forward and drove her shoulder into the man's gut —it felt like tackling a tree—and pain lanced through her back as he brought the bat down on it, but there was no real power in his strike, and Zandra gripped the backs of his knees and heaved and rode him to the floor.

The bat came around and struck her directly on the bullet wound in her shoulder, and another wave of nauseating pain crashed through her, but she grabbed the man's forearm and sank her teeth into his wrist all the way to the bone, and when he screamed and bucked underneath her and tried to shove her off of him, she drove her knee into his balls as hard as she could, and did it again.

The man made a horrific gurgling sound and this time he did buck her off, but as Zandra rolled away from him, she took the bat with her, and before she'd even made it back to her feet, she swung it like a hammer at the man's legs. The bat cracked into the floor, the tiniest fraction of a second too slow as the man scuttled away from her, gasping and holding his wrist to his chest, and Zandra realized Jordan was losing his mind outside, barking and howling like a rabid beast.

Zandra used the bat to push herself up, agony still radiating from her shoulder and her back, her vision swimming, but she drew back the bat and set her feet to charge—

And stopped.

The man stood by the door. With her gun in his hand.

"You wouldn't stop," the man hissed, his voice high-pitched and grating, like sand sliding across metal. "I gave you every opportunity. All I wanted was solitude. All I wanted was to be left alone." The man's words cut through Jordan's beyond-frantic barking. "This town is mine. Can't you comprehend that? It belongs to *me*. But you... you and that infuriating storm… you ruined everything. *Everything.* And now I have to ruin you."

The man raised the gun and aimed it at Zandra, point-blank, dead-bang, and she watched his finger tighten on the trigger, and the living room exploded as Jordan's massive body smashed through the picture window in a cascade of razor-edged glass shards and sprays of blood. The man whirled to face him as Jordan's teeth caught the man's wrist —the same wrist Zandra had bitten—

But those teeth hadn't closed on the hand that held the gun. The hand that held the gun swung down until its barrel rested between Jordan's eyes, and Jordan gave the man's wrist one final shake, and the gunshot crashed through the room and Jordan yelped and thudded to the floor, the hair on the top of his head burning.

Zandra threw the baseball bat as hard as she could, watched it crack into the man's elbow, watched the gun fly from his spasming fingers, and only when the man in black leaped through the broken window and sprinted away into the darkness did Zandra realize she'd been screaming.

Her scream ran dry and her throat cracked as she dropped to her knees next to Jordan's broken body. A swiftly expanding pool of blood stained the floor around them.

* * *

Once Zandra had dropped him off at his townhouse, Colin spent the next couple of hours trying and failing to find something to occupy his brain. He stared into the refrigerator, picked a meal, prepared and ate it. He spent twenty mindless minutes scrolling through Instagram. He watched an episode and a half of a Finnish cop drama on Netflix, paused it to use the bathroom, and realized he couldn't remember a single second of either episode. He picked up his phone and opened his contacts. Zandra's name sat there on the screen, staring at him, and his thumb hovered over it. Dipped down but moved away. Dipped and moved.

Finally Colin stuck the phone in his pocket, walked out the front door, and wandered down to the cluster of mailboxes at the edge of the townhouses' parking lot. He didn't expect to get anything, since he'd only turned in his temporary change of address form a few days ago, but he couldn't stand to stop moving, either. It had gotten dark, and the frogs, katydids, and cicadas all seemed to be competing with each other for which species could produce the most white noise.

The only thing in his mailbox was an advertisement from a local car dealership, with a cheap plastic key fob attached to it. He paused under one of the parking lot's streetlights to read it. The ad announced that if Colin removed the little tab on the fob, and the number displayed matched the one printed on the flier below it, he'd be eligible for a massive bonus upon trading in his old vehicle. He pulled the tab, saw that the number did indeed match—just as he was sure it would on every single ad the dealership had mailed out—and dumped the whole thing in a recycling bin on his way back up the hill.

When he was a few feet away from his front door, the door to the unit next to his opened, and two people emerged, engaged in what sounded like a lively conversation. The first was a black man, dressed in lightweight coveralls and tennis shoes, holding a bucket filled with cleaning supplies in one hand and a broom and a mop in the other. Colin couldn't tell how old he was, maybe twenty-five, maybe forty-five, with a broad, gap-toothed smile and an impressive head of natural hair that bounced and bobbed when he moved. It took Colin a few seconds to connect the coveralls and cleaning products with the van parked two spaces down, which bore the logo of the GOLD-SMITH CLEANING COMPANY, along with a phone number and website address.

Following the man out the door was a blond white woman who *definitely* looked to be in her forties, though Colin thought she might have been a few years younger, especially if she'd spent time abusing a tanning bed. She wore sandals and yoga pants and a beige silk blouse, and Colin spotted some tasteful yet serious diamonds both on her hands and in her earlobes.

The blond woman said, "Tell Nicole if she wants that recipe, she'll have to come and ask me for it." The woman had the Red Springs accent, but a slightly tamped-down version of it that made Colin wonder if she'd spent time in another part of the country.

"No doubt, no doubt," the man in the coveralls said, reminding Colin of the way Karlos had talked, back at Aunt Petunia's. "Same time next week?"

"If you'll have me!" the blonde answered, and threw her arms wide and hugged the man around the neck, both of them grinning. Colin realized he was staring, but couldn't quite make himself stop. The energy between the two was that of old friends, and not at all what he'd come to expect from the town's populace.

The blonde woman saw him standing there and stepped away from the man, her grin still in place but taking on a note of curiosity. "Hey! You the new neighbor?"

Charity's words sprang into Colin's mind: *Be nice!*

He stepped forward and stuck out his hand. "Colin. Colin Massey. Yeah, I just moved in."

The woman shook his hand, and right behind her, so did the man, the same friendly, curious smile on his lips. The woman said, "I'm Sara, Sara Duck, and this here's Lorenzo Goldsmith."

Lorenzo Goldsmith produced a business card out of thin air and pressed it into Colin's hand. "Owner and operator of the Goldsmith Cleaning Company. We put the hurt on dirt!"

"More owner than operator, these days," Sara said, pride in her voice. "How many crews you got going now?"

"Five." Lorenzo had set down the mop and broom to shake Colin's hand. He picked them up again and gestured toward the van. "Let me stow all this."

As Lorenzo went to the van, Sara focused on Colin. "So what brings you to Red Springs? Let me guess—you work for Volkswagen. We're gettin' an awful lot of out-of-town types showing up here, now that the big plant's open in Chattanooga. Lots of Germans! You're not German, are you? You don't sound like it."

"Uh, no. No, I'm from Connecticut."

"Picked a fine time to show up, let me tell you. That twister did quite a number on us."

Lorenzo had come back by then. He said, "Bad for the town, but good for business! We can't do like Servpro, whole restoration thing like after a fire, but we're gettin' *plenty* of calls 'cause of damaged roofs and such. Y'know, somebody comes home after the storm, water got in where it wasn't s'posed to, and do they feel like cleanin' up the mess? Not when they got us!"

The easy friendship between Sara and Lorenzo continued to baffle and fascinate Colin. It didn't seem sexual at all. More like the way he'd seen Zandra and Perry interact. Above all else, it seemed filled with genuine *respect*. Colin gestured at Sara's townhouse. "Did the storm damage your place?"

"Oh, no, not at all. Lorenzo just comes out once a week and gives it all a top-to-bottom spit-shine. I keep telling him he could just send one of his crews, but—"

"I can't do sub-contract for an old friend!" Lorenzo smiled at her. "Your place needs the *master* touch."

Sara rolled her eyes. "You're so humble."

"Ain't braggin' if you can back it up."

Colin began to feel the positive energy these two were putting out take hold of him. Trying not to grin like an idiot, he said, "So you guys are old friends?"

"Known each other our whole lives," Sara said. "Survived the Cartauga County public school system together. Got our finance degrees from Dalton State together. I was maid of honor at his wedding."

Lorenzo said, "Then she went an' bought a car wash, and I started the Cleaning Company, and shit, now it's been, what, twenty years?"

"Shut your mouth," Sara said playfully. "My kids make me feel old enough already."

Lorenzo peered around Colin. "You, uh, you do your own cleaning?"

Colin shook his head. "I've got Merry Maids coming in twice a—"

Lorenzo interrupted with a loud raspberry. "Amateurs! You want the real deal, you just call the number on that card I gave you. You got kids?"

"No—no, it's just me."

Sara's left eyebrow quirked up. "No wife, either?"

Lorenzo made a big show of elbowing her in the side. "*Down,* woman! Man just moved here! Let him get his legs under him!"

Sara sighed, and said, "Please ignore him. What do you do for a living, Colin?"

What indeed? Colin said, "I guess I'm sort of a consultant."

Lorenzo's eyes widened, sparkling with mischief. "Oooh, mysterious! You work for the CIA? You gonna have to kill us if you tell us what you really do?"

Colin laughed. He couldn't help it, and as he did, he realized he didn't *want* to help it. He didn't think he'd laughed, not like this, since he'd arrived in Red Springs. He tried to think of a suitably snappy comeback to Lorenzo's question when his phone buzzed in his pocket. He pulled it out and saw *Zandra Seagraves* on the screen.

Colin held up a finger. "Sorry, sorry, I need to take this, hang on." He hit *Accept.* "Hey, what's up?"

Four minutes later, barely missing one of the gas pumps, Zandra's Camaro skidded into the parking lot of the MegaStar on Dahlonega Highway—the one where she'd convinced Larry the self-mutilating junkie to let his counter-clerk hostage go. That memory felt vague to her. As if it had happened decades ago. Thirty seconds later, Colin's rented Hyundai came zooming in and screeched to a stop next to her. He jumped out, his face pale, as Zandra hurried around to the Camaro's passenger side.

"What happened?"

Colin wasn't panicked, but she didn't think it would take much to get him there. She lifted Jordan, wrapped in a blood-soaked blanket, and settled into the passenger seat with him on her lap. "You've got the address I texted you?"

Colin waggled his phone. "Yeah, it's already in Waze."

"You're driving. Get us there. Break every fucking speed limit you have to, but do it. Now! Come on, let's go, *let's go!*"

Colin jumped in behind the Camaro's wheel, adjusted the seat and the mirror, and threw the car in gear. He seemed to take her at her word about the speed limit thing, because he drove like the proverbial bat out of hell. After a minute, shouting to make himself heard over the rushing wind, he said, "What happened? Tell me! Are you hurt?"

Zandra stared through the windshield, feeling as if her body were about to shake itself apart. Her vision swam in and out of focus, and every time Jordan let out a soft whine, Zandra thought her heart would stop. "You just concentrate on driving. We need to get there. We need to *be* there already."

Colin did as he was told. The Camaro's engine whined as they shot past eighty miles per hour and climbed toward a hundred. The car whipped down the 775 spur to I-75, turned north and blew through the Georgia-Tennessee border, and almost came up onto two wheels as they took the Rossville Boulevard exit and headed into Chattanooga. If Zandra hadn't been as close as she was to an emotional meltdown, she might have been impressed at how well Colin drove. A couple more high-speed turns put them on Amnicola Highway. Zandra's heart thudded against her ribs as the sign for the 24-hour animal hospital came into view.

At some point in the last few minutes, Jordan had stopped making any sound. Zandra wasn't even sure he was still breathing. It didn't matter. He'd put her life ahead of his own, and she was determined to do the same.

After the doctors and nurses had come and taken Jordan into the back—he wasn't dead, not yet, not quite—Zandra and Colin sat in the hospital's emergency waiting room. She leaned against him, her head on his shoulder.

Colin said, "You going to tell me what happened now?"

Zandra didn't move. "He was in my house. The motherfucker was *in my house.* Came after me with a baseball bat. And he shot my dog with my own fucking gun."

Colin laced the fingers of his right hand through her left. Gently he brought her knuckles up to his lips and kissed them. "Jordan's tough. He'll make it."

She didn't recognize her own voice. "You should've seen him. What he did for me. I'd be dead if not for that dog. I'd be dead and gone."

A door on the far side of the waiting room opened, and the doctor in charge—a young white woman named Vanessa, who looked about twenty-five—came through it and beckoned to Zandra. She shot up out of her chair, Colin right behind her. Vanessa said, "The glass from that window really did a number on him. He's got multiple deep lacerations, we've got to repair a lot of muscle tissue, and one of the shards pierced a lung. He's lucky that no major tendons or ligaments got severed. Jordan's going to have a long road ahead of him. But he'll make it."

Zandra had all but forgotten about the damage from the window glass. Every time her eyes closed, she saw the muzzle flash from her Glock, heard Jordan's agonized, truncated yelp. "What about the bullet wound?"

Vanessa blinked at her, but a second later waved a hand. "We've got that stitched up. It was superficial."

Zandra's jaw fell open. "*Superficial?* Doc, he got shot in the head!"

The doctor shrugged. "Glancing. He lost some skin and hair, but it was just a graze, really. Most pit bulls have awfully thick skulls, and your boy's no exception." She paused. "Ordinarily I'd be writing up a police report, and I'm still going to need one for our records, but I'm assuming you'll handle that for now? Sheriff?"

Zandra threw her arms around Vanessa and hugged her tight. "Thank you, Doctor. Thank you, thank you, thank you so much." Zandra turned her loose and stepped back to arm's length. "I can't let him die. You understand that, don't you? I *can't.*"

Smiling, Vanessa said, "And he won't. He was in bad shape when you brought him in, I won't bullshit you about that, and he'd lost an awful lot of blood. But you got him to us in time, and he's in good hands now. He'll be fine."

Zandra hugged her again, relief flooding through her like water from a cool mountain brook.

But she closed her eyes when she did it, and all she could see were the silver-mirrored lenses of the man in black's demon face.

3 2

It wasn't until Zandra caught sight of her reflection in one of the Farmhouse's windows that she realized how beaten and bloody she looked. The man in black's assault had torn open the bullet-dug trench in her shoulder, and the sleeve of her shirt was soaked in blood. Other sprays of blood crisscrossed her face and chest. She wondered how much of it was hers, how much was the man in black's, and how much belonged to Jordan.

It was just past 8:00 a.m., and Zandra sat on the wrong side of her own desk, staring across it at Special Agent Danette Yu. Zandra hadn't slept. "I assume you've got your forensics people back out there?"

"They've been there all night. This is a huge break for us, as I'm sure you're aware. The guy bled all over the place."

"I'll leave these clothes with you before I go, of course. Plenty more DNA to share."

Yu leaned toward her. "Sheriff, this puts us a lot closer than we were. Which is why I'm not going to string you up for contaminating an active crime scene. Never mind what Agent Hirsch told you." Zandra nodded. She'd wondered which way Yu would go on that. A knock sounded at the door, and Zandra looked around to see Vocker standing there with a bunch of empty evidence bags.

As Zandra stood, Agent Yu said, "I'm glad you're all right, Sheriff. And I'm glad your dog is going to make it. But I haven't changed my position about your involvement here. Please. Go somewhere else. *Anywhere* else. Let us deal with this."

Zandra said nothing as she left the office.

Ten minutes later, now dressed in Sheriff's Department sweats and an old pair of flip-flops she'd found in the bottom of her locker, she walked out into the lobby waiting area to find Colin perched on one of the intensely uncomfortable plastic chairs. He popped to his feet. "Sweet outfit. The flip-flops are a nice touch, too. Very Red Springs."

She walked past him. "Yeah, they needed to wring the blood out of my clothes. And the Camaro. Is there anything to eat at your place?"

He followed her. "Do you like avocado toast?"

Zandra had never had avocado toast. "I just need to think." Once they got out into the parking lot, she stopped by his car and turned to face him. "You've talked to Agent Yu. Right?"

He nodded. "She called me in yesterday. Took my statement."

"Did she tell you to hang around?"

"Actually no. She said I could go back to Milford."

"Then why are you still here, Colin? Are you nuts?"

She watched as smart-ass answer after smart-ass answer passed across his face. But finally he lost his grin. "Zandra. Come on. Is it not obvious by now?"

She shook her head and opened the passenger door. "Crazy white boys." The whole ride back to his townhouse, Zandra tried to come up with something to say, but her brain kept misfiring. She was in pain, and exhausted, and needed food and sleep, or maybe sleep and then food, and she didn't trust herself not to say something stupid, so she kept her mouth shut.

Colin turned in to the lot, aiming the car for his townhouse, but halfway to his parking space he hit the brakes so hard Zandra lurched in her seat. She said, "What the hell, Colin?" But he only pointed mutely out through the windshield. Zandra raised her head to look—

And saw Horace Pounder sitting on Colin's front steps. He wore sneakers and basketball shorts and a plain green t-shirt, no trace of the department about him. No trace of white robes, either. He sat hunched over, his elbows on his knees and his broad, pale face in his enormous hands, and when he raised his head, Zandra saw that he'd been crying.

Colin looked over at her. "What do you want me to do?"

Zandra's exhaustion doubled. She had to drag the words out of her own throat. "He's not going to pull anything crazy, I don't think. Go ahead and park."

Pounder got up and came to her side of the car as she and Colin got out. Zandra saw Colin watching them out of the corner of her eye, and imagined how helpless he must have felt at the thought of trying to resist Pounder physically—and then almost laughed out loud when Colin, no trace of fear in his voice, said, "Hey, Deputy? See this phone I'm holding? Yeah, we're streaming live now. So fucking watch yourself."

Pounder's expression didn't change as he looked over at Colin and his phone. It just stayed miserable. Quietly, or as quietly as he could manage with his megaphone voice, Pounder said, "Boss, I can't tell you how sorry I am. I ain't got nothin' like an excuse. But I can tell you the reason for it. If you'll let me. Can we talk?" Another glance at Colin. "In private, maybe?"

Zandra said, "Colin, I think you can stop recording. Let's all just go inside where it's cooler. And you can say your piece." Colin hesitated, but she gestured toward the door, and he reluctantly went and unlocked it. Zandra followed him inside. Pounder blocked out the light from the doorway as he came in and closed the door behind him.

"This's a really nice place you got here," Pounder said, looking around. "I ain't never been inside one o' these." He turned to Colin. "You, uh... you ain't movin' here to stay, are you?"

Colin leaned against the back of the sofa with his arms folded. "All due respect, Deputy, Zandra told me about you and your pointy white hood. If you've got something to say, why don't you go ahead and say it?"

Pounder said, *"Zandra."* Reverently. Almost in a whisper. His meaning—*She lets you call her Zandra*—hung there in the room with them. Pounder stood awkwardly for another few moments, but Zandra flopped down in one of the living room's easy chairs, so he tentatively settled his bulk on the other one. The chair groaned under his weight.

Colin said, "I guess I'd be a bad host if I didn't offer coffee at this time of the morning. Who wants some?" Zandra held up a hand. Pounder shook his head. "Okay, well, I'll be in the kitchen." A little louder: "Right over here. Where I can see you both." He drifted out of the living room.

Pounder stared at the spot on the carpet between Zandra's feet. "I ain't proud o' what I'm gonna say. It ain't good. But I'm gonna tell you why I was there, talkin' to Shep Curtis, an' wearin' what I was wearin'." He paused. Took a couple of deep breaths and dragged his eyes up to meet hers. "Pounders has always been in the Brotherhood. Back from the time it started. The Brotherhood… the Brotherhood's what started Red Springs, Boss. Right after the War Between the States."

Colin snorted loudly.

Zandra shot him a look and said, "Let's let the man talk."

Pounder went on. "I know, I know, it was a civil war. I learnt that in school. But that goes to what I'm talkin' about. Boss, the Brotherhood of the Holy Cross of Red Springs split off from the regular Klan, an' they started this town. Hell, them's the ones got Cartauga County chartered in the first place. You ever thought why there ain't hardly no black folks around here? I can tell you why. It's 'cause they used to get lynched. An' they knew to stay away. An' that's wrong, it's horrible, I know that. I always known it. Boss, I loved your brother. He was like a second daddy to me. An' I…" He choked up. "I love you, too, Boss, I do, I swear to God Almighty, you're like family to me."

Pounder paused again. Zandra thought he was waiting for a response from her. She didn't give him one.

"Red Springs… red, like the blood o' the lamb, my granddaddy always said… It got a little better after World War II, but not much. Turned into a sundown town."

Colin came back from the kitchen with a coffee mug in each hand.

He handed one to Zandra and sat down on the couch with the other. "The fuck is a 'sundown town'?"

Zandra said, "It's a town where black people know not to get caught after dark. During the day they'd just get glared at. Maybe spat at. But once night fell, it was open season."

Colin winced. "Jesus."

Pounder nodded. "I know it. I know it. I know it's awful. But my granddaddy, he said a Pounder wasn't a real man till he put those robes on. That's what he taught my daddy, and it's what my daddy taught me. And I didn't—I never did put 'em on. When you saw me, that was the first time I ever touched 'em."

Zandra frowned. "But *why?* If you know it's so awful, why would you?"

Pounder seemed to shrink in on himself. "My daddy… my daddy's dyin'. I ain't said nothin' to you about it, 'cause it's private. Somethin' else Daddy always said—'Keep your dirty laundry to yourself.' Ain't nobody's business what goes on in a family. Behind closed doors. But he's… he wasn't doin' great to begin with. Started in his heart. It's got a tumor in it, and he wouldn't go see a doctor for the longest, and now it's spread, he's all eat up with it. And I was sittin' there, side of 'is bed, and he said, *Lemme see you in them robes, son. Lemme see you be a real man.*" Pounder pulled up the hem of his shirt and mopped at his eyes with it. "So that's why I called Shep, an' said I was ready."

Pounder stood, wobbling a little. He crossed the living room to Zandra's chair, and sank down onto his knees at her feet, and bowed his massive bald head. "I was just doin' it for my daddy, Boss. But seein' you… seein' your face, when you saw me…" He looked up, and fresh tears welled in his eyes. "I ain't never been sorrier about nothin' in my life, Boss. I can't… I don't wanna let my daddy down, but I can't do this for somethin' that shoulda died 'fore it was ever born. Please forgive me, Boss. I'm so sorry. Please forgive me."

Zandra leaned forward and reached out a hand. She laid it alongside Pounder's face, gently, and used her thumb to wipe away one of his tears. "I thought I'd lost you. I thought the man I trusted and respected hadn't ever existed in the first place."

Pounder brought one colossal hand up and covered hers. "I'd do anything for you, Boss. I just—if I ever see your face lookin' like that again, I swear it'll kill me. I'll fall down dead."

She smiled, and said, "You're forgiven," and Pounder let the sobs come and slumped down against her knees.

"I'm so ashamed," he said, his breath hitching. "I'm so ashamed."

"Come on." She patted him on his shoulder. "Go sit back down, okay? We've got some things to discuss."

Pounder nodded, and used his shirt to mop at his face again, and made his way back to the chair. Colin picked up a box of Kleenexes from an end table and tossed it to him. Pounder caught it, and thanked him, and blew his nose a couple of times. It sounded like a lighthouse horn. When he could speak again, Pounder said, "What'd you want to talk about?"

Zandra said, "Well, first off—this doesn't need to go past the walls of this room, all right?"

"Anything you say, Boss."

"All right. It's looking like Shep Curtis might be involved in something to do with the dungeon."

Pounder's jaw fell open. "Huh? How?"

Zandra told him about Sheriff Bigelow's cell phone, and the text messages, and the turn of phrase she and Colin had associated with Shep Curtis. "It's not proof. It's not even close to proof. But I was going to talk to him about it when I ran into you."

Pounder drummed his fists on his knees. "Well then let's go talk to him about it right the fuck now!"

"Hold on. Has anybody told you what happened to me and my dog last night?"

Pounder blinked. "Nope. I was wonderin' where the pooch was. What happened?"

Zandra explained about the attack at her house.

As the story went on, Pounder's jaw clenched, and his teeth audibly ground together. His fingers dug into the arms of the chair hard enough that Colin said, "Hey, uh, I'm renting this furniture, too, so could you not...?"

Pounder relaxed his grip. "Sorry, bud." To Zandra: "So… what do you think needs to get done? An' how can I help y'all do it?"

Zandra stared at the now-extinguished fireplace. She couldn't help seeing Jordan there, stretched out, warming his belly. "I got Hirsch to get a warrant from Facebook. Trying to track down where these messages are *really* coming from. And it supports my whole theory in one way, but it's useless in another. Because he said they were all coming from the Wilkins house."

Pounder frowned. It made his face look like a pale jack o' lantern. "How's that possible?"

"It's not. Unless… well, I had an idea. It's not a great idea, I don't think. Because if I'm right about it, I'm going to kick my own ass for missing something so simple. The Wilkins place—is it still under active surveillance?"

Pounder shook his head. "Wasn't nobody goin' back there, even tryin' to go back there, and forensics took all they was gonna take from it. I mean, it's still taped off, it's an active scene an' all. But ain't nobody stakin' it out now."

Zandra nodded. She chewed on her lower lip. "I'm supposed to be staying away from this case, and I think Agent Yu would most likely notice if I went and rented a piece of heavy equipment. But… how do you guys feel about shovels?"

33

After giving it further thought, Zandra took Pounder with her but left Colin at his townhouse. When Colin protested, she said, "Look, I don't know that we're going to find anything. But if we do, it's going to be a police matter, and I'm already going off-book enough as it is. Having you there would only gum up the works even more."

So Colin stayed behind. Once it got dark, Zandra went with Pounder to his house, where he got a couple of shovels out of his garage, and together they drove out to Mrs. Daywood's place and walked to the wreckage of the Wilkins house, their path lit by a couple of high-powered flashlights. Pounder almost had to go to his hands and knees to get under the police tape strung up around the property.

"How you gonna explain this, Boss?" Pounder asked as they walked to the edge of the exposed basement. "Ain't we about to do some serious compromisin' of a crime scene?"

"Agent Yu wasn't interested in anything I had to say about it," Zandra replied, speaking as much to herself as to Pounder. "If we don't find anything, I'll apologize for moving dirt around. If we do find something—depending on what it is—she'll thank me for it. I hope."

Pounder twirled his shovel like a drummer twirling a stick. "Let's get to it, then."

Zandra said, "Hang on." She turned in a slow circle, playing her light around the property, letting it slide out to the trees. The katydids and frogs were at full strength, chattering all around them, but nothing moved. Zandra felt as if she and Pounder were the only two humans for a thousand miles.

She flexed her fingers. The impact from the baseball bat hadn't broken any bones, and though gripping the shovel handle hurt, it didn't hurt badly enough to make her reconsider. She tried to move a shovelful of dirt. If she held her arm just right, she could do it without getting flares of pain from her shoulder, and a determined grin stretched her lips. "All right. Yeah. Let's get to it."

The walls of the basement were old, rough brick, and broad flagstones made up its floor, but she and Pounder focused on the west end —the end obscured by the small-scale mudslide Zandra had noted when she'd first seen the place. They started at the top, at ground level, clearing the now-dry dirt away, moving steadily down toward the basement floor. The work increased swiftly as the mudslide grew thicker, and in only a few minutes Zandra and Pounder had both broken significant sweats. She was glad for the gentle breeze that moved the muggy summer air around, and glad she'd remembered to bring gloves, since otherwise the palms of her hands would have been masses of blisters.

After half an hour, Zandra took a break and leaned on her shovel, her back aching thanks to the awkward placement of her feet on the steep slope. She watched Pounder as he kept working. "Thanks."

Pounder flipped another shovelful of dirt over the edge—they'd agreed not to let any of it roll down into the basement, so as not to compromise anything the CSIs had catalogued—and leaned on his own shovel. "You ain't got to thank me, Boss. I meant it. I'll do anything you say."

"I appreciate that. But this might be nothing. We might just be out here, digging away like fools, and all we'll end up with is more brick."

He shook his head. "It don't matter. You think it's worth doin'. So I'm doin' it."

She let a smile play across her lips, and Pounder returned it, his broad, smooth face boyish in the indirect illumination from the flashlights. They both bent to the task once more.

Eighteen minutes later, the tip of Zandra's shovel hit something with a *clunk.* She exchanged looks with Pounder, and the two of them attacked that area, swiftly removing dirt until they had uncovered the source of the sound: set into the decades-old brick of the basement was an unmistakably modern doorframe, and in the frame stood a gray-painted metal door. Pounder prodded it with his shovel. "You reckon that's gonna open in? Or out?"

"With my luck, it'll open out, and we'll have to move this entire damn mudslide. But let's uncover the hinges and see."

Another bout of work exposed the top third of the doorframe and several more inches of the door itself, and Zandra recited a silent prayer of thanks. The hinges were on the other side. The door opened away from the basement. Pounder said, "Well, we sure as shit found *somethin'.* You wanna call Agent Yu now? Or Hirsch? Somebody?"

Zandra chewed on her lower lip. "No. Not yet. We need to know what's on the other side. I don't want to drag everyone out here for a broom closet."

Pounder nodded. "I figured you'd say that. Need to get down to the doorknob, then, right?"

Zandra dove back into shoveling by way of an answer. Pounder joined her, and as the moon slid across the sky overhead, peering down at them through low-hanging clouds, they moved several more cubic feet of dirt, exposing the top half of the door as well as the latch, a plain black lever-style handle. Zandra pushed it down with her booted foot. The latch clicked open.

She and Pounder both wore their sidearms, and his bear-paw-like hand drifted to the Glock at his hip. Zandra drew her own gun. Still with the latch disengaged, she pushed the door open and shined the beam of her flashlight into the darkness on the other side.

A tunnel stretched away before them. Flashing her light around,

Zandra thought it looked hand-dug, the surfaces rough. Starting about twenty feet into it, what appeared to be railroad ties were set into the walls and ceiling, reinforcing it. Pounder had hunkered down, peering in alongside Zandra, and he whistled through his teeth. "How many people you reckon built this shit?"

Zandra glanced over at him. "You think it was more than one?"

"Well, if them're railroad ties? Looks like they're the old kind. Wood soaked with creosote. And them things is *heavy*. Not like concrete heavy, but still, really fuckin' heavy. If one guy did this? Damn. I'm fixin' to be impressed." He paused. "You still wanna wait to call somebody?"

Zandra wasn't sure how many times she'd been warned off of this investigation by now. Yes, finding a tunnel like this was significant, but if it ran for a few dozen feet and dead-ended, she'd still have egg on her face if she called in Hirsch and Yu. "I want to see where it goes. Then we can call someone. You in?"

Pounder blew air between his lips. "Ain't you been listenin' to what I been sayin'?"

"Okay, next question. Can you fit through here? Or do we need to dig some more?"

"Shit, if I don't never pick up a shovel the rest o' my life, I'll be just fine with it. Don't worry, boss. I'm like a octopus. I squeeze through tight spaces."

Keeping her skepticism at that to herself, Zandra sat down on the edge of their excavation and dropped into the tunnel. It looked to be an inch or two over six feet high, so she could walk in it comfortably. Behind her, Pounder shimmied and grunted and cursed until he popped through the opening and thudded down to the tunnel floor. Zandra said, "Watch your head," just as Pounder stood up and banged the top of his head into the tunnel's ceiling. He cursed some more, but adopted a stooped-over posture that made him look like an enormous, pale, hairless gorilla.

"Okay, Boss. Lead the way, I guess. 'Less you want me to squeeze back out, and let you out, and come back in. 'Cause I don't think I can get past you down here."

Zandra had holstered her sidearm when she entered the tunnel. She drew it again and, with a motion of her head, directed Pounder to follow her.

Zandra moved as quietly as she could. The only sound in the tunnel came from Pounder trying not to breathe hard behind her. The tunnel stretched away in as perfect a straight line as a hand-crafted underground passage could achieve, she thought, heading due west, and as she went, she tried to judge where they were relative to the surface. Not long after they started traversing its length, the tunnel dipped into a steady slope for about twenty feet, and the railroad tie reinforcements for that section grew more frequent. She figured they were passing under the road that led to Mrs. Daywood's house.

"Horace," she said quietly, over her shoulder. "What's due west of this place? I can't bring it to mind."

He took a few moments to answer. "Bunch o' thick woods," he finally said. "And, uh… past that… I reckon you'd get over to Lawson Lake."

Zandra grunted, her cognitive map clarifying. "Lake" was pretty generous. The body of water was more like a large pond, with three or four old houses around it, most of which had sat for years, unoccupied and rotting. A chill trickled down her spine as she realized *old and rotting* had described the Wilkins place, too. Zandra wondered if the tunnel would dip again and dig underneath Lawson Lake. She hoped it wouldn't. "Hey. How far you think we've come?"

"Dunno. Quarter mile, maybe?" Pounder's hand closed on her shoulder. "Boss. Up ahead. Look."

Zandra squinted. Just at the edge of their flashlights' reach stood another door. Zandra took a deep breath. "Get ready."

They approached the door slowly. Carefully. Guns trained on it. It was metal, like the one they'd uncovered, but painted black instead of gray. Zandra heard nothing from the other side of the door. She carefully pressed her ear against it. Still nothing. The handle turned easily under her touch, the latch disengaging, and the door swung inward toward her.

The room beyond the door was small, barely big enough for her and Pounder to fit into, with cinder block walls and a concrete slab floor, a single bare bulb sticking out of a socket in the ceiling. More like a closet than anything else. In the far wall stood another door, this one wooden, and faint light seeped around its edges. Zandra listened again, heard nothing, and, Glock at the ready, opened the wooden door just a crack. A smell assaulted her nostrils, a punishing, heavy miasma thick with earth and oil and... what? Something like *leather*. The scent rocketed Zandra back to the time when she'd bought a jacket from a leather goods store.

"What's out there?" Pounder breathed at her shoulder. "What d'you see?"

It took a moment for Zandra to make sense of it. She peered into a long, wide room—another basement, she felt sure—that had been divided into sections by lengths of long black sheets suspended from the ceiling. Though the floor, like the room Zandra stood in, was a flat concrete slab, and the parts of the walls she could see appeared to be cinder blocks coated with water-proofing tar, the scene reminded her, bizarrely, of a furniture store, in the way that such a place often divided itself into "rooms" to highlight individual bedroom or living room suits. Tiny red Christmas lights hung in random loops and arcs everywhere, draped over nails banged into exposed ceiling beams, casting the entire space in a deep blood red. She caught glimpses of beds and chairs, and the arm of a threadbare couch...

...and people, occupying those spaces.

Zandra's breath quickened with recognition.

In the center of the nearest room, Angelique Currant sat in a folding camp chair, her legs crossed, a drink in one hand.

She wore nothing but a pair of dark glasses.

Zandra waved to her. Beckoned. When the girl didn't move, Zandra whispered, "Angelique! Angelique Currant! Come here!"

Angelique acted as if she couldn't hear anything. So Zandra opened the door, her head swiveling right and left, and crept across the space to the girl's side, her voice still pitched low. "Angelique! Are you all right? What is this place? Do you—"

Zandra touched Angelique's shoulder, and recoiled, and in that instant she

understood

everything.

Everything.

Every second since she'd first laid eyes on the blood-encrusted table in the dungeon. Since seeing the status updates on the teens' Facebook pages. All the souvenirs. All the photos. Everything came blasting into Zandra's brain at the same time, and under the onslaught of the revelation she staggered backward and thumped into Pounder and fell to her knees on the concrete floor.

Pounder dropped down at her side, his hand on her back. "Boss, what is it?" His enormous head swung back and forth, looking from her to Angelique and back. "What's wrong?"

In the chair, Angelique's skin slid slowly off of the wood-and-wire frame underneath it and folded in half at the waist, flopping onto her lap like a discarded sweater, and Horace Pounder turned and emptied his stomach onto the concrete floor.

Zandra tried to speak, and had to cut herself off, because the words wanted to come out as a scream, and she knew that if she started screaming now she might not stop. Struggling not to hyperventilate, she clung to Pounder, wrapping her arms around one of his mammoth knees. She had to say it. She had to speak the words. Zandra raised one badly trembling hand and pointed at what had once been Angelique Currant.

"She's been… she's been… oh God." Zandra pounded her fist into her unwounded thigh and forced herself to whisper. "Horace, she's been *stuffed!*"

Pounder gasped for air, his body heaving, and she realized he was sobbing and vomiting at the same time.

Zandra said, "Stuffed and… and mounted. He's a taxidermist. The guy. From the dungeon. The guy who was in my *house*. He… he takes the kids, and makes them give him all their information, and *stuffs* them."

Pounder stood. Slowly. She heard his tendons creak. He wiped his mouth on a handkerchief and stuffed it into a back pocket. "So..." His breath trembled. "So that's where those pictures came from? On the computer?"

Zandra gripped his wrist and pulled herself upright. Her breathing still rapid, she felt the shock shifting into anger, into *fury*, and she wanted to scream and tear all the sheets down and find the bastard, find him and empty her gun into him, shoot him and shoot him until he flew apart. The killer had stuffed and mounted these innocent teenagers, and posed them for photos, and pretended to *be* them. Zandra pulled Pounder down closer to her lips. *"He could still be here. We've got to secure this place."*

Pounder nodded. They separated, and slowly, methodically swept the space, moving from one black-sheet-divided faux room to the next, pushing the sheets aside as they went, until they reached another door at the far end. This one had a little window set into it, and Zandra looked through to see an old, decrepit stairwell leading upward.

Pounder tried the knob. It turned easily. "Want me to check upstairs?"

"Together."

Zandra took the lead again. Pounder followed her up a moldy staircase into the house proper. She said, "No wonder this didn't arouse any suspicion." The house had all but fallen in on itself. Moldy, half-collapsed walls, hardly any ceiling left. Floors that sank alarmingly under Pounder's weight.

"There's nothin' here, Boss."

"Almost nothing." Zandra pointed to a thick cable running through a glass-free window and down through a hole drilled in the floor. "That's where he's getting his power. Tapped into the grid somewhere nearby."

"Okay. Ain't no*body* else here right now, though."

"Right. Let's head back down."

Once they'd entered the taxidermist's... what? What should she call a place like this? Zandra didn't know. She wedged a chair under the knob, and—now that they weren't actively looking for a killer there—allowed herself to take everything in.

This basement wasn't much like a furniture store after all. It was more like a prop room. One area held racks of clothing. Another had bin after plastic bin of items like sunglasses, beer bottles, and beach balls. A space along one wall was the only part of the basement not bathed in red light. Instead, sunlight LED bulbs lit a green backdrop, and beside the backdrop sat a camera on a tripod, as well as a workstation with a computer and two big monitors. Pounder came over and stood beside Zandra as she stared at the setup.

"This is how he did it," Zandra said, her voice hollow. "He posed them here. And he Photoshopped different backgrounds. That's... that's why we never saw their eyes. In the pictures. He knew the eyes wouldn't fool anyone."

Slowly Zandra turned, half-forcing, half-allowing herself to gaze out at the basement's true horror.

At least two dozen stuffed, mounted black teenagers sat or lay on various pieces of furniture throughout the place. Every one of them stripped naked. Zandra swallowed a lump of bile that had risen into the back of her mouth.

"But... but *why?*" A kind of desperation colored Pounder's voice. "Why would anybody *do* this?"

A cheap metal cot with a stained mattress lay in the nearest section, and stretched out on the mattress was the taxidermied body of a beautiful black girl. She lay there in a pose that almost achieved *peaceful*—except that her legs were parted in a way that struck Zandra as unnatural. *Unnatural even for this place,* she said to herself, along with *I'm going to have nightmares until I die.* Zandra moved closer to the girl's body, and something between the girl's legs caught her attention, and she focused her light.

This time Zandra threw up.

Not much. And she did her best to keep it from touching any of the objects around her, just let it pool on the floor at her feet. Pounder appeared at her side, steadying her, asking if she was okay, what was wrong, what upset her so. She pointed.

"There. It's—embedded in her. A…"

Pounder took a step closer, shining his own light where Zandra had indicated. One of his hands flew to his mouth. "Holy fuck. Holy *fuck*. Boss, that's a, that's a…" He didn't seem to be able to get the words out.

Zandra knew the words. *Sex toy.*

The killer had embedded a rubber appliance designed to mimic a vagina into the girl's taxidermied body, turning *her* into a sex toy. An object for his use. Zandra forced her feet to move, to take her closer to another still, lifeless form. This one was a boy, a lean, beautiful boy of eighteen or nineteen, and a whimper flew from Zandra's throat when she recognized him. It was Jimmy Biddles. The whimper turned to a choke when she saw that the boy's penis and scrotum had been removed and replaced with a big black rubber dildo.

From back at the workstation, Pounder said, "Boss. Boss! C'mere!"

Zandra staggered over to where Pounder stood, staring down at the computer. Its monitors had come to life, one of them displaying a message about a system update. A photo storage application was running. Zandra looked closer, and saw the words, "Photos uploading automatically," and watched as three new photos appeared on the screen.

Each one was of the front door of Colin's townhouse.

And each one was closer than the one before.

34

Zandra tore back through the tunnel. She didn't know if she could get any reception while inside it, so she left Pounder to make his way back up into the house and call dispatch from there. She'd also given him Colin's number and told him to call until he fucking well got through.

The night sky's stars flickered between the trees, visible through the half-door-sized opening she and Pounder had dug at the tunnel's other end, and Zandra dove headlong through it, skidding on the loose surface of the mudslide that had hidden the door to begin with. She rolled to her feet, the hot night air flooding her lungs and the chatter of the katydids all around her, and sprinted across the broken, chewed-up tornado path back to Pounder's truck, his keys in her hand.

As she ran she dialed Colin's number herself. "Pick up," she breathed, lungs burning. "Pick up, goddammit!"

Colin's voicemail greeting played in her ear. At the beep, she screamed, "Get out of the house! Colin! He's there, he's at your place, get the fuck out of there!"

Zandra climbed up and wrenched open the Ram's door and settled behind the wheel, cranking the engine to life before she'd even fully stopped moving. The truck's tires spun in the gravel driveway, digging trenches down to the red clay beneath, before they took purchase and thrust her out onto the road.

She could barely breathe for her heart beating. She had to grip the wheel hard to keep her hands from shaking off of it. The wail of distant sirens reached her over the roaring of the air past the open windows. Good. That meant Pounder had made the calls. That must be what it meant. Unless there was some other emergency, some teenager in a car wreck or old man with a heart attack. She clenched her jaw and squeezed the steering wheel until her hands ached. It *had* to be deputies on the way to Colin's townhouse. It *had* to be.

Zandra whipped around the shoulder of Angel Ridge and took the curve up the ridge's east side. She heard sirens ahead of her, more approaching behind her, and skidded around the curve beside the row of townhouses into a sea of glittering blue lights. She almost T-boned a Lexus as the truck screeched to a stop, and she didn't bother cutting the engine as she threw the door open and charged toward Colin's front door.

The Sheriff's Department had divided Cartauga County into four quadrants, with two deputies patrolling each quadrant on twelve-hour shifts. Now, counting the two that came roaring into the parking lot behind her, all eight department cruisers were clustered around the place, and Zandra saw that someone had already broken the front door open. Lights glared from every window. Neighbors up and down the row had emerged from their own houses, coming to try to see what was going on, and a couple of patrol officers were waving them back.

Bill Coyle and Kenny Roach stepped out the front door just as Zandra got there, and her words slammed out like crashing waves. "Is he here? Colin Massey, is he here?"

Bill shook his head. "Ain't nobody here." His eyes creased, and he gestured inside. "You need to see this, though."

Bill and Kenny led her to the kitchen, where the back door also stood open. The whole kitchen was in shambles. Chairs overturned, pots and pans lying scattered about—and a knife block had been flipped off the counter, knives of varying sizes and weights spread across the floor. Zandra said, "Are all the knives—"

Kenny got there ahead of her. "Near's we can tell, the biggest one's gone."

Zandra stepped through the back door. A light bulb burned above it, and shined down on a smeared, bloody handprint on the doorframe. "I want a BOLO for Colin Massey, white male, early to mid-twenties, six-foot-two, 170 pounds. Brown hair, blue eyes. Whoever took him could be in a vehicle, so get the word out to all neighboring counties. They might be on foot, too, so I want deputies all over this fucking ridge. This *just happened*, people! They can't be that far away! Fucking *move!*"

Bill and Kenny snapped to, leaving Zandra there in the doorway, and she heard them relaying her orders. Her mind spun, faster and faster, and to keep herself from spiraling out of control she called Pounder. He answered on the first ring.

"Yeah?"

"Where are you?"

"On my way. I got Krista and Summer with me. They came an' picked me up."

Krista Dempsey was the department's sole K-9 officer, and Summer was her highly trained, highly expensive, highly unfriendly Belgian Malinois. Summer was all business, all the time, and had bitten more than one officer who'd gotten too familiar with her. The thought of any dog put Zandra's heart back at the vet's office with Jordan. If anyone or anything could track whoever had taken Colin, surely to God Summer could do it.

If she got there in time.

Whoever had taken Colin. Zandra knew who. The tall, lean, demon-faced man who'd almost killed her in her own home. The man in the ski mask, with the mirror-lens eyes.

She played her flashlight over the terrain behind the townhouses. Manicured grass went back about thirty feet until it hit a stacked-stone retaining wall. The steep face of the ridge rose up above the wall, thick with trees, the woods unbroken for another quarter mile or so before the big, fine houses started. The ridge had looked a lot different when she was a girl, running around up here with her brother. Back before there were any houses at all. Just trees and old hunting trails...

Zandra's skin prickled. She stooped and swept her flashlight across the grass, and almost choked when the beam picked up a flattened section. Footprints through the dew-shining blades. They curved up and around the retaining wall, and before Zandra had even fully formed a thought, she broke into a sprint. The footprints vanished as soon as the neatly trimmed lawn did, but she knew what was up there, in the woods. She knew the trails, if they were still there. And she knew of one in particular that, if she remembered correctly, ought to be just through *here*—

Zandra burst through the branches and undergrowth and onto a hard-packed path that led north across the face of the ridge.

In the middle of the path lay a butcher knife, its blade slick with blood, its handle the same design as the ones from Colin's knife block.

Zandra was barely even aware of the words she bellowed into her radio as she sprinted along the path. She thought she heard men's voices, shouting from somewhere behind her. Her lungs began to burn again as her legs worked, carrying her through the woods fast as a mountain lion, and—

She skidded to a stop. The sound of her own footfalls on the hard earth might have been playing tricks on her. No! From ahead, somewhere ahead, faint but undeniable, she heard Colin's voice.

Screaming.

The beam of her flashlight picked up drops of blood on the trail ahead of her. They swiftly grew closer together. Bigger around.

Zandra bolted ahead. The trail curved to the right, heading up part of the ridge so steep she would've had to grab onto trees and rocks to help pull herself up, but the screams came from straight in front of her. Zandra crashed off the trail, arms held up in front of her face as she bulled through swatting branches, her shins tearing through clinging vines and bushes. A wild blackberry cane sank its thorns through her pants and into her flesh, but she paid it no mind.

The land dipped down, a long, steep incline heading for the base of the ridge, and she saw lights ahead of her.

Colin screamed again. Closer.

Zandra tried to figure out what the lights belonged to, but leaving the trail had disoriented her. Something moved in front of one of the lights, but she couldn't tell if it was a person, or just a tree branch swaying in a night breeze. She also knew the beam of her light, swinging wildly back and forth as she ran, was a dead giveaway of her position, but it was the only thing keeping her from running straight into a tree or off a cliff, and she took a calculated risk.

"Colin!"

She shouted as loud as she could, but the trees seemed to absorb the sound, just took it and folded it away into some secret silent place. The lights grew brighter, and she heard another scream—

But that wasn't Colin.

Holy shit.

Zandra burst out of the trees and stopped, blinking, the blue-purple glare of mercury-vapor lights almost blinding her. She stood in a small open area behind—what was that? A house? Some blocky structure. As her pupils contracted, twenty feet in front of her she saw two men struggling, writhing on the ground in a tangle of limbs and fists and blood.

The man in black, his mirror-eyes flashing, pinned Colin to the ground and straddled him, and drew back a fist that flashed with a short, broad blade, and just as he brought the blade down, Zandra's booted foot smashed into the side of the man's head and sent him sprawling like a string-cut marionette.

Zandra crouched next to Colin, who'd made it up onto his elbows and was pushing himself away from the mirror-eyed man, digging his heels into the ground and scooting on his ass. Blood poured down his face from a laceration on his forehead that disappeared up into his hair. It pooled under his wide, frantic, staring eyes, and before Zandra could ask him how badly he was hurt, Colin said, "Oh shit oh shit oh *shit,*" and she spun to face the man in black again.

He'd sprung to his feet, the blade still in his fist, and Zandra's gun leapt into her hand, its barrel leveled at the center of his chest. "Don't move," she said, her words shaking, and she was going to say it again, but the man's hand flickered and the short, broad knife buried itself in the heel of Zandra's hand. Her Glock thumped to the ground at her feet and the man in black folded her in half with the force of his tackle.

The world spun around her as she and the mirror-eyed beast tumbled over and over again. Zandra fetched up hard against the corner of something huge and metallic, and some dim, pain-hazed part of her brain recognized it as a dumpster, just as the smell of rancid garbage hit her nose. The man in black slammed her shoulders to the ground and mounted her, just as he had Colin, handling her as if she weighed no more than a paper doll, and Zandra knew that if she let those fists rain down into her face that he would beat her to death.

She pulled the knife out of her hand and buried it in his ribs.

It was as if she had set a grenade off, the way he hurled himself up and off of her. Up and off and away, the man in black staggered, staggered past the dumpster and around the edge of the square building she'd seen earlier, and Zandra realized where they were. She'd come out of the woods to find Colin and his abductor right behind the Sav-A-Ton gas station at the edge of town.

And if that son of a bitch made it to a car, he could get away clean.

Zandra shoved herself up to her feet. The world spun, and when she touched the back of her head—the spot that had connected with the edge of the dumpster—it came away bloody. She couldn't move the hand the knife had struck very well, but she curled the bloody fingers of her other hand into a fist and staggered after the man in black.

When she came around the edge of the building, she saw the mirror-eyed man stumbling toward a couple of motorists at the gas pumps: a chubby teenage girl filling up a banana-yellow Beetle, and a lean, grizzled man dressed head to toe in camouflage, standing next to a mud-spattered Ford Ranger pickup. The hilt of the knife still protruded from the side of the mirror-eyed man's chest, and the teenage girl started screaming, and Zandra surged forward and drove a foot into the back of the man's knee. He collapsed, and this time Zandra rode him to the ground, and she drove her undamaged fist into the side of his head again and again and again until she felt him go limp.

"You are under… arrest… motherfucker," she wheezed, and cuffed his hands together behind his back. She looked up at the teenage girl, who was standing there recording video on her phone, and barked, "Hey! Quit fucking filming us and call 9-1-1!"

"Zandra."

She yelped at the sound of the voice. It didn't sound like the slithering, grating menace she'd heard in her house.

It sounded familiar.

The man spoke again. "Zandra. You can take this mask off me now."

She moved off of him. Over to one side, where his face was turned. "No. No way. No *fucking* way."

"Do it. It's me. *Do it.*"

Zandra reached out with her good hand and gripped the ski mask. It peeled up and off his head easily, and dislodged the mirrored sunglasses as it went, revealing the long, sad scar.

Zandra sat back on the pavement, staring. Dimly aware that a small crowd was gathering. Dimly aware that Colin had arrived, and was kneeling next to her, his hand on her shoulder. Her world had narrowed to a pinpoint. The identity of the killer. The taxidermist.

Gush Parsons's uneven face stared up at her. But now, instead of the dull, cow-like gaze he'd had ever since the motorcycle accident, a fierce intelligence gleamed in his eyes. Malice spilled out of them like invisible searchlights.

"Surprise," Gush said, and smiled. It made Zandra feel cold and greasy. He winced. "Ooh. Good work with the knife. Nothing too vital punctured, I don't think, from the feel of it. I'm impressed with the amount of pain, though. You might have…" he shuddered and gasped "…might have hit some kind of nerve cluster."

Zandra got closer to him. That dim awareness let her know that a fleet of glittering blue lights bore down on them, and she thought she might have heard the voice of Special Agent Danette Yu coming from somewhere. But her attention stayed on Gush. "This is... Gus, it's not your fault. When you—when you had the accident, it, it damaged you. Damaged your brain. That's why you've done all this. You couldn't help it."

Gush's smile grew nastier. "That would... make you feel better, wouldn't it? Well, let me tell you... a secret. Come here. Come closer."

Zandra felt a hand on her arm, maybe Colin's, maybe someone else's, but she shook it off. Red lights bore down on them now. She knew the ambulance was pulling into the parking lot, but she put her face down at Gush's level, looking him in his uneven eyes. "What? What secret?"

Gush whispered, "I was on my way back from getting rid of Sharmelle's body when I *had* the accident."

Zandra gasped. The gasp caught in her throat, locked it down tight. She couldn't breathe.

Gush said, "That wreck was the best thing that ever happened to me. It gave me a mask, you see? No one saw me after that. I was hidden. I could move about as I pleased."

EMTs swarmed all around them, and someone asked her to step back to give them room.

35

The next day, after spending half the night in the emergency room and the other half in her office talking to Agent Yu, Zandra sat next to Gush Parsons's bed in the hospital. He kept drifting in and out of consciousness. His hands and feet had been immobilized by thick leather straps, and Zandra kept well out of bite range, but she wanted to talk to him. She needed to.

Zandra stayed out of the doctors' and nurses' way. Someone came in to check on him about every fifteen minutes.

She'd been sitting there for just under an hour when Gush opened his eyes and focused them on her.

"Sheriff. You look like you have questions for me."

Zandra leaned closer to him. Not close. Just closer. "I have a *lot* of questions. But they say you were right. I didn't hit anything vital. So we'll have time for everything else down the road."

He blinked. Slowly. Like a lizard. "Everything else but…what?"

"Why was Sheriff Bigelow's cell phone there at the Wilkins place? What did he have to do with what you were doing?"

A tiny, self-satisfied grin seemed to push Gush's head farther down into his pillow. "I had two wooden boxes in my Workshop. Did you find them?"

"One had a bunch of souvenirs in it. The other one was empty."

"Ah…okay. Yes. That explains a great deal."

"How so?"

"The first one did indeed hold souvenirs. The second one, though… well…"

"What? What was in it?" She scooted her chair an inch nearer his bed. "Tell me."

"You see, Sheriff, I've been… watching… the citizens of Cartauga County for many, many years. Since before I got my mask. Back-yards… decks… crawlspaces… I moved freely about, you see. Watching. I got very good at watching. And hiding. No one ever saw me. But I saw you." He chuckled. Dry. Brittle. "Oh, I saw you all. I saw all of you."

Trying her best to ignore the gooseflesh that rose all over her body, Zandra said, "And this relates to an empty wooden box how?"

"I began collecting things, Sheriff. Important things. Secret things. The keys to… well, to everything, weren't they? Date books… photos… thumb drives… The little things that let the county's people do what they most wanted to do. Hide what they wanted to hide. I suppose you could say I collected little bits of their souls."

Zandra swallowed. "And the cell phone was one of those little bits."

"It most certainly was. But not the *only* bit. No, no, no. Not by a long shot."

"All the messages on the phone. All the dates, and codes. What do they all mean?"

"Well, Sheriff, I'm *sure* I don't know. It was password-protected, wasn't it? You see, when I saw Cyrus Bigelow run his car off the road, I just *had* to sneak over and take a look at the wreckage. And the phone was right there. Just lying there, out in the open. At the time I thought Bigelow might live. So I took it. Just in case."

"You're saying you had nothing to do with Bigelow? What he was into?"

Gush's Picasso face shifted into what might have been an attempt at broad, cartoonish innocence. It came off as nightmarish. "I just picked up a phone, Sheriff."

Zandra worked to unclench her jaw enough to speak. "What else was there? In the wooden box?"

A grin stretched his mouth wide. "Enough to fill it, yes? But now the box is empty. Who knows what else there was? Or where all the little bits ended up? A tornado is a powerful, unpredictable thing, Sheriff. I can't begin to tell you where everything else went." He laughed. "Not that I ever, ever would."

Zandra left him there, chuckling to himself. The harsh lights and stinging antiseptic smell of the hospital corridor made her want to vomit. She had to take slow, deep, careful breaths in the elevator.

Crossing the lobby, she saw a tall man walk through the front doors, a bouquet of flowers in his hands. The glare of the morning sun from the parking lot silhouetted him until he'd gotten much closer, so that she was only ten feet away before she recognized Shep Curtis.

He showed her his big teeth. "Why, Sheriff Seagraves, what an unexpected pleasure!"

Zandra realized she was legitimately too exhausted to muster up any strong feelings for or about him. "What are you doing here, Shep?"

He shook the flowers in her direction. "Ministering to my flock, of course. Yours isn't the only drama in Red Springs, you know. I'm here to provide spiritual comfort to an ailing church member." After the briefest of pauses: "I can give you counsel as well, Sheriff. If you need it. Must've been quite the shock, seeing your deputy wearing his true colors."

Zandra's eyes narrowed. The existence of the Holy Brotherhood of Whatever the Fuck They Called Themselves wasn't explicitly illegal. But she moved closer to Shep Curtis, and as her exhaustion faded, she put an edge in her voice that made his smile falter. "Listen to me. I've got my eye on you and all your pointy-hood motherfuckers. I'm going to be on you like stink on shit. Every time you scratch your *balls*, I'll know about it." Shep inclined his head, revving up his best condescending smile, but she went on. "Also? 'Curtis For Sheriff'?"

The smile cracked and fell apart.

"Oh, you didn't know I knew about that? Yeah. In your fucking dreams, *Shep*." She jabbed a stiff finger toward his face. "Red Springs is *my* town. Understand? I'm not going *anywhere*."

Zandra walked out of the hospital before Shep Curtis could come up with a response. Billy Coyle was waiting for her, and gave her a ride over to the Farmhouse. A couple of the other deputies had fetched her Camaro and put it in her reserved spot.

Half an hour later, having decided that she was close to delirium and that the rest of the paperwork could fucking well wait, Zandra walked out the side door and stopped in her tracks.

For just a second, when she saw Colin there leaning against her Camaro, his scalp bandaged, she thought she might have been hallucinating. That suspicion grew stronger when Jordan's front half popped out of the Camaro's passenger window. His tongue flopped out of his mouth and rested on the inside of the big plastic cone ringing his bandaged head.

Colin said, "We were both going to be standing here waiting for you, but he really wanted to get in the car."

Okay, yes, Colin was real. But she barely had enough energy to get back to her house, much less deal with… whatever situation she had with him.

Her house. It belonged to her again. Now that Gush Parsons had been apprehended, the sense of violation and betrayal she'd felt while inside it had evaporated. It had been immediately replaced, of course, with the even more overwhelming sense of violation and betrayal at the revelation that Gush was the killer, but she still found herself looking forward to sleeping in her own bed.

"Hi yourself." She walked past Colin to Jordan. He'd pulled his front legs back inside and stood there in the passenger seat, wiggling his rear end. Zandra winced when she saw the bandages wrapped around his shaven chest and back. Her own right hand was a mass of bandages, courtesy of Gush's knife, so she petted Jordan carefully with her left. "Is he really okay to come home? The vet released him?"

Colin came around and stood beside her, looking down at the

huge black dog. "Yeah. You're supposed to keep him inside except for walks, and don't let him run around like a loon, but yeah, they said he was *incredibly* strong, and would most likely recover better at home." He pulled a white paper bag out of one pocket. "I've got all his medication here."

Zandra kept scratching Jordan's chin, but turned to meet Colin's eyes. Their brilliant shade of blue seemed to have dulled to a metallic gray.

"He rang the doorbell, Zandra. He just walked right up and rang the doorbell, standing there, looking all alone and pitiful. He said he'd gotten lost, and wanted to use my phone to call his mother. And I turned the alarm off and just let him right in."

She put her good hand on his arm. "I'm sure that's how he got close to everyone he went after. It was… something he'd spent years perfecting, I think."

"Well, it worked. Next thing I knew, he had that fucking mask on and came at me with one of my own knives."

She searched his face. "Any sane person would be on a plane right now. Getting as far away from here as possible."

The corner of his mouth twitched. "Well… I didn't get a chance to thank you. You realize you saved my life last night, right? I fought him off and ran, but he caught me. He would've killed me."

Zandra didn't blink. If she had, the darkness, however fleeting, would have been filled with still, lifeless faces and horribly violated bodies. She knew Colin didn't fit Gush's pattern. He wasn't young and black.

Gush had tried to take Colin specifically to hurt her. It made her guts twist up tight.

"Okay. You're welcome. I, uh… I should be thanking you. For sticking around. For giving me a place to stay. For not… um. For not escalating things when I wasn't thinking clearly." She walked around to the driver's door. Colin stayed where he was. Jordan whined and pushed his nose under Colin's hand until Colin started scratching him in the same place Zandra had.

She opened the door. "But seriously. There's no need for you to stay in Red Springs anymore. You can go back to Connecticut now." When Colin didn't respond, Zandra climbed in, shut the door, and cranked the engine.

Colin leaned down, looking in at her through the open passenger window, and said, "Could you give me a little room here, bud?" Jordan *whuffed* at him, turned, and carefully stepped between the seats. He lay down in the backseat and propped his cone-surrounded head on the center console.

Zandra sighed.

Colin folded his forearms and rested them on the window frame. "I might not have escalated things while you were blitzed. That doesn't mean I don't want to escalate them at all."

She drummed her fingers on the steering wheel, grateful for the first time ever that the Camaro had an automatic transmission. Driving a stick with only her left hand functional wouldn't have been easy. "Look. Colin. There's just—it's not—it's just not a good idea."

His face darkened. "Why not?"

"Just trust me."

"I'm afraid I can't do that, Sheriff. I'm going to have to hear some concrete reasons."

"Colin…"

"Hey, it's your town, maybe you understand things around here better than I do. Maybe you know some things I don't know. Maybe you've got some solid, convincing reasons why you and I shouldn't at least give it a shot. If that's the case, I'll do like you said—get on a plane and fly my sorry ass back to Milford. But if there are reasons, I want to hear them. I'd like to think I deserve that much."

Zandra let her head fall back against the headrest. "Okay! Okay, fine. There's three. Three really good reasons. If it was only one, or even two, then maybe, *maybe* we could see where things might go. But all three? No way. Three strikes and you're out. And you, Colin, are out."

He nodded. "Okay. Lay them on me."

She held up her index finger. "One. You're a yankee. Not only are you openly fucking horrified at the culture around here, but you'd also stick out like a gangrenous thumb no matter what you did. If you're looking for a place to belong? A place to maybe call home? This will *not* be it for you."

Colin shrugged faintly. "Fair enough. Go on."

She held up her middle finger beside the index. "Two. You're white. You are *alabaster* white. And in case it hasn't sunk in, this is not the most racially enlightened town. You don't *ever* see a white man dating a black woman. Not in public, anyway. You'd be on the receiving end of exactly the kind of hostility and prejudice that's freaked you right the fuck out the whole time you've been here."

Colin stared at the empty passenger seat. "Hmm." He thought about it. "Huh. Okay. What's number three?"

Zandra didn't bother putting up her ring finger. She just let her hand fall into her lap. "Colin, you're a *baby*. I'm thirty-nine! I'll be forty in October! I don't have any business running around with somebody who should be going to frat parties and doing keg stands. Even if I wanted to go for the whole rob-the-cradle cougar thing, what would we even have to talk about? I don't know anything about Instagram stories or YouTube stars or colleges with *safe spaces*, and I don't care about learning, to be perfectly honest. I—hey. *Hey*. Are you grinning?" He *was* grinning. Colin lowered his head so that his forehead rested on his arms, but she could see his body shaking with poorly stifled laughter. "What's so goddamn funny?"

Colin looked up, grin still in place. "How old do you think I am?"

"Uh." His attitude stopped her dead in her tracks. "I don't know. Twenty-two? Twenty-three?"

He drummed his fists on the window frame. "Zandra, I'm thirty-four!"

Her jaw dropped open. "What? Bullshit. Bullshit!"

Colin pulled out his wallet. "Here! Look at my driver's license!" He slid the card free and handed it to her.

She stared at the listed date of birth for ten long seconds before she handed it back to him. "Fucking hell, Colin, have you *ever* had to shave?"

He replaced the license and put his wallet back in his pocket. "So. That's only two out of three. And I figure I can deal with the first two."

Zandra groaned. And groaned louder. Her groan got bigger and bigger until Jordan whined at her. Finally she said, "Get in the damn car," and Colin did as he was told, his perfect teeth on full display.

She put the Camaro in reverse, about to back out of her parking space, but when she glanced in the mirror, she saw someone standing behind the car. It took her a second to connect the face to a name: Savvy Horne. One of the students at Red Springs High School. Savvy just stood there, and Zandra couldn't quite parse the look on her face, so she got out of the car and approached the girl.

After a couple of seconds, Colin got out as well.

"Savvy, right? That's what everyone calls you? Short for Savannah, isn't it?"

Savvy's face crumpled with grief. Tears spilled from her eyes, and Zandra moved closer to her and put her good hand on the girl's shoulder. "What is it? What's wrong? Are you okay?"

Savvy tried to speak, but it just came out as sobs. She rubbed the back of her hand across her face, wiping away tears and snot, and walked a few paces toward the road. "I'm so sorry, Sheriff. I'm so sorry, I didn't mean to do it, I didn't mean it, I'm so sorry."

Zandra went to her and put a finger under Savvy's chin. Lifted her face up. "Hey. Hey, look at me. It's okay, all right? Whatever's happened, you're safe now. Just tell me. Do you want to go inside? We don't have to talk out here in the open."

Savvy sobbed again. "I did it, Sheriff! I didn't mean to, I was—I was trying to—" She scrubbed at her face. "I was trying to kill my grandpa! That's why I went with him! That's why I was out there on the ridge!"

Colin said, "What's she talking about?"

And Zandra knew.

Bile rose into the back of her throat.

Her knees felt weak.

Savvy said, "I was aiming at him. At my grandpa. Because he… he beats me, and, and, in front of my friends, in front of everybody, and I was going to make it look like a hunting accident, but then he moved, right when I pulled the trigger he moved, and I missed…"

Colin put it together. "Oh God."

Savvy wailed, "I didn't mean to shoot your brother! I swear I didn't mean it! It was an accident! I'm so sorry! I'm so sorry, Sheriff!"

Behind them, the side door opened, and Horace Pounder stepped out. "Everything okay, Boss?"

Zandra couldn't really feel her arms or legs. She wasn't sure the words were coming out of her mouth, because she couldn't hear them over the roaring in her ears, but she put her arm around Savvy's shoulder and gently steered her toward Pounder. She told her mouth to say, "Savvy, I want you to go with the Major, all right? I want you to tell him everything you just told me. And he'll take care of everything else. Can you do that?"

Savvy nodded, and said, "I'm so sorry," again, and went to Pounder.

Pounder got a look at Zandra's face as she turned, and his eyes went wide. "Boss! What's, what're you—"

Zandra shook her head. "I'll… I'll deal with it later. Just take her statement and put her in a room."

Pounder nodded, and he and Savvy disappeared into the Farmhouse. Zandra turned and half-embraced, half-fell against Colin, and he wrapped her up in his arms as she stared into his chest, stared through him, wondering where her own tears were.

"An accident," Colin said, his voice sounding as scooped-out as Zandra felt. "Perry died because of an accident."

"Not an accident," she murmured. "Attempted murder. Plus manslaughter."

"And she's, what, fifteen? Sixteen? I can't even begin to—I don't understand. A girl that young, does something like this, and now she'll spend the rest of her life in jail."

Zandra pulled away and looked up at him with exhausted eyes. "Are you kidding? She's an underage white girl. Who accidentally killed a black man. In the Deep South. She'll get probation. At worst."

Colin's words seemed to have run out. He just shook his head.

"Come on," Zandra said, and took his hand.

Colin followed her mutely back to the car.

317

THE END

ACKNOWLEDGEMENTS

The Storm would not have been possible without some brilliant, supportive, very patient people.

For Falstaff Books: John Hartness and Melissa McArthur.

For Excellence in beta reading: Zach & Sarah Caylor, Clint & Doris McInnes, Brandon Jerwa, Haris Orkin, Karen Jordan, and the irreplaceable Zandra Wilkerson, who lent me her namesake as well as her insight.

For analysis above and beyond the call: Shon Jason Medley.

For making a suggestion that drastically improved the story: Alexander Robb.

For valuable music advice: Daniel Harris.

And for the Catoosa County Sheriff's Department: Sheriff Gary Sisk, Lieutenant Andrew Dodson, and all the officers who took part in the Catoosa Citizens Academy. Anything to do with law enforcement that I got right is thanks to them. Anything I got wrong is entirely on me.

ABOUT THE AUTHOR

Dan Jolley began writing professionally at age 19. Starting out in comic books, Dan has worked for major publishers such as DC (*Firestorm*), Marvel (*Dr. Strange*), Dark Horse (*Aliens*), and Image (*G.I. Joe*). He soon branched out into licensed-property novels (*Star Trek*), film novelizations (*Iron Man*), and original novels, including the Middle Grade urban fantasy series *Five Elements* and the urban sci-fi *Gray Widow Trilogy*.

Dan began writing for video games in 2007, and has contributed storylines, characters, and dialogue to titles such as *Transformers: War for Cybertron*, *Prototype 2*, and *Dying Light*, among others.

His latest work includes the best-selling Audible Original Middle Grade urban fantasy audiobook *House of Teeth*, and a Middle Grade post-apocalyptic sci-fi novel series for German publisher Fischer Verlag called *Bad Tide Rising* (published in Germany as *Waterland*).

Dan lives with his wife Tracy and some largely inert felines in northwest Georgia. Readers can learn more about him on his website, www.danjolley.com.

FRIENDS OF FALSTAFF

Thank You to All our Falstaff Books Patrons, who get extra digital content each month! To be featured here and see what other great rewards we offer, go to www.patreon.com/falstaffbooks.

PATRONS

Dino Hicks
John Hooks
John Kilgallon
Larissa Lichty
Travis & Casey Schilling
Staci-Leigh Santore
Sheryl R. Hayes
Scott Norris
Samuel Montgomery-Blinn
Junkle